P9-DMJ-384

CRITICS PRAISE LEANNA RENEE HIEBER AND *THE STRANGELY BEAUTIFUL TALE OF MISS PERCY PARKER*!

"A compelling, engaging novel that drew me in from page one. Bravo!"—M. J. Rose, Bestselling Author of *The Reincarnationist* and *The Memorist*

"I want more! NOW! Such a beautifully written book.... The story is fantastic in more ways than one. A gorgeous writer. . . ."
—Maria Lokken, President, Romance Novel.tv

"A strangely beautiful tale indeed! An ethereal, lyrical story that combines myth, spiritualism and the gothic in lush prose and sweeping passion."
—*USA Today* Bestselling Author Kathryn Smith

"Tender. Poignant. Exquisitely written."
—*New York Times* Bestselling Author C. L. Wilson

Strangely Beautiful

Tresses of lustrous, snow-white hair tumbled from their cloth-bound imprisonment, streaming like a waterfall down the young woman's back. In an effort to make his student more at ease, Alexi did his best to appear wholly disinterested as she carefully removed her protections with delicate, private ceremony. But then she turned to face him, clutching those items that had held her unusual features in mystery: glasses, gloves, long scarf.

"As you would have it so, Professor, here is your pupil in all her ghastliness."

Though Miss Parker's hands clearly trembled, her voice did not. Luminous crystal eyes held streaks of pale blue shooting from tiny black pupils. A face youthful but devoid of color, smooth and unblemished like porcelain, had graceful lines as well-defined and proportioned as a marble statue. Her long, blanched locks shimmered in the candlelight like spider silk. Upon high cheekbones lay hints of rouge: any more would have appeared garish against her blindingly white skin, but she had been artful in her application. Her rosebud lips were tinted in the same manner.

"You see, Professor, even you, so stern and stoic, cannot hide your shock, surprise, distaste—"

"Distaste?" he interrupted quietly. "Is that what you see?"

The Strangely Beautiful Tale of Miss Percy Parker

LEANNA RENEE HIEBER

LEISURE BOOKS NEW YORK CITY

To Alan, the muse

A LEISURE BOOK®

September 2009

Published by

Dorchester Publishing Co., Inc.
200 Madison Avenue
New York, NY 10016

Copyright © 2009 by Leanna Renee Hieber

All rights reserved. No part of this book may be reproduced
or transmitted in any form or by any electronic or mechanical
means, including photocopying, recording or by any information
storage and retrieval system, without the written permission of the
publisher, except where permitted by law.

ISBN 10: 0-8439-6296-8
ISBN 13: 978-0-8439-6296-3
E-ISBN: 978-1-4285-0732-6

The name "Leisure Books" and the stylized "L" with design are
trademarks of Dorchester Publishing Co., Inc.

Printed in the United States of America.

10 9 8 7 6 5 4 3 2

If you purchased this book without a cover you should be aware
that this book is stolen property. It was reported as "unsold and
destroyed" to the publisher and neither the author nor the publisher
has received any payment for this "stripped book."

Visit us online at www.dorchesterpub.com.

ACKNOWLEDGMENTS

Pardon the list, it takes a village ...

Thank you to Paul Peterson, my first and beloved audience.
To Andy Waltzer, who loves Percy as much as I do.
To Michael Dixon, who inspired me to finish the book.
To my family, for everything, always.
To Marijo, for the brain cell.
To Marcos, for caring.
To the RWA NYC, an awesomely supportive resource.
To Isabo Kelly, for teaching me tons of things.
To my agent Nicholas Roman Lewis, for always believing in this story.
To Marianne Mancusi, I promise to pay it forward.
To Chris Keeslar, editor extraordinaire, thank you for this blessed moment.

The Strangely
Beautiful Tale of
Miss Percy Parker

PROLOGUE

London, England—1867

The air in London was grey. This was no surprise; but the common eye could not see the particular heaviness of the atmosphere or the unusual weight of this special day's charcoal clouds: the sky was pregnant with a potent wind, for The Guard was searching for new hosts.

On to London they came, and that wind full of spirits began to course through the streets of the city; merciless, searching. Around corners, elbowing aside London's commoners and high society alike, nudging their way through market crowds and tearing down dirty alleys, they sought their intended. A candle burst into flame in the window of a marquess's house. The tiny cry of a young boy summoned his mother into the drawing room. Similar sounds went up in other parts of the city, confused gasps growing into amazed giggles before being subdued into solemnity. One by one the intended targets were seized.

Six. Five . . .

Where is Four? Ah . . . Four.

Now, Three.

Alone and unaccompanied, the children left their respective houses and began to walk.

And, Two.

Searching for the final piece, the greatest of the possessors paused, a hesitating hunter. Deliberate. And, finally . . . the brightest, boldest, most promising catch of the day.

One, and done!

A sigh of relief. The city's infamous fog thinned.

Only a bird above espied the six drawing toward London's center; weaving through a maze of clattering carriages, stepping cautiously over putrid puddles, a sextet of children looked about the cluttered merchant lanes and sober business avenues with new eyes and saw strange sights. There were ghosts everywhere: floating through walls and windows, they rose up through streets and strolled beside quiet couples! One by one, each transparent form turned to the children, who could only stare in wonder and apprehension. In ethereal rags, spirits of every century bowed in deference, as if they were passing royalty.

Drawn in a pattern from all corners of London, the six children gathered in a knot at the crest of Westminster Bridge. Nodding a silent greeting to one another, or curtseying, the youths found each other's faces unsettlingly mature. Excitement tempered only by confusion crept into their expressions as they evaluated their new peers, in garb ranging from fine clothing to simple frocks, their social statuses clearly as varied as their looks.

A spindly girl whose brown hair was pinned tightly to her head kept turning, looking for something, clutching the folds of her linen frock and shifting on the heels of her buttoned boots. It was her tentative voice that at last broke the silence: "Hello. I'm Rebecca. Where is our leader, then?"

A sturdy, ruddy-cheeked boy in a vest and cap, cuffs rolled to his elbows, gestured to the end of the street. "Hello, Rebecca, I'm Michael. Is that him?"

Approaching the cluster was a tall, well-dressed, unmistakable young man. A mop of dark hair held parley with the wind, blowing about the sharp features of his face, while timeless, even darker eyes burned in their sockets. His fine black suit gave the impression of a boy already a man. He reached the group and bowed, his presence magnetic, confident . . . and somewhat foreboding. In a rich, velvet voice deep as the water of the Thames, he spoke. "Good day. My name is Alexi Rychman, and this has turned into the strangest day of my life." He glanced at the spindly brunette next to him, who blushed.

"Hello, Alexi, I'm Rebecca, and I feel the same."

Alexi firmly met every child's gaze in turn, prompting introductions.

"Elijah," a thin blond boy said, his features sharp and his eyes a startling blue. He was garbed in striped satin finery that seemed rakish if not foppish on such a young man, and he was clearly the wealthiest of the lot.

"Josephine," added a soft French accent belonging to a beautiful brunette, olive-skinned and sporting the latest fashions. Two shocks of white hair framed her face.

"Michael," chimed in the sturdy boy with a brilliant, contagious smile.

"Lucretia Marie O'Shannon Connor," replied an Irish accent, shyly, and its owner stared at the cobblestones, dark blonde hair falling to veil her frightened face. Her plain calico dress bespoke modest means.

"Pardon?" Elijah's drawn and angular face became even more pinched.

"I suppose you could call me Jane if that's easier," the girl murmured with a shrug, still staring at the street.

"I'll say," Elijah laughed.

Alexi's eyes flashed with a sudden unfocused anger. "And here I thought all my life I'd be a scientist. It seems forces at large have other plans. I don't suppose any of you has the slightest idea what we're supposed to *do*?"

Everyone shook their heads, just as surprised with their new destinies as he.

"Then, let me ask a mad question." Alexi's tone was cautious. "Does anyone, all of a sudden . . . see ghosts?"

"Yes!" everyone chorused, relieved that if this were madness, they weren't alone in it.

"Can you hear them speak?" he asked.

"No," was the universal reply.

"Neither can I, thank God, or we'd never have another

moment's peace." Alexi sighed. "Well, I suppose we'd better get to the bottom of this. I . . . saw a chapel. But I've never been there and don't know where it is."

Rebecca, still blushing, pointed. "I . . . I think that raven can show us."

Above, a hovering black bird was waiting for them. The new Guard looked up and nodded, then followed through the bustling heart of the city.

The crow stopped at an impressive edifice labeled ATHENS ACADEMY. The red sandstone building had appeared all of a sudden, nestled impossibly among several less-interesting lots. The multistoried construction was shuttered, clearly unoccupied by staff or students. It was the summer holiday, after all. Yet it was occupied by ghosts. And, as the wide wooden doors opened for the six children, these ghosts pointed the way toward an interior chapel, as if everything here had been waiting.

While the others walked ahead, Alexi lingered, studying what seemed to be a normal school, normal halls and stately foyers, hoping to find further clues. When he at last reached the chapel doors, the candles upon the altar burst into flame. The ladies in the group gasped.

Alexi lifted his palm—and the candles extinguished. He furrowed his brow. A young man of methods and proofs, he was; such happenings defied his knowledge of a more definite world.

The bright white chapel was of simple decor, with a painted dove high above a plain altar. A hole formed in the air before them, first as a black point but growing into a rectangle. This dark portal opened with a sound like a piece of paper being torn, surely leading to a place more foreign than the children had ever seen. They approached it in silence.

"This must be a sacred space for us alone," Michael quietly surmised, peering into the void, seeing a staircase that led to a beckoning light below.

Alexi set his jaw, strode forward and descended the stair. The others followed.

The room below was circular, lined with Corinthian pillars but blurred in the shadows, as if this were a place at the edge of time, a dream. There was a different bird depicted in stained glass over their heads, not a dove but something great and fiery. A feather was engraved in the stone below the glass, with an inscription. Alexi read it aloud: " 'In darkness, a door. In bound souls, a circle of fire. Immortal force in mortal hearts. Six to calm the restless dead. Six to shield the restless living.' "

Immediately, a circle of blue-coloured fire leaped up. Everyone gasped except Alexi, who was looking curiously at the cerulean flame, wondering how on earth such a thing was possible: the fire remained in a perfect circle around them, at a height of a few inches, and gave off no heat.

"Alexi, look!" Rebecca cried, pointing to his hands. He'd been contemplating the possible chemical compounds inherent to the fire, not noticing the licking tendrils of that same blue conflagration emanating from his palms and trickling down to the circle. Another ripping sound tore through the room, this one far greater, and at a new portal threshold there suddenly stood an indescribable woman.

Alexi forgot the fire, and the fact that it was coming from his hands. He forgot his troubled, logical concerns. He could only stare, overtaken. His mind, body and heart exploded with new sensations.

The woman was tall and lithe, glowing with a light of power and love, with features as perfect as a statue and hair that was golden. No; it was lustrous brown. No, rich red . . . She shifted from one hue to the next, maintaining her breathtaking beauty but seeming to radiate all colours at once. Diaphanous material wrapped her perfect body, sweeping layers and transitioning hues like the rest. Her eyes were crystalline lamps, sparkling and magnetic. There was no other answer but that she was a divine creature.

She spoke. Her voice held echoes of every element; an orchestra of stars.

"My beloveds. I've not much time, but I must inaugurate you, as I have done since your circle began The Grand Work in ancient times. You won't remember those who came before. Nor has what's inside *overtaken* you. It heightens you. You are heroes of your age. The Guard picked you six because your mortal hearts are bold and strong.

"There has never been a more crucial time than this century, this city. Your world is filled with new ideas, new science, new ideas on God and the body . . . and most importantly, spirits. There's never been such talk of spirits. You are the ones who must respond."

She turned to Alexi, and he felt himself stop breathing. Her gemlike eyes filled with tears that became rubies, then emeralds, then sapphires as they coursed down her perfect cheeks and tinkled to the stone floor before vanishing. Unconsciously, Alexi reached out a hand to touch those tears, though the woman remained beyond his reach within her portal.

"Alexi, you are the leader here. Inside of you alone lives what's left of my true love, a winged being of power and light—the first phoenix of ancient times. Murdered by jealous Darkness, he was burned alive. His great power was splintered but not destroyed. This fire from your hands is your tool. It was the weapon used against you long ago, but now you control the element and are born again within it. My love lives on in you, worthy Alexi, and you will fight Darkness by bearing the eternal flame of our vendetta." She turned to the others, and breath stole back into Alexi's lungs.

"The power that inhabits the rest of you comes from great beings in those days—Muses, forces of Beauty that chose to follow our broken phoenix as votaries, to keep chaotic Darkness from infiltrating this world. Together you are the new Guard, and this task is yours."

"The Guard?" Rebecca piped up, confused.

"That is what you will do: guard the living from the dead wandering the earth, whom you now see but cannot hear. Your Grand Work is to maintain the balance between this world and the one beyond, beside. Darkness would run rampant over your great city and beyond—and will, unless you silence his emissaries. Hold fast, for the struggle will worsen. Darkness will seek to destroy the barrier pins between worlds. And to fight this, a prophecy must be fulfilled. A seventh member will join you. She will come as your peer to create a new dawn."

Suddenly, their oracle winced as if struck. Alexi rushed forward—to protect or comfort, he did not know—but the divine apparition put out a hand that stopped him dead. "But you must understand that once the seventh joins you, it will mean war."

The group couldn't help but shiver, even if they didn't understand.

"Who *are* you?" Alexi asked, unable to hide the yearning in his voice.

She smiled sadly but did not answer his question. "I hope you will know her when she comes, Alexi, my love. And I hope she will know you, too. Await her, but beware. She will not come with answers but will be lost, confused. I have put protections in place, but she will be threatened and seeking refuge. There shall be tricks, betrayals and many second guesses. Caution, beloved. Mortal hearts make mistakes. Choose your seventh carefully, for if you choose the false prophet, the end of your world shall follow."

"A sign then—surely there will be a sign!" The boy named Michael couldn't hold back a string of desperate questions. "And *when* will she come? And how will we know how, and what, to fight against?"

"You'll be led to fight the machinations of Darkness by instincts within you. But you shall not always be fighting. You are also as you were—your mortal lives and thoughts

remain unchanged, though they are augmented by the spirits inside you. Each of you has a specific strength."

She looked to Josephine, then, naming her "the Artist,"
turned to Jane, "the Healer;" then to Rebecca, "the Intu-
ition." Michael she named "the Heart," and Elijah, "the
Memory." Then, finally, Alexi: "the Power."

"As for a sign when she has come, your seventh, look for a
door. A door like this"—the woman gestured to the portal
in which she stood—"should be your gauge. But don't go
in," she cautioned, glancing around herself woefully. "You
wouldn't want to come here.

"You'll see this threshold together, all of you, I'm sure, when
it is time. As for when your seventh will come . . . I cannot
say. I'm powerful, but only the great Cosmos is omnipotent.
Time is different where I am and we are in uncharted waters.
But she *will* be placed in your path. And once she is, you
won't have much time. Then, a terrible storm."

There was a disturbing sound from the darkness behind
her. The woman glanced back, fearful.

"What is your name?" Alexi insisted, desperate to know
more.

The woman smiled sadly, and her glimmering eyes
changed hue. "It hardly matters. We've had so many names
over the years—all of us." She surveyed the group before her
eyes rested once more on Alexi. "Especially you, my love:
please be careful. Listen to your instincts and stay together.
A war is coming, and it isn't what you think. Hell isn't down,
it's around us, pressing inward. And it will come. But your
seventh will be there when it does, or she will have died in
vain."

"Died?" Alexi cried. It seemed some new horror appeared
at every turn.

The woman smiled again: wisely, sadly. "One must die to
live again." Then, blowing a kiss to Alexi, she disappeared.

The sacred space faded, returning the dazed group to the
empty chapel. In overwhelmed silence they filed out the

back doors into a quiet London alley. The group looked at one another in alarm and wonder.

Alexi stalked off. There was something bitter in the air indicating unity was wise, but he was wracked with emotions he could not decipher and was unable to face his new friends for the shame of his confusion. Rebecca started after him, even called his name, but his head throbbed. He wished to lock himself *away,* to go back to simpler days of pillaging the secrets of science.

And yet, that oracle—that *goddess*—had given him a task. He was meant to be a leader.

The new power coursing through him could not calm his inner tumult. His head spinning and his heart pounding; transformed in one afternoon from boy to a man craving an otherworldly woman, he retreated to his family estate.

It was his first mistake. He found chaos. It was as if an angry hand had swept down and smote the entrance foyer and staircase. At the foot of the stair lay his elder sister, Alexandra, crumpled in a heap of taffeta, her body unnaturally twisted. Alexi's grandmother, clutching her heart, all fine lace and severe looks, was bent over her.

"Alexandra!" he cried as he rushed forward, scared to touch his sister's body lest he somehow break it further. The girl was whimpering, staring from their grandmother to him alternately, paralyzed from the waist down. "What happened?"

"Something terrible," their grandmother wheezed, in her heavy Russian accent. "A force . . . Oh, I cannot describe. Evil swept through." And suddenly the woman's eyes grew bright. Always had she demonstrated a frightening knowledge. "There's something different about you," she pointed out, and then began speaking in Russian: "The firebird— that's it. There is a darkness coming, my boy. And you must light the darkness with your fire." Then, taking a shuddering breath, she eased back against the wall. She did not breathe again.

Alexi felt the blood drain from his face. Could he, with his new power, have prevented this? Did failure mark his very start? He'd meant to be a man of science, not . . . whatever he now was. How could he lead when he couldn't even believe what he'd seen and heard? Clearly he was a mortal, as were the others in his charge. The coming battles would not be easy. But that powerful stranger, that strange seventh . . . Maybe his goddess would return.

CHAPTER ONE

London, England—1888

A young woman, the likes of which London had never seen, alighted from a carriage near Bloomsbury and gazed at the grand facade before her. Breathless at the sight of the Romanesque fortress of red sandstone that was to be her new home, she ascended the front steps beneath the portico with a carpetbag in tow. One slender, gloved hand heaved open the great arched door; Miss Percy Parker paused, then stepped inside.

The foyer of Athens Academy held a few milling young men, papers and books in hand. Their jaws fell in turn. In the diffuse light cast by a single chandelier they saw a petite, unmistakable apparition. Dark blue glasses kept eerie, ice blue eyes from unsettling those stares that she nervously returned. Much of her snow-white skin was hidden from view by a scarf draped around her head and bosom, but only a mask could have hidden the ghostly pallor of her fine-featured face.

The sudden tinkling of a chandelier crystal broke the thick silence. Percy's gaze flickered up to behold a young man, equally pale as herself, floating amid the gas flames. The transparent spirit wafted down to meet her. It was clear from the stares of the young men of solid mass, rudely focused on Percy, that they were oblivious. She herself acknowledged the ghost only subtly, lest she be thought distract as well as deformed.

The spectral schoolboy spoke in a soft Scots brogue. "You'd best give up your pretensions, miss. You'll never be one of them. And you're certainly not one of us. What the devil are you?"

Percy met the spirit's hollow gaze. Behind her glasses, her opalescent eyes flared with defiance as she asked the room, her voice sweet and timid, "Could someone be so kind as to direct me to the headmistress's office?" A gaping, living individual pointed to a hallway on her left, so she offered him a "Thank you, sir," and fled, eager to escape all curiosity. The only sounds that followed were the rustling layers of her sky blue taffeta skirts and the echo of her booted footfalls down the hall.

HEADMISTRESS THOMPSON was scribed boldly across a large wooden door. Percy took a moment to catch her breath before knocking.

She soon found herself in an office filled to overflowing with books. A sharp voice bade her sit, and she was promptly engulfed in a leather armchair. Across the desk sat a severe woman dressed primly in grey wool. Middle-aged and thin, she had a pinched nose and high cheekbones that gave her a birdlike quality, tight lips twisted in a half frown. Brown hair was piled atop her head, save one misbehaving lock at her temple.

Blue-grey eyes pierced Percy's obscuring glasses. "Miss Parker, we've received word that you're an uncommonly bright girl. I'm sure you're well aware that your previous governance, unsure what to do with you, supposed you'd best be sent somewhere else. Becoming a sister did not suit you?"

Percy had no time to wonder if this was sardonic or understanding, for the headmistress continued: "Your reverend mother made many inquiries before stumbling across our quiet little bastion. Considering your particular circumstances, I accepted you despite your age of eighteen. You're older than many who attend here. I'm sure I needn't tell you, Miss Parker, that at your age most women do not think it advantageous to remain... *academic*. I hope you know enough of the world outside convent walls to understand." Headmistress Thompson's sharp eyes suddenly softened and something mysterious twinkled there. "We must acknowledge the limitations of our world, Miss Parker. I, of course, chose to run an institution rather than a household."

Percy couldn't help but smile, drawn in by the headmistress's conspiratorial turn, as if the woman considered herself unique by lifestyle inasmuch as Percy was unique by fate. But the woman's amiability soon vanished. "We expect academic excellence in all subjects, Miss Parker. Your reverend mother proclaimed you quite proficient in several languages, with particularly keen knowledge of Latin, Hebrew and Greek. Would you consider yourself proficient?"

"I have no wish to flatter myself—"

"Honesty will suffice."

"I'm f-fluent in several tongues," Percy stammered. "I'm fondest of Greek. I know French, German, Spanish and Italian well. I dabble in Russian, Arabic, Gaelic... as well as a few ancient and obscure dialects."

"Interesting." The headmistress absently tapped the desk with her pen. "Do you attribute your affinity for foreign tongues to mere interest and diligence?"

Percy thought a moment. "This may sound very strange..."

"It may shock you how little I find strange, Miss Parker," the headmistress replied. "Go on."

Percy was emboldened. "Since childhood, certain things

were innate. The moment I could read, I read in several languages as if they were native to me." She bit her lip. "I suppose that sounds rather mad."

There was a pause, yet to Percy's relief the headmistress appeared unmoved. "Should you indeed prove such a linguist, and a well-rounded student, Athens may have ongoing work for you next year as an apprentice, Miss Parker."

"Oh!" Percy's face lit like a sunbeam. "I'd relish the opportunity! Thank you for your generous consideration, Headmistress."

"You were raised in the abbey?"

"Yes, Headmistress."

"No immediate family?"

"None, Headmistress."

"Do you know anything of them? Is there a reason . . . ?"

Percy knew it was her skin that gave the woman pause. "I wish I could offer you an answer regarding my colour, Headmistress. It's always been a mystery. I know nothing of my father. I was told my mother was Irish."

"That is all you know?"

Percy shifted in her seat. "She died within the hour she brought me to the sisters. Perhaps I was a traumatic birth. She told Reverend Mother that she brought me to the Institute of the Blessed Virgin Mary because the Blessed Virgin herself had come proclaiming the child she bore must be an educated woman. And so she left them with that dying wish . . ." Percy looked away, pained. "My mother said her purpose had been fulfilled, and, as if she were simply used up, she died."

"I see." Miss Thompson made a few notes. It was well that Percy did not expect pity or sentiment, for she was given neither. "Miss Parker, Athens is unique in that we recognize all qualities in our students. We've a Quaker model here at Athens. We champion the equality of the sexes and I happen to believe that learning is not bound in books alone. It is my personal practice to ask our students if they believe they possess a gift. Other than your multiple languages, do you have any other particular talents?"

Percy swallowed hard. She was unprepared for this question. For anyone else it may have been a perfectly normal inquiry, but Percy knew she was far from average. "I have a rather strange manner of dreams."

The headmistress blinked. "We all dream, Miss Parker. That is nothing extraordinary."

"No. Of course not, Headmistress."

"Unless these dreams come more in the manner of visions?"

Percy hoped the flash of panic in her eyes remained hidden behind her tinted glasses. Years ago, when Reverend Mother found out about the visions and ghosts, she'd put aside her shock to caution Percy about speaking of such things. Neither was something the science-mad, rational world would celebrate. Percy knew her appearance was odd enough, let alone seeing the dead or having visions. It was lonely to be so strange, and Percy wanted to confess everything she felt was wrong with her and have the headmistress accept her. But she also recalled the horrible day when unburdening her soul had caused a priest to try to exorcise her best friend, a ghost named Gregory, from the convent courtyard. She'd never find anyone who could truly understand. Thus, she would not associate herself with the word "vision," and she would most certainly never again admit to seeing ghosts.

She cleared her throat. "Those who claim to have visions are either holy or madmen."

The headmistress was clearly taken aback, as much as her patrician façade might indicate: she arched an eyebrow. "As a girl raised in a convent, do you not consider yourself a woman of religion?"

Percy shifted again. Miss Thompson had unwittingly

touched upon a troubling topic. Percy could not help but wonder about her faith. Those in her abbey's order, the oldest of its kind existing in England, had withstood innumerable trials under the empire. Every novice and sister took fierce pride in their resilience and that of their elders. But Percy, a girl who kept and was left to herself, felt out of place, the colourless curiosity of her skin notwithstanding; her restless disposition had difficulty acquiescing to the rigours of the cloth. Only the presence of a spirit out of its time—such as her Elizabethan-era Gregory—had made her feel at home. No, doctrine could not explain the world as Percy knew it. An unsettling sense of fate made her ache in ways prayer could not wholly relieve.

But none of this was appropriate to discuss in present circumstances. "I am a woman of . . . *spirit,* Headmistress. By no means would I commend myself holy. And I'd like to think I'm not mad."

The raucous shriek of a bird came close to Miss Thompson's window. The sound made Percy jump. A raven settled on the ledge outside. Percy couldn't help but notice an oddly coloured patch on the large black bird's breast. Percy didn't stare further, lest she seem easily distracted. She waited for Headmistress Thompson's gaze to pin her again, which it soon did.

"Dreams then, Miss Parker?"

"Yes, Headmistress. Just dreams."

The headmistress scribbled a note and frowned curiously at an unopened envelope in Percy's file before placing it carefully at the back of the folder. Before Percy could wonder, the headmistress continued. "We have no dream study, Miss Parker. A girl like you doesn't have many options, and so I would advise you to make the most of your time here. It seems fitting your focus should be languages; however you must maintain high marks in all courses in order to continue at the academy. Do you have other interests, Miss Parker?"

"Art has always been a great love of mine," Percy stated. "I used to paint watercolours for the parish. I also adore Shakespeare."

A scrawl into the file. "Dislikes?"

"I'm afraid the sciences and mathematics are beyond me. Neither were subjects the convent felt necessary for young ladies."

The headmistress loosed a dry chuckle that made Percy uneasy. "There is no escaping at least one mathematics or science sequence. I am placing you in our Mathematics and Alchemical Study."

Percy held back a grimace. "Certainly, Headmistress."

Miss Thompson cleared her throat and leveled a stern gaze at her. "And now, Miss Parker, I must warn you of the dangers of our unique, coeducational institution. There is to be no—and I repeat, no—contact between members of the opposite sex. Not of your peer group, and most certainly not with your teachers. The least infraction, however innocent it may seem—the holding of a hand, the kiss on a cheek—will require immediate dismissal. You must understand our position: any word of fraternization or scandal will doom our revolutionary program. And while I hardly think any of this would be an issue for you in particular, Miss Parker, I must say it nonetheless."

Percy nodded, at first proud the headmistress should think so highly of her virtue; then came the sting as she realized the headmistress meant her looks would garner no such furtive conduct. Worse, Percy felt sure she was right.

"Classes begin Monday. Here is a schedule and key for Athene Hall, room seven."

As Percy took the papers and key, she was gripped by a thrill. "Thank you so very much, Miss Thompson! I cannot thank you enough for the opportunity to be here."

The headmistress maintained a blank, severe stare. "Do not thank me. Do not fail."

"I promise to do my best, Headmistress!"

"If it be of any interest to you, a meditative Quaker service is held Sundays. You'll find none of your Catholic frills here. But indeed, Miss Parker, the school keeps quiet about all of that, as I am sure you may well do yourself, living in intolerant times."

"Yes, Headmistress."

"Good day, Miss Parker—and welcome to Athens."

"Thank you, Headmistress. Good day!" Percy beamed, and she darted out the door to explore her new home.

Inside the office, Rebecca Thompson stared at the door, feeling the strange murmur in her veins that was part of her intuitive gift. Her instincts were never clarion, but they alerted her to things of import. Miss Parker, her gentle nature evident in the sweet timbre of her voice, had set off a signal.

Rebecca considered the envelope in the girl's file. *Please open upon Miss Parker's graduation—or when she has been provided for,* it read. "I daresay a girl like you won't find yourself 'provided for,' Miss Parker," Rebecca muttered.

Turning to the window, she opened the casement, and the raven outside hopped in and strutted over the wooden file cabinets, occasionally stopping to preen his one bright blue breast feather that indicated his service to The Guard.

"It's odd, Frederic," Rebecca remarked. "I can't imagine that awkward, unfortunate girl has anything to do with us; it doesn't follow. It *shouldn't* follow."

Growing up, as The Guard chose their mortal professions, it was agreed that a few of them should remain near the chapel and portal of The Grand Work on the fortresslike grounds of Athens. Rebecca and Alexi were the perfect candidates for academia, and for twenty years now had followed that path. Athens was a place where Alexi and Rebecca were known as nothing other than upstanding Victorian citizens providing for the intellectual improvement of the young. The two had agreed to never bring The Grand Work upon their students. The school was the one place where it seemed they controlled destiny rather than destiny controlling them—and they had fought to keep it that way.

Yes, the secrets of The Grand Work were matters for the world beyond the school walls. Their prophetic seventh had been named a peer, and that meant these students were not subjects of scrutiny. No, while Miss Parker did not appear a "normal" girl, and though she happened to spark interest, she was likely nothing more than a child deserving a solid education.

Rebecca sighed, easing into her chair as Frederic hopped onto her shoulder. She considered inviting Alexi to tea, then allowed he would be steeped as usual in solitude, frowning over texts of scholarship, his favourite companions. As predicted, their personalities and desires had not changed when the six great spirits entered them. Still, Rebecca and her friends' lives revolved around duty, a reality that Rebecca resented more with each passing year. Privately she wished those spirits had taken her heart when they arrived, for it was a terribly lonely destiny, and even The Grand Work couldn't change that.

CHAPTER TWO

Percy entered into Athens's courtyard, a large rectangular space surrounded by archways. Covered corridors with sparkling, diamond-shaped panels of Bavarian glass joined each building, and every facade sported the same Romanesque features hewn from red sandstone. The dormitories rose at the narrow ends, while the academic halls constituted the clerestory length of the rectangle. Athens was sealed entirely by walls from the bustle of London beyond, a sanctuary where only the ambient sound of a throbbing city washed over the stones like the lap of waves.

The centerpiece of the cobblestone courtyard immediately took Percy's interest. An angel towered over a fountain of deep bronze, a book in her upraised hand. Lilies at her feet spewed water from their widening buds.

Next, the ladies' student quarters caught her eye, and she saw they were smaller than those of the gentlemen. As she was surely to be an outnumbered female in her classes, Percy began to realize the differences of this world—a world that held infinite possibility. Percy had long dreamed of romance. Aided by dear Gregory, that genial middle-aged spirit, she'd played every Shakespearean heroine in the privacy of her convent room. However, interactions between Percy and living men, who of course didn't speak in pentameter, were uncommon. Should occasion call for masculine contact, the abbey specimens were dour men of the cloth who barely acknowledged Percy as human let alone female. Recalling the well-assembled, handsome young men here who'd gaped rudely upon her arrival, Percy remembered Miss Thompson's pointed remarks on her age and state . . . and resigned herself to scorning rather than soliciting romantic prospects.

Years ago she'd fallen in love with Mr. Darcy, as she supposed every young woman had done while reading Austen and first discovering her femininity. Romance and imagination were elemental to Percy's heart. She'd never been in love with a real man, of course, for her skin and convent shelter kept her from ever being noticed or appreciated by any suitable candidates—and she supposed it was safer to relegate love to the realm of fantasy, anyway. But whether she ever might feel the reality of love, the ache of its absence she understood well.

Perhaps, she rallied, she might follow the headmistress's independent example and someday run a school of her own, full of unfortunates like herself.

Gazing at her surroundings, she let out a spate of fateful

murmurs to stave off the aching prospect of life without love. She was here to learn, not frolic! Recalling the headmistress's mention of possible employment, she reminded herself to be grateful: an unfortunate such as herself was lucky to get anything at all.

Strolling along the courtyard, Percy found she could easily keep her delicate skin safely beneath the shadows of an arched walkway; the sun would do her no damage here. And realizing that each hall branching off the yard had a variant name of a Greek god or goddess etched above its wooden entryway, Percy smiled.

Stepping onto the small landing of Athene Hall, she threw her slight weight against the thick door to open it and slid into a paneled foyer. Below narrow stairs beyond, a sour-faced woman sat surrounded by lists, notices and unopened post.

The woman started at the sight of Percy. "My, my. Good afternoon, miss, are you a student here?"

"Yes, madame, I only just arrived," Percy replied. "My name is Percy Parker." When the woman at the desk blinked dull eyes, Percy's fingers nervously intertwined. "Room seven?" she added.

The matron broke their locked stares to skim a list of names. "Ah, yes. P. Parker. I'm Miss Jennings. You'll find me here should you dream of slipping out after hours, no matter what your appearance. Your room is just upstairs," Miss Jennings finished, and eagerly returned to her lists.

Room seven was marked with gold paint upon a dark door. The room was small but far airier than the brick of Percy's former quarters at the abbey. A window inset with Tudor roses faced the door. A still life hung above the iron-framed bed: wildflowers beside a pomegranate, the fruit's reddish skin parted to reveal glistening ruby seeds so ripe they appeared bloody. This innocuous image made Percy shudder, and she turned to unpack her meager belongings.

Opening a velvet box, she took out a silver necklace. Near

the door was a long mirror, and Percy donned the necklace and stared: a silver bird with outstretched wings and a tail of flame now flew over the fabric around her neck. She unwound her layers of scarves and lace, freeing her length of pearlescent hair to tumble around her shoulders and down her sides. In the mirror, a barely corporeal reflection stared back.

She touched her face and sighed, confirming that she was indeed flesh and blood. Then she tucked the phoenix pendant below the folds of her dress, out of sight but close to her heart. An ancient and pagan symbol, she could never wear it on the outside of her clothing at the convent, but she had always kept it close, as it was the only thing her mother left her.

A movement near the window caught her eye, and a spirit in a mess of a Regency gown stuck her head through the panes. When Percy met the girl's transparent eyes, the girl made a face and withdrew as quickly as she had appeared. Percy shook her head. London had an incredible number of ghosts, and she felt like she'd seen every single one on her journey from York.

She'd wished to take the train, but Father Harris had insisted upon a carriage. Percy knew he dared not be seen at the York station platform in the company of such an odd charge. The city had grown slowly before her eyes as they rode: an intricate, messy, living creature. Country pastures speckled with cottages had given way to stout brick houses that narrowed and nestled closer and closer together. Houses compressed into apartments, gardens were traded for window boxes; flower petals began to kiss from one wooden trough to the next before there ceased to be flowers at all, and living quarters were stacked haphazardly amid pubs, banks, shops and city halls. All surfaces had grown progressively darker, choked by the immense soot of the city that added a grim weight to the London fog.

In the heart of the city, stately facades were followed by

dark lanes increasingly peopled by spirits. Shadowed door-
ways containing desperate, shivering figures opened onto
malls where hansom cabs trotted in conspicuous display, grit
coupling with grandeur. Down every cluttered lane, wraiths
of every station represented the vast spread of life that had
built the city over the centuries. Percy's sight was full of
them walking next to unsuspecting humans, floating in and
out of wooden pub walls and up from the sewers, turning
eerie heads as she passed, acknowledging her.

One disheveled bricklayer floated near a window on Tot-
tenham Court Road, his labouring spirit edging mortar that
had long since hardened with a transparent trowel. A society
lady in a grand gown passed down the same avenue, vanished, and repeated her journey, perhaps awaiting deferential
hails or an escort that never came. Percy could never have
imagined the veritable crowds of London spectres. Smiling,
she entertained the thought that they welcomed her.

London was a tangled mess of streets rebuilt after the Great
Fire and according to ancient maps. Roads twisted, took
full-corner turns and vanished completely, began and changed
names at strange places and disorienting angles, wound
around masses of cramped architecture. From the Thames
one gained one's bearings, but a block up the bank there was
no hope to see anything but the fresh, stately spires of Parlia-
ment. She noticed only one Catholic chapel, its gothic windows nestled between a cobbler and a butcher. Finally, a
fortress the colour of a sooty autumn maple leaf hove into
view, tucked within half a city block in the district of
Bloomsbury on a road that remained nameless. It had seemed
that her destination, Athens, a place the reverend mother
had referred to as "London's best-kept secret," was perhaps
a good place to keep one's own secrets. Percy certainly
hoped so.

Allowing a sudden exhaustion, she sank onto her new bed
in her new room. Her eyes felt strange, as if a curtain were
drawn across them, and a vision followed: Tendrils of mist

emanated from a dim opening, and a white glimmer appeared at the bottom of the widening black portal. A skeletal hand crept to the edge of the hole. Another hand appeared at the opposite corner. Another, and another . . . The bony host of hands clicked as they reached upon each other, and there came murmuring whispers of a thousand years. From the shadowy center of the door, something shifted into view—the huge head of a ghoulish dog. Wide canine eyes glistened and shone with an alien, crimson light. A dripping, gruesome snout sniffed as if the beast were on the hunt, preparing to race off and consume its prey . . .

Percy shrank back, the vision fading. She had no idea what the creature might have to do with her—and she didn't want to know.

From the eternally dim shadows of the Whisper-world a voice resonated like a deep, angry bell tolling three o'clock: "Where. Is. She?"

"I've no idea, dear," replied a softer, feminine voice. "Was I supposed to do something about her? I thought you've been looking all this time. While you've only just noticed, it's been eighteen of their years. She could be anywhere. She's not my responsibility, you know."

The deep voice grunted. "Do. Something."

The woman sighed, her fair skin glowing in the moonlight. Placing her hands to her coiled tresses atop her head, she found something sharp. With a hiss, she brought her thumbs back into view; their pricked pads sprouted thick, dark jewels, garnets that began to overflow and weep. Lifting up her hands, she watched in fascination as the crimson trail spread from her thumbs onto her palms. She turned her hands one direction, then the other.

"Hmm," she said after a long moment.

"Well?" pressed the voice in the shadows.

"London," she replied.

"Something wicked, then?" the voice gurgled.

The woman turned and smiled, nonchalant. "By all means, let the dog loose."

There was a grinding of stone. A ferocious growl erupted from the deep, before a barking, snarling, ugly cloud leaped into the sky. It vanished into the shimmering portal opposite the shadows where the woman's master stood brooding, a portal where now rose the Tower of London.

The voice tolled again from the shadows. "There will be hell to pay."

CHAPTER THREE

London's fashionable dead populated Highgate cemetery, near the suitably gothic moorland of Hampstead Heath. It was fitting that the estate of Professor Alexi Rychman was as striking, dark and brooding as its master had grown up to be, a building nestled at an equidistant point from those two eerily beautiful expanses of rugged flora and carved stone.

All in black, greatcoat billowing about him, a wide-brimmed hat low over his noble brow, Alexi strode toward the wide carriage that had sped to a halt at the end of his drive.

"Evening, Professor," called the driver from up top, bushy sideburns peppered with grey and a handlebar mustache framing a familiar jolly grin.

"Evening, Vicar Michael."

"Evening, Alexi," Rebecca Thompson echoed from within.

"Evening, Headmistress." Alexi nodded as he climbed into the carriage, removing his hat, dark eyes flashing with banked fires. He loosened the signature red cravat about his throat as the moonlight fell through the carriage windows onto those striking features his friends hardly ever saw fixed in anything but unbreakable concentration.

"Bon soir," said a soft French voice across the carriage.

"Evening, Josephine," Alexi replied, nodding to her as well. "Do you have your piece?"

Josephine indicated she did, holding up a small canvas wrapped in paper.

Josephine Belledoux was an artist whose impressive credits included a painting in nearly every major English museum and countless private residences. However, no one seemed to remember her name. Her shimmering, calming pictures produced such a profound effect that they were immediately forgotten . . . and thus never removed. And there were other effects. The British Museum owned a few of her paintings, the work fulfilling vigilant duty to the Crown in keeping the treasure of the empire free from spectral disturbance.

Josephine had grown into the sort of beauty that could prompt a war. Tonight, her shocks of prematurely white hair were wound into the elaborate coiffure atop her head. Those bold streaks had been there as long as any could remember, since that very first day on the bridge. Out of respect, no one had ever asked why, and Josephine never told.

Alexi closed his eyes and felt within himself for the Pull. The Guard all knew that unmistakable alarm of spectral disturbance. His mind coursed the streets of London, as if tracing a specific drop of his own blood; the massive arteries of London were superimposed upon his own, and wherever there was a spasm, there was his destination.

Rebecca watched Alexi's brow furrow in mild strain. Alexi's inner cartography was keen, but her own was unmatched.

"South of Holborn . . . north of Embankment this evening. Am I right?" He eyed her.

She smirked. "Indeed you are. Impressive." Each of the six tried to outdo the others on pinpointing their subjects, not only to an address but often giving a specific floor and room. Once, Rebecca had even identified the victim's attire.

The carriage cleared the countryside and was soon rattling through the dark, bustling streets of London, in and out of gaslit avenues both wide and narrow before slowing on Fleet Street.

"Prepare ye!" Michael's merry voice sounded from above.

Screams usually alerted The Guard that they had arrived. So it was this time: strangled cries and intermittent bestial growls came from a shattered window a few stories above. A crowd had gathered, murmuring low and excited. The Guard's carriage stopped nearby, and Vicar Michael Carroll descended from the driver's seat to help the ladies disembark. He took particular care with Rebecca, and made sure to linger on her arm for a bit longer than mere friendship would require, but Rebecca didn't notice; her attention was on Alexi, as usual. A raven was hopping on the roof of the carriage and making noise.

Lord Elijah Withersby stood upon the dim, cobbled street pretending to be a bystander, but his fine, rich clothes screamed that he didn't belong. At his side stood a hearty, dark blonde Irishwoman wearing a modest dress and a distant smile. She still had an incredibly long Catholic name that had been shortened to Jane.

Once assembled, The Guard formed a line and took hands, and Frederic the raven flew to the window. Something magical was undoubtedly present. A wary cry came from the window above.

Alexi's commanding voice pierced the evening, a single word plucked on the lyre of an ancient language known only to The Guard. The foreign declaration reverberated down the street, and the eyes of the six gleamed too brightly as they turned to gaze upon the bystanders. One by one, as if tired or bored, the crowd wandered off, returning to their various points of origin. Wiped from their memories was the incident; it was as if nothing odd had occurred at all. England's populace at large was not involved with The

Grand Work. Neither were the denizens of London to know about it.

The raven returned to Rebecca's shoulder, biting her ear fondly. He pecked at her shoulder rhythmically, and she passed along his information:

"Frederic reports one priest, two parents and a little girl—inhabitant volatile."

Alexi nodded. "'Once more into the breach, dear friends, once more.'"

The company stepped to the landing. Alexi summoned Michael forward with a command: "Come, the gentle heart opens many doors."

The vicar stepped ahead, placed bent fingers in front of his chest, and the locked front door swung open with a strange metallic sound. The Guard swept inward, and the six tore up the stairs to the flat on the second floor, where Michael's fingers rose again and the flat's door swung open with the same odd noise. Passing through the parlor and dining room toward an unnatural light spilling from the bedroom, Alexi flung the unlocked door wide.

Inside was an eight-year-old girl who lay rigid upon her bed, her skin glowing.

"Luminous!" Alexi declared her state as a matter of protocol—of course all could see that the girl was possessed. Planting his imposing presence at the foot of her bed, he looked at the parents, then at the priest, and smiled broadly. "Good evening! It would appear you have an intruder!"

Before the horrified parents or the priest, midscripture, could react to this additional invasion, Elijah fixed them each with an intent stare. The three relaxed at once, and their gazes misted contentedly over. Elijah patted each on the head, satisfied with their submission.

Michael placed a hand on the priest's shoulder and indicated his own Anglican vestments. "Bless you, Father—and not to worry," he added to the fellow clergyman who would remember nothing. "You're doing a lovely job. We're just helping." He always felt the need to explain himself.

Alexi, his expression fierce, tossed off his black greatcoat and suit jacket and began rolling up his charcoal-coloured shirtsleeves. He lifted his hands, conjuring the usual inexplicable blue flame before him. As he turned his palms outward, more fire issued forth, and he began to weave the hovering wisps into a graceful dance. A circle of flickering blue now framed the little girl's body, but a sick grey light pulsed like a heartbeat within, illuminating her skeleton and shuddering organs.

Rebecca and Michael took positions across the room, while the other three continued various stages of their chores. Josephine ripped paper away from a shimmering painting, and she hung the dynamic portrait of a winged, airborne angel in the center of the wall.

"Name of victim?" Rebecca asked with crisp efficiency, taking notes on a small pad.

Elijah bent over the girl and pressed his hand to hers. He gasped, pictures searing his mind with their psychometric power. "Emily. A quiet child. Inhabitant came upon her during evening prayers. Inhabitant is angry and dangerous—responsible for a death half a century ago. It won't show me how."

Rebecca nodded. "That shall suffice, Elijah. Thank you for your talents."

"It's cruel. But it isn't that Ripper," Elijah went on, shuddering, wiping away the sweat that had burst forth upon his brow.

"Damn," Alexi muttered.

Remaining unobtrusive, Michael moved to Elijah's side and gave his friend a serene smile. He gently pressed Elijah's hands in his, calming him with the effects of his enormous heart. Indeed, an endlessly kind soul could achieve almost anything.

"Thank you, Vicar," Elijah breathed, and returned to maintain control over the girl's family and priest.

"Emily," whispered Josephine, standing at the foot of the girl's bed. The child's eyes, squeezed shut in great pain, now opened to stare at her and plead for help. Josephine directed the child's gaze to the painting of the angel. "Stare long and hard, Mademoiselle Emily." She herself fixed her eyes on the shimmering seraphim. "This is your guardian, Emily. Look here, he will ease your pain."

Moving to the parents, who were staring dreamily at the ceiling while Elijah so bade it, Josephine placed a hand above them and turned her palms. Like marionettes, their heads followed her movements toward the picture on the wall. "That is never to be removed," she commanded.

The little girl began to choke. Michael breathed in a steady rhythm, guiding everyone's breath by example, and Jane moved opposite Alexi, standing on the other side of the bed. The Irishwoman placed two suddenly glowing hands upon the circle of azure flame that Alexi had summoned to contain the inhabitant, and the rigidity of Emily's limbs eased.

There came an indignant rumble. Emily's back arched unnaturally. Blood dribbled from her chapped lips. Jane's fingers bent as if playing the keys of a piano, and the blood vanished.

"Name of inhabitant?" Rebecca asked, and turned another page of notes on the conditions of the evening: weather, locale, persons present, services rendered, etc.

Elijah bent again, this time touching Emily's shoulder, where the spirit inside strained against her little limbs. "Muezzin," he gasped in pain. Michael moved to place a hand upon Elijah's collar, and began to laugh quietly. Elijah's face twisted but, after a moment, a sigh escaped and he was able to nod and smile.

"Muezzin is a title not a name, but I suppose it will do," Rebecca replied, and she began to recite a text that the spirit would recognize and heed. Such literary knowledge was particular to Rebecca, and not strictly a required part of the ritual, but she had found it useful in commanding spirits' at-

tention and respect. "'Alike for those who for Today prepare, and those that after some Tomorrow stare, A Muezzin
from the Tower of Darkness cries, *Fools! Your Reward is neither Here nor There*.'"

The transparent, skeletal form gave a jolting movement in
response.

"Nicely done, Rebecca, what was that? And what did you
mean, a title not a name?" Elijah was flipping through the
Bible in the priest's hands.

"In life, this spirit was a muezzin, calling all men of Mus-
lim faith to prayer," Rebecca clarified. "But I sense it began
to denounce Allah for his mercy and peace, turning away
from faith and from him. No, it will *not* disperse quietly. I
don't know that anything will—" Rebecca suddenly whimpered, overwhelmed by the helplessness the spirit hoped to
foist upon them.

Michael stepped forward to dispel the dread, kissing her
gently upon the forehead. Her face relaxing, she gave him
thanks.

Rebecca then repeated the verse pulled from *The Rubaiyat,* recently translated by an Englishman and indeed perfect
for the occasion. The muezzin's spirit moved in Emily, as if
trying to respond: a few gurgling sounds were transferred
from the passion of the spirit to the numb lips of the child.
The sounds resembled actual words, a distant tongue. Then,
sensing it could not use the child's mouth as it wished, the
spectre shifted out of her face and strained a ghastly head
away from Emily's body. Its unnatural mouth contorted in
spasms.

"It speaks," Jane noted ruefully.

It was a particular nuisance of The Grand Work that The
Guard was granted a modicum of control over troubled spirits, but no direct communication. They could hear the occasional murmur, but could not always understand.

"Regardless of it knowing my translation of *The Rubaiyat,*
I cannot speak its language," Rebecca spat. "Why is one of

us not a translator, Alexi, for the tiny bits we can hear? Though for that matter, why should we need one? Alexi, why are we mediating spirits from the East? Since when do we traffic in international trade?"

"Yes, Alexi," Jane piped up. "Nonnative spirits have increased dramatically. Eight within recent months have traversed the whole of the Atlantic and more to rattle our isle. That damned American war alone will have us reeling until we die. And every year it grows worse."

"I suppose it could be a sign," Alexi replied. His voice was quiet.

Rebecca stopped and stared. "You mean, a *sign?*"

Emily began mumbling. The spirit was contracting and wrestling more fiercely against her face, desperate to win the child's mouth.

"Sh...she...she's coming," Emily murmured. "She's coming!" Then suddenly: "SHE IS COMING!"

Everyone gasped. Jane held Emily down as the child shook, and Alexi bound the spirit tighter with violent swipes of his hand and flame.

"You don't suppose Emily means Prophecy is coming...does she?" Michael asked, surprised.

The group stared, apprehensive. They'd begun to think it just a dream, a hallucination they'd all shared, regardless of any other proof they had of the night. It had been so many years since that incredible woman told them such improbable tales in their chapel, and they weren't quite sure what to believe anymore. Though, they could not doubt The Grand Work which they now performed.

Alexi set his jaw. "I will believe nothing until I see the foretold signs, and I urge you to do the same. Until then, words are just words. Remember to beware of false prophets." From his tone, the matter was clearly closed to further discussion.

"Bind with us, Alexi. It gathers vehemence," Michael warned, reaching out his hand.

Elijah whispered to the parents and priest, and those three continued to stare blankly at Josephine's painting. The Guard joined hands in a circle around the bed.

Emily's arms flew out, rigid again at her side. There came a horrible crunching noise from her hands—bones breaking—and the child screamed. Jane set her jaw and disengaged from the circle, taking the child's damaged flesh in hers, bestowing a misty sphere of glowing light upon each fingertip; then she again joined the circle.

"Hold on, Emily, dear heart, this will be over soon."

"Cantus of the Eviscerate," Alexi proclaimed, and magnificence coursed through him, making him a brilliant, powerful conduit. The Guard began to chant something low and lovely that formed in the air like particles of heaven. It was full of music, as if accompanied by an orchestra of a thousand, yet barely rang louder than a whisper. They were the simple words of their private, ancient order, words which Emily's possessor hated.

The blue flames wound tighter and tighter on their own, sinews binding the spirit without Alexi's conducting. The spectre opened its jaws as if howling. Emily manifested the nightmarish sound, making it twice as horrible.

The child's skin became brittle. Hairline fissures, like the cracking of a porcelain doll, began to spread across her arms and legs. Blood, thickened by possession and steeped in a glowing grey light, slowly dribbled up through her splitting flesh. Jane tried to counteract this veinlike spread across the child's body, but the wounds held no parley.

Intense beams of grey light shot from the cracks in Emily's skin and a strange mist began to pour from all orifices in her face. The vapour clung outside the girl's body, growing into a shuddering human form that curled into the fetal position, cowering as she lay sobbing.

"Emily, look to the wall, to your angel, sweet child," Josephine urged.

The parasitic vapours next wrapped around the child's

neck, cursing her for the accessible soul that drew the spirit in, then imprisoned it with the righteous fear that was ultimately the body's savior: Emily's unspoiled heart would rather let the beast destroy her than turn violence upon others. The Guard wasn't always so fortunate. Weaker subjects could always be found and driven to unspeakable things. London's mysterious Ripper was likely evidence enough of such horror.

The cantus reached its climax, an unyielding "Shhhh" in which The Guard released their clasped hands and placed a finger to their mouths, and the intruder burst apart like ashes in a gust of wind. It blinked out, leaving behind only a tendril of mist.

Emily lay silent. Her bloodshot eyes were fixed to the painting across the room, and she looked as ghastly as ever.

Jane sat by the child's side and began to sing a lullaby, brushing hair from the girl's face with a glowing hand. She placed illuminated fingertips on each of Emily's hands, and the glow spread. The blood that had risen to the surface retreated again, and the child's flesh regained the smooth perfection of youth. The tiny spheres of ivory light that had been left floating above Emily's mending fingers merged into a larger ball of light that returned to Jane's abdomen. A shiver worked up the Irishwoman's spine as the power reentered her.

Michael scooped Jane into a warm embrace, softly murmuring what an amazing job she'd done. Josephine bent, whispering a French benediction upon Emily's forehead. The child responded by falling into a comatose slumber. Alexi's shoulders fell, and he moved to lean against the wall, rubbing his temples.

Michael moved next to gather Rebecca in his arms; then, with a contented giggle, he gave her a smacking kiss on the cheek. Rebecca made a face and batted her eyelashes at him. Michael's giggle turned into his very special laugh—a necessary part of the night. The laugh was contagious. All six now laughed loudly and openly, and the dark energy that had permeated the room was banished. The room, and each soul within it, was cleansed.

The mesmerized priest's fingers closed around his Bible, his eyes vacant as Elijah sent him out the bedroom door with a pat on the back. Elijah then patted the parents, who drifted off, dazed, to their respective bedchambers. In the morning the trio would remember nothing.

Rebecca finished her notes before moving toward Alexi. She carefully parted a lock of black hair on his damp forehead and kissed his cheek, then forced herself to retreat. Alexi's lips twisted into a weary smile as his eyes flickered across her, but the expression faded as he looked out the window with a melancholy stare. Such extraordinary circumstances never failed to stir up emotion. Tears rolled down Josephine's smooth cheeks, and she made no effort to stop them.

Alexi straightened into his typical, formidable presence. "Well done, my compatriots."

"Time for a drink!" Elijah declared, his fist high in the air. "To Café La Belle et La Bête!"

Everyone filed out of the building and into the night.

Alexi, exhausted, took one final moment to contemplate an alternate history where he might have become a renowned scientist instead of an academic who chased ghosts. But The Grand Work had its own agenda, and his mortal desires were in no way considered. Prophecy suggested, of course, that someday his empty heart would be warmed and refreshed, but until he could be sure, until *she* came forward and his divine goddess could again speak to him, everything, including Alexi, was holding its breath—and choking on it. A little girl on Fleet Street might be safe for the moment, but the rest of London was not.

Still . . . she was coming, wasn't she? She'd best show herself before the last of his hope died and he didn't recognize her at all.

CHAPTER FOUR

Percy woke with a terrible start, roused by nightmares of her first day of class. The dreams had climaxed with a hundred eyes that bored so deeply that her skin peeled away piece by piece, leaving only bones beneath as she sat at a classroom table. A single bell struck softly somewhere above: it was only Sunday.

She dressed and left her chambers, entered Promethe Hall, following a small stream of people—and an equal number of spirits—to the school chapel. Thankfully the grey shadows of morning, together with the cover of her soft blue shawl, kept her from attracting attention; living or deceased, no Sunday morning penitent whispered, pointed or even stared at her.

Percy would not have thought to find such a unique chapel within a Quaker school. The place seemed . . . alive. Rows of amber stained-glass angels burned with inner light. White pillars supported smooth, arched rafters, and made the tiny building appear larger than possible, as if a portion of heaven itself had been annexed by it. An elegant fresco, a white dove of peace, covered the dome above a modest altar dressed in white linen. To Percy's delight, the shape of the bird's outstretched wings, and the generous spread of light about its feathers, reminded her of the pendant she wore against her skin.

The service was sprinkled with long, reflective silences for the benefit of meditation. It was peaceful, vastly different than elaborate Catholic rituals. Yet, oddly, something here felt like home.

Leaving the chapel in a daze, Percy wandered back to her

hall and sat in the shade of the front stairs. Listening to the splash of the fountain in the courtyard, she eventually found herself roused from her reverie by the anxious sound of a young lady struggling to say an English word. Behind her stood a pair, one of whom attempted to overcome a thick German accent. The other, a plump brunette, stared blankly.

"I'm sorry, miss, but I don't understand you," snapped the brunette, and walked away.

The German girl watched the other girl depart, baffled. Clad in an elegant, russet-coloured traveling dress, she put her pretty face into her hands. Her blonde hair, set in elaborate braids atop her head, shuddered as she began to cry.

Percy rose with a hesitant smile. *"Guten tag, Fräulein. Was ist seine Problem?"*

The young lady looked up with a priceless expression and turned to see who spoke. Percy expected the girl to gape, and was surprised when there came no reaction to her odd appearance.

"Oh!" the girl exclaimed happily, and flew into a torrent of German, stating that she'd lost her room key, wasn't sure of her hall assignment, what to do about it or with whom to speak.

"Kommen Sie mit mir," assured Percy, leading the way toward the headmistress's office.

"Danke! Danke!"

"Bitte." Percy smiled. *"Ich heisse Percy. Percy Parker."*

"Ich heisse Marianna Farelei! Forgive me, I try English. I need speak as much as I can to be better student, yet some words I always . . . *vergesse.* I'm especially bad when others are impatient."

"Well, I'm happy to assist, Marianna."

"Thank you so much . . . Percy. How happy I was to hear Deutsch!" The girl's pleasure was obvious.

"It must be overwhelming for you here in England," Percy pointed out.

"Ja, ja. How do you know to speak my language?"

"I love all languages." Percy smiled warmly. "I suppose you could say I collect them, and have since long before I came here."

"How interesting," Marianna said. "Your previous place of study must have been very nice."

Percy paused. "I was raised in a convent. *Eine Kirche.*"

"Ah."

Marianna had finally taken the time to consider Percy's face. This prompted Percy to explain, "I was born with this terrible pallor. Forgive me if I frighten you."

"Frighten? No, I think it is lovely, your face. You are like a doll—I do not know the name . . . one of those that break if you drop them. I used to have one. She was my favourite."

However awkward, Marianna had chosen the perfect words. Percy smiled at the girl's kindness. "What happened to your doll?"

"She broke. I dropped her." Marianna bit her lip. "I am sometimes very clumsy."

Percy giggled. Marianna stole a glance at her, then started to giggle, too.

With one quick trip to the headmistress's office, the two solved Marianna's problem, facilitated by Percy's translation whenever necessary. The girls then strolled back across the courtyard toward their dormitory.

"What are the words on each building?" Marianna asked.

"They are odd variants of Greek names. I've never seen them written quite like this."

"Greek names?"

"Yes, tributes to Greek gods—like my name is."

"Yours? I do not remember a 'Percy' goddess."

Percy smiled. "It's a pet name of sorts."

"Are you the same age as me?" Marianna asked, peering at her. "I cannot tell. You could be young, or much older, with that face."

"I am eighteen, older than most here. I was matriculated due to my . . . circumstances."

"Ah, I see. I am . . ." Marianna fought for an English number. "Fifteen."

"And how did you find Athens?" Percy doubted the German girl was sent away due to any oddness, like herself.

Marianna shrugged. "I desire school, my parents did not and hoped I would change my mind if they applied far away, somewhere quiet like this. But I would have done *anything* to continue." She smiled suddenly. "Of course, if they truly know what I wish to do . . ."

"And what is that?" Percy prompted.

"I would give my heart to be . . . *eine Speilerin*."

"An actress?" Percy repeated.

"*Ja,* but my father would run me through with a sword!"

Percy laughed then mused, "An actress. The only plays I have ever seen were Nativities at the abbey. I loved them, of course. They were magical. But I have read all of Shakespeare, and—"

"*Ich liebe* Shakespeare!"

"Good, then we'll have much to quote each other, you and I!" Percy felt a rush of pleasure at having found a possible friend—a *living* friend—to share her time here.

From behind her glasses, she squinted at the blue-grey sky and added, "I never knew my parents. I wonder about them, though, and imagine how it would be to look like everyone else. To consider dreams, and futures, like they do. Of course, were I to dream of the stage, I'd only be fit to play Hamlet's ghost." Percy sighed.

Marianna's eyes lit, and she exclaimed excitedly, "Or Ariel or Titania!"

Percy grinned as she realized this was perfectly true.

Inside, they reached their respective chamber doors, and Marianna said, "I must . . . settle in and write letters now. Percy, will you sit with me at first meal?"

"I'd be delighted," Percy replied. A sliver of desperation edged her words as she added, "I would like to consider you a friend. May I?"

"Of course you are a friend! Why do you ask?" The German girl seemed surprised.

Percy stared at the cobblestones. "I look strange, Marianna. I'm nothing like the others. If things are the same here . . . well, people will whisper and scoff, repulsed by the look of me. I don't want to make you uncomfortable, and—"

"I speak different. You do not . . . look at me strange when I talk. You help. And you think you look *frightening?*"

Percy shrugged. "My skin, my eyes, my hair . . . No single aspect of me is normal."

"Your hair is white? Your eyes, too?" Marianna asked, peering closer.

Percy nodded, wondering if she should take off her glasses.

Marianna shrugged. "You are . . . pretty as a sculpture is pretty. Do not be ashamed," she ordered.

"I am grateful for your kindness."

"And I for yours," Marianna replied.

"Indeed. I shall see you soon."

"Yes, my friend. Good afternoon!"

Percy returned to her room, spirit uplifted. She listened to greetings spoken loudly in the hallways, friends returning and catching up, and decided she was not yet brave enough to make any other forays toward interaction. She would leave such bravery for another day.

On the edge of the Whisper-world, the shadows rang with the voice of Darkness. "What has the dog found in London?"

His female servant sank onto the eternally cold stones, stretching out languidly, attempting to look inviting. The shadows didn't move, and the woman scowled. "Only East End whores. Fitting, don't you think? Isn't that what she is—a whore?"

The shadows grunted. There was a slow, methodical

sound: footfalls, back and forth. "Whatever is left of that bird . . . I'll burn him all over again."

The woman waved her hand. "Yes, yes, I'm sure you will. And, her? When it finds her, will you tell the dog to bring her back alive? Or shredded into pieces?"

The shadows roared, and the woman realized she'd misspoken. Still, there was no going back. "Why, you truly *miss* that troublesome wench, don't you?"

CHAPTER FIVE

Blood was everywhere, drenching the dirty stones of Hanbury Street, flooding the gutter below a wooden gate. A bleary-eyed crowd, growing despite the ungodly hour of the morning, gazed down in horror at the mangled corpse. Constables and a haggard investigator crawled the scene like insects; real flies buzzed alongside. Rumours and shrieks filled the air, and the word "Ripper" was on everyone's lips.

A lean, severe woman stood just beyond the horrified East End crowd. Her brown hair was pinned tightly beneath a simple touring hat, save for one renegade lock, and Rebecca Thompson folded her arms and gazed down at the scene from the steps of an adjacent tenement. At her elbow was the usual tall, formidable man in a long black greatcoat, and he tipped his top hat and squinted upward, his mop of dark hair rustling in the breeze.

"My God, Alexi," Rebecca murmured, brushing her gloved hand across his forearm before resting it again upon the buttons of his sleeve. "Darkly Luminous work this must have been, to have produced such an effect." She shuddered. "Is this a sign of something new?"

A distracted hum was his only reply.

"Alexi, are you listening?"

"There are gargoyles atop this shabby roof. How odd," Alexi mused. "Yet they neglected their sole duty—to deter whatever demon struck here. Poor girl. Poor dead girl."

"You're *not* listening to me."

"I always listen, Rebecca." He turned dark eyes to hers, and his sculpted lips softened into a slight smile; a rare occurrence. "It indeed may be a sign. But we cannot know for sure until this"—he gestured grimly toward the body—"is added to something more substantial. Until we see all that was foretold."

"I confess, I'm shocked we've had so long to wait for Prophecy."

Alexi's jaw hardened. "As am I."

"May she actually help us," Rebecca muttered, squinting at a flock of ravens sweeping around a nearby spire. As Frederic, that unique bird with a patch on his breast, hopped down from a rafter to squawk at them, she waved a mollifying finger. "Forgive me for asking, Alexi, but could you . . . could you have neglected her along the way? Could we have missed her? We're not growing any younger. If . . ."

His stern gaze halted her speech. "'Placed in my path,' it was said. No one has been placed in my path that we have not considered and discounted. Please don't distrust my sensibilities, Rebecca."

She hurried to say, "Of course, I was never suggesting—"

"Please trust that I'm well aware of my age, and that I will remain all the more alert for it!"

Rebecca sighed. "Why do you dislike talking about Prophecy so?"

"Why? Because it's private."

"Private? What's private about a public prophecy?" Rebecca scoffed. "There's nothing private about the fact that our number of six will become seven."

"The . . . fate of the seventh and myself is private."

Rebecca groaned and clenched her fists. "You're still going on about that? About the two of you? Alexi, in what part of her speech did your goddess say you were supposed to love the seventh? Those words were never spoken; love has nothing to do with it!"

He turned and pinned her with his eyes. "I've always believed it, Rebecca. You alone know this. Unless . . ."

Rebecca held up a hand. "I've never said a word."

"And you must not until the time is right. I can only imagine the dreadful gossip." He grimaced, pained. "Elijah wagering on my intimate thoughts . . . The years have proven that my fellow foes of Darkness are drawn to melodrama and rumour." He ground his teeth. "A bond of love *is* implicit in Prophecy, Rebecca, though you claim otherwise. I've made my life choices accordingly, difficult as that has been."

"No, no. *Convenient* as that has been," Rebecca muttered.

Alexi folded his arms and eyed her. "Pardon?"

"It's very convenient for a man as stoic as yourself to decide you'll simply wait for Prophecy like some arranged marriage. None of that dreary mortal pining; none of that average human mess of emotions for you. No, you'll just wait for something divine, and when 'all the appropriate criteria have been met,' like one of your algebraic equations . . . huzzah, you have a bride!" She turned away, hands clenching the folds of her skirts.

After a moment, she whirled on him again, as if she could keep silent no longer. "Should you be right, would you even know what to do with her? No, Alexi, I daresay you wouldn't. And as you persist in thinking of Prophecy as some sacred love affair rather than an order of business, you're making it more complicated for yourself—and more dangerous for us. Mortal hearts make mistakes. They are cruel, unpredictable things." There was a tense silence as Rebecca caught her breath.

Alexi's jaw worked slowly as he stared down at her. "Is that all?"

Rebecca's eyes flashed. "Hardly. But I'll stop there."

"Why are you so adamant that I am mistaken?"

Rebecca simply stared at him. She opened her mouth and closed it, shook her head, defeated.

The crowd shifted, and she and Alexi caught sight of the dead body again, now being placed gingerly on a board and hauled away. The scene had accumulated much to-do. "Enough to give one nightmares for months, that," Rebecca murmured.

Alexi tilted his head. "Of course. But we've seen such horrors before."

"When?"

"One lifetime or another," he replied, absently holding out his arm. Rebecca took it, and he continued speaking, stepping down from the landing. "And this tragedy may be only the cry of poor Whitechapel, nothing more. We've no concern with human crimes, no matter how ghastly. If it becomes our Work—if the supernatural becomes evident—we will act."

"Patience, eh? It never fails to surprise me when that is your counsel, Professor."

A brief spark passed through his eyes. "Was that not what we just discussed, my dear? If I had no patience, I'd have gone mad long ago."

Entering the dank shadow of a nearby alley, Rebecca sighed. "Fifty Berkeley Square is causing trouble again," she remarked. As was often the case, she was the first to feel the burning in her veins.

"The usual? Noises?"

"Yes, and moving lights. Books ejected from second-story windows, blood dripping from their bindings. It will be rather a mess."

Alexi sighed. "Shall we clean it up, then?"

She shook her head. "Let me handle it."

"Rebecca, Bloody Bones is a trial. It's not a task for you alone."

"Alexi, please. You've enough to worry about," she assured him. When he raised an eyebrow, she asked, "You truly think I cannot arraign the subject myself?"

Alexi was silent.

"Shall we bet on the matter?"

Alexi's lips curved. "Why, Headmistress, you surprise me. I didn't think you a wagering woman."

"You press me to strange deeds, Professor."

"Indeed. Well, then: a bottle of my favourite sherry. It shall await me at La Belle et La Bête upon your failure. I do believe Josephine keeps several in stock—perhaps for just such an occasion."

Rebecca grimaced. "While I have every faith in my success, I do wish your tastes were less expensive. But, a bottle of sherry it is. And now we'd best get back to Athens."

"Should we?" he asked.

"It *is* the first day of class, Professor, and you have students to terrify."

"Ah yes, so I do."

The small student body of the academy bustled noisily through the halls. Percy, however, prepared in quiet.

Her linen gown of her favourite light blue colour was simple yet elegant. She tucked her silver phoenix pendant lovingly between the layer of her chemise and dress, and felt the familiar comfort of its chain around her neck and its solid form below her breast, a hidden fortitude. In a manner of ritual necessity, Percy shrouded herself further. She draped a blue scarf about her head, circling her neck with the soft fabric and folding its edges into the neckline of her bodice. She buttoned satin gloves that hid her deathly pale hands. But donning her tinted glasses as her final barrier, she was seized by a fit of nerves—despite a hint of rouge upon her cheeks and lips, there remained no cure for her unmistakable pallor.

Glancing once more at her first class assignment, she gathered her books and opened the door into the busy hall, hoping to remain as inconspicuous as possible. But the instant she appeared, it began. And while the reverend mother had warned her, Percy couldn't have known the ongoing shock of being stared at so intently and by so many. Whispers and curious peering created a cacophony of sound and sensation, and Percy felt riddled by pinpricks. The journey down the hall and through the foyer was a gauntlet filled with snickers and gasped comments, students poking one another and pointing.

After overhearing one young lady ask her friend when they'd begun to admit carnival attractions to Athens, Percy had quite enough, and threw her slight weight against the front door, grateful to slip into the outside breeze. The welcome sight of Marianna, smiling at her and waiting on the steps, lessened the weight of her circus novelty.

The girls walked toward Promethe Hall, where they had a literature class together. "I see now, Percy," the German girl offered quietly. "How people look at you."

"I must admit, Marianna, I was not prepared for the extent of it."

"You are, how do I say . . . ? *Attractive,* Percy. You 'attract' many looks."

Percy smiled wearily. "I suppose you could say that."

"In time you will no longer be a surprise," her friend stated with confidence.

"I hope. Have you met other girls in our hall? I've remained solitary."

"A few ladies came by and introduced themselves. They were polite."

Entering a book-filled room lined with tables, the two girls took to the corner. A few students nodded at Marianna as they passed, and one civil young man deigned to smile at Percy as well.

Marianna poked Percy's arm. "That one looks nice."

"Hmm?"

"The boy who just passed us and smiled. He is . . . handsome." Marianna peered for a bit at the student in question.

"You may look, Marianna, but I beg you to recall the headmistress's speech. She gave it to you as well, did she not? We are to have not the least bit of contact with men, however handsome."

Her friend just shrugged and, as roll call was read by the instructor who entered—a round woman named Mrs. Henrick, who spoke in a shrill tone—paid particular attention to the name of the young man she had noticed: Edward Page.

Mrs. Henrick went about the room and asked students to name their favourite author. Marianna answered "Goethe," and Percy answered "Shakespeare." Percy felt the teacher's eyes upon her, as well as those of the other children, and was grateful for her glasses. Though they were a meager shield, they were nonetheless some protection.

Mrs. Henrick pried further. "Favourite play?"

"Hamlet," Percy replied, and immediately felt a pang for her dear ghostly friend Gregory, to whom she had played Horatio a hundred times, holding his dying—already dead—body.

Mrs. Henrick prated on, and Percy became confident the class would pose no trouble. She also pledged to help if Marianna got behind in her reading.

After class, the girls were forced to go their separate ways, heading in separate directions down the academy's various halls. Marianna strolled off to a composition class, and Percy became nervous. The very name Mathematical and Alchemical Studies sounded both exotic and threatening, a true barrier to what she imagined would otherwise be effortless study here.

It was hard enough to ignore the murmurs of the living, let alone those of the dead, who also sprinkled the school grounds. Percy heard everything, despite attempting to hide beneath her numerous accoutrements as she crossed the courtyard. Living students wondered if she was a ghost haunting the academy, while the dead wondered the same. She prayed to someday grow accustomed to this trial.

Alongside her, nineteen other students shuffled into a chamber that looked more like the nave of a gothic church than a classroom. It was filled with long tables, lined with stone beams and bordered by stained-glass windows of mythical creatures.

Sitting near the back, Percy tried to become invisible. However, pale as she was, transparency was impossible. She wished she could join those around her, the dead floating through the walls. Some spirits paid avid attention to the assembling class; some simply hung in a wandering breeze; while others chattered softly about the woes that tethered them to this world.

Percy began to curse inwardly. She denounced the gift that alienated her from both populaces; she cursed her ability to see and hear those she more closely resembled, and also her kinship to the living who would never understand the strange sights that her eyes now found commonplace. It was as if she watched distant members of her family on both sides, but through windows that precluded her from joining them. Yet the family could not be ignored; there was always noise to keep them in mind.

A door burst open, and the assembled company, ghosts included, started. Out from an office at the front of the room strode a tall figure in black, and the ensuing silence was deafening.

The newcomer turned to face his students. Percy's breath caught. Here stood the most striking man she had ever seen. Lustrous dark hair hung loosely to broad shoulders. A few locks turned out in an unkempt manner contrary to the rest of his appearance, while a few strands clung to his noble, chiseled features—a long nose, high cheekbones, defined lips like a Grecian sculpture and impossibly dark eyes. He was dressed in a long professorial robe that hung open over a smartly buttoned velvet vest, and a crimson cravat at the throat was the only colour this distinguished figure sported.

Percy gaped a moment before coming to her senses and shutting her mouth, her face growing hot. The professor's hair was not greying, yet a few creases upon his regal forehead betrayed years of deep thought. Percy guessed that he might be twice her own eighteen years—and yet, as she looked around, she found her male peers plain and unremarkable in comparison.

She felt a pang of recognition, too, that bothered her greatly. Percy would never have forgotten seeing such a man. And there was something in his personality, in his commanding presence, which was beyond the limits of mortality.

As the two other females in the room appeared wholly unaffected, Percy ordered her heart to stop racing; its intoxicated pace was alarming, and she chided herself for such a foolish, hasty spark. Nonetheless, her distaste for science suddenly seemed an extraordinary misfortune, as she hated the thought of doing poorly in a class taught by someone so breathtaking.

The newcomer wrote a name upon the board in scrawling script. His voice took hold of his audience, a richly resonant, unparalleled baritone. "I am Professor Rychman. Welcome to my class."

He swept the room with his eyes, coolly evaluating his new students. When his gaze found Percy, it lingered. Caught in that stare, she shrank into her chair.

Though his eyes widened, she could see him make an effort to remain polite. After a moment, Percy realized his expression wasn't one of disgust, mockery or even surprise; it was confusion. Odd.

He began a roll call, managing to steal just one more glance in her direction. Then he arrived at her name. "Miss P. Parker?"

"H-here, sir." Percy raised her hand.

The professor looked up from his roster. All eyes were upon her. Percy squirmed. The professor nodded slowly, as if he were trying to decipher a riddle. Then he moved on to the next name, and Percy could breathe again.

Class began. Professor Rychman was ruthless with his subject matter, and he flew through what he considered background material and began scribbling unending sequences of letters and symbols in all manner of baffling arrangements. Percy attempted to take notes but was soon lost. Hypnotized by the stern yet melodic sound of his voice, she found herself swept away by the cadence of his speech. Every movement and sentence held impossible confidence. His eyes managed to stare down every student over the course of the lecture, and even when his back was turned, his presence gripped the room. And by the end . . . Percy had a page full of numbers, dashes and circles, but not a clue as to their meaning.

Over the course of his second class of the day, Alexi repeatedly found himself staring past the spirits that floated through his classroom, focusing instead on a living girl who looked like one of their number. He would never admit to his students that he saw spirits; it was not something a man of science or sanity admitted. Still, he could not help but think *Luminous* as he stared at Miss P. Parker, imagining her a body possessed, like little Emily. But this student seemed in no distress, other than her nerves, perhaps, and none of his internal alarms was raised.

He wondered at the age of this unmistakable Miss Parker, for while it was clear her smooth cheek was young, there was something that distinguished her from youth, her pallor notwithstanding. A timelessness.

It did not signify. The true Grand Work would not involve his students.

Percy and Marianna met again in the dining hall, a room with wooden rafters and low chandeliers with portraits of dour men and women parading the paneled walls. Cliques of other young ladies sat chattering. Percy and Marianna sat near a bay window that looked out onto the courtyard, sharing their thoughts on various teachers and what they foresaw as potential strengths and difficulties. Marianna was particularly worried about a speech barrier in her last class, while Percy couldn't forget Professor Rychman.

"I'm afraid I'll be made a fool in mathematics, I'm dreadful at the subject. But, oh, the professor! He's magnificent!" she breathed.

"Yes?"

"Oh, yes, Professor Rychman. I can't say I've ever . . ."

"Ever what?"

Percy had to turn away and butter another piece of bread to hide her blush. "Seen anyone like him," she finished, attempting to sound nonchalant.

Marianna leaned forward with a smile. "I would think he has never seen anyone like you, either."

Percy bit her lip. Though she'd been tortured over Mr. Darcy as a girl, she was terribly unprepared for being smitten with a living man. A blazing bonfire deep inside now sent lightning flashes to wake dormant dragons all over her body at any moment she thought of him, pictured him or spoke his name. But she knew better than to relay this to her new friend, so she and Marianna finished dinner and returned to their respective rooms.

That evening, as Percy readied for bed, she was struck by a vision: a floating feather, something on fire, the flapping of great wings; herself running barefoot down a long and misty corridor . . . She could ignore it no longer. The visions were coming more rapidly than ever before in her life, perhaps once a week now rather than every few months. She thanked heaven that the images usually waited until she was alone.

Suddenly she was overcome by the first vision she remembered ever having, and as it presented itself once again Percy groaned. It *hurt*. There were . . . spirits in the sky. Hungry and searching for something. These spirits, smoky tendrils on the wind, were part angel. Beautiful yet dizzying, they darted helter-skelter under a bloodred canopy, their pelting forms a wonder. They descended rapaciously, looking, careening about the streets of London. One by one, they found new homes. A jolt shook her, a deafening thunder both outside Percy and within. Something was about to merge . . .

The vision faded and Percy collapsed onto her bed, gulping for air and drowning in yearning. It was times such as these when she needed to believe there was a God of love and comfort, a Being of peace and beauty who could one day offer meaning. Her body shook until sleep won out . . . but even in sleep there was no rest. Someone kept screaming her name, over and over, matching the rhythm of her heartbeat, and the person screaming was very, very angry. Just as Percy was looking for answers, someone else was looking for her. She prayed she found her truths before her pursuer found her.

CHAPTER SIX

Headmistress Rebecca Thompson owed Professor Alexi Rychman a very expensive bottle of sherry. Luckily, spirits—liquors as well as ghosts—were in ample supply at Café La Belle et La Bête.

The spectres came and went as they pleased, now and then troubling to adjust the glassware, to the owner Josephine's unending irritation. One pair of Restoration wraiths kept to a corner, eternally interested in gossip divined from the liv-

ing. One former army general never left his post at the end of
the bar. And of course there were many, many others.

Everyone inside, living and dead, turned as the door
opened and the scowling Rebecca entered.

"Good afternoon, my dear Miss Thompson!" hailed her
jovial, rosy-cheeked friend in a modest suit, rising from a
table by the window to press her hand. The other gentleman
at the table, more finely dressed, waved a limp hand and resumed gazing out the window.

"Hello, Michael . . . Elijah," Rebecca murmured with a
curt nod.

Vicar Michael Carroll, maintaining his affable grin, pulled
out a chair. "And what has you so flustered?"

"Alexi, of course," she spat, taking a seat between them,
removing her hat and gloves to replace stubborn locks of hair
falling from her coiffure. She failed to notice Elijah roll his
eyes.

"What now?" Michael asked, twirling his grey-peppered
mustache.

Rebecca sighed, adjusting the gathered folds of her navy
skirt with a pronounced rustle. "Do you recall the trouble at
Fifty Berkeley Square?"

"What of it?"   •

"Alexi seemed to think I was outmatched. But as we often
perform alone, I never dreamed—"

"Old Bloody Bones got the better of you, eh?" Michael
grinned.

"Yes," Rebecca muttered. "What a horrid sight. And
stench. It wouldn't stay still long enough to bind properly!
I'm afraid I made a mess of it."

"Alexi's been hard on you, then? Did he come to your
aid?"

"Yes, yes. He was right. It took the two of us to dispel the
bloody devil." Rebecca glowered. "So, as was our wager, I
owe him a bottle of sherry. His absurdly expensive label, of
course."

"Ah! A bet against Alexi?" Michael shook his head. "While I admire your pluck, my dear, I must say I'd have foregone that temptation. Now he will be gloating and unbearable."

Elijah sniggered against the window.

Rebecca turned. "Good afternoon to you, too, Lord Withersby. Your impeccable manners are always a balm."

Elijah turned, as if he hadn't yet noticed Rebecca or heard her previous greeting, and inclined his head in an exaggerated bow. "Miss Thompson. Delighted."

Michael laughed. "You know, Elijah, you match the consumptive artwork Josephine has on these walls. You really should sit for Rosetti. Or . . . I suppose we could simply leave you in your seat and hand you a gold frame to hold over your face."

Elijah pursed his thin lips in annoyance.

"Oh, is that a new one of Josephine's?" Rebecca pointed to the opposite wall and rose to examine the indicated canvas. Michael followed, always eager to be near her side. Elijah remained seated . . . and held a peppermill over Michael's tea.

A clatter of glasses above the polished oak bar brought the lovely, olive-skinned Josephine, cursing in French, out from a back room. Brandishing a wet towel, she waved it in the air with a few words that were not French but instead The Guard's strange and ancient tongue. The towel passed straight through the portly body of that spirit in military uniform who was trying to unsuccessfully help himself to a glass of wine. Glumly, the general heard the odd words, felt the tickle of the towel and went again to sulk in his usual place.

It was good the four friends were the sole living occupants of the bar, Rebecca mused; the afternoon was shaping up to be a bit of a production unfit for outsiders. Improper familiarity across class lines was one thing, but blatant interaction with the dead was another.

"Ah, Rebecca!" Josephine, tucking one thin lock of silver hair behind her ear, moved to kiss her friend on both cheeks. She drew back, noticing Rebecca's sour look, and her French accent made her words all the more provocative. "What, what is zat face you give me?"

Rebecca grimaced as she drew a stack of notes from her reticule. "Josie, would you fetch me bottle of sherry—your best, if you please? And tie a ribbon or something around it."

"Ooh! And what might the occasion be?"

"Alexi," Rebecca muttered. "We wagered on a . . . spiritual matter, and I lost."

Josephine clicked her tongue and shook her head, rolling back the sleeves of her blouse. "Someday we'll find something he can't master, and we'll drink sherry on his remittance for a change." She refilled Elijah's cabernet, then set off to procure the prize.

"Where's Jane?" Rebecca asked the assembly.

Michael shrugged. "Off on her own, as usual."

"Never trust the Irish. Never know what they're up to," Elijah muttered.

Michael cleared his throat. "Rebecca, forgive my cold heart that I haven't yet inquired. Did you and Alexi discover anything at that last Ripper site? Can we help?"

"I'd have preferred a waltz with Bloody Bones than to have seen that poor wretch . . ." Rebecca shuddered. "But, no. There's nothing to do but wait and listen."

Michael ignored this. "London's terrified." ❧

"I know," Rebecca replied. "And so am I. Such gruesome evil is usually within our control—is part of our Grand Work. But these murders on Buck's Row and Hanbury Street . . . we had no warning, no feel of the supernatural. I'm worried about our school. What if one of our girls wanders out? They're all so innocent—and my responsibility."

"How was the start of term?" Michael asked, trying to access happier fare. He inched his hand toward Rebecca's but at the last moment lost courage and withdrew.

"Only a few new students," Rebecca replied, oblivious. She shifted uncomfortably, thinking of Miss Parker. "One girl is startlingly unique. Must have some sort of condition, poor thing. Deathly pale skin, the whole of her white as snow. Glasses shaded her pale eyes, which, through their glass, appeared almost violet."

"You're certain she's mortal and not Luminous?" Michael asked, again twirling his mustache.

"You think I can't tell the difference? Still, it is eerie to see a living girl so similar. And the spirits gaze at her so. Perhaps they are just as curious."

"What do they call people without colour?" Michael scratched his head, ruffling a patch of grey-peppered hair and not bothering to comb it back into place.

"Albinos," supplied Elijah.

Rebecca nodded and continued her musing. "Eerie, indeed. A timid girl, orphaned, raised in a Catholic convent. When asked if she considered herself gifted in any way, she replied that she had a strange manner of dreams. I tried to clarify whether these were dreams or visions, but she didn't know or want to admit."

Elijah snorted. "Damn Catholics. Don't they all think they see things—Christ in a spoon or the Virgin in a crumpet? Delusional fanatics. God bless Mr. Darwin for setting us straight."

Michael waggled his mustache. "Please, Elijah, your compassion is leaking onto the tablecloth, and it's making an awful mess."

Elijah's hand hovered over a butter knife.

"No silverware duels today, gentlemen. Please," Rebecca implored.

Michael leaned over the table, not to be dissuaded. "Mr. Darwin, Lord Withersby, was a man of God. As a scientist, he believed in the sacred process of life designed by an omnipotent Creator. Men who lack imagination will say he's not of God for their own purposes." He turned away. "Now, what of this girl's dreams, Rebecca?"

"I wasn't at liberty to press her. Timid as she was, I doubt she'd have shared."

"You are rather intimidating on the job, *Headmistress* Thompson," Elijah mocked, though kindly. "You and Alexi, both—our resident gargoyles."

Rebecca offered Elijah a cold, cautionary smile.

"Did Alexi think anything of the girl?" Michael asked.

Rebecca shook her head. "I've no idea. The students are simply our employment, and bless them for that. We decided long ago that we should bring none near our madness, and that has served us well. I therefore leave Alexi to his own impressions regarding her. The girl was nothing to bring to account, merely interesting, that's all." When Michael raised an eyebrow she added hastily, "But I do worry about a girl like her, and about all of my students in this increasingly dangerous city."

There was a long period of silence as the three friends picked like birds at the dry biscuits before them.

"We're overdue for a meeting. The air is sick with forces. There may yet be more murders," Michael finally said. "Supernatural or no."

"Two less harlots on the streets," Elijah offered, his bony fingers toying with his fork.

"Sunshine, you are," Michael replied. "A joy to all mankind."

"I do my best," laughed his friend.

Elijah punctuated his words by threading his dessert fork into the lace of Rebecca's cuffs. She responded by tossing a piece of biscuit at his head. It bounced and hit the window, and a voice scolded suddenly in a thick French accent.

"*Mon Dieu!* No refinement! Even you, Rebecca, whom I hold to a higher standard than these heathens at your side.

You let them goad you into misbehaving?" Josephine strode toward them, cradling a bottle of fine sherry upon her arm.

"Josie, now, don't curse your kin," Rebecca replied, blowing the other a kiss.

Josephine glared, but the men at the table gasped. "Did you see, Josie?" Elijah exclaimed. "Her Arctic Highness just sent you a token of affection floating on an icy breeze! Come, a smile is due at least for such a novelty."

"You give me no credit!" Rebecca cried. "I'm never as frigid as you all make me out to be."

Michael clapped his hands to his arms and rubbed them furiously. "Elijah, what on earth could be causing that draft?"

Rebecca folded her arms and scowled.

"She simply awaits a man's embrace," Elijah blurted. "That alone will remedy her chill."

Michael choked first on his biscuit, then, taking a drink of tea, choked once more—this time due to Elijah's work with the peppermill.

Rebecca's hand flew to her snug collar, her heart seizing. She masked her sudden wound with bluster. "If I wasn't bound to you by damnable fate, if you were *proper* gentlemen, you might consider etiquette, for such talk surpasses scandal!" She rose from her chair, throwing down her napkin, trying to deter further scrutiny. "I'll never know why you tease Alexi and I so, Elijah, when *you* are the impossible one!"

Elijah grinned, unrepentant. He looked innocently at his fellows. "Me? And what of me would you tease, when Alexi so much more deserves it? *I* do not stalk about like one of those gothic *vampir* onstage at the Royal. Nor do I brood with dramatic zeal, nor can I start fires of my own accord, nor daily dress as if in mourning. Nor do the first bars of Beethoven's Fifth seem to burst forth each time I enter a room!"

"Shameful! All of you!" Josephine scolded, though she

fought back a smile. Removing her apron, she dusted the bottle in her hand briefly before sliding the white linen garment down the bar, where it passed through the head of the general whose transparent body was folded over, asleep.

"Poor Alexi," Rebecca huffed, collapsing into a chair. "If he only knew how he was abused. To think that the serious boy of so many years ago—"

"If we didn't know and love him, this would be cruel," Elijah interrupted. "But as all of us adore his brilliance—insufferable though he is—and though he appears a dark thespian rather than a chemist, we gladly admit we'd fall apart without him."

"Alexi Rychman, melancholy prince of Denmark!" Michael proclaimed, pounding his fist on the table in delight and raising his teacup to drink a toast. The others followed suit.

Through their laughter, they failed to hear the door open and click shut, and a tall, cloaked, formidable figure dressed all in black approached. His stoic features were offset only by his blazing eyes. Alexi Rychman stared down at his friends with a frown.

"Something amusing?" he asked.

At the sound of his low, rich voice, the group looked up and shrieked, delighted. Elijah cried out the first notes of Beethoven's Fifth, unable to help himself. This did nothing for the others' composure. In fact, Michael, head thrown back in a wail of laughter, lost balance and fell from his chair. No one bothered to stand and greet their leader properly.

"You really should have your own personal orchestra, Alexi!" Elijah gasped for breath.

"'To be or not to be . . . !'" Michael wailed from the floor, waving an arm above him grandly.

"An appropriate theme for you, you must admit!" Elijah continued, offering Alexi a sharp-toothed grin.

Rebecca, flushed, stood with an uneven breath and handed Alexi the sherry bottle with its dusty ribbon tied lopsided around the neck. "Professor, your prize. I acquiesce to your eminence and superiority—sir," she stated with a curtsey. There was a hint of a smile as she did so, however, and Josephine masked a sputtering giggle with a cough.

Alexi snatched the sherry from Rebecca's hand. "Whenever you heathens can regain a modicum of sense, it's time for a meeting," he stated coldly. This quieted the group enough for him to continue. "There now. Sanity has returned to La Belle et La Bête, but I'd best speak quickly as I fear its presence is fleeting. But before we begin . . . could someone go and remind our grey friend down the street not to push the actors into their places quite so hard? Since the discovery of his dead body during the renovations, his ghost has become increasingly meddlesome, causing many complaints."

He waited a moment for one of his companions to volunteer for the routine policing of Drury Lane's most infamous spectre. Then: "Fine, you lazy fools, I'll go. Considering your present behaviour, I'd not trust one of you to admonish this spiritual hooligan. Clearly, I ought to do it myself. But I warn you: sharpen yourselves." He turned and promptly exited, his long black cloak billowing behind him. Throughout his exodus, a few more bars of the Fifth Symphony were hummed.

Outside, Alexi took a deep breath. Irrepressible chortles and a smattering of "Whether 'tis nobler in the mind" could be heard erupting inside.

"Infidels," he muttered, taking the alley toward the Theatre Royal at a purposeful clip. "Will they forever be children?"

CHAPTER SEVEN

The third floor of Promethe Hall, not often used, was a basic yet stately affair; an open foyer with wide windows looking onto the school courtyard yet draped in white fabric, making the whole area softly but generously lit by the dawn. Two weeks into classes, Headmistress Thompson was ascending to this area when she stopped abruptly at the top of the stairs. The sight that greeted her had never before been there.

Shimmering and flickering like a candle, a large, transparent feather made of glittering wisps of blue flame floated two feet above the seal of Athens Academy, which was engraved on the floor below. Rebecca approached in awe. As she moved close, the feather brightened and seemed to dance, almost as if it were happy to see her.

The room had arches at either end, leading to the north and south wings of the hall, and the usual trickle of morning students began to pass through. A rush of nerves caused Rebecca's skin to moisten, but she took care to mask her amazement and maintain her composure. The students passed by with a nod of deference and nothing more. As their headmistress hoped, they could not see the large, hovering feather that spontaneously burst into flame.

Rebecca exhaled slowly. "Things like this are supposed to stay relegated to our sacred circle and the chapel, thank you very much," she muttered, scolding the phenomenon.

She glanced down at the seal of the academy, a golden eagle bearing a lit torch in its great claws. The school's motto was inscribed below, first in Greek, then translated:

AS THE PROMETHEAN FIRE WHICH BANISHED DARKNESS,
SO KNOWLEDGE BEARS THE POWER AND THE LIGHT.

The feather, ephemeral as smoke and delicate as spider's thread, gave off no heat or sound, but its blue flame was instantly familiar to her, as it would be to all her coterie. Slowly returning down the stairs, she eyed the feather to the last before scurrying to her office. She had often wondered if there was more to the building than it cared to tell. Urgently, she sent Frederic to fetch Alexi.

"Your English has improved greatly, Marianna." Percy sat at the feet of the courtyard's statuary angel, twirling the water in the fountain's basin with distracted fingertips.

Marianna reclined beside her, finishing her picnic breakfast. "I am trying. I wish we spent more than one class together, but I have made a few friends."

"Wonderful," Percy replied in earnest, before glancing away. "You remain my only friend. At times I see that Edward boy. Every now and then he nods a greeting. Everyone else is afraid. I can't blame them. I do look like a ghost—"

"No, Percy. Do not make excuses," Marianna said. When her friend stayed silent, gazing at the angel above, she declared like an elder sister, "I accept melancholy for one moment, Percy, but that moment has passed. So. Are language classes still your favourite?"

Percy smiled. "I wish they were more challenging, but they do provide lovely escape to different worlds. It makes me forget myself—how I am, what I am—if only for a moment."

"Ah! Doth I hear melancholy again, my dear Hamlet?" Marianna chided. Percy laughed. "There. Much better. Is that Alchemic—what is it called?—class still giving you trouble, despite your 'magnificent professor'?"

Percy groaned. "Oh, that class remains my bane! I pay attention, take countless notes, but all I remember is the sound of Professor Rychman's voice. Every syllable he speaks is like a hypnotic delicacy, like dark velvet. I try to grasp his explanations, but all I can see is how his robe sweeps as he moves, how his presence commands the room, how his brow furrows in thought, how his eyes blaze, how he calmly brushes a lock of dark hair from his noble face . . ." She trailed off, horrified by the vividness of her descriptions. With a fearful glance at Marianna, she folded her hands in her lap.

Marianna's eyes gleamed as she whispered in Percy's ear, "Someone is most certainly smitten!"

Percy swallowed. "Marianna, you mustn't say such a thing—even a suggestion could get me expelled! This institution, in its unique position, cannot be too careful with the men and women under its protection. While I admit I may be . . . intrigued by him, this man is my professor, Marianna, and nothing more. You must realize that! Perhaps one day"—it was Percy's turn to take a sage tone—"you'll realize that there is a supreme delicacy to such matters."

There was a long pause, and Marianna bit back a grin. "Does he wear a ring?"

"No," Percy replied.

Marianna smiled. "I see. Who is this dashing hero? Have I met him?"

"You'd know if you had, I assure you. Wait! Oh, why, speak of the devil!" As if on cue, from Apollo Hall strode an impressive figure. Engrossed in his thoughts and ignoring the students sure to dive clear of his path, he strode briskly toward Promethe Hall. His academic's robe and dark locks billowed about him, giving him the appearance of a great, swooping bird, and he looked up as if sensing Percy. His dark eyes pierced her to the core and all breath flew from her lips. "There," she whispered.

The two held each other's stares for a moment, student and teacher, and Percy was paralyzed, unable to break from his eyes until he led the way, snapping his head to the side as he moved across the courtyard.

Marianna shuddered slightly. "Goodness, Percy!"

"What?"

"Well, he is striking indeed—but grim!"

"Distinguished, regal, elegant, fascinating . . ."

"Eerie," Marianna argued.

Percy turned suddenly, removed her glasses and pinned her friend with a stare. "Eerie, you say? 'Eerie' should daunt me, should it? What am I, then?"

Though the light hurt her eyes, the desired effect occurred. Percy's irises flashed in the sunlight, the tiny blue and white slivers of colour glowing. Marianna gasped. Percy replaced her glasses and closed the lids of her eyes, favouring them from the pain to which she'd just subjected herself.

After a moment, Marianna spoke. "Well, Percy, I will give you this. There is certainly *something* about the man."

"Yes. But I cannot know more of him."

Marianna sighed. "My dearest Percy, welcome to the ranks of the unrequited."

Percy turned, grave. "You must refrain from such statements. Such talk is scandal. The only reason he affects me so is that I feel . . . strange around him. I sense he knows something that I need to know. I've had such an odd sense of things my entire life, Marianna, such dreams while awake, such beautiful and haunting images! It must lead to something."

"And you think your professor of science may have answers?"

"That's just it: the thought is absurd! Of course this could just be a fascination which I dare not foster, but nonetheless I wonder . . . Please, Marianna, never one word of this."

Her friend held up a hand, her obligation to duty clear.

Professor Rychman continued walking, and the two girls continued watching. Just outside the arch into Promethe

Hall, Headmistress Thompson waited. Percy and Marianna observed as the professor held out his arm. She took it, and they fell into immediate, intense discussion.

"They know each other well," Marianna stated, watching closely.

Something the headmistress said must have irked him, for Rychman glared at her as they turned to go inside. She patted his hand, to which the professor responded by lifting his head high.

"Very well indeed," Marianna continued, giving Percy a grimace. "By the look of them, they deserve each other."

Percy found she could not argue. She watched the professor's great, robed arm open one of the tall doors of Apollo Hall, and he motioned his equally severe companion inside with a familiarity that surely only great intimacy could create. Percy yearned for his intoxicating stare one more time, but she wasn't so lucky. Indeed, she felt oddly abandoned.

Marianna anticipated her, and gave a gentle inquiry. "Are you all right?"

"Of course I'm all right. Why wouldn't I be?" Percy retorted.

"Indeed. Come, my dear girl, let us bemoan your fate over tea and cookies," the German lass offered. She giggled. "Loneliness should never be faced on an empty stomach."

Percy whimpered. "Marianna, look at me, then remind yourself not to joke in such a manner. A lonely fate is all too probable, thank you very much."

"Somehow I do not think so. I think fate will provide."

"I can only hope." Percy chose to adopt her friend's optimism. "Come, then, tea and biscuits! Then, on to our mountain of studies."

Alexi and Rebecca stared at the feather of blue fire floating at the center of the foyer.

"Incredible," Alexi stated, approaching. "What an omen."

"Indeed," Rebecca murmured, following.

"And here we were worried about signs being too subtle to detect."

Alexi drew close. The transparent feather responded to his proximity, its fire leaping higher. The image danced and shimmered, inviting Alexi to reach out a hand. Rebecca steadied him, cautious, but he shirked her warning and allowed his fingers to tickle the edges, to pass through the phantom image.

Rebecca clamped her hands across her mouth to hold in a cry of surprise. Though she knew her students could not see what she saw, she would not take chances; she had cordoned off the entire floor, claiming repairs. But . . . Alexi had turned into an angel. Huge, phantom wings burst from his back, made of that same bluish, wispy flame, and he was snapped into place atop the school seal by a force unseen, the feather emblazoning his torso. He stared, wide-eyed, at the gossamer wings and robe whipping about his ankles with great force.

"My God," he declared. "Perhaps that myth of ours is true after all . . ."

It was past time for their meeting as they assembled. Five of the six Guard entered the chapel at intervals, filing past the amber stained-glass seraphim in the windows, whispering devotions and phrases in a tongue long unheard and long forgotten. A warm blue glow grew in the air, beginning as tendrils of mist upon the marble floor before lifting like a breeze to the rafters above and hanging there like a cloud.

The five figures soon stood silently at the altar beneath the white bird of peace and closed their eyes in meditation. The stained-glass guardian angels glowed. The blue cloud of power trembled.

The door of the chapel was thrown open, and the formidable Professor Rychman swept in, his black garments accented by a flourish of burgundy at his throat. Six candles upon the altar immediately burst into flame. Alexi's voice broke the silence. "Good evening, friends. To our sacred depths," he commanded, "where I'll tell you of our omen. And perhaps the goddess will return to tell us more!"

With a slight rending sound, the altar became their large black door, bluish light dancing around it, a corridor and staircase beyond. The Guard filed past and down, into their sacred space. A strange music, a low chant of mysterious vintage, floated up through the air.

Closing, the door once again gave way to a plain altar, and the chapel was left empty.

From the far reaches of the Whisper-world, there came a pounding sound of organic matter against stone. The woman in the silver moonlight winced as the shadows rumbled in anger.

"What to do, then, if she cannot be found?" asked the tolling voice of Darkness.

"Give us time, dear," the woman answered. "You've been without her for many mortal years. You could do with a bit of patience."

"They. Are. Protecting. Her."

"I rather think she's protecting herself," was the woman's muttered reply.

"Then we must shake down the city. The world. Until we find her. Undo it. Take down the barrier, rip it open."

"Really?" The woman brightened, her lips suddenly wet. "Loosening the pins? Why, Master, that's quite bold of you after all these years."

"Desperate. Times."

"So it would seem!" the woman breathed, excited. "I'll tell the Groundskeeper to attempt the Undoing. Chaos, heed the cries of waking war!"

CHAPTER EIGHT

A doorway surrounded by light. A wispy ring of feathers floating at the center of a portal before shifting into flame. There
were glyphs, like those in Egypt . . . Behind the door, music—

Percy's mind returned to class.

She had been soaring through all her courses except one.
She had endless pages of notes in Mathematical and Alchemical Studies, but nothing to show for them save a loss of
breath whenever she beheld her professor. She was certain
she was failing the class. Failing and falling . . .

Her eyes narrowed on Professor Rychman, who had mo-
mentarily paused at the chalkboard midscript, an equation
in progress. Subtly he cocked his head, as if sensing something or catching a note of faraway music. His lecture began
again soon enough.

Percy realized she had no idea where in the lesson she had
left off, or where she might pick back up. Looking hopelessly
at her lesson book, she wanted to cry. Worse, the vision refused to leave her mind. Seizing a piece of paper and a bit of
hardened charcoal that she kept in her pencil box, she began
to purge the image by transcribing it onto paper.

She ought to have waited until her drawing class for such a
flurry of creation; she knew that. But even then, all she was
allowed to do in Professor Bryan's class was sit with a tedious
still life while the woman moved about the room with her
thumb in the air measuring perspective. This searing image
could not wait.

Class ended and students began to file from the room, but
Percy remained oblivious to even her professor's unmistakable presence.

"Miss Parker?"

That stern, rich voice was so sudden and startling. Percy jumped, staring up in horror. How long had he been watching her scribble? "Oh! Yes, Professor?"

"Meet me in my office at six, Miss Parker. Room sixty-one, upstairs."

"Y-yes, Professor."

Professor Rychman stared at her, his noble face expressionless for a moment longer; then he strode out of the room, his robe billowing behind him.

Percy shed a few anxious tears, chided herself and left the classroom. She stepped into the lavatory to adjust her shawl, dry her eyes, apply a bit of rouge and attempt to stop trembling, but it was no use. She went back to her bedroom and paced and shook until it was time.

RYCHMAN was carved in bold golden script across the large wooden door above the number sixty-one. Percy knocked hesitantly. "Come." The resonant voice emanating from the other side was impossibly both monotone and melodious. Percy opened the door.

The professor's office was large, filled with tall bookshelves and decorated with paintings and relics. He sat across the room at a marble-topped desk, a fire blazing behind his throne of a leather chair. Twilight shone through a narrow stained-glass window that stretched nearly floor to ceiling on the left wall, and faint slivers of light fell upon the charcoal-coloured frock coat he'd donned outside of class. Two candelabras bearing flickering ivory tapers sat at either end of the desk. The room was filled with a warm, antique light.

An inscrutable yet pervasive power emanated from Professor Rychman's person like a scent, something heady and alluring, almost magical. Percy stared at him in wonder for a very long time until at last he looked up.

Her face coloured; Percy could feel the mottling, rosy patches burst forth upon her cheeks in a patchwork blush, and she stared, mortified, at the floor, knowing that her skin's deformity was now further evidenced. Out of the corner of her downcast eye she noticed a spirit hovering by the window, staring at nothing in particular, and she wished that she, too, could vanish through the wall.

The professor removed thin wire reading glasses and beckoned Percy sit across from him at the desk. She sat, but did not dare remove her glasses in turn. Instead, she chose to examine the art on the walls. There were angels, figures in robes—some looking heavenly, others dark—and a few ancient religious icons. Percy stared at a stately bird against a bloodred sunset for a long moment, seeming to forget where and who she was. A spirit appeared via one of the professor's bookcases just as another wafted in, then out through the window, merely passing through. She couldn't tell if they regarded her with interest or pity, and they didn't say.

"I see you fancy art, Miss Parker," Professor Rychman scolded quietly.

Percy fixed her eyes on the patterns in the marble desk before her. "I–I am so terribly sorry for drawing in your class, Professor. It will never happen again."

There was a long pause. Too timid to glance up past her tinted glasses, she could feel his intense scrutiny. She shrank into her chair and began to count the tiny specks of tea leaves scattered about the desk.

"You fancy art. You do not, it would seem, fancy the sciences?" His tone was snide, and Percy bit her lip. "Please, Miss Parker, do be honest," he continued. "You won't be graded—yet."

"It isn't that I dislike the sciences, Professor. It is more that I don't have the mind for them."

The professor frowned, looking disappointed. "Well, Miss Parker, it is true that you are doing rather poorly in my class. Am I, perhaps, unclear in my lectures . . . ?"

She dared glance up. "Oh, no, Professor, it isn't you. It most certainly isn't you!"

"Then what, Miss Parker, happens to be the trouble?"

Her cheeks burned hotter. "Me, sir. I–I cannot make a bit of sense of the subject," she fumbled, and a tear escaped her cheek to splash on the marble desk. She tried to wipe it away before he noticed, but she was certain nothing escaped him. "I want so badly to learn. I'm just—"

"Preoccupied?"

Percy cleared her throat. "Perhaps. I—"

A flash of pain suddenly worked its way through her. She saw herself in the middle of a stone hallway, immersed in a shaft of bright light. The light transfixed her core, as if she were a butterfly on a pin. She heard anxious voices far away, and something very angry, growling.

"Miss Parker?"

As quickly as it came, the intense vision vanished. Percy's head snapped back as she focused again on her professor, whose angular features sharpened as he stared at her.

"Oh, goodness—forgive me, Professor!" Percy panicked. "Heaven knows what comes over me, these little flashes. I'm terribly sorry, pay me no mind, please don't think me rude! It's never happened when someone is near, speaking to me. I don't know what's wrong, but—"

"Slow your tongue, Miss Parker. Flashes, you say?"

"It's nothing, Professor, please forgive me."

"Miss Parker, you seemed in pain for a moment. Please explain."

"I'm . . . I'm fine, sir. There are moments—tiny dreams, no, I mean to say a splitting headache, and then gone."

"Visions?" he posed quietly as Percy wrung her hands. "Do you have the gift of visions, Miss Parker?"

She shook her head. "I'm not mad, Professor. I dream. Headmistress Thompson said dreams are not 'gifts.' Gifts mean academic excellence or one keen particular talent—"

"I know what gifts are, Miss Parker, for heaven's sake."

Percy shrank back in her chair.

The professor drew a measured breath and leveled his tone. "Miss Parker, I'd rather not remove you from my class for your poor grades. However, I demand that you pay better heed to my words. No drawing! I am, in addition, forced to begin a private tutorial so that I may more directly monitor your progress. If I see no improvement, I will have to remove you from my class and the headmistress must determine what is to be done with you. Such are our rules."

"Yes, sir." Percy nodded, commanding her tears to remain at bay.

"Look at me please, Miss Parker."

Percy looked up, and she was sure her glasses only half hid her fear. Neither the professor's rigid expression nor his dark eyes—as inscrutable to her as her own dark lenses must be to him—softened.

"A series of tutorials will commence, dependent on your progress. We will begin tomorrow at six in the evening. Do I make myself clear?"

"Yes, Professor."

"You are dismissed."

"Yes, Professor. Thank you, sir, for your gracious patience with my inability."

"Try not to test that patience, Miss Parker, for it does not run in ample supply," her instructor offered blandly, returning to his paperwork.

Percy rose, attempting to be as unobtrusive on her way toward the door as possible, but Rychman's voice halted her. "Trying to make yourself invisible is to no avail, Miss Parker, no matter how hard you try," he declared. She did not turn around, for she was at the exit. But then he added, "You have to know the correct spell."

Percy raised her eyebrows and spun, expecting to perhaps see that he was joking, which she would have found very odd. But his face was stoic as ever, which was just as disconcerting.

"Also, Miss Parker, it would . . . seem you have good eyes." He tilted his head as if to invite a challenge of his assumption. "I merely ask you not practice other visionary work in my class."

"Th-thank you, Professor. I promise I'll try, I—"

"Enough. Stop stammering, we both have work to do. Tomorrow at six."

"Yes, sir!" Percy opened the door to his office and felt a cool draft tickle the hem of her dress.

"Miss Parker," Professor Rychman called, just before she fled. "Before you go, answer me one more question." His voice was careful.

"Of course, sir." Percy turned back into the room, but she kept herself pressed against the exit.

"What was that door you were drawing?"

Percy wrung gloved fingers together. "I do not know, sir. I saw it in a ... dream." There was a long pause. The weight of the professor's stare was heavy. "If you don't mind, Professor, why do you ask?"

Rychman leaned back in his chair, tapping his fingers upon his desk. "It reminded me of something."

Percy smiled timidly. "Well, if you could decipher the meaning, Professor, I'd be much obliged."

"Indeed." He held her with his stare a moment longer. Percy hoped she had calmed her blush, but she couldn't be sure. The professor returned his attention to his paperwork. "Good day, Miss Parker."

"Good day, sir." She curtseyed and left the room.

Alexi watched the door close slowly behind his student and listened to her darting footfalls recede. He unlocked a drawer in his desk and pulled out a notebook. As usual, he ignored the spirits wafting in and out of his office, even if they were trying to speak to him in words he was unable to hear. He wished he could hear them for just a moment, enough to determine if they knew about Prophecy or had a message from his long silent goddess. But, to his infinite chagrin, since that first day in the chapel she'd never again been seen. Still ... this girl had just drawn a door. That was the sign.

And yet, this wasn't an actual portal he'd seen or would

see; it was just a picture. He couldn't base the fate of his world on the sketch of a young woman, however unique. Prophecy decreed the seventh would be his peer. *This* girl was his student not his peer, and there were rules. It was his job to teach here, not to look for his destiny; he had to set aside foolish notions.

Opening the leather-bound volume he'd withdrawn, Alexi hummed a melancholy little tune as he thumbed the pages. Finally arriving at a blank one, he scrawled a few hasty sentences into the book before closing it. He then stared at its cover, black and plain save for a tiny circle of feathers, and demanded his heart slow its uncharacteristically brisk pace.

A man in a dusty coat bent with a hammer and chisel over a particular piece of rock on a distant coast. A remote and once sacred place, it was now unguarded, and the Groundskeeper hummed, brushing stray locks of multicoloured hair from his weather-beaten face that was both old and young. The only unchanging thing about him was his caste; his voice shifted and melded into every servile accent of the ancient and New World, with a few conquered dialects between.

"So much work to do. Loosening the Sepulchral Seals! My sweet, milky white lady . . . I work for you now that Majesty's gone! Loosening, loosening, to slit the seal!"

He threw his weight against the stone and it turned like a screw in a piece of wood. A wet exhalation sounded, and vapour lifted from the rock like a puff of tobacco smoke from an ancient pipe. A sound of glee gurgled in the man's throat. "Only a few more, my dear!"

The Groundskeeper pressed his head to the stone. A sound rattled from behind it. A skeletal finger shot from the crevice, but the Groundskeeper swatted at the protruding digit. "Patience, you'll have your time! But give me leave. So much work to do for my lady, and so many seals yet to break!"

CHAPTER NINE

Percy could not calm down. She and Marianna had been studying in her room when the bell tolled half five, and now she jumped to her feet with a distracted whimper.

"And where are you off to?" her friend asked, looking up from her books.

She had been too embarrassed to tell Marianna prior to the engagement. "Since I'm a disaster at mathematics, I'm required to attend evening tutorials with Professor Rychman."

The German girl raised an eyebrow, grinning. "Tutorials with *him?* In private? Is that even allowed? Well . . . I suppose you are a bit of an exception here to begin with."

Percy collapsed upon her bed with a groan. "Oh, how he intimidates me! He speaks the one language I can't understand. Yet, there's so much to commend him. Art and books fill his office. He writes by candlelight, not gas lamp. So melancholy, a philosopher of the world whose heart is cool, but deep within . . . in the moments when he almost smiles, those eyes . . ."

"Listen to yourself, Percy!" Marianna fought back a laugh.

Percy winced. "I know. I know, God help me. I'm utterly hopeless, and this talk will be my undoing." She picked up her books, adjusted her glasses, drew her shawl tighter around herself as if it were armor and set off.

Hurried, nervous steps carried her toward Apollo Hall, and her quaking, gloved hand knocked clumsily on door sixty-one.

"Come," said the voice within.

Percy mused that if she heard a voice from Olympus, her

professor's might sound similar. She pressed her hand to her collarbone and the pendant hidden under her dress. She felt the weight of the phoenix against her flesh and it bolstered her, as it always had.

She slipped into the office and stood quietly at the door. The warm firelight was inviting, at odds with the professor's cool demeanour. He stood before one of his massive book-cases, long fingers running slowly over several spines. He plucked a volume, nodded to Percy, moved to his desk and gestured for her to have a seat. They both sat and took a long moment to evaluate each other.

"Miss Parker." The professor finally broke the silence. Percy started.

"Yes, Professor?"

He fixed her with a measured stare and folded his hands upon his desk. "After some reflection, what seems to give you the most trouble?"

"The actual mathematics, Professor. I have no problem with remembering terminology. That is simply language. I'm actually very good at languages—"

"Numbers are no different, Miss Parker. They are a language in and of themselves."

"I wish my mind could consider them as such, sir."

"You are the verbal type, I see."

Percy offered a tiny smile. "Well, actually, sir, I'm rather quiet."

"Your mind prefers words to numbers," the professor clarified, unamused.

"Y-yes, Professor."

"I see. Read the following for our next meeting. This book covers basic mathematics I've not thought to review in class, as they should already be commonly known." He handed her the book, open to a specific chapter.

Percy nodded, feeling very small. "I am sorry, Professor."

"Do not apologize. Not all of us can be mathematicians or master chemists," he replied with a passing, lofty air.

"I suppose not," Percy agreed, setting her jaw. She forewent pointing out that she would have nothing at all to do with the subject matter were it not an absolute requirement to continue at the academy.

"Return with this book next session, and with any questions that you may have. I will do my best to translate."

"Thank you, sir."

"Not at all," the professor replied. After a moment: "You are quite proficient in language, then, Miss Parker?"

"So it would seem, sir," she replied. She was careful to maintain her modesty.

"What tongues are known to you?"

"Latin, Greek, Hebrew, German, French, Swedish, some Spanish, Portuguese, Italian, Gaelic..."

"Rather studious of you, Miss Parker. Convent education alone?"

"Yes, sir."

"You learned all these in your time there?"

"Mostly, sir. They came to me... easily, as if I had heard them before. But I suppose that sounds terribly strange."

"It would surprise you how little I find strange, Miss Parker," the professor said, tapping his fingertips upon the marble desk.

"How odd," Percy mused. "Headmistress Thompson expressed a similar sentiment. In exactly the same fashion."

"Did she now?" Professor Rychman smiled slightly, as if Percy had referenced some private amusement. There was an awkward pause; then the professor rose from his chair, towering above her, and Percy looked up, her eyes unable to hide her awe. "Miss Parker, I don't suppose you might hazard a guess as to the only question you answered correctly on your last exam?"

"Ah." Percy nodded ruefully. "'What symbol crowns the alchemical pyramid?' The phoenix."

Something flashed across the professor's face before it became again his usual cool, disinterested expression. "Transformative power. Rebirth," he said, narrowing his eyes. "What do you think of the symbol, Miss Parker?"

Baffled, Percy considered her reply, unconsciously pressing her hidden pendant to her flesh. "I . . . I think him beautiful, and comforting."

The professor seized on her words. "*Him?* How so?"

"The phoenix myth has always captivated me—the idea that, if something lovely perishes, it might have the chance to rise again."

The professor's eyes were fixed upon her with an intensity she found thrilling. Percy shyly took folds of her dress into her hands; the fabric rustled in the silence that followed.

"Indeed," he muttered with an odd sharpness, breaking contact with her and turning away. "Good evening, Miss Parker."

"Good evening, Professor." Percy rose awkwardly and moved to the door.

"Dream well," the professor added.

Percy stopped in her tracks but did not turn around. She nodded slowly, allowing his words to sink in, then opened the door and disappeared into the hall.

Into Alexi's notebook went the record of his conversation about the phoenix, another possible clue. But if he was gathering data from Miss Parker, which he shouldn't, he needed to also be looking elsewhere. He needed to be out collecting probable sources, data and proofs outside in London where a peer was meant to be placed in his path. Prophecy would never come so young, so meek, so unlike the goddess he had long expected. She'd come in a blaze of light, glory and beauty. Not quietly. And yet, something was keeping him rooted to Athens, keeping him looking for the next moment he'd talk with this ghost of a girl . . .

★ ★ ★

Before she knew it, there were the bells again, luring her to
the professor. Alarmingly, it seemed to Percy as if no time
had passed. Had she merely daydreamed the minutes into
oblivion? There had been two full days of classes between
tutorials, two days she did not actively remember. She had
only thoughts of him. And, oddly, she recalled the rumbling
and constant bark of a dog.

At room sixty-one, Percy knocked. The idea that she
might be living solely for the moments spent in the professor's private company concerned her; her entire body had
thrilled in class today when he'd asked her to visit.

"Come," the unmistakable voice called from within.

Percy entered the office yet hovered at the door, waiting
for an invitation to sit. The professor sat writing at his desk
and did not glance up. He had replaced his professorial robe
with a long black frock coat and new cravat, a cloth of a distinct shade of crimson that hung slightly askew. He waved a
hand to the chair opposite. Percy slowly took that seat, silent.

The professor set his papers aside. Percy could see him
parceling her by pieces: her snow-white face with length of
scarf about her head, her high-collared dress, gloves and
tinted glasses. Percy watched him watch her and was prepared for more questions.

"Before we begin today, may I ask, Miss Parker—?"

"About my appearance, sir?"

The professor tried to smooth the pause that followed
with a strained, unsuccessful smile. He said nothing.

"Ask anything you wish, Professor. You may stare in wonder. Gape, even. I've grown accustomed to it all."

"I hope you would not consider me so rude," her instructor retorted.

Percy offered a conciliatory smile and was appalled by the
subsequent spots she felt bloom upon her cheeks like fiery
carnations. "Of course not, Professor. I did not...I mean,
you have never gazed at me in a way...in that way...I

mean, in a rude manner. I—" The words had tumbled forth, but now her gloved hand flew to her lips to stop the hemorrhage. Terrified that her private fascination could be seen through her awkwardness of speech and the transparency of her skin, Percy prayed she would not be sent away immediately. Humiliated, she took a long breath and tried to begin anew. "I was born with this skin, Professor. I'm well in health, my pallor has never been indicative of my constitution. Except, of course, that while I do enjoy sunlight, it isn't very kind to me."

"I see. And the glasses?" Professor Rychman asked.

"I have quite sensitive eyes as well, sir."

"Ah. I hope you find yourself comfortable here? In my office?"

"Yes, thank you. I've always been most comfortable by candlelight."

The professor nodded. "It's always more of dusk than daylight in here, as I tend toward the nocturnal." He plucked a book from behind his desk and leafed through the pages, not glancing up at her.

"As do I, sir. The night is full of mystery and magic— though sometimes the magic may tend toward nightmare. My stars of birth are governed by the moon."

"Ah, we have a romantic in our midst. And an astrologer as well?" Percy could not tell if the professor's tone was cordial or disdainful. His expression, however, was stern. "Before we continue, Miss Parker, I must find a more basic guide than the one I previously gave you—your work in class over the past few days has shown several new deficiencies. If you have any interest, you may peruse my library while I look for something suitable."

Percy winced. Never before had she been the handicapped student; she'd always excelled. Nevertheless, she rose and glided across the room while the professor hunted for what she felt sure would be a grade-school primer.

As she expected, many shelves were devoted to mathematics and the sciences, natural and arcane. She was delighted to discover various books of drama as well, including a *Compleat Works of Shakespeare,* and the collected works of other great poets. But what engaged her most was a particular shelf bookended by Pythagoras and Liebniz. In the middle of these treatises by academia's gods of logic sat books on ghosts, possession, exorcism, mesmerism, witchcraft, demons, angels and all manner of unexplained phenomena.

"Fascinating," Percy couldn't help but murmur.

"Hmm?"

"Oh!" Percy started, whirling around to find the professor standing close. "I didn't mean to disturb you, sir."

"What are you—?" The professor looked up briefly from the book through which he was flipping. "Ah. I see you have found my particular collection on the occult." He returned to the contents of his tome as he walked back toward his desk.

"Yes," Percy breathed in wonder. "I assumed that, as a man of science, you would discount such things."

"There are many types of science, Miss Parker," was the professor's sharp reply.

"Quite right," Percy agreed. "Quite right indeed." She glanced at the shelf below, which was filled with books on the mythologies of manifold cultures. "Ah." She smiled, spotting a popular modern volume, which she retrieved. "Dear Bulfinch. I rather say he had me inventing my own myths at an early age. I'll never forget when Reverend Mother brought a copy from the city. I must have read it a hundred times." Percy felt a glow of pleasure, her true, passionate nature sneaking past her timidity. But when she stole a glance at Professor Rychman, he was staring at her with impatience.

She looked away. "I'm sorry, Professor, I do not mean to prattle on—"

"Bring the volume with you if you must, Miss Parker, but take your seat. We're well into our time."

"Yes, sir." Percy hurried to her chair, the book still in her grasp.

The professor glanced at the copy of *The Age of Fable* clutched in her hands and admitted, "I always found the ancient religions far more entertaining than England's sober Christianity."

Percy raised an eyebrow, surprised by such a personal comment. "Do you not consider yourself a Christian, Professor?"

He regarded her for a moment. "Forgive me, Miss Parker. I forget I speak to one who was convent educated. Worry not for my soul. I am . . . a man of spirit."

"Of course, Professor." And Percy nodded, compelled by the fact she had similarly described herself to the headmistress.

Her teacher continued to stare at her. "Perhaps you consider your faith of stronger mettle, Miss Parker, having been raised as you were?"

Percy had not expected to be asked further questions on the topic, especially not such a private one, having just been reminded it was past time for their lesson. "Well, to be quite honest," she began awkwardly, "and I hope the Lord will forgive me for saying so, but I have seen so many strange things that I do not know exactly what to believe. Raised as I was, sir, aspects of the Christian faith fascinate me, but I feel so much is left unexplained . . ."

"Indeed," the professor replied. He opened his mouth as if to continue along this course of discussion but at last seemed to think better of it. "No matter. We stray from the subject at hand. You are here for a mathematical tutorial, after all."

"My apologies, Professor."

"No need for apologies," he replied. "I was the one asking the questions."

"Thank you, sir."

"And there's no need to thank me!" the professor snapped.

"I'm sorry—Oh dear!" Percy murmured, biting her lip and yearning to retreat into her corset. Two ghosts at either end of the room had stopped swaying and turned to evaluate her. It would seem they were laughing.

Professor Rychman chuckled, himself. However, though the noise indicated amusement, no such sentiment was reflected upon his face. "Miss Parker, you'll never learn from me if you fear speaking incorrectly, out of turn, or, dare I say, against popular opinion. I am perfectly capable of commandeering a conversation should it be necessary. I speak when I please. I suppose I cannot begrudge anyone else the same."

"Even if I am a woman?" Percy asked. When the professor raised an eyebrow she added, "Miss Jennings said that, even if I could speak every language known to man, no matter, it remains far better to be seen than heard."

The professor put his book down. "And who is this sage Jennings?"

"Our dormitory chaperone."

"Ah," replied Rychman. "I should hesitate to regard your dormitory chaperone's words as gospel, Miss Parker. In my presence you will speak, ask questions and answer mine whenever I pose them. As for my thoughts on circumstances when men and women should best be silent . . . they are not covered in today's lesson."

Percy, at a loss, said nothing, but allowed a slight smile to grace her lips. The professor seemed satisfied that he had been understood.

He opened her class book to several previously assigned pages and gestured. "These basic mathematics, Miss Parker. What did you make of them?"

"The geometry I understood more than all the rest, Professor." She produced the corresponding homework, a piece of paper with a few numbers and scribbles a lesser mathematician might construe as equations.

The professor peered at the paper, grimaced and hastily penned over the entire page. "It would seem that the geometric problem was the single thing you managed to answer correctly, Miss Parker. As for the rest of your answers, they might as well be one of your foreign tongues." He furrowed his brow over a particular notation. "I assure you, I speak all forms of mathematics but the one you've created here."

"I was afraid you might say as much, sir."

The professor spent the next half hour attempting to explain where Percy had gone wrong in her figures, and to discern at which step she had lost her way. At long last he sat back in his chair, put his fingers to the bridge of his nose and gave a sigh. Percy drew her scarf about her cheeks, trying to hide from both his regard and her own shame.

"Miss Parker, now it is I who cannot understand." The professor spoke in an even tone. "You are quite adept with language. The mathematics involved here is a language. Look at these rules, and think of them as if they were the same as conjugating a verb. Think of these symbols as if they are simply a foreign alphabet!"

"I've tried, sir," she cried. "I understand how to read the formula, and I can translate, partially, but it's in the wrong tense. I could list every element in the pyramid chart on the wall behind you, but if you were to ask me how to configure a compound, I'm at a loss."

Professor Rychman sighed and rose from his chair. He turned to the fire behind him and muttered irritably in an archaic tongue, a long-dead dialect. What was it? All Percy knew was that, after a moment, the words became clear: *"None shall weave of my teaching who cannot first grasp a thread. And why am I wasting my time when there's so much else to be done?"*

In response, Percy raised her eyebrows and replied in the same archaic tongue, *"One must wish to weave if she is to excel at the loom. But if you've more important work, Professor, is there a way I may be of assistance?"* The conviction with which she spoke surprised them both.

The professor faced her, amazed. His expression quickly returned to its usual cold and careless façade, but not before Percy's heart missed a beat. "You are a linguist indeed, Miss Parker. Aramaic. Impressive. I spoke hastily in a language I assumed you would not know, and I have been proven a fool."

Delighted with herself, Percy fought back a smile. "My apologies, Professor—and I'd never call you a fool. But," she added sheepishly, "if you wish to mutter something secret, I suggest sticking to a Chinese tongue. I'm quite insufficient in Mandarin, for example."

The professor smiled. "I'll bear that in mind, Miss Parker. Tell me again how you learned so many tongues while behind convent walls."

Percy shrugged. "I wish I could explain, sir. But they just come to me, like the melodies of long-forgotten songs."

"Interesting, indeed." He gestured to her assignment. "I can only hope the meaning of mathematics is similarly long forgotten yet waiting to be discovered. *Comprende?*"

"*Sí, Señor.*"

"*Versteht?*"

"*Ja, Herr Rychman.*"

The professor set his jaw. "I suppose I could continue to ask, and you'd continue to understand , wouldn't you?"

"*Oui, Monsieur.*"

"Every tongue except mathematics."

"I'm afraid not, sir. Forgive me."

"I expect all those problems finished to the best of your ability," he commanded abruptly, pointing to a new page in her text.

"Of course, Professor. Thank you."

"You're very welcome. Good evening, Miss Parker."

"*Do svidaniya,*" Percy replied.

The professor's ears perked up and a smile toyed at the corner of his mouth. "My grandmother was a Russian immigrant," he admitted, looking as if he had found something long misplaced. "I've not heard a word of that language in many, many years. It is a beautiful sound, and I thank you for it. Good night, lady of all lands."

Feeling a little silly but nonetheless pleased, Percy blushed, gave a tiny wave and scurried out the door.

Unable to sleep for nerves, Percy took to the library to dive into the company of her dearest friends: books. She shouldn't have been in the library at Apollo Hall at such an hour, it was against the rules, but Miss Jennings was frankly scared of her and let her come and go as she pleased. As if she were a ghost. And, Percy confessed to herself with a little thrill, the idea that she was in the same building as Professor Rychman, whose candelabras she'd seen lit from the courtyard window, produced a titillating effect. She wondered what he was reading, thinking, doing . . .

A book about Newton's deterministic universe lay open at her fingertips. She'd been hoping a grand theory might crack open the mysteries of mathematics. The theory was fascinating, the calculations daunting.

The librarian, an elegantly featured, black-skinned woman to whom Percy hadn't had the courage to introduce herself, was shutting down and trimming the lights at her desk when she saw Percy at a back table and gasped. Percy looked up, flushing. She'd removed her accoutrements due to the lateness of the hour, but she hastily put on her glasses. Perhaps she was less frightening with her glasses.

"I'm sorry, Madame Librarian, I'm sure I'm well past a reasonable time . . . I . . . couldn't sleep." Percy stood. "I'm Percy Parker, I'm fairly new here."

The librarian was dressed in a modest, freshly pressed dress, her black hair pinned tightly beneath a sensible dark bonnet. She smiled, her brown cheeks dimpling.

"No, miss, it is I who should apologize. I thought you were . . ."

"A ghost," Percy finished. She'd heard that phrase so often. "It's understandable."

The librarian came closer. "Of all the things," she said softly, her tone rueful. "Of all the things a woman like me ought never do is react to a person's skin colour as if it were shocking."

Percy blinked. Then she smiled. Perhaps there were oases in Athens, places where she could be on some level understood. Certainly a woman such as this had withstood plenty.

"I'm Miss Mina Wilberforce," the woman offered. "Pleasure to meet you, Miss Parker."

"Wilberforce?" Percy breathed. Such a famous name, that: the man who had ended English slavery.

Mina grinned. "No relation. But I decided I'd take the name of an emancipator rather than any from a master."

Percy grinned back. "Brilliant."

"Shall I leave you to your studies? I can't get enough of these books. I think a woman should read every one that's ever been written. So, you've got a deal of work to do, Miss Parker. Just drop the latch on your way out."

"Thank you, Miss Wilberforce."

"Mina, please. And if you ever get tired of the harsh stares, come sit with me. We'll stare at each other, unflinching, for a good long while."

Percy laughed. Mina turned and shut the door behind her.

Buoyant, Percy sat back down to her studies and didn't notice the sudden chill on the air, nor the pale hovering figure beside her until it spoke. "Ah, Newton . . ." cooed the wispy, feminine voice.

Percy jumped slightly. She looked up to find a young woman much like herself both in pallor and age, but with the distinct difference that this young woman was transparent and floating. The female spirit glided backward, obviously startled to see Percy's eyes meet hers.

"Yes, I can see and hear you," Percy clarified, familiar with the reaction. Many spirits spoke to mortals. Few received a reply.

"Indeed! Most exciting!" exclaimed the spectre. Tightly spiraled curls floated about a face cherubic save for dark, sunken circles around the eyes. The frayed dress was dated; the open neck of the gown hung loose on a frail frame. "My name is Constance."

"Hello, Constance. I'm Percy."

The two girls nodded, knowing they could not take hands.

"Percy? That's a woman's name, is it?" the spirit asked.

Percy smiled. "It stands for something ancient."

"You do not look a bit ancient."

"Well, I'm not," Percy admitted.

"No, but you do look like one of us. How did you learn to see my kind?"

"I've always had the ability," Percy explained. "But I've dared not speak of it, else I'd be thought mad."

Constance batted Percy's stack of books with a hand that passed right through. "Mortals know nothing," she scoffed. "I thought I knew everything when I sat at that table. On the other side, you realize how little you really know."

"Really?" Percy breathed.

"Indeed. I now know the most important lesson: not everything can be explained. When I was alive, I thought I understood the whole of science, life, God . . . Went quite mad because of it."

"Is that why you travel this hall?" Percy asked.

"My body lies in a tiny plot behind. I come into this room looking for something"—Constance made one floating turn around the table—"but I cannot, for the death of me, recall what I seek. Here I drift, looking for a once-insignificant item that now means peace."

"And you think you'll find it in this hall?"

"I spent inordinate amounts of time here when the academy first opened, years ago," the ghost explained. "The first in the area to let young women attend a full curriculum. My family disowned me when I told them I wished to become a scientist. No daughter of theirs would become educated beyond eligibility, doomed to a field meant only for men! I was a revolutionary, here by the grace of the founder . . ." Constance trailed off. "Ah, well. I shall keep looking. I don't have much choice." Her hollow face took on a hopeless expression, and she glanced around, her ethereal curls quivering in a nonexistent breeze. "It's something over there, perhaps," she murmured, and began to fade.

"I hope you find whatever you seek, Constance."

The spirit looked her in the eyes. "Same to you, Percy of the spirit flesh." The ghost faded a moment, then brightened, as if an afterthought increased her link to the world of the living. "And do be careful. London is going absolutely mad."

Percy shivered. "How so?"

Constance failed to answer; she simply disappeared. The lamp grew brighter and the air warmer.

Percy gave a yawn, closed Newton and turned down the lamp. Moonlight fell in great pearly slabs against the bookshelves as she made her way to the library door, which clicked softly shut behind her. Percy then slipped through the darkened corridors of Apollo Hall and back to her bed. Despite all that she'd learned, she knew exactly what would occupy her dreams until morning. It wouldn't be ghosts or mathematics or Newton's deterministic universe, but something—someone—infinitely more corporeal.

"The Groundskeeper reports destabilization. Shall I go and see for myself? I've an idea where to find them," the servant of shadow stated, one toe on the threshold between the eternal and the mundane.

The Darkness shook and roared. "Go! For the love of the Unholy, go already!"

"You don't have to be such a brute about it." The woman made a fierce face and turned in a huff, her elaborate skirts of the latest human style swishing across the portal and onto a cobblestone street. "You know, you'd best be nice to me. Or I'll switch sides and join *their* fight instead!"

"You wouldn't dare."

The woman narrowed emerald eyes. "Are you threatening me? I'd advise against that. You'd best consider a promotion, too. Minor Arcana status? I'm insulted. I'm far too talented not to be better recognized. If you knew what was best for you, you'd replace her with me."

The shadows roared, but the servant expected it and did not flinch.

"Then treat me better, or I *will* turn on you. It's high time I was important to someone."

CHAPTER TEN

Josephine arrived at the table with several glasses of red wine. She tousled Elijah's hair and mimed a kiss—but only when her friends weren't looking.

It wasn't that fraternization within The Guard was prohibited, of course. There were several miserable triangles of unrequited affection, at the very least. Elijah and Josephine had simply decided to love each other in private.

Just as Elijah was about to reach around to give Josephine a surreptitious but deliciously inappropriate pat, Alexi whisked in through the door of the café, his black robes swirling, and halted the frivolous chatter of his friends with one quiet question. "I don't suppose any of you has seen a door?"

The group blinked up at him.

"You mean a portal?" Michael clarified.

"Of course I mean a portal," Alexi snapped.

"No. Why? Whom have you met?" Rebecca asked. Everyone looked at her, unable to mistake her sharp tone.

Alexi held up a hand. "Don't be hasty, Rebecca. It's nothing. I'm simply on guard," he explained. "As we all should be." He seated himself in a chair but then fidgeted. "At our last meeting in the chapel I assumed we'd get some sort of help or direction, but . . ."

Michael laughed. "I gave up hope of ever seeing that goddess again years ago." Only Rebecca noticed the flash of profound sorrow that passed over Alexi's face.

Elijah leaned forward, pulling a gold-plated notebook from his vest pocket. "Now that you mention it, *I'm* adding a name to our list."

Alexi raised an eyebrow. "You think you've met a candidate?"

Lord Withersby smiled. "My dear professor, I just saw the incomparable Ellen Terry play Lady Macbeth." He placed a dramatic hand over the sumptuous silk of his breast pocket. "She brought the lyceum to its knees. She channeled raw power. The spirits trembled. *I* trembled. I'm sure she could do wonders with us. Even if not, we'd get a hell of a performance."

Alexi grimaced as he stared at the list before him on the table, the notebook of candidates with nothing to recommend them but either beauty, prominence or sham spiritualist credentials; every one had been a failure, at least to his mind. "Come now, Elijah, we considered and crossed Queen Victoria off our list. You truly think an actress, however talented, will prove to be our woman?"

Getting a private audience with Her Royal Highness had been a feat only Lord Elijah Withersby had been able to manage, and then only because the poor woman was hysterical, desperate to see her dear Albert on the other side. Alexi had apologized, explaining that it wasn't their job to reunite the living and the dead, even for royalty. As with everyone else they interviewed, The Guard had been forced to wipe Her Royal Highness's memory clean, and they had departed a bit more worried about the crown than ever before.

"I daresay Terry is a visionary," Elijah promised, penning the name in bold strokes at the bottom of the list. "I'll try and obtain a private audience with her soon."

Josephine eyed him, then turned to The Guard's leader. "You must admit it's thrilling to consider, Alexi. Why *shouldn't* Prophecy be famous?"

Alexi simply shook his head. "It's not *that*. But . . . one would think none of you sees any excitement of your own. Chasing celebrities and actresses—"

"We can't, the lot of us, be above everything like you, Alexi. We must take our pleasures when they're thrown at us . . . or try and get in their way," remarked Elijah.

"Above everything?" Rebecca scoffed. "Please. Don't encourage him. He already thinks himself omniscient. Omnipotent. Tortured."

Alexi rose from the table, long folds of black fabric rustling. He offered his companions both an expression of pity and the comment, "How little you all understand."

"Of course we don't," Elijah mocked. "Only you do. Only you ever have." The others laughed, albeit nervously.

"If you're all so brilliant, discern Prophecy," Alexi snapped. "Oh, but *do* be looking for a door while you're out chasing actresses. Don't forget that. Remember, a door's the one sign we were given. I doubt it'll be a stage door." And with those words, he made a grand, sweeping exit—with Elijah, of course, humming a bit of Beethoven in his wake.

"He couldn't have been *truly* offended," Josephine tittered once the door shut behind him.

"If he didn't maintain such an absurd stoicism, we'd have nothing to tease him about. And then how would he know we care?" Rebecca smiled suddenly, thinking of something else, something from long ago. "You know, our dear professor wasn't always as omniscient and omnipotent as he now pretends. There was a time when he was just learning. Michael, would you like to tell this, or shall I?"

Grinning, the vicar gestured for her to continue.

"We weren't yet fifteen when Alexi started first experimenting with alchemy, thinking his powers granted him insights beyond the books and treatises he'd already devoured. So there he was, hovering over an array of powders, books and bottles when Michael and I came to escort him to a meeting. Flowers were bound by metal clamps at the center of the room. He was muttering things, swirling fingers in the powder. He gestured to the flowers . . . and the stone wall opposite him burst into flame. Poor Michael nearly lost what little mustache he was trying to cultivate!"

The company chuckled as Rebecca continued. "Alexi cursed and the fire extinguished itself, leaving a charred wall. Best of all, though, bits of exploded flower landed on his head and he didn't notice. Alexi replied—in that voice of his, mind you, while wearing a crown of daisy petals— 'Bloody hell, I'll never be able to explain that to the help.'"

The table rang with laughter—a sound that bound the group together through happiness and strife. Michael's hand, shaking with his guffaws, found Rebecca's, and the shared amusement made all The Guard feel for just a moment as if they were once again young.

Out on the street, Alexi paused. Inside La Belle et La Bête he heard laughter, but he was not included. He never was these days. And he couldn't help but wonder, couldn't help but fear that he had nothing to look forward to but an empty life of monotonous spectral policing until his body gave out from the strain. Perhaps Prophecy was all a lie, a carrot to keep The Guard trotting along a life of service with no reward. He felt like a failing actor who no longer believed his own lines.

One of the neighborhood spirits was acting up, but Alexi

had no desire to give chase. He was contemplating ignoring it altogether when he bumped shoulders with a cloaked figure moving quickly in the opposite direction.

"Oh!" the figure exclaimed, with a feminine gasp. The hood of her cloak fell back to reveal the most beautiful woman he had ever seen. The woman and Alexi both stopped and stared at each other. After a moment Alexi recovered himself, bowed and tipped his hat.

"Don't I know you?" the woman breathed, her beauty lighting up the alley. Her perfectly coiffed, raven black hair glinted blue in the falling twilight, and her green eyes sparkled with mystery.

Alexi's heart faltered, for he remembered the words of his goddess. She had hoped they would know each other instantly. But . . . "Pardon me, miss. I don't believe we've met. I am Professor Alexi Rychman."

The woman blinked and seemed to recover herself. "Of course. Do forgive me, Professor. You merely reminded me . . ." She shook her head. "Ah, I grow distract. My name is Miss Linden, and I've only just arrived unaccompanied in the city. I know how that must seem to a gentleman, a man of letters such as you. Please forgive my desperate air, but do you have any idea where I might find shelter? I . . ." Her voice broke. "I'm sorry, but I . . . I am on the run from something terrible." There was a pause. The woman's emerald green eyes shimmered with tears.

Alexi ruminated. His goddess had said the prophesied seventh would need refuge.

"I am aggrieved to hear it, Miss Linden. Might I recommend this very café before you?" He gestured to La Belle. "I know the owner and clientele well. Though you are in trouble, I know it to be a place of safety."

Miss Linden looked immediately relieved. She glanced from the café to him again, the creases easing across her brow. "Thank you, kind Professor. But, were you just leaving?"

"Yes, I . . . I have work I must attend."

"Of course. And thank you." She smiled demurely. "Perhaps we shall cross paths again."

Alexi chose not to respond to that, no matter how tempting. "You are welcome. Good evening, Miss Linden." He bowed and stalked off, fighting the urge to glance back. He was used to ignoring urges.

His racing blood calmed after several blocks. Until there was a critical mass of evidence, he could not allow his thoughts or sentiments to run ahead. There was no margin for error, not when one was blessed or cursed with his fate. Mortal hearts were known to make mistakes, but Alexi Rychman would make no more.

The door of the café opened, and a woman entered whom none of The Guard would ever forget. She pulled back the hood of her cloak, worry on her face, hands shaking. She looked up, met Josephine's welcoming gaze and offered a strained smile. Elijah and Michael both stood, bowing slightly. She nodded to each in turn, and took a few steps inside.

Josephine, as hostess, attended the new guest. "Mademoiselle, welcome to La Belle et La Bête! I am Mademoiselle Belledoux, proprietor." She collected the newcomer's cloak and placed it in an alcove nearby.

The newcomer had a flawless face and raven black curls piled delicately atop her head, and she well surpassed the average patron of La Belle et La Bête. She was truly a vision, a beauty clad in a mixture of deep crimson velvet and satin brocade. A slender, gloved hand flew to the cameo at her throat. Her emerald eyes glowed warm and hopeful.

"Greetings, mademoiselle. Forgive my intrusion, but I, seeking a bit of refuge, was sent here by the kind professor I just met outside."

"Kind?" Elijah snorted. Rebecca elbowed him.

"We are honoured that you take refuge here. Please, have a seat. What may I procure for you this early evening,

mademoiselle? Tea, perhaps? Or"—Josephine leaned in—
"we have been known to tempt royalty with our special
cabernet."

The woman smiled. "How can I refuse?"

"Compliments of the house, mademoiselle!" Elijah stated,
rising from the table. Josephine turned to the wine cellar and
flashed him a glare, but he simply beamed at her in response.

The newcomer's lips curved into a wide smile. "Why,
thank you, sir! What a relief to find a haven in such an out-
of-the-way place."

Elijah hurried to settle her at a table. "Please allow me to
introduce myself. Lord Elijah Withersby, miss, at your service." When the woman offered it, Elijah took and gave her
satin-gloved hand a kiss.

"Miss Lucille Linden. A pleasure to make your acquaintance, Lord Withersby."

"And may I introduce my esteemed colleagues? Miss Rebecca Thompson, Mr. Michael Carroll and that French tart
fetching your wine is—"

"My mutually esteemed colleague, Lord Withersby, curb
your heathen tongue or I'll not hesitate to remove it," Josephine called from the cellar stair.

Rebecca also scowled at Elijah, and she turned to address
the newcomer. "Please forgive Lord Withersby. He ought
not be allowed out in polite society, for reasons which should
be clearly evident to a lady such as yourself."

"Terribly sorry, Miss Linden. I am a cad," Elijah admitted. He paused a moment before grinning wickedly. Rebecca and Josephine both shook their heads.

Miss Linden brimmed with amusement. "So it would
seem, Lord Withersby. A scandal to your class."

"Thank heavens I'm a second son and my family's all
abroad, else I believe I'd have been shipped off to some tedious war somewhere rather than slumming about in this
tedious city," Elijah said with a casual wave.

Josephine set one glass of wine before her guest, kept a

glass for herself and raised it. "To new acquaintances! Not many fresh faces find us here, but when they do they are always welcome."

"I, too, shall raise a glass!" Elijah cried.

"Pity you don't have one, Lord Withersby," his secret mistress replied; and she and the newcomer shared an innately feminine smile as they toasted and sipped the blood-red liquid.

"I offer you my sincerest appreciation, my new friends!" Miss Linden exclaimed. But then her hand rose to her throat again, and she leaned forward, her beautiful face clouded with worry. "May I call you friends? To be honest, I am in most desperate need of them. I realize this is a great imposition after so short an acquaintance, but . . . I need to hide."

"From the law?" Vicar Michael asked. He was determined to be careful. They couldn't have the law snooping about, not if they intended to continue their Grand Work unhindered.

"No. From a . . . beast of a man," she said at last.

"Your husband?"

"Of sorts. My master . . . He's—oh, I do not wish to bore you with my unfortunate, improbable details. I've lived a strange life. You'd not believe me were I to explain."

"You might be surprised," Elijah suggested. Rebecca gave him a warning glance.

Miss Linden raised an eyebrow. "I just need shelter," she explained after a moment. "I cannot go to my family; he'll know where to find me. I have to throw myself upon others' kindness and wait out this terrible storm. Any suggestions you may have, I would deeply appreciate."

Josephine looked at Elijah, Michael and Rebecca before finally ending on Lucille. She seemed to come to a decision. "There is a room two floors above. You may call it your own, so long as you don't bring the law or your master's wrath down upon us. We are a secretive group but kind. You need pay only what you can afford—if that is anything at all."

Tears filled the newcomer's eyes. "Bless you. Bless all of you! My new life begins," she murmured. "But now, you must forgive me again. This may seem frightfully forward, but as my life has come undone at the very seams I have little to lose. Tell me more about your professor." As Elijah began to chuckle, Miss Linden's face flushed. She hurried to add, "Perhaps I spoke too hastily. I—"

"Professor Alexi Rychman," Elijah interrupted. "Our Master of Ceremonies, Minister of Revels, our Melancholy Prince of Denmark."

Michael failed to contain a chuckle. Miss Linden appeared confused.

Rebecca stepped forward. "I am truly sorry, Miss Linden. Our ill breeding again rears its ugly head. We can beg only the excuse of weariness and the trying fact that we've spent far, far too long with one another. Please forgive us."

"I think you're charming," Miss Linden assured them, as if their particular quirks were nothing out of the ordinary. "Clearly, this Professor Rychman is a friend of yours."

"Like it or not, he's stuck with us," Elijah agreed.

Miss Linden smiled. "Well, forgive my boldness, but I am glad. I hope to see him again. There are few into whose path I would rather again be cast."

"Indeed?" Rebecca said.

"Indeed." Miss Linden's eyes glittered warmly as she took another sip of cabernet.

Elijah turned to Rebecca, clearly surprised, mouthing the words, "Placed in our path?"

Rebecca's lips became a grim line. The blood in her veins murmured, churning up her instincts at the introduction of this new and beautiful face. Miss Linden had indeed been placed in their path seeking refuge.

CHAPTER ELEVEN

Percy's latest recurrent vision was a hazy one where she was standing in the middle of a circle, surrounded by shafts of light. Music—inhuman, beautiful, incomprehensible—was everywhere, playing inside of her and out. This music, which she had no words to describe, lingered on in faint strains throughout the day.

It was while Professor Rychman was in the midst of a tutorial lecture of particular eloquence that Percy roused from the vision to find him snapping his fingers in front of her face. She started, fumbled an apology, wrung her hands. "Oh, Professor! I've no d-doubt that your patience for me is at an end," she stammered. "But I swear on my life that I listen to your every word and—"

The professor sighed. "Miss Parker, I wish you felt more at ease here. If you did, you might take to things with more surety."

"I am, sir. At ease, I mean. Well, I . . . Oh, dear." Feeling a fool, she looked away.

"At ease. Indeed?"

Percy folded her hands upon the desk. "I suppose not. Forgive my timidity. It undermines any hope I have for collected composure."

"Your composure, Miss Parker, is nearly regal," he replied. "That is, it would be if you stopped hiding."

Percy blinked through her glasses at him. "Hiding?"

"With your shrouds and your shields I cannot tell when you are comprehending what I say. It is common knowledge that the eyes are the window to the soul, but your windows are shuttered. What they have to say has been muted."

"But sir, the sun, the light—"

"Does the sun shine here, Miss Parker? You told me you were comfortable."

"Well, I am, sir. Here the room is perfect but, outside, people stare and—"

The professor interrupted without pity or pause. "Do you include me in that number, Miss Parker? I would hope you realize that I have more important things to do than gawk as if you were a museum piece." He leveled his gaze at her before returning to transcribing notes from a text.

"Of course, sir," Percy replied. "Of course I realize that."

"I call it hiding," the professor repeated.

Percy let out a brief sigh, knowing she had no choice but to muster a bit of courage. She feared his reaction more than she could say, but he left no other option. "Very well, sir," she remarked with quiet resolution. She rose from her chair, turned her back to him and began to remove her barriers.

She had not realized the entirety of the feeling of security they gave until she was confronted with her protections' absence. After her careful hands removed glasses, gloves and long scarf, Percy felt naked. Vulnerable. *Indecent.* Yet, she reminded herself, it had not been her idea to lower her defenses. If the professor was to be disgusted—which was her greatest fear—it was through no fault of her own.

The thought brought no comfort.

Tresses of lustrous, snow-white hair tumbled from their clothbound imprisonment, streaming like snowfall down the girl's back. In an effort to make his student more at ease, Alexi did his best to appear wholly disinterested as she carefully removed her protections with delicate, private ceremony. But then she turned to face him, clutching those items that had held her unusual features in mystery. He forced his eyes to his book.

"As you would have it so, Professor, here is your pupil in all her ghastliness."

Alexi looked up. Though Miss Parker's hands clearly trembled, her voice did not.

His furrowed, generally disapproving brow rose slightly, and he leaned back in his chair and took her in. Luminous crystal eyes held streaks of pale blue shooting from tiny black pupils. A face youthful but devoid of colour, smooth and un-blemished like porcelain, had graceful lines as well defined and proportioned as a marble statue. Her long, blanched locks shimmered in the candlelight like spider silk. Upon high cheekbones lay hints of rouge—any more would have appeared garish against her blindingly white skin, but she had been artful in her application. Her rosebud lips were tinted in the same manner.

She was attuned to even the most minuscule response. Her merciless, hypnotic gaze found his and she frowned. "You see, Professor, even you, so stern and stoic, cannot hide your shock, surprise, distaste—"

"Distaste?" he interrupted quietly. "Is that what you see?"

If Percy had taken the time to truly consider his response, she would have noticed that his tone was far from distasteful; it was, in fact, flattering. But she plowed on, choosing hurt. "What else can one feel when they behold living flesh that looks dead?"

"You assume ghost and not angel?"

Those words in regard to herself made Percy's heart con-vulse. Surely he could not have intended a compliment. "I . . . I would never presume to liken myself to anything heavenly, Professor."

"Indeed? Then it would seem that you, Miss Parker, are more modest than I." If there had been an admiring look in his eye, it was quickly gone. The professor blandly donned his glasses. "Now, come take your seat. No more hiding, not in this office. Never again."

"That is still your wish?" Percy asked.

"It is."

Percy put down her things with a sigh. But as the lesson continued, she began to relax, seeing that he looked at her with no other quality but the expectation of fastidious attention. Once his lecture was complete, she was excused with an assignment and a curt nod. Percy donned her scarf, her gloves and her glasses with delicate deliberation, preparing to walk out again into the world. But halfway to the door after bidding the professor a quiet farewell, books in hand, she stopped and turned around.

The professor, busying himself at his desk, could evidently feel the weight of her stare; he looked up after a moment. "Yes, Miss Parker?"

"Thank you, Professor."

"For what?"

"You are . . . the only man who has not made me feel as if I were on display."

The professor blinked, his face expressionless. "You are a student and not an exhibit, Miss Parker. Good day."

Percy curtseyed in response. Exiting the office, she felt heartened and keenly alive. Her blood murmured strangely in her veins. She wasn't sure she'd ever been so happy.

As soon as the door closed behind Miss Parker, Alexi opened a drawer, withdrew his notebook and hurled it onto his desk. His pen flew. He did not allow himself to think of the implications of this previously unknown anxiety that was building inside.

"Miss Parker," he said aloud as he wrote. "A ghost? Not my goddess in colours, but in fact the mirror opposite. Colourless. And yet, uniquely beautiful. Could her ghostly yet angelic appearance actually be a warning? Is she to be trusted or avoided? Why am I not dismissing her entirely, as I ought? She is a *student!* Why dare I even consider her?

"More the goddess is that ineffable Miss Linden, with her own clues, all those familiar words . . . And yet I sense in Miss Parker a gentleness similar to my goddess of two decades past. Which of them is the true seventh—if indeed either? Neither gentleness nor beauty, no matter how unusual, make Prophecy!"

He slammed the book closed, knowing the fate of the world rested on his shoulders.

"I've found them. I'm Lucille Linden now. Isn't that a lovely name?" the servant of shadow said proudly, having crossed the threshold back home. She spun, appreciating the rustle of her fine, blood-coloured dress, the exotic sculpting of her body beneath her corset, the absurdity of her bustle, the useless but fashionable layers of doubled skirts.

Darkness growled. "Why. Do. They. Live?"

"Come now!" Lucille smiled broadly. "Let me have a bit of fun. One of them in particular I want to toy with. How I've missed mortal games."

"Is she *with* them?"

"No. I've not seen her. Or anything like her. Perhaps she's abandoned them, too—just like she did you." She couldn't help pointing this out, and shrugged when Darkness growled. "Oh, stop. I'm sure she'll be along soon; she can never stay away. She's so pathetically predictable."

"Don't be long," Darkness commanded.

Lucille waved a languid hand. "Remember my warning. I want to be important. For that reason, I shall take the time I please and make my own choices, thank you very much. I don't see that you have much alternative."

CHAPTER TWELVE

Reaching down into one of his office's myriad hiding places, Alexi withdrew a small wooden container and handed it to Josephine. Opening the lid, she saw how the sealed vials of coloured powder shimmered in the fading light. Her slender fingers closed protectively around the box. Alexi's alchemical study hadn't been for naught. He'd found a way to transfer blue fire directly into paint pigment. Useful, for The Guard's artist to employ upon her ethereal canvases.

"Use it sparingly," he cautioned. "It's a powerful mixture this time. I eagerly await your creation, Josie. I expect it to be ravishing."

There was a knock upon the door.

"Come."

A slender figure entered the room, shawl draped around her bowed head as if she were votaress for a goddess. Per the professor's request, she threw back her wrap and removed her dark glasses.

"Ah, Miss Parker!" Alexi boomed.

The figure jumped, smiling nervously at the professor before her eyes riveted to his lovely companion in her impeccable gown. Josephine was similarly taken aback by the sight of this unparalleled girl, and she gasped upon surveying those unearthly, crystalline eyes.

The newcomer shoved her tinted glasses back on her face, tossed her shawl over her head and turned to the professor with a strained expression, as if he had betrayed her. "Forgive me, Professor, I did not mean to interrupt—" She choked, stealing another furtive glance at his ravishing companion before moving toward the door.

"No, no," Alexi assured her. "I'm completing a matter of business. Miss Parker, this is Mademoiselle Josephine Belledoux, an esteemed colleague of mine. Josephine, this is Miss..." He hesitated, realizing he did not know how to continue. He did not know her first name.

"Percy," she supplied.

"Thank you. Miss *Percy* Parker, one of my students."

"*Enchantée,* mademoiselle." Josephine bowed her head.

"*Merci beaucoup,* mademoiselle, *et moi aussi.*"

"*Ah, Français!*" Josephine beamed, basking in the warmth of her native language.

"Miss Parker is adept at many tongues," Alexi explained.

Percy gazed ruefully at the floor. "Unfortunately my talent doesn't apply to mathematics." Contemplating the presence of this other woman in Professor Rychman's office, she felt her heart fall in an alarming fashion.

"That's quite all right, Miss Parker," Josephine said softly. "Personally, I detest mathematics and all sciences. So I paint."

"Oh?" Percy looked up at this woman who was surely years older than she, yet showed no sign apart from the contrast of her hair. Dark brown locks were swept up into an elaborate knot, and two white streaks framed her face.

"It would seem, Miss Belledoux, that you two are of like minds. Miss Parker would rather be sketching her dreams than paying attention in class."

Percy cringed.

"Can you blame the young lady?" the Frenchwoman replied, kindly.

The professor ignored his friend's smile, gesturing broadly to the south wall and speaking for Percy's edification. "My paintings are Miss Belledoux's own, and I am in the process of commissioning a new piece."

"Your work is *tres belle,* mademoiselle," Percy breathed, looking around.

"*Merci, ma amie.*"

"Miss Belledoux, I must now uphold my duty as Prometheus, bearing the torch of education to darkened minds," the professor declared.

Josephine raised an eyebrow. "Well, aren't we *se donner de grand airs?*" She bowed and moved to the door, giving Percy a knowing grin. "Don't let him fool you into thinking he bears any such light," she whispered. "It's been nothing but darkness for ages."

Percy couldn't help herself, and the two women shared a smile.

"Excuse me!" The professor shook his head and glowered. "There will be no slander in this shrine of knowledge!"

"All right, so he's brilliant," Josephine offered, but she winked as she opened the door to the hall. "It's his social graces that leave something to be desired."

"Out, I say!"

"Au revoir!" And with a carefree laugh, the Frenchwoman disappeared.

"Infidels, every one of them," the professor muttered, gesturing for Percy to sit.

"Who?"

The professor sighed, irritated, searching for his pen. "My colleagues. Social graces? Ha! I hope you're ready to learn something."

"Certainly."

"You've forgotten," the professor remarked, gesturing.

"Oh." Percy removed her shawl again. Sliding her glasses from her face, she steeled herself a moment for the brief flash of distaste she was so accustomed to seeing. But the professor launched directly into his lesson without a moment's pause, never once shying away from the sight of her. He hadn't changed, and the fact filled her with joy.

The professor could condense entire philosophies into a graspable twenty-minute speech. Nonetheless, when he turned again to the processes of mathematics, Percy's eyes fell on the open book of Shakespeare at the corner of his desk. She leaned in and saw notes and scribbles in the margins.

The professor, evidently aware she had lost focus, sighed. "Miss Parker, what now . . . ? Oh. *Hamlet*?"

"I promise I was listening, sir. It's just that this play is my favourite."

"I acquiesce," he muttered to himself. "The grip of this mathematical theory is not to be regained. And so, if nothing else, I'll commend your theatrical taste." After a moment he inquired, "Have you heard of the recent production in town where Hamlet marries Ophelia at the end?"

Percy's jaw dropped. *"What!"*

"I suppose this day and age cannot be trusted with a good tragedy. So, you do not approve?"

"Of course not, Professor! I hope you'd give me that much credit!"

"As a professed Romantic, I wasn't entirely sure."

Percy rallied a meek rebuttal. "I have standards, Professor."

"Indeed? Well, get out of my office before I raise your standard of attention. I may have even had you for fifteen minutes before you wandered off."

"Professor, I assure you that I always listen—"

He shrugged. "Never mind, I have work to do. I must go home and gather my wits for a whole night of study. I have a ride ahead of me." But as the professor shooed her from his desk, his face seized with a flash of discomfort. His hand flew to his temple.

"Professor, I'm s-sorry," Percy stammered. "Are you all right, sir?"

"As my 'social graces leave something to be desired,' will you be so kind as to see yourself out? Good evening, Miss Parker," he replied, clutching his forehead.

Realizing he wanted her companionship no longer, Percy stumbled out. "Good evening, Professor, do feel better." But as she tried to shake him from her mind for the rest of the day, it was a matter as difficult as grasping mathematics.

★ ★ ★

The female calling herself Miss Lucille Linden leaned out the window of the tiny room she'd graciously accepted in the floors above La Belle et La Bête. Her new friends were eating dinner below. Feigning illness, she had declined their generous invitation. Instead, she stared out over London's sooty, dirty rooftops.

A growl sounded, and she turned to see a cloud of horror awaiting direction. "Go ahead," she said.

The cloud turned tail and dove through the roof. There came a cry from below, and then the voices of Lord Withersby, Miss Thompson, Mr. Carroll and the Irishwoman introduced as Ms. Connor. The foursome sounded afraid but determined. There were the continued noises of a fracas.

Lucille grinned, her mouth watering. "Listen to them play!" she crowed.

A knock on her door and a strained command interrupted her pleasure. "Miss Linden," a voice called out, "it's Josephine here. There's an intruder down below so you must lock yourself in. The gentlemen are taking care of him, all right?"

"Yes, yes, of course," Lucille replied, ducking back inside the window and feigning innocence.

She appreciated the illusion they were trying to keep up. They assumed, of course, that she had no idea of their true nature. They also assumed that she was a harmless, powerless young woman. It was time to be honest on both sides.

Though . . . perhaps honesty was not ideal at this exact moment. Especially not if one of them was about to die.

An infernal thing the likes of which The Guard had never seen passed through the structure of La Belle et La Bête and descended upon their table. Snarling horrific, snapping teeth in their faces and shredding tablecloths, the abomination was a huge cloud of black smog that became one dog and then one hundred, a chimerical, shifting creature that was at first incorporeal and could pass through walls, but which then flickered into something deadly with claws, jaws and horrible red eyes. In the next moment it became a cloud again, impossible to catch.

"What in God's name is this?" Rebecca shrieked, scooping up her wool skirts as she spun and dashed to the door, her companions following. "Josie, Miss Linden's upstairs. We'll not test her with a thing such as this. Have her lock herself in!"

Josephine raced upstairs.

Elijah backed down the alley outside, staring at the demon cloud with horrified fascination as it followed, floating at the level of their heads and taking up nearly the entire width of the alley with its bulky canine body and flickering profusion of heads. It hunched forward, ready to attack.

Michael took Rebecca's hand on one side, and Jane took the other. A powerful wind whipped around them. Josephine, having bade Miss Linden stay within, swiftly joined their ranks. She took Michael's left hand.

"Elijah, come," Rebecca commanded.

The beast lunged, but Withersby ducked out of the way. "Please tell me this is just the Black Dog of Newgate," he exclaimed, joining his friends in their circle of clasped hands. London's most gruesome tale of spectral revenge was much less horrifying than entertaining thoughts of a whole new breed.

Rebecca shook her head. "No," she replied. "We've never seen this."

The dog whipped around to face them, snarling. But as it prepared its next attack, Rebecca shouted a command in the ancient language of The Guard. The hellish thing cocked its head, opened its many maws wide and jumped—only to disperse at the last moment into a grey mist and pass through them.

At the other end of the alley the creature coalesced and

hurtled off in the opposite direction. The Guard gave chase, Elijah trailing after, cleaning up any mess that might give away their battle. They all gave thanks that none of London's passersby could see ghosts, as their spectral quarry would have caused a riot. They simply had to deal with being considered lunatics.

As they ran, Josephine sought to pinpoint Elijah's reference. "Wait. The Black Dog... Was that the sorcerer?"

"Yes," Rebecca answered, panting as they turned a corner. "The scholar imprisoned in Newgate centuries ago for sorcery."

"The one where the starving inmates ate his body and then a huge, avenging black dog tore them limb from limb?"

"That would be the one. But this is not that dog."

Michael seemed just as eager to make this beast something they knew. "What about the stench of decay that follows the Newgate dog? You smell it now, don't you?" There was comfort in the familiar, even one of London's most macabre spectres. More importantly, the Newgate dog was something they could best. They already had.

"No," Rebecca replied, breathless. "I smell brimstone. This is not that beast! Do you feel anything in your blood? Any of you? I feel nothing. We can't track this, we can't sense it..." Any further commentary was cut off as she stumbled, losing her footing on a cobblestone. Michael was quick to catch her arm. "Damnable heels," she muttered, righting herself. "Why don't they make a boot a woman can run in?"

"Hello, friends!" A fierce form on a black steed and trailing black robes appeared at the opposite end of the street. Staring up at the floating, shifting beast, Alexi cried, "What the hell is this?"

A snarl and a swipe knocked his hat off his head. Alexi growled right back, jumping off his horse and shrieking a curse in the ancient language of The Guard. Blue flame leaped from his hands, and it singed the spectral dog's many noses. The blue flame streamed a circle around the shifting cur, which hunkered down opposite Alexi and seemed to be tensing its haunches. However, instead of attacking Alexi, when it found a weakness in its fiery containment the beast turned and swarmed back the way it had come, tearing off down the street in a gruesome splintering of canine forms— and through Elijah. Lord Withersby groaned and collapsed in a heap.

"Coward, face me!" Alexi cried, mounting his horse after glancing down worriedly at his unconscious friend. Elijah had been swept up into Jane's arms, her healing powers at the ready—if she was not already too late.

Rebecca ran toward Alexi's horse. "Alexi, don't you dare—" But he was already after it, yelling curses and chasing the monster down the next avenue with bolts of blue fire.

While he knew he couldn't destroy the hellish thing on his own, Alexi felt the least he could do was reverse the game, be the fox tracking the hound. For that reason he gave chase, spurring his stallion, Prospero, into areas of London he preferred to forget, the city's dark and dirty underbelly. Urchins, beggars and streetwalkers beckoned, unaware of the terror that had just flashed past. He hissed at their advances, stricken into anger at their desperation.

One particular young woman, barely more than a child, called up to him, asking if he wanted company for the evening. Alexi gritted his teeth and cried, "Find shelter, for God's sake! Don't you know something terrible is on the loose?" He flung coins into the street as he passed.

"I know, sir," the consumptive waif called back, darting to pick up his offerings. "Where lurks the Ripper? But we've nowhere to hide. We've got no choice. Bless ye for the shilling!"

It was too much. Alexi reined in his horse, suddenly turning back toward the form silhouetted in dim gaslight, locks of hair piled haphazardly beneath a moth-eaten bonnet. She, thinking perhaps that she had procured a client after all, gave him a practiced, inviting look far more desperate than attractive.

He shook his head and emptied the entirety of his pockets into her hands. "Find as many of your lot as you can and take them to spend the night in safe shelter."

The young woman gazed up in awe. "Are ye trackin' 'im, then, good sir? Are you the detective?"

"Of sorts, dear girl," Alexi replied.

She reached up to stroke his horse's black neck. "Then you're our guardian angel."

Reins in hand, Alexi could neither acknowledge the sentiment nor look the waif in the eye, knowing he must fail at guarding all the poor wretches society cast onto the street. "Don't take long, and don't part company," he commanded gruffly, and set off.

"I won't, sir!" she cried. "Bless you, sir. I was a friend of Annie Chapman, may she rest in peace! By God, she's lookin' out for me by sendin' you this night!"

These wards were the poorest, the most hopeless. Their inhabitants were the dregs, hapless souls who had come to this city seeking fortune and finding no love in the bosom of the empire. All street lamps ended at Commercial Street and Whitechapel Road. Alexi had forgotten that fact, because when summoned here in the past, in the course of his work, there had always been ethereal light to guide his way. Spectres cast their own illumination. Tonight, the sector was black. Even the ghosts were hiding.

Heaven must have felt a bit of pity, for the clouds above thinned to allow a dim grey moonlight to filter down. It was just enough for navigation at a slow plod. Prospero stamped impatiently, messily splashing muddy puddles and then clacking forward across the cobblestones.

Past a wide corner just inside the dim sooty haze of Duffield's Yard, just off a set of train tracks, Alexi drew the horse to a halt; he'd caught sight of something amorphous rustling in a space between two miserable brick buildings. He could only make out sounds, however, because there was a black hole ahead, a pitch-black deeper than night itself, snuffing out all existence. Alexi gave a cry, shouted a command, a verse in an ancient rite of which he was the master. The shadows shifted. Two bloodred eyes fixed on him. Then ten. Then came a swish of air and a muffled cry, changing suddenly into an ungodly gurgling noise. There came the smell of blood.

Prospero reared. The cloud of evil rose, a flickering mass of violence and vermin, shifting doglike shapes floating up into the night sky. Alexi's heart exploded with hopeless fury at the lifeless heap he dimly saw crumpled below.

He dismounted and ran, his hand flying to his mouth upon closer inspection: the woman's throat had been slashed open, and there were also cuts visible on her cheeks. The victim's eyes suddenly shot open—or so it seemed. Alexi retreated a step, watching as a ghost lifted from the woman's body, creating a double image: the lit, monochromatic form of the spirit, unmarred and superimposed upon the still-bleeding corpse. In a frayed dress, the spectre rose to a standing position where both Alexi and she could evaluate the particulars of her bodily remains, which had been spared the more severe mutilation of the Ripper's other subjects. But the beast hadn't finished. Would it therefore strike again?

He turned to offer the victim's ghost what paltry benediction he could, but her defiant face stared back at him. Her arm lifted and she pointed west, toward the black cloud roiling with horror, toward that bestial form floating above the crumbling tenement roofs near Aldgate. There was hatred for the beast in her eyes, and her transparent lips mouthed the word "Go." Alexi hurried back to his horse.

The trouble was in the tracking. There were no direct paths. It was only a five-block stretch of sharp turns down bleary alleys and dank gutters clogged with refuse and the occasional corpse of an animal, but the course was painstaking. Alexi fought not to trample any huddled, sleeping children, the saddest of all the ward's forgotten horde tucked into the endless shadows. Veering his course from the train yard, he kept his eyes fixed on the malevolent mass passing low in the sky. But then it stopped suddenly and plunged below the rooftops. Alexi loosed a string of curses and spurred his horse down another dark street.

As he rounded the corner of Mitre Square, an incantation died on his lips at the same moment the beast's next victim did. Surrounded by brick, the small square was now her open, bloody mausoleum. A wispy ghost, a weary young woman confused and wide-eyed peeled upward and into the night sky. There was no sign of her killer.

Alexi murmured a benediction in the spirit's direction, watching her ascend. He prayed that she would continue upward into what was now a calm haze of silver moonlight, rather than return and be tethered to the unspeakable reality of her mortal remains below. Ruffled skirts and pooling blood from a torn abdomen and something that was now hardly a face remained turned toward him on the ground, and Alexi wondered if the sight would ever leave his mind. He choked back a wail and darted back out the walled block, well aware that there were officers on patrol who would soon find her. Everyone was vigilant these nights, but no one was of any use. Not even him.

But Alexi no longer doubted that he had found the source of Whitechapel's recent woe.

His pale eyes flew open and he gasped, and Elijah found himself in Michael Carroll's modest sitting room.

"Elijah, thank God," Jane murmured in her soft brogue, returning glowing hands to her sides.

"Where are the others? Are they safe?" he asked.

Another voice answered: Josephine. "Yes, we're all here. Michael's home was the closest to where you fell." She placed a gloved hand upon Jane's broad shoulder. "Nicely done."

"Thank you, Josie," the Irishwoman replied. Seeing that her hands were no longer glowing, she brushed damp hair from Elijah's face.

He grinned. "Jane, darling, Irish or no, please know we're nothing without you. You can place those healing hands on me at any turn."

Jane frowned. "Lord Withersby, that was a rather frightenin' display, and by the Holy Saints don'tcha ever repeat it." Anxiety and exhaustion had heightened her accent.

"You think I planned it, do you? It passed through me with no warning—"

"We know. We saw," stated a new voice. Another figure stepped into the light.

"Why, my dear Miss Thompson, you look dourer than usual."

"Hush, you reckless infidel!" Rebecca retorted. Her expression softened into a fatigued smile but a moment later her tone was again sharp. "Elijah—truly, we thought we lost you."

Glancing around, he frowned. "Where is our fearless leader?"

There was a tense silence. "On his way," Rebecca replied.

Elijah shook his head. "Don't tell me he *pursued* it?"

None of them wanted to answer. "Yes," Rebecca finally murmured.

"Why aren't you following him?" Elijah cried, struggling to get out of bed. "He needs our help!"

"I don't, but London does." The door of Michael's sitting room flew open, and Alexi entered in a storm of dark robes, his face ashen. "Two!" he cried, pacing the room and pounding his fist against a window frame. "It shredded two women tonight! There was nothing I could do! I don't understand what it could want with those poor wretches! What is it, and what does it gain?" He collapsed on the settee only to stand again and continue pacing. "It isn't a ghost. We deal in spiritual disturbances, when spirits and humans mix poorly. This is a *demonic* force. I..." He trailed off, clearly not liking where his thoughts were leading, and walked over to peer down at Elijah. "Are you all right?"

"Yes, thanks for asking," his friend replied. "Jane pulled me back from the brink, apparently, though it has taken her since you left."

"Good." Moving to the window, Alexi looked across London toward Athens, to where the first light of dawn was licking the horizon. He pounded a fist against the sill. "Damn it all! Those poor girls. It was my fault. I should have stopped it somehow."

"Alexi, it was *our* fault," Rebecca corrected, taking a step closer. "We should have stopped it. You cannot take it upon yourself—"

"What good are we if there are things beyond our power?" he cried. "In the end, are we just useless mortals?" After a long, tense moment, he turned to Rebecca. "Headmistress..." he began.

She anticipated him. "Yes, Professor. We'll inform the students. And we must place guards there. For our peace of mind, we must implement whatever protections we can."

"What do we do?" Michael asked, for the benefit of those who were not involved in the school. He moved to place a hand on Rebecca's shoulder, which was trembling ever so slightly.

"We attend to whatever work we can manage. And pray Prophecy becomes clear," Alexi replied.

"How cowardly," Michael murmured. "This creature preys only on single, unaccompanied women. We must pray most heartily for their peace."

The Guard nodded, sitting in uncomfortable, dangerously unresolved silence.

Alexi gazed out the window. "I need you now," he murmured against the glass, yearning for his goddess. "Proclaim yourself before more innocents die." But then a sudden thought occurred to him. "Miss Linden. Where was she during all of this?"

Josephine replied. "I told her to remain at La Belle, locked in her room. She knows nothing of what transpired. Should we mention it to her?"

Alexi breathed a sigh of relief. "Heavens, no. I'll not let a stranger in on our business until they give me good cause." He scowled. "No matter how intriguing."

Yet, it was time to consider Miss Linden. It was time to see if she was more than just beauty and a few leading clues. War was coming, just like his goddess had foretold. Or maybe he and his friends had missed the beginning and were running late to the front lines.

CHAPTER THIRTEEN

Athens's students stumbled into the auditorium, having been abruptly roused by their house wardens at the break of dawn. In the front of the room, near the raised lip of the stage, several professors milled about, their arms folded as if in effort to contain themselves. As they'd filed through Promethe Hall, it immediately went up as rumour among the students that the murderer, the Ripper, must have come close, was perhaps in their midst or had perhaps struck down one of their own in the night.

The chamber where they assembled was a mix of function and form, with a vaulted, frescoed ceiling depicting birds on wing, and the center of the stage's crimson curtain now parted as Headmistress Thompson stepped forward, dressed in her usual prim and conservative layers of grey. The ambient yellow glow of the gas lamps, set in golden sconces at intervals across the scalloped walls, created warmth in sharp contrast to her cold expression. The assembled faculty took their seats. Mina Wilberforce scanned the crowd, found Percy, and the two shared a nervous smile before Mina turned back to the headmistress.

Percy felt her pulse quicken as there was a flicker of movement from stage left: Professor Rychman entered from a dark wing. He bowed to the headmistress, descended the stair to the floor and stood by the edge of the stage like a sentry, head swiveling, eyes searching. Unable to change her focus Percy waited, praying for him to find her where she sat in a shadowed seat to the side, Marianna fidgeting nearby. When their intent gazes at last met, his eyes actually lingered a moment as he gave a subtle nod. Percy thrilled. Had he truly been assuring himself she was safe?

Only an astute observer could have noticed the extent of the drawn looks, the hard weariness in the eyes of both Professor Rychman and the headmistress, but Percy had made a habit of studying them—especially together—and so was deeply concerned.

"Ladies and gentlemen, esteemed students and faculty of Athens," the headmistress began. "I regret many things this morning. I regret the necessity of having to gather you. I regret that there must be a change in school policy. And I regret most deeply to report that there were two additional murders last night."

The auditorium burst into hushed murmurs and a few soft cries. The headmistress took a step forward and the sound quieted to a hiss. "In response, there will be guards posted at every doorway, entrance or egress of Athens."

The room buzzed. As Professor Rychman ascended the stage, there fell immediate silence. The ferocity of his expression would still a screaming infant, and his voice resounded throughout the chamber. A collective shudder went through the crowd.

"I am sure the sensationalistic rags of this city will address every question you may have, and relate every heinous, disgusting detail of the murders," he remarked bitterly. "But let me come straight to the point. The murders fit the Ripper's profile; he continues to attack the young and defenseless. For that reason, though the violence remains so far centered in Whitechapel, we shall take every precaution." He cast a pointed glance at a few known pranksters among the crowd, those most likely to sneak out late at night. These few students had the good sense to stay silent or nod. "Our buildings are not fortresses. But until this violence is no longer a threat, our *grounds* shall be." Alexi cast a sweeping stare across the auditorium; then he deferred to the headmistress.

"I expect full cooperation," she continued. "I do not expect anyone to question the measures which we might be forced to enact other than the guards . . . but for now classes will remain on their regular schedule, and there are no substantive changes to protocol or to events. I wish I could offer a message of comfort and inspiration this morning, but until we hear more from the authorities, any such statement would be a contrivance. You are dismissed."

Percy and Professor Rychman caught each other's eyes once more before she filed out of the auditorium. There was something in the lines of his face that was new and infinitely more complex, as if something in this great tragedy was striking a personal chord. Percy didn't know why this instinct fluttered in her mind, other than that studying him so intently perhaps gave her strange ideas. Her imagination was simply too vivid.

Marianna looked ashen. She took Percy's hand as they exited into the hall, and Percy heard her utter a few Lutheran prayers. In the courtyard, many students were glancing up at the sky and doing the same. Percy noticed the dawn sparkled oddly.

There were already guards posted at the doors. Percy recognized some of them as janitors, some as teaching assistants, and a few were faculty themselves. This gave Athens a new air, as if both the school and London were preparing for a siege, and before her first class Percy took out the small pearl-beaded rosary that Reverend Mother had entrusted to her. She prayed it several times. It had been too long since she had said even a word of the elaborate liturgies that she knew by rote, and she resolved to be better about her personal rituals of faith. She had a sense London could use every prayer it could muster.

A soft baroque melody crackled from a wonder of modern technology, the phonograph sitting in the corner of Professor Rychman's office. He and Josephine clinked aperitif glasses, choosing to offer this toast to mankind's finer sensibilities.

"I've noticed the guards. I hope they leave everyone with some small comfort."

Alexi nodded. "We must be careful. Still, I'll be damned if our Grand Work will affect the operations of this school. It's the only thing Rebecca and I have to remind us that we're really human and not merely freakish hosts to guardian angels," he remarked mordantly, sipping his liqueur. Turning to survey the covered canvas she'd brought, he added, "So, you're finished? Such expediency with this painting, Josie. I'm impressed—especially after the work we've been forced to do . . . and after your rude exit last time you were here. At least my students still respect me."

"Fear you, appreciate you," Josephine corrected with a meaningful smile. "Indeed, that ivory girl with the amazing eyes seems to appreciate you a good deal. Bless her gentle heart, I think she was rather put out by my presence in your office."

Alexi scoffed. "What? Who? Miss Parker?"

"Eyes like that can't conceal the way they look at you," Josephine replied.

"Don't be ridiculous."

"A beautiful girl. She's an inspiration."

"If only she could hear you say that, Josie." Alexi looked

thoughtful. "The poor woman considers herself repulsive. I think that's hardly the case . . ." Josephine blinked at him as he trailed off, so he shifted and grumbled, "Of course, who am I to say, seeing as my 'social graces leave something to be desired.' I do say, Josephine, it is one thing to taunt me to my face, another entirely to undermine me in front of a student."

"Ah, is the impenetrable professor actually concerned with what the young lady thinks?"

"That is uncalled for," Alexi warned. "And dangerous to make any such impli—"

"There is something about that girl, Alexi," Josephine cut him off. "In fact . . . I've worked so fervently on this piece, I've hardly slept." Her saffron gown kissed the floor as she swept over to her covered canvas. Draining the last of her liqueur with dramatic flourish, she drew the curtain aside. Beneath was a sunlit seascape. Upon a jagged shore, two robed figures stood against the growing shadow of a dark cave entrance: a pale, regal young woman was being led into the increasing darkness by a man with luminous skin and unkempt auburn hair falling about naked, muscular shoulders. The woman's pale hair blew before her, as if the locks were desperately reaching out, seeking purchase in the wind. A third figure stood near a rock, cloaked and hooded, raising a clenched fist. The clouds on the horizon were ominously black.

"Well?" Josie asked.

"Oh, my," Alexi breathed. But the painting, while gorgeous, left a bitter taste in his mouth.

"Your student will like it, I trust. She was the muse, heaven alone knows why. As always, I chase inspiration." The Frenchwoman sighed, pressing her hands to her eyes and taking a seat. "Also, Alexi . . . I must confess there is another reason I have worked night and day. I am frightened. Ever since that attack by *la bête* . . . I cannot sleep for the nightmares."

"Change is upon us," Alexi agreed.

Josephine noted the edge to his tone as he moved to hang her new work by the door. "You are scared, too."

"It isn't that I mind the idea of change. It's the possibility we might react improperly." He clenched his jaw and changed the subject. "So, you think there's something to Miss Parker, do you?"

Josephine shrugged. "*Oui*. Miss Linden, too, but I do not know what."

"Hmm." Alexi's eyes lingered on the painting, contemplating the shadows into which the slender woman was being led. Then the clock chimed and his brisk manner heightened. "It is six, my dear. Time for the arrival of the very girl in question."

"Ah, *oui*," Josephine murmured.

She had just risen from her chair when there was a brief knock upon the door.

"Come!" Alexi called out. "Now, good day, Josie, and thank you for the painting."

Through the professor's door, Percy heard music. She heard also her cue to enter but nonetheless hovered outside, drinking in the delightful sound. Her estimation of the professor's cultural refinement was ever increasing.

A call from behind the wood made her jump. "Miss Parker, we cannot conduct a tutorial with a door between us, can we?"

She hurried into the room with a murmured apology. As she did, Percy noticed Josephine, and drew back for fear of interrupting. But the Frenchwoman beckoned her forward before amiably waving farewell and slipping out. Percy's gaze did not follow Josephine out the door, and so she did not witness the knowing wink, nor Alexi's glare in return. Instead, Percy glided to the desk and began removing her protections.

The lesson passed as usual and without event. The professor spoke, and she listened. But Percy's mind was far from the mathematical lecture. While integers and equations might prove an impassable gulf, she sensed their time together was of grave import aside from education; but she had no idea how to say so.

The professor handed over an assignment with a sigh and leaned back, pressing thumb and forefinger to his nose in characteristic thought. Percy bit her lip and read this as her cue to leave. With the same unconscious ceremony as accompanied her disrobing, she reversed the process. Wrapping her length of blue muslin about her head and neck, donning gloves and glasses, she rose from her chair and lifted books into her slender arms.

She didn't know how to bring up the subject of the Ripper, yet she felt she must before walking out the door. Quietly she said: "It is good that the school has taken precautions, considering the recent state of affairs. It's such a frightful thing—and it troubles you greatly, doesn't it, Professor?"

"Yes, Miss Parker, it does," Professor Rychman replied. He and Percy stared at each other, and she felt compelled to ask his further opinion, but the gravity of his expression stilled her inquiry.

He glanced past her, a smile flickering across his face. "On your way in, Miss Parker, did you notice the new addition?" he asked.

"Oh, no, Professor, I didn't," Percy replied, seeing Josephine's newest painting. Her books fell from her arms. Papers scattered. Choking, she sank to her knees, glasses falling from her face and into the folds of her dress.

"Miss Parker?" Professor Rychman called out.

Dimly, Percy saw him rise from his desk and rush to her side. But compelled by the force that had overtaken her, she began to speak in a voice that was not quite her own, one that spoke in Greek, and her senses were no longer in England: *"No, I'll yearn for the sea,"* she insisted, glancing fearfully at the cave entrance before turning back to the shore. *"I hear crying. Who's crying?"*

"You are."

An overwhelming smell accosted her nostrils; a very specific fruit. A beautiful, unearthly man touched her arm and she chilled. Light bounced off the sea before her. Darkness was behind. In the sunlight ahead, out on the rocks, a figure reached toward her in anguish.

"No." She shook her head. *"Don't take me just yet; give me one more hour . . ."*

"Your time has come, love," said the eerie man, and his cold hand seized her shoulder to lead her into the darkness.

She reached out to the figure who wept in the light. The sweet smell of fruit turned her stomach. *"Shall I never see them again? Him?"*

"Perhaps someday, in some other era. But never the bird again. Never that bird." And the luminous man pressed something into her hand.

"Miss Parker!" Alexi said, kneeling before her. The girl's eyes looked unseeing into the distance. He took her outstretched hand and squeezed it, hoping to bring her gently back from her sudden transportation. A soft breath escaped her lips, but she remained far away.

Staring at her with fascination, he tightened his grip about her fingers. A breeze rustled through the room, and he felt his powers rise. What was happening in that moment was unparalleled. He'd never encountered anything like it. And while there was no visible door to indicate Prophecy was occurring, this was unmistakably a sign. Perhaps his goddess was trying to speak through Percy Parker.

"Yes, come to me," he breathed.

A sound came across the waves, a whisper to rouse a dreamer. Percy felt something in her hand and so she opened her palm.

Seeds. Juicy, ruby red seeds.

She stifled a cry. How could she be parted from her angel?

There was a sensation upon her outstretched fingertips, feathery like wings, which she heard rustling. And a murmur so like the waves called to her again and spoke a name that sounded vaguely familiar. She wanted to go to that voice. It was calling her.

"Miss Parker," Alexi said again, patiently.

He felt her fingers stir in his palm and draw away. He murmured an ancient benediction known only to The Guard, then pressed his fingertip first to her forehead and then to her collarbone. She was still lost. He couldn't help but notice her resonant beauty, captured in the passionate throes of this faraway vision.

Finally, clutching her by the arms: "Percy." A gentle yet firm command.

"He'll come for me, I swear it. Please don't let the dark take me again!" the girl cried, her words at last returned to her native English tongue. Her eyes were full of horror as they snapped into focus. The spell was broken.

Percy stared up at her dear professor, who now knelt before her, firmly holding her arms in his hands. Terror overwhelmed her and she scrambled to her feet. The professor rose and, with swift control, seized her.

She stared deeply into his eyes, blushing, and shook her head. "Please, Professor, don't send me to an asylum! I'm not mad, I swear to you. Forgive me, I had no warning, I don't know what that w—"

"Miss Parker, shhh." He forced her to meet his gaze. "No one is going to commit you."

"Oh, Professor, good God, what you must think of me." She began to cry.

"Calm yourself, Miss Parker, there is no need of tears. All is well. Whatever held you for a moment is gone. No one will take you anywhere."

Percy had never been so close to him, and her senses swam.

Her blush could grow no more fiery, and her tears would not stop, yet she had no choice but to believe her stern professor. She took a long breath.

He released her arms. They both looked at the place where his hands had been. She looked at him shyly as she bent to collect her books and papers, trying desperately to think of something redeeming she might say, but her tongue was shackled. Her shaking hands placed her small, dark glasses back upon her face.

The professor calmly watched her fumble for her things. "You have no idea what had you just then, Miss Parker? Were you aware you were speaking Greek?"

Percy picked up the last of her papers and stood. She shook her head. "I have no idea, Professor. No idea at all!" she murmured helplessly. "But I owe you so much. My life is in your debt. If you had not brought me back . . . I wonder if I might ever have returned!"

Scurrying to the door, she gave no further explanation but was careful not to give the painting a second glance. The door half open, she turned again, murmured another few thank-yous and apologies brimming with emotion, and disappeared into the hall.

Alexi sat heavily at his desk, making notes. His head swam.

Miss Parker had not been his goddess speaking to him. She hadn't come with answers; she was as lost as he in this place of waiting and wondering. She didn't seem to know what she was, or what she might be; so he couldn't be sure she was Prophecy. Not yet. And there was too much at stake to guess.

But she had, in a way, dealt with a door. It was a portal that only she had entered. Could Prophecy be interpreted broadly?

"One step at a time, or everything will be ruined," he muttered. "The goddess warned caution. It could all be a trap. Everything could be a ruse, and you dare not fail." But his stomach tightened when he thought of how it had felt to grasp Miss Parker's delicate hands in his own, and he burned with an exotic shame.

No! Students were not involved in the Grand Work. He and Rebecca had long ago pledged this, for the school was a boundary. It was both a wall and a link—a bridge between an average human life and the strange fate foisted upon him, the fate that made him an outcast in the very society he was sworn to protect. An outcast like Miss Parker. Maybe she would understand...

"You are her teacher," he reminded himself. "She is not a peer, so you cannot be more." But a foreign sensation was waking inside of him, churning with emotion locked tightly away.

On the opposite side of the academy, Percy burst into Marianna's room and collapsed upon the bed. Her friend sat at her desk with a book. Starting with surprise, she shook her head. "And what is it now, my dear?"

"I had a vision tonight, a vision that pulled me in and would not let go!" Percy wailed into a pillow. "When I came to, I was kneeling in the professor's office. I must have appeared absolutely raving!"

"What? A vision... took you in?"

"It was as if I was suddenly in a dream, and I collapsed—Oh, dear Lord! He was there before me, trying to bring me back. Oh, Marianna, it was humiliating!"

"I'm sure it was."

"And I was speaking Greek." Percy loosed a sickly laugh. "The professor asked how I liked his new painting. It was as if I went *into* the painting! My vision was the painting come to life. I had no power to resist; it was as if it had all happened before."

"This is so strange, Percy," Marianna said. "What shall you do?"

Percy shrugged, helpless. There was a long silence. "Could he have something to do with it?" she murmured at last.

"Your professor?"

Percy shook her head, feeling ill. "I must clear my mind of this. I must find some distraction."

"Well, I'm having a frightful time with *The Odyssey,*" Marianna admitted. "You might assist me."

"Wonderful!" Percy cried. She spent the rest of the evening helping Marianna grapple with Homer. It was much easier than dealing with the fact that her inscrutable professor was unquestionably part of her destiny.

CHAPTER FOURTEEN

Percy's heart faltered as Professor Rychman opened the door to his classroom. Today she feared not only what he must think of her, but the repetition of an uncontrolled vision. There was the additional terror of the day's Alchemy and Mathematics exam.

He stalked quietly into the room, glancing at each student in turn as he discussed the usual manner of his examinations. She heard the rustling of his robe behind her but couldn't bring herself to look up when he passed her table. He paused nearby. Percy's pulse quickened.

"... And I do, ladies and gentlemen, expect your answers to be in English and no other language." The professor then offered Percy a soft aside, in Greek. *"Do I make myself clear, Miss Parker?"*

Her eyes shot up and she gave him an expression of helpless apology. He rewarded her with a kindly smirk. Relief flooded her body, and she returned the smile: he didn't hate

her, wasn't wholly put off by that inexplicable encounter last
night. He nodded briefly to indicate the subject a closed
matter, and then the classroom echoed with the remainder
of his exam particulars.

After taking the test, Percy spent the entire afternoon be-
moaning it. Alternately she dwelled upon his little smirk and
gracious understanding. Before she knew, it was nearly six
and she was rushing off to see him.

On his office door there was a folded piece of paper marked
MISS PARKER. The note inside read:

> *I shall likely be otherwise engaged at the time of your arrival,
> Miss Parker. The door is open; you may enter and await me
> inside.*
>
> —*Rychman*

Percy folded the note with care and tucked it into her corset, placing the lovely spiral script next to her heart. Dreaming it a note of a more personal bent, she suddenly flushed,
appalled at how easily her fancy took flight.

Glancing furtively about the room, she couldn't help but
make a bold dash to the professor's phonograph, a luxury of
which she was sure her convent would never have approved.
Her skirts fluttering as she knelt, Percy rifled through ornate
boxes of Bach and opera before her eye fell upon a cover
edged in red velvet, with gilt letters: "Requiem" by Wolf-
gang Amadeus Mozart. Her choice was made.

Placing the thick disk upon the turntable, she turned the
crank and the needle made contact. Voices and orchestration
burst forth. The melody began as a simple, ascending line of
strings, mournful and glorious, and it halted Percy's breath.
She stepped away, beaming, relishing every note. It was the
Lacrimosa.

But as the choir began to sing, their voices ebbing and
flowing, a most intriguing thing followed. Within the first
few bars, as if a summons bell tolled, spirits began to pour

through the walls, windows and ceiling of Professor Rych-man's magnificent office. Each note drew a new soul from the fabric of the air, as if all the spirits of Athens Academy had been beckoned to fill the room in rapture.

Percy stood amazed and delighted. In addition to the more familiar haunts, the spectral retinue of the nearby British Museum must have also been invited. Spirits of all times, cultures and classes twirled around her, dancing and reveling to the gorgeous death mass, singing in unison with the choir. Some looked down and evaluated Percy. She returned their hollow gazes and they were greatly pleased.

Like a butterfly shedding its chrysalis Percy tossed her shawl, glasses and gloves upon the desk and abandoned herself, as the spirits did, to the music, sharing a bond with them that went beyond colouration. Her skirts spun out around her.

Constance, haunt of the science library, wafted near. Her spiral curls bounced weightlessly. "Hello, Miss Percy! This one, it just so happens, is our favourite! However did you know?" Percy just giggled and spun beside her ghostly friend, closing her eyes in a moment of ecstasy.

The entire lot, human and spirits, failed to notice as the office door quietly opened and shut.

Alexi stood just inside the threshold to his office and raised an eyebrow at the spectral bedlam. Setting his jaw, he stared at the veritable army of spirits that had collected in his office uninvited. As he folded his arms and shook his head, a veritable column of black fabric, the haunts began to notice. He shooed each off with a wave of his hand, and they knew enough not to disobey.

Miss Percy Parker. What a curious one she was. He wished the mortal young woman could see what kind of chaos she had stirred up, but surely she couldn't.

One spirit remained unaware of his presence, staring at Miss Parker with such longing that he reluctantly decided to let it stay. The spirit, a hollow-eyed girl with ringlets and clothing from long past, reached toward Percy, wishing to touch her. Alexi understood. When left to her own devices, Miss Parker was neither shy nor awkward; she was radiant.

After a moment, the spirit turned and caught Alexi's gaze. He nodded a slight greeting. The ghost's eyes widened and a hand flew to her lips, suddenly delighted, though he wasn't exactly sure why. He shook his head and stalked to his desk.

Hearing sudden, firm footfalls against the wooden floor, Percy opened her eyes and cried out, embarrassment surging. Fervently blurting apologies, she ran to the phonograph to stop the music. Professor Rychman halted her.

"Let it play, Miss Parker. Perhaps you will better absorb your studies when they are underscored by Mozart."

"Th-thank you, Professor, for yet another instance of your kind patience. I am—"

The professor narrowed his eyes, clearly wishing to hear no more. Percy scurried to her seat as he gracefully took his.

Constance floated to her side. Percy glanced up and tried to nod the ghost toward the door. Constance just grinned and shook her head, refusing. Percy pursed her lips.

The entirety of the lesson passed with Constance hovering just behind and to the side of Percy's chair in what appeared to be an attempt to distract her. Dread that the professor might finally snap under the strain of her odd behaviour and send her packing from the academy made Percy's hands shake, but she certainly could not explain to him that she was having difficulty concentrating because the deceased was breathing down her neck. How could yet another mad admission aid her credibility?

Once the professor had finished a complex little lecture, he sat back in his chair and folded his hands in his lap. Constance, who had watched the lesson as if she, too, were his pupil, leaned in, her translucent face just above Percy's head. Feeling the cold draft in the ghost's wake, Percy batted at her hair in irritation.

"That will be all for today, Miss Parker," the professor declared, promptly picking up a book and burying himself in it.

Percy gathered her shrouds in haste. Constance took this opportunity. She whirled to Percy's side and whispered, "You realize, Percy, that he can see me, too."

"What?" Percy breathed.

The professor glanced up from his book. Percy stared at him, wide-eyed, then at the ghost, and then back at the professor. Professor Rychman furrowed his brow, looked at the ghost, then back at Percy.

"You can see Constance?" Percy squeaked.

Professor Rychman frowned. "Constance?" He nodded slowly. "I did not know the two of you were...acquainted."

"But you can see her?"

"If you mean this transparent woman with curled hair and dated fashion, yes, Miss Parker, I can."

Percy nearly wept with joy.

"You, strange one, who never cease to surprise me, how do you know that she is Constance?"

"She told me, sir."

"Told you?"

"He cannot hear me, Percy. That is the difference between the two of you," Constance explained.

"Yes, sir, she told me."

"You can see *and* speak with them?" the professor clarified.

"Yes, sir."

"My, my, Miss Parker. How very useful," he mused.

Percy narrowed her eyes. "I beg your pardon, sir?"

"Never mind. When did this ability of yours begin?"

It took the professor nodding encouragement to convince her to continue.

"It has been with me since I can remember, Professor,"

Percy admitted. "My earliest memories are of Gregory, an Elizabethan spirit. In life his daughter was trampled by a horse and I became a surrogate to his restless soul. It was only because of my fondness for him that I knew I had any sort of ability. I never thought anything amiss until I unwittingly told Reverend Mother. She, of course, was quite shocked . . ." Percy chuckled as memories washed over her. "Dear Gregory, I do hope he has found peace!" She suddenly remembered herself. "Oh, but forgive my prattling on, Professor!"

"It's fascinating," he replied in earnest.

"Could you always see them, Professor?"

"No," he replied simply, and seemed taken by sudden memories himself.

"When did it happen that you could, sir?"

"I'm afraid, Miss Parker, that would take more time to explain than I have to give. Did anyone other than your mother superior know of your ability?"

"No. She did not want anyone to declare me mad. Of course, there was the day she sent a priest to exorcise Gregory. I made a terrible fuss, screaming that they didn't dare take my friend away. Can't say I endeared myself to the priesthood after that, and Reverend Mother made it clear to keep my sight a secret ever after. But Professor, how happy this makes me! To know I'm not the only one, and that perhaps you may know why—"

"Do not expect answers from me, Miss Parker," he said, stemming Percy's excitement.

"Forgive me. It's just that I've prayed desperately for someone who knows something—"

"We are all looking for something, Miss Parker," was his reply. When Percy glanced at Constance, she nodded in agreement. "And on that note, *I* happen to need to look for something, so I bid you adieu."

Percy rose, dazed. "Thank you, Professor. Have a lovely evening."

"Same to you, Miss Parker," he replied, furiously scribbling down several notes.

Percy once again gathered her things, gestured for Constance and left the office. "He could see you! I am amazed!" she exclaimed to the ghost as they entered the hall.

Constance was gliding at her side. "There is something to all of this, Percy. I can feel it." A fellow student was walking up the stairwell, so the conversation paused as they descended the steps. Constance resumed speech as soon as Percy was free to respond. "I saw the way you gazed at him when he wasn't looking . . ."

Percy experienced an odd ache and said nothing. She shook a finger at her noncorporeal companion, a firm warning not to speak of such things again. "Until next haunting," she said.

The two friends waved good-bye. But as Constance vanished through a nearby wall, Percy could hardly contain herself. Surely fate was beginning to find her.

Alexi was brooding more than usual.

"Why did you come to my office for tea?" Rebecca asked wearily. "So I could watch you scowl? I assure you, I've seen quite enough of that through the years."

"A prophecy. How ridiculous! What respectable man of science lives his life in accordance with some mad vision?" Alexi was lamenting.

"Only you, I'm sure. It isn't like anyone else has our lot in life."

"Waiting for a promise I can't prove and a woman I can't see, blindly trusting that someone is going to waltz in and change everything . . ."

"Well. Has she?" Rebecca asked.

Alexi pinned her with a cool stare. "What?"

Rebecca sighed. "Has someone waltzed in and changed everything, rearranged the order of your world? You normally aren't so forthcoming in your laments."

Alexi lapsed into silence. After a while, he voiced the true reason for his visit and pinned her with a stare. "Do you know one unmistakable Miss Parker?"

Rebecca shifted uncomfortably in her chair, but her face remained neutral. "Yes, what about her?"

"She *sees* ghosts."

Rebecca raised an eyebrow. "Does she now? And how did you find that out?"

"The girl's wretched at mathematics. I'm giving her tutorials. Our sessions have led to several interesting revelations."

This was the first Rebecca had heard of it. "Private lessons? You have a chaperone, I hope." She leveled her gaze upon Alexi, all the while shaking her head. "Although, with you I've nothing to worry about. You've never been one for an affair, much less taking liberties with an oddity. Still, perhaps just for propriety we should send someone—"

"She can also *speak* with ghosts," Alexi continued angrily. "She draws strange symbols that relate to our work, and recently was transported by a painting, crying out in Greek. If those aren't signs, I don't know what are."

"And was there a portal?" Rebecca asked.

"No," Alexi sighed. "And, she's not our peer. Yet, I cannot help but wonder. Do you think we are looking for a literal portal, or might we accept the suggestion of one? Is Prophecy flexible? Miss Parker *is* extraordinary." His eyes flashed as he processed his friend's previous statement. "Honestly, Rebecca. To call her an oddity? I'd expect more kindness, considering our fate makes us no less—"

"What of Miss Linden?" Rebecca interrupted. "She has most certainly been 'placed in our path.' She keeps inquiring about you at La Belle. Why are you avoiding her?"

"I'm not avoid—"

"Yes, you are. All of us except Jane, who isn't impressed by anything, find her charming. She speaks cryptically, as if she's scared to admit her powers just as we are. Remember the part of Prophecy that said she would be escaping something? Well, Miss Linden is now our guest, and we suspect she's—"

"Please don't say it."

A long silence passed as they stared at each other. Rebecca finally reached out a hand and placed it on his. "Your goddess isn't coming back, Alexi. Not in the way you may think. That's what you're struggling with; I know it. You're looking to find her, the former lover of whatever possesses you. But that isn't to be, and it wasn't what was foretold. You are here, a mortal. With us, other mortals. There's work to be done and choices to be made. Business. It's just business, Alexi. So come and be present with your friends rather than hiding in your office."

Alexi furrowed his brow. "I'm supposed to love her, Rebecca."

His friend's eyes flashed. "For the last time, Alexi, love has nothing to do with the prophecy!"

"Goodness, Rebecca, it's nothing to be upset about."

"Of course it's something to be upset about! The fate of many lives hangs in the balance! Love will only complicate matters, don't you see?" She rose from her chair and went to the window. After a long moment she turned, her expression pinched. "Don't tell me you've fallen in love. If you're avoiding Miss Linden . . . Don't tell me *Miss Parker* has your interest. That simply cannot be—"

"I'm not in love with anyone, Rebecca," Alexi replied. "Other than the goddess, my intended, the only woman I felt I was ever allowed to—"

"Bloody parasites is all they are, commandeering our futures without a care for *our* hearts, *our* needs!" Rebecca cried out. "Your goddess isn't coming, Alexi! And she didn't love you. She loved what was taking up residence inside you."

Alexi froze, his friend's words touching down violently in a vulnerable place like a flash of lightning. He hadn't re-

ally thought of that. He'd never wanted to think that his
goddess never loved *him;* but, truly, what did she know of
Alexi Rychman? What could she know? He was just a vessel,
after all.

Slowly he rose from his chair and turned to the door. He
wanted nothing to do with this, any of this, anymore. "To
hell with Prophecy, Rebecca. Let the war come. I'll just
teach mathematics and we'll all die alone."

As he flung the door open and exited, Rebecca cried out,
"Alexi, no! Don't take it in such a manner! Come back and
sit with me . . ."

The door shut.

Pounding her fist on her desk, Rebecca collapsed into her
chair with a string of curses.

Alexi went home to his cold, empty estate, which represented everything he was. Throwing himself into his leather
throne of a library chair, seizing a snifter of brandy and seeking to lose himself in volumes of scientific journals, he felt an
irrepressible anger begin to boil up. "If you won't help me,
Goddess, if you've no care for me, then you can't ask me to
suffer your cryptic riddles," he hissed. "No more. Prophecy
be damned."

It wasn't until he caught a whiff of smoke that he realized
his anger had set the room on fire. Actual fire. He had sway
over candles and the occasional gas lamp but inadvertent ar-
son hadn't previously been in his repertoire. He raised his
hands and the flames went out, and then he cradled his head
and fell into a wretched sleep.

Having transported himself a full continent south of his previous travails, the Groundskeeper grunted, wiping sweat
from his furrowed brow with the sleeve of his long grey coat.
The ash caked on his cuff smeared dark lines across his forehead.

"So much work, my lady! If you've gone before to help,

seems your work's been undone. The seals hold fast. Damn those mortals!"

He brought his chisel down hard, its metal singing against the glassy base of a lava flow. The surrounding rock seemed to shudder, almost to belch, and a fresh, thin layer of dust began to settle over his skin and begrimed clothes.

"Ah..." He pressed thin lips into a smirk. "Loosening, loosening, for chaos to come." His song was like the voice of a strangled bird.

CHAPTER FIFTEEN

His eyes burned as Alexi read the letter to his sister he'd too-long failed to write. "Dear Lord, Alexandra, what more can I do?" he murmured bitterly. "I'll visit when I can."

There was a knock at his door. He didn't want to see or speak with anyone, but it was time for Miss Parker's tutorial, and of all the people in his life she was the one he least minded. "Come!"

Nodding with her usual deference, she entered, and Alexi noticed a lightness to Miss Parker's step. As she sat in her chair, he held out an expectant hand. She produced her assignment, though the fingers of her left hand danced busily out of sight. Alexi signed his letter, sealed it hastily and abruptly began a lecture.

To Percy it seemed as if Professor Rychman would rather be anywhere else. It troubled her that she should be so attuned to his energy, to the key changes in the music of his presence. As his lesson came to a close, she leaned forward to gather her things. "Are you well, sir?" she asked, daring to look up at him.

He waved a dismissive hand.

"Truly?" she pressed.

The professor raised an eyebrow. "You know, for a meek young lady you can be dreadfully persistent. My life outside of this campus, Miss Parker, is trying. Not that it's any of your business. Also, someone close to me is not well."

"Ah. Miss Thompson," Percy guessed.

"What? No. Why her?" The professor narrowed his eyes.

Percy shrugged, staring into her lap. "Well, sir, I thought perhaps you and she—"

"She and I? Nonsense, whatever it is you're insinuating," he barked. "My sister is ill."

Percy wished she had remained silent, and yet she suddenly felt overjoyed. Was her professor actually free from attachments after all? It seemed that neither the French-woman named Josephine nor Headmistress Thompson laid claim to him. "My prayers shall be for your sister," she murmured, rising to her feet. "And for your life here and outside."

"Are you well, Miss Parker?" the professor asked. "You've been fiddling with something all evening that has nearly driven me to distraction." He looked pointedly at her left hand.

"My apologies, Professor. I haven't been able to part with it all day. I just received it," she confessed, holding up an ornate little cross, "for my birthday, along with my favourite book of fairy tales. Reverend Mother is so thoughtful."

"Fairy tales?" When Percy cringed, the professor spoke with less disdain. "Which is your favourite?"

It never failed to surprise her when he asked questions that bred familiarity. "Well..." She hesitated, looking away. "Beauty and the Beast," she said finally. "I identify with the characters."

"Because you think yourself the Beast."

Percy bit her lip and tried to stare through the floor so as not to cry.

"Foolish girl," the professor said, and Percy could not tell if his intent was gentle, condescending or both.

Feeling both ugly and childish, Percy put on her glasses to hide her tears and drew her scarf tight about her head and neck. At the same time she reassured herself that his words were meant as an encouragement.

"Have I rattled you so very much?" he pressed, his voice like faraway thunder.

She paused. Then, in a moment of fleeting bravery she removed her glasses and stared into his eyes. "Always."

The professor almost smiled. "Finally, you are honest with me."

She was quick to reply. "I've never been dishonest."

"Be of good cheer, faint heart, you are too easily hurt," he chided.

"My heart is fortified with passions, Professor; it is my confidence that is too easily undone."

The professor just pursed his lips. Percy lingered a moment in the power of his stoicism. She reminded herself she'd been treated no differently than any other here, beast or no, and she would be forever grateful to him for that fact alone.

"Until next time," he stated, releasing her from the bondage of his stare with the wave of a finger. But as Percy opened the door, feeling she would breathe easier once she reached the hallway, he called, "Miss Parker?"

"Yes, Professor?" She turned, a hitch in her breath.

"Happy birthday. Which is it?"

"Nineteen," she replied.

"Nineteen," he repeated, evaluating the number with a slight grimace. "Well, Miss Parker, may your birthday wish come true."

Percy felt a bright smile cross her face and she curtseyed. "Thank you, Professor!" But recalling the particulars of her birthday wish, Percy disappeared out the door before her professor could note her guilty blush.

As she exited Apollo Hall, dreaming what her professor's birthday embrace might feel like, a dozen pink roses suddenly appeared from behind a courtyard pillar. Percy leaped back. The boy she recognized from her literature class, Edward, peered out from around the pillar, his eyes aglow. Percy blushed and put gloved hands over her cheeks to hide.

"Alles Gute zum Geburtstag!" Marianna cried, jumping out on the other side of Edward. "Happy birthday!"

"Marianna, Edward—thank you both! How sweet you are!" Percy giggled. Edward mimed taking her hand and kissing it chivalrously, not quite daring the wrath of the school should he actually do so.

"Merry natal day!" he cried, bowing with an exaggerated flourish. The walking stick he carried made him look the youthful, endearing dandy.

The three strolled to the fountain, where Edward begged leave to attend his studies. He leaned in to mime kissing Marianna's hand. The German girl's face turned pink, but her eyes were bright and gay. A courtship of stares must have been building between the two in their class, Percy assumed, but this connection was a bold new step.

As Edward backed away from the fountain, still staring at the hand he had imagined kissing, he stumbled. He spun upon the culpable stone with mock fury, trouncing it soundly with his walking stick while the girls laughed. Marianna's cheeks grew increasingly flushed, and Percy wondered if her friend just might swoon right then and there into the fountain.

"How was your lesson today, alone in that room with your dear professor?" the German girl whispered airily, abruptly turning the tables.

Percy replied calmly, refusing to betray herself with giggles. "It was professional and uneventful. He said he hoped my birthday wish came true."

"If only he knew," Marianna murmured.

Percy turned and clapped a hand over her friend's mouth. The German girl squealed with glee, but the sound was stifled.

"You will be my undoing, Marianna. I swear, that talk of yours will get me expelled!"

"No, I promise, Percy, your fascination remains our secret alone!"

In some ways, Marianna's friendship with Edward could not have come at a better time. At dinner in the ladies' dining hall, as Percy and her friend sat sipping a bland soup, a few chattering girls brought in a length of paper. In a matter of moments a banner posted above the dining room doorway proclaimed:

IF YOU WILL PATIENTLY DANCE IN OUR ROUND AND
SEE OUR MOONLIGHT REVELS, GO WITH US!
AUTUMNAL GALA OF 1888
SATURDAY, 8 P.M.

A girlish cheer went up about the room, and the usual topic of conversation—young men—changed to something new: dancing. The anxieties over Jack the Ripper, whose name had been ceaseless in its flow through the dining hall for the past month, especially with all the newspaper coverage, vanished in the excitement. For the first time all year, the girls of Athens would actually be able to touch the opposite sex without reprimand. How else could they dance?

"*Eine Tanz,* Percy! I must send home for my gowns!"

"'If not, shun me, and I will spare your haunts,'" Percy murmured.

"What?"

"Titania's next line is more appropriate for me."

Marianna sighed. "Ah. Is that your poetic way of declining the invitation?"

"Why attend? I was never taught to dance." Percy's attempt at disinterest failed, however, for fantasy had got the better of her and she imagined elegant couples aglow with cheer, chandeliers, music . . .

"You must attend," Marianna said gently. "For such nights are the stuff dreams are made of."

"What could I expect other than cruel whispers and derision? No, I cannot go," Percy replied. She tried to return to her soup, but a sudden vision of a bloody dog's muzzle appeared and ruined her appetite.

Many blocks away, The Guard sat by their usual window at La Belle et La Bête. The circle was not complete, to be honest, for Alexi and Jane were again missing, but their party included a beautiful new face.

Alexi hadn't spent time in the café for a number of days, and Rebecca was quieter than usual, her shoulders tight and her words clipped. Jane had visited earlier for a cup of tea, but upon hearing news of Miss Linden's arrival she excused herself, stating that she simply didn't have a use or inclination for any more friends.

A candle at the center of the table dripped onto the tablecloth, and Elijah was absently gathering wax on his fingertips into a ball. Josephine hovered nearby, pouring more tea.

"What a shame, Miss Linden, that you've come to London during a spate of such horror," Michael remarked.

Lucille agreed softly. "But it would always be daunting, to be a lone woman in London, would it not?"

"That is why we make friends, Miss Linden," Rebecca replied.

None of them had inquired further regarding Miss Linden's past, and she hadn't volunteered. It was not proper to pry. But they took her warmth toward them as evidence of her goodwill and gratitude.

"Never worry, Miss Linden. I am here for your protection," Elijah assured her with a wide smile.

Josephine, standing over him and pouring tea, stepped on

his toes and said, "Fear's never been so prevalent." She took a seat.

Rebecca hummed, her brow furrowed, her eyes pained. "Even Alexi is affected. I've never seen a look on his face like I did when..." She halted herself and began again, "I'd never seen such a face when he heard the latest news."

"Ah, Alexi. Why haven't I seen that professor of yours?" Lucille asked.

Rebecca replied through clenched teeth. "I cannot answer for him, Miss Linden." Then, struck by an idea, she exclaimed, "The gala! That would be the perfect opportunity. Our academy is about to have its annual soiree. It will be so good for the poor dears, as our students are not accustomed to guards at their doors; they must feel like they're imprisoned. Professor Rychman thinks the festivity stuff and nonsense ... so I'll arrange the chaperone list to include his name." Rebecca smirked. "Elijah, if Miss Linden cares to attend, would you escort her?"

"I'd be honoured," Elijah replied—a bit too eagerly for Josephine, who surreptitiously picked up her dinner knife and held it near his fingertips. But when below the table he placed a tiny object atop the many folds of fabric over her thigh, Josephine glanced down to see he had fashioned his little ball of wax into a tiny heart. Her immaculate olive cheek gained a hint of colour.

"You once told us you hail from Bath, Miss Linden," Elijah remarked. "You must be no stranger to a fine soiree."

"Belle of the ball, I'm sure," Michael declared, raising his glass.

Miss Linden's eyes sparkled. "You flatter me, Mr. Carroll. Lord Withersby, indeed you are correct—I'm no stranger to a ball. There were so many, you'd think Bath had nothing else to do. All the faces, eager eyes, the flitting fans of young ladies in tense clusters or tucked on a divan, vying so desperately for a glance or a dance ..."

Rebecca snickered. "Well, then, you'll love gala night at

Athens. It's the only time students are allowed even the slightest fraternization, and it's the very picture of ineptitude."

"I most heartily look forward to it," Lucille exclaimed. Her eyes grew misty as she suggested, "A dance where no one would find me. I might finally feel free, be part of society once again." She glanced away as her voice faltered. The Guard, embarrassed for her, found fascination in their steaming teacups.

After a moment Josephine asked an almost inaudible question. "Do you think the Ripper is finally finished? There has been no recent violence, *seulement les fous* in the paper, and . . . well, I was hoping it might be done." Below the tablecloth, Elijah placed his hand over the little wax heart he'd given her, and the pressure of it through the fabric of her dress was a tiny comfort.

"Something is searching for an answer," Lucille remarked. "And I pray it has something to do with us." When everyone stared at her, surprised, she smiled graciously and explained, "I personally comfort myself with the idea that truly terrible things are only omens of better days to come."

The Guard glanced at one another and looked around for a door.

CHAPTER SIXTEEN

A shimmering grey form burst through the wall as Percy made her way toward the professor's office. "Oh, Percy, the gala!"

"Goodness, Constance, don't startle me so!" Percy laughed softly, careful to make sure they were alone.

"Do forgive me, but each year I forget how delightful it is."

"I'm sure the gala is lovely," Percy muttered. "If I could float invisibly, as you do, I would gladly attend."

"But, Miss Percy, the dancing—"

"I never learned. Now, please, Constance, I mustn't be late."

"You ought to have the professor teach you. A cultured, learned man such as he? I wouldn't doubt a waltz—"

Percy's hands flew to her face. "Constance, I beg you!"

"There's nothing scandalous about a dance lesson. He's a teacher. He'd be teaching you."

"I . . . wouldn't dare hope," Percy replied.

A strange look came over the ghost's face. "Hope? Just remember. Alive or dead, we are all looking for something."

A flurry of students appeared, and Percy was unable to reply. Constance pinned her with a stare before vanishing into the paneling.

Percy knocked upon the professor's door. Above the din, she barely heard his reply. She scurried into the office and closed the door on the cacophony of excited students outside. The professor was pacing behind his desk, powerful as ever but seemingly angry and tired. Percy wondered at his mood; surely he couldn't be anxious about mathematics alone.

"Damnable gala," he muttered, making a face. "Sends the entire school into a juvenile tizzy."

"Yes, it's all the girls can speak of," Percy admitted. She took her seat, watching him. "Do faculty attend?" Constance's suggestion nagged at her thoughts.

"Many serve as chaperones. We take turns year to year. I suppose you're looking forward to it, Miss Parker?"

"No," Percy replied, removing her accoutrements in the ritual pattern. "I shan't attend."

The professor raised an eyebrow. "Why not?"

"Look at me," she stated, glaring. When he stared back, undaunted, she explained, "I'm abnormal, and I don't know how to dance. I'd look a disastrous fool. The sight of a ball gown with one of my scarves draped about it . . . They'd wonder what nervous phantasm plagued their fete."

"Nonsense. You're no ghost, Miss Parker."

"Thank you, Professor. And while you're someone who would know, I wish I could share your optimism."

"I'm sure it's not been easy for you, Miss Parker, but not everyone thinks you frightening."

She allowed herself to smile. His unfaltering acceptance was the dearest thing she could imagine. She nonetheless looked down and bit her lip. "I suppose I should try to not be so timid."

"Is it the world that frightens you, Miss Parker? Or the strange things that you see? What exactly is it that you see?" the professor asked. He'd clearly been wondering. Percy was lost for a moment, intoxicated by his concern, enjoying how every rich syllable he spoke lingered in her ears.

"Many things," she finally breathed. "Many . . . nightmarish visions."

"You admit to visions at last, Miss Parker?" the professor asked. When she glanced up in panic, he held out a hand. "Miss Parker. Did I call you mad when you transported yourself to Greece? When you spoke to spirits? You ought to think better of me. And you might be surprised what people other than yourself see . . ." There was a strange light in his eyes.

Percy's melancholy vanished. She gasped, "You have visions, too, Professor?" Turning, she leaned forward and reached out across the desk.

His demeanour shifted abruptly, and the professor pulled back. Still, there was a thoughtful look on his face as he added, "No, Miss Parker, I do not. And we have strayed long enough from our lesson."

Excitement and disappointment churned through Percy as she handed over her assignment. The professor scrawled notes upon the page and slid it back. "The left column is correct; the right, incorrect. You have an amazing capacity to learn what I teach—in halves." As he began to elaborate upon where she'd gone wrong, Percy sighed. Her heart raced and she prayed he could not hear it pound. She was enraptured by his explanation, when suddenly her eyes blurred and she was watching a whole new scene. Another vision. People, fire, colour . . .

And then it was gone. Percy jumped as her eyes focused again on the professor, who was waiting for her to reinhabit herself. "If you're going to leave your corporeal form when I am midsentence, Miss Parker, at least have the courtesy to tell me where you travel," he declared.

Furrowing her brow, she took a hesitant breath. "There was music"—she bit her lip—"and people in a ring, and there seemed to be some sort of blue fire . . ."

Oddly, the professor's jaw clenched. "How familiar."

Percy fought back shock. "You know more than you've shared, Professor!"

He gave a curt nod. "I know far more than I've shared—and that I'm willing to share."

Percy could not help herself. "Why do I have these visions, Professor?" she asked. *And why are they even more frequent around you?*

The professor shook his head. "I assure you, I do not know. Now, review these conversions from class. And take this to the library." He handed her a note with a filing number. "Perhaps you'll understand general theorems better in Italian."

Percy took the paper and grimaced. She was being dismissed.

As she shrouded herself in her scarf, a knock sounded at the door. "Come," was Rychman's response. Headmistress Thompson entered, her presence in the office nearly as commanding as the professor's. She evaluated Percy, eyes narrowed, and Percy held her breath. Finally the woman nodded and turned to address the professor.

There was a terrible awkwardness that Percy could not help but notice, and it made her uncomfortable. There was surely something between these two, no matter what the professor said. Percy chided herself for jealousy, but it would not be quieted. Miss Thompson's voice was amused, her face twisted in an uncharacteristic smile. "We are rotating the gala's chaperone list this year, Professor. You have been voted in. I told the committee I would relay the information to you in person."

"Thank you for the message, Miss Thompson," he replied. "You're a dear." Percy giggled in spite of herself, and the professor turned a stony glare in her direction. With one finger he pointed, saying, "Silence. You are dismissed, Miss Parker. May your next vision include some correct answers for tomorrow's lesson."

Percy bit her lip, bowed to both the professor and the headmistress and fled.

"Good evening, Miss Parker," Rebecca called out as the student left. When the door slid shut, she stared a moment and murmured, "What a strange child."

Alexi nodded. "An interesting young woman, indeed—and clever in every subject but mine. Now and then she overcomes her skittish nature, but . . . I do believe I intimidate her."

Rebecca laughed. "You don't say."

He ignored her tone. "New elements have come to light regarding her."

"Really? What?" Rebecca sat straighter in her chair.

Alexi chewed on his lip, thoughtful. "I already told you of the ghosts. Miss Parker has visions, too. Visions I believe relate to our work. I think she might even have seen our chapel. But . . . I still have a hard time believing we would be sent a student when we were told our seventh would be a peer. And to pursue it further, to involve her in—"

"I wholeheartedly agree," his friend interrupted. "Be

careful what you ask her to do. I shouldn't want to be forced
to expel the girl."

Alexi made a face. "Rebecca! I'll hear no insinuation
from you! And you needn't worry; I'm through searching. This nonsense is driving me mad. Let Prophecy come
and hit me over the head if she's going to come at all. I'm
sick of the whole preposterous game. As I said last time we
spoke—"

"Ah, yes. You're giving up after all these years. How noble," Rebecca scoffed. "Remember ten years ago, when Elijah decided he'd had enough? How he stopped coming to
meetings? Do you remember how the papers rang out with
ghost stories, how we had to run around in cloaks so as not
to show our faces since he wasn't there to wipe scenes clean,
how the spiritualists had a ball, how a child actually died
because—"

"I remember it well," Alexi growled. He'd been the one
to fetch Elijah and give him a ferocious set-down.

"Then stop posturing. You're no more done with Prophecy than it's done with us. Alexi, you *must* come to La Belle.
It's absurd, you avoiding us. You must talk with Miss Linden. You must determine her importance to us, if she has
one. As I said before, she asks after you all the time. And
Alexi, I—"

Alexi gritted his teeth. "As I said before, if I have been
avoiding our haunt it was not a conscious choice. My life
need not revolve solely around this institution and that pub,
Rebecca. How tedious has been our routine."

His friend shook her head. "Goodness, listen to you com-
plain! You should know more of Miss Linden, that's all. She
spoke last night as if everything happening in London was
meant to bring us together," Rebecca explained. "If she's
our seventh . . . Well, to be perfectly honest, I thought that
seemed possible."

Alexi's expression clouded. "Indeed." There was an uncomfortable pause as Rebecca waited for him to elaborate and was disappointed when he did not.

"Indeed," she snapped, bristling as she rose and walked to the door. "Do recall the task we've all been set. You cannot discard your mantle of responsibility, no matter your frustration or . . . interest in a student. If anyone should be interesting, it should be Miss Linden! It's not like she's hard on the eyes. Now, good evening. As for the ball, are you so melancholy that your duties take—?"

"I'll attend the blasted ball! And for you to implicate me in scandal, then push me toward Miss Linden makes me wonder what's possessed you."

Rebecca slowed, suddenly contrite. Turning, she said, "Forgive me, Alexi. I've been inappropriate. You would not dare impropriety. If I've spoken in error—"

He shook his head. "Rebecca, please. No apologies. I value your opinion, as always." But while his words were forgiving, his tone was cold. "Do tell Lord Withersby he owes me the research assigned him—he causes trouble if he's not busy."

Alexi returned to his work, then, and Rebecca nodded and silently took her leave.

Marianna chased her friend into her bedroom in Athene Hall. "You must attend, Percy."

"I told you, I cannot."

"But our dear little Edward will so be unhappy if you are not there. If you fear he will fill my dance card and not yours, I am certain—"

"Marianna." Percy placed a pale hand on her friend's anxious face. "You dear, dear girl. I know that you fancy him, and that he fancies you. Please, do not trouble yourself over me. I'm very happy for you both, and all I want is—"

"I want you to have someone, too."

Percy smiled sadly, patting Marianna's hand and staring out her window.

For the second time that day, Constance startled her by bursting through the wall. "Forgive my intrusion, Miss Percy, but you simply must come to the Apollo lot!" The ghost's transparent eyes were sparkling. "If you don't, you surely will regret—"

Percy motioned the spectre to silence. She wasn't sure how Marianna would feel about Constance and had not yet brought up any of her abilities regarding the dead. She had no idea how to begin.

"Percy?" the German girl said, seeing her friend's shifted focus.

"Marianna, my dear," Percy replied, deciding to take a chance. "Would you like a little adventure?"

"Always."

"Come on then." Gesturing for the ghost to lead the way, Percy dragged Marianna to her feet and out the door.

"What are we—?"

"The night is beautiful," Percy explained. Then, "Out for a bit of fresh air, Miss Jennings!" she called as they rushed past the front desk.

"You won't get beyond the courtyard!" the woman shrieked.

"Don't worry, we're not trying!"

"Where *are* we going?" Marianna breathed.

"There." Percy pointed.

"The little graveyard behind Apollo Hall? Why? Are we allowed? Is there a guard?"

"Don't worry," Percy promised. "We're still within school grounds."

"Who lies buried there?" Marianna asked.

"I was told it's for students and professors who have no other family. Oh! I suppose *I* might be buried here someday . . ."

Constance hovered nearby. "Once a year, Miss Percy, near my headstone, the ghosts of two professors celebrate their wedding anniversary. I thought you might appreciate it."

Through an open arch in the courtyard, behind Apollo
Hall, the two living girls and one spectre approached a
heavy, spiked gate bordered by a rough stone wall. Marianna
remained at the entrance, shaking her head.

Respecting the limits of her friend's comfort but unwilling to turn back, Percy opened the hefty gate enough to
wedge herself through. Gliding up a stone path that led to an
inlaid circle, she took in the sight before her: two transparent figures in midcentury clothes, a man and a woman,
waltzing. Their weightless feet spun gracefully above the
ground, and their featherlight forms held each other with
confidence and care.

"Oh, to dance... To merely be *touched,*" Percy whispered, dropping to her knees. Constance hovered silently
nearby.

"What is it you see?" Marianna called.

Percy gave an aching sigh, which was caught by the
breeze. "A waltz."

The sound of voices in the courtyard below drew Alexi away
from the book he read by candlelight. He drifted absently to
the rear window of his office, and suddenly the ghost Miss
Percy Parker called Constance appeared, pointing emphati-
cally below.

"What do you want?" he asked, irritated.

The ghost pointed again.

Gazing down from his window, he saw an incredible
sight: two glowing, floating figures twirling above the tiny
collection of graves. A third figure knelt nearby, long white
hair billowing in the breeze, and Alexi recognized Percy,
arms outstretched as if to embrace the dancers. He sighed,
feeling a strange and tearing discomfort. Constance gestured
with great detail, emphatic.

"All right, I'll do it. I'll teach her tomorrow." Alexi
paused. "Stop staring at me, I said I'd do it. You've never
bothered me before. Is the sole purpose of your afterlife to

meddle in my affairs? Or is it Miss Parker to whom you're so drawn?"

Constance simply gave an enormous smile.

"You shouldn't, you know," Alexi grumbled. "Meddle. It's dangerous." No one knew better than he.

A stone gave way, and from a gaping hole in the Southern Hemisphere spirits floated free, amazed and gleeful, hell-bent on trouble. Their eyes were gleaming. The Groundskeeper giggled as each emerged. "Come on, come on!" He gestured them onward. "We're about to undo the wall between! If we can't find her, we'll shake the whole world till she tumbles out!"

Watching from across a portal, Lucille turned to the impatient Darkness, who rumbled, "I want you to kill them."

"What would be the point? They'll just inhabit new bodies. They always do. Don't you understand? This will never end. This vendetta of yours will never be settled until an all-out war is waged. You realize that, don't you?"

"But. Where. Is. She?"

Lucille took a deep breath. "I do not know."

Thunder crashed. "Break all the seals! Shred them! War!"

Lucille's eyes burned with emotion. "Not yet, my lord. Listen to me. It will all come together. We will find her. When I have them in my hands, she will follow."

The thunder turned to a hopeful whisper. "She will?"

Lucille reached out a hand. The long, thin fingers of Darkness reached back.

"There now. At last. Trust me, for once, would you? They've no idea the surprises that await."

Chapter Seventeen

Alone in the scientific library, her bone white fingers absently tapping the table, Percy bent over a tome of Italian mathematics. She could not concentrate. Out of the corner of her eye she noticed a man enter the room, meander half-heartedly to a shelf and begin poking at a few spines. After a moment he procured an armful of books. Evaluating his cargo with great disdain, he moved to sit opposite her.

Percy looked up in her usual meek manner. The finely dressed gentleman, incredibly lean and sharp-featured, bowed his head in acknowledgment. His eyes went wide as he took in her coils of snow-white hair and spectral appearance, yet this was his only reaction. Percy returned to her work. The gentleman, casting one last sideways glance, did the same.

It was not long before he tired and rose from his seat, books balanced precariously in his arms. He moved past Percy to return the volumes, one by one. On the fourth pass, his last book fell from his hands and an irritated sigh escaped his lips. She felt his eyes dissecting her.

"Here, sir," Percy offered, bending to pick up the volume.

"Thank you, m'lady," the man replied.

As he took the book, their fingers brushed. Percy felt something overwhelming sweep through her, as if a thunderstorm broke open her veins. The two gasped in unison, and the gentleman's eyes clouded and his face contorted as if he'd seen something horrible.

It was best that the kind yet protective Miss Wilberforce had gone, lest she imagine an impropriety was taking place.

Percy removed her glasses. The man seemed to be reeling from the odd moment, and reeled again from the vision of her irises. "Oh, my," he exclaimed. "Allow me to offer an apology, Miss..."

"Parker," Percy supplied.

"You are...quite unique." It was a failed attempt at flattery.

"So I've been told," Percy remarked. "Now, if I may ask: who are you, sir, and what did you just do to me?"

The man blinked, confused. "Well, my name is Withersby. Lord Withersby. And I...touched you, Miss Parker. Accidentally."

"Lord Withersby, accidental brushes do not cause such...palpable shock."

"Ah. Yes. Well. That was rather odd, wasn't it?" He seemed at a loss.

"Indeed. So I must ask: was it you or was it me?"

"I'm afraid it must have been my doing. Unless, Miss Parker, you are in the habit of such exchanges...?" The man's eyes narrowed.

"No."

The two considered each other for a long moment. Withersby finally said, "The incident was entirely my fault. Do forgive me." With a bow, he turned to depart.

"But Lord Withersby," Percy called. "What *happened?*"

He halted and turned. "Have you, Miss Parker, ever witnessed someone burn to death?"

Percy recoiled, horrified. "N-no. Not that I recall!"

"No, no. Of course not. My mistake."

"Is that what you saw?" Percy pressed. "You touched me and saw *that?* A vision?"

"No, no," he said. "Nothing to trouble yourself about. Now, if I may...?" He held up a hand, intending to take his leave.

"Wait, please," Percy begged.

He huffed. "Yes?"

"I have dreamed of fire, Lord Withersby. You see, the strangest things have happened all my life. Things like this. I yearn to find others who might be able to explain. I believe one professor here at Athens—Professor Rychman—might be just such a man. Do you know him? Is that why you are here?"

An odd look crossed Withersby's face. "As a matter of fact, Miss Parker, I *have* heard of him. I hear he's a mean old codger. And yes, he's why I'm here."

Percy laughed. "Oh, the professor can be quite severe, it's true. But he's brilliant. He's been so tolerant of me and . . . I owe him much. If you are here for him, may I speak to him of you?"

The man gave her an inscrutable smirk. "If you like, Miss Parker. If you like."

"I do, Lord Withersby, and I shall. What do you call what you just did?"

"Well . . ." The nobleman shrugged. "I just call it a 'cognitive touch.'"

"And this happens whenever you have contact with another person?" she marveled.

"Person or thing," the man admitted, squirming. "But really, Miss Parker, we should not be having this conversation. It's improper. In *many* ways." Languidly, he waved a hand across Percy's face and seemed to be waiting for something to occur. After a moment, he furrowed his brow. Percy blinked at him, equally baffled.

"Well, damn!" the man declared. Without another word, he turned and vacated the premises.

"Indeed!" Bewildered, Percy wandered along the shelves, glancing at the spines of the books he'd been replacing, wondering what to make of the encounter. How many were there in the world who had powers beyond explanation?

Passing a case wedged between the wall and a staircase, one she'd never before approached, she felt the air around her grow cold. The chill seemed to be emanating from a moldy book, which Percy took down and opened to find old theories on biology. There was a note in the margin:

> *Constant is my care for you, sweet girl, my Constancy. All I ask is that you, for one blissful moment, put aside your obsession long enough to look into my eyes.—P.*

Percy gasped, turning to the front. There she found a faded name: Constance Peterson. Another inscription was written next to a diagram of the human heart:

> *Can science explain everything, my Constancy, when my heart beats only for you?*

On the opposite margin, there was a shaky reply:

> *Dear P., though you share my library table, I cannot commit any part of my heart, for I fear I do not have one to divide. The course of my blood flows toward science alone.—C.*

"Oh, Constance," Percy breathed. "Have I found your lost treasure at last?"

The doorbell echoed hollowly through his dark estate. Grumbling, Alexi rose from his study chair and made to answer. He was not expecting visitors.

"Well, well," he remarked blandly, staring down at Elijah Withersby, who stood on his front stoop, smirking. "What do you want?"

"Aren't you going to invite me in?"

Alexi turned and walked inside. "Would you like something to drink?" he asked, inviting his friend to enter with a casual wave and then leading him to the library. It was one of the few rooms in the sprawling estate that he maintained.

Elijah smiled. "Some rare and exceedingly expensive sherry, perhaps?"

Alexi went to a cabinet and returned with a little glass filled with the precious liquid. "Here." He placed it in Elijah's outstretched hand, trying not to look as begrudging as he felt. "Enjoy."

"Such a host."

"You weren't invited," Alexi reminded him.

"I know." Elijah sighed. "Auntie kicked me out of her parlor. I was driving her mad."

"I can't imagine," Alexi muttered. "Tell me you did something useful today."

"I did that research you assigned me. Ghostly dogs." He dropped some parchment with a summary on a nearby table. Alexi noticed it was dreadfully short. "But while I was in the library, I met a student of yours. Ghastly pale girl."

"Ah." Alexi clenched his jaw and folded his hands. "Miss Parker."

"I recall Rebecca mentioning something about her at La Belle, something at the start of term about a ghostly addition to your academy, and I—"

"Rebecca didn't say a word to me about her then," Alexi interrupted, grumbling. "I wonder that—"

"Well, I'm telling you now, Lord and Master."

"Don't call me that," Alexi snapped.

"Your Royal Eeriness? Melancholy Minister of the Constant Sneer?"

"I do not sneer."

Elijah snorted. "I beg to differ, Your Eeriness, but perhaps I alone see your disdainful glances."

"Lord Withersby, I'd sneer at the devil to halt your endless flow of drivel."

Elijah bowed, delighted. "Anyway, that student of yours," he continued, "seemed awfully fond of you. I cannot, upon my life, understand why."

Alexi shook his head. "Is that why you've come? Well, our friend Josephine suggested something similar, but I think you both daft. I don't want to hear another word about it."

Elijah looked taken aback. "Josephine? How did she meet Miss Parker?"

"In my office," Alexi replied.

"Indeed? In your office. Beguiling your students in the evening hours? Alexi, I'm—"

"Elijah!"

The nobleman wouldn't be silenced. Adopting a contemplative mien, he mused, "She'd be a fitting match for you, Alexi. Really, she's suitably haunting. You'd make a pair indeed; dark and light, quiet and bombastic. But isn't it forbidden to—?"

"There is nothing to forbid, and you are a lecherous fool!"

"Oh, but Alexi, you're all riled up! We've been waiting years for any sort of fancy to sprout up in your cold and dreary life, and now this? What fun! Well, Rebecca won't be happy."

"Lord Withersby, you are—"

Elijah cut him off. "There's one awkward thing, which is why I've come. I tried to get away before the girl asked me any questions, but...I brushed her by accident and, well, she sensed my power. I tried to wipe her clean of the memory but it did not take." He braced himself for a reprimand.

Oddly, Alexi just smirked. "Miss Parker has talents unlike anyone I've ever met. She is a unique young lady."

Elijah laughed. "Yes, she seems to fancy you, and that's odd indeed."

Alexi shook his head, disgusted. "Get out of my house."

Elijah rose with a chuckle, drained the rest of his sherry and slipped toward the door. As an afterthought he added, "Oh, because I'm sure you're yearning to know, when I touched the girl, I saw a figure in flames. I'll be damned if I know what that means."

"A figure in flames?" Alexi leaned forward. "Did it resemble a phoenix? Was there a door?"

Elijah furrowed his brow. "Oh. Are you thinking...?"

He shrugged. "While I admit she's intriguing, she's hardly a likely candidate for Prophecy. Didn't Rebecca tell you? Our seventh is most certainly Miss Linden. We're just waiting for the right sign. To that end, since you have neglected to visit us, I have been directed to bring her round to see you at the academy ball. So . . . dress pretty!"

Alexi's expression was grave. "Please, Elijah. Tell the group. No jumping to conclusions until we see all the facts."

"Yes, well, we're sure." Elijah grinned suddenly. "But why not? If you think our seventh is Miss Parker, why don't you touch her and see what you find out?"

As the clock struck six, a familiar form burst through Alexi's office wall. She fixed a gaze upon him until he gave her some acknowledgment: "I know! For God's sake, I'll teach her. Now leave me be." He batted his hand at the spirit. Constance smiled, satisfied, and vanished as there came a knock at the door.

"Come."

Miss Parker hurried in. She removed her scarf, causing her white hair to tumble around her shoulders, and removed her glasses. It occurred to Alexi that he had never seen her without her accoutrements outside of this room, and found himself pondering whether she was ever without them or if this ritualistic disrobing was alone for him and her bedroom mirror.

Perhaps she was conscious of being examined, for colour flooded her cheeks and she blurted, "A fascinating few days I've had."

Alexi lifted an eyebrow. "Oh?"

"I met a man who brushed my hand and had a vision. Have you ever heard of such a thing?"

"Once," he replied, suppressing a weary chuckle.

"Really? Please tell me about it!"

"Sadly, I don't know any more, Miss Parker. I only heard of it. Now, your lesson, if you please."

The young woman sighed, riffled through her books and produced a paper. Each corner had a symbol scribbled upon it that Alexi noted with growing interest.

"A ring, a flame, a bird and a door? What are these? Surely not equations," he stated, turning the paper on its end to study the absentminded sketches.

White hands fluttered out across the desk. "I'm sorry, Professor, my mind wandered. I—"

Urgency filled his voice as he interrupted. "If a ring, a flame, a dove and a door were variables in an equation, what would be their values? If you had to give a meaning to these, what would you make of them?"

Miss Parker blinked. "I don't know that I could make anything of them, mathematically."

"Do they mean nothing, Miss Parker?"

"Alone, the symbols are self-explanatory. Together . . . perhaps, components of a legend? They are symbols that have haunted me since birth, feel fraught with significance, and yet I do not know more."

"Fascinating," Alexi murmured. "Have you ever seen a door?"

"Pardon me?" She stared at him blankly.

"A portal. A void. Have you seen one, other than in your visions? Has one ever, say, opened to you—as if it were part of the wall one moment and suddenly, in the next, a gate to another realm?"

"Well, no, not like that. Why? Have you seen a door like that, Professor?" Her eyes were wide.

"If I did," he reminded himself quietly, "it would be best not to enter."

Miss Parker shifted in her chair, at a loss and a bit fearful. "Well. My equations—are they correct, Professor?"

"Hmm? Oh, yes." He tore himself away from his reverie

to examine her work. "Let's see. On the last five, your mind evidently was on doves and doors. If only we knew why."

"Professor, I promise it's no fault of yours." Her shoulders rose and fell helplessly. "I'm past hope, I suppose."

Alexi shook his head. "You know, Miss Parker, you are too intelligent to be so melancholy."

Her eyes slowly rose to meet his. They glittered, pinning him with an unintentionally merciless stare. "Your contemporaries might say the same of you." Her bold moment then faded. "B-but you flatter me, sir. You have seen nothing of my intelligence, only my ineptitude."

"There are as many types of intelligence as there are sciences. That's the reason I continue these sessions, as I've given up on you ever truly mastering mathematics." Alexi paused as she gasped, having expected it. "Come now—don't look mortified, little spectre."

Her hands clenched. "Please, sir, I ask you never to call me such a thing. Never!"

"There, finally! *Spine,* Miss Parker. Thank you," Alexi replied, smiling. Then he turned his attention to the book he had been underlining when she arrived, flung it down and launched into a lecture, ignoring that her mouth was still agape.

"Now. Here the *Y* value is manipulated. You will graph these. The lines follow a certain pattern, but you must follow the equation not merely sketch a line. You might catch hold of this, merging as it is geometry with algebra."

Percy struggled to catch up. "It is?"

"Well, not exactly—but think of it as such and you'll like it better. That will be all."

Miss Parker shook her head and gathered her scarf. "Yes, of course. Good evening, sir." With a curtsey, she scurried to the door.

"Did I say you were dismissed?" he called.

She whirled. "You said, 'That will be all . . .'"

"For the *first* lesson." Alexi rose and went to a shelf. "Turn the phonograph handle," he instructed, "and place the needle on the disk."

Miss Parker's pale face lit up. She did as instructed, and the phonograph bell crackled; the glorious sound of strings lifting sinuously into the air. Alexi moved toward the open floor of his office.

"The pleasant surprise about music and mathematics, Miss Parker, is that it's all numbers," he began casually. "And so is a dance."

The music became distinguishable as a lilting waltz. Miss Parker's eyes widened and a hand flew to her mouth. "Oh, Professor!" Joy radiated from her like a sunbeam, and for a brief moment, Alexi forgot what he was about to say.

"Hush, hush. Don't make me regret taking the time to do this. Come here, silly girl."

Percy darted forward, but when she stood before him, looking up, she became so frightened that the professor might read her mind that she shrank back, embarrassed and awkward.

His own composure remained cool as he offered a noble bow. "That is your cue to curtsey, Miss Parker."

"Oh, yes, of course. How stupid of me." She curtseyed, and the professor closed the distance between them to a decorous familiarity. She stared up at him. Her pounding heart made her mind swim. The professor placed a hand around her waist and took her right hand. When they made physical contact, Percy thought she might faint. Actual, voluntary human contact from a man she so admired . . . Tears rolled down Percy's white cheeks.

"My goodness, Miss Parker, if I thought this would upset you . . ." Alarmed, Professor Rychman withdrew. "Of course there is an academy rule of no contact, but a dance lesson is most certainly an exception, and if you fear—"

"Oh, no, my dear professor! You must understand. In the convent, the only man I ever could call a friend was a ghost. We could never so much as take hands . . ."

There was a moment, as they stared at each other, where Percy thought they shared a keen understanding of loneliness. The professor's dark eyes softened. He respectfully held her gaze until she bashfully looked away; then he held out his hand, patiently allowing her to approach when ready.

Percy wiped her eyes and stepped forward. His hand closed again over her waist. Her fingers alit upon his other palm, and he coaxed her hand into his, squeezing gently.

"Your fear of me simply must cease," he commanded.

"It . . . it isn't that I'm *afraid,* Professor."

"If I'm not mistaken, Miss Parker, you quake."

"Not out of fear, I assure you!" But after this declaration, more mottled patches burst upon Percy's porcelain cheeks. She was terrified anew that he'd expel her on the spot.

The professor cleared his throat and simply said, "The rhythm guides us, Miss Parker. One-two-three, one-two-three." He tapped time upon her finger. "Your feet must do the same. Place your other hand on my shoulder."

Percy complied. She was far too nervous to look at him. Instead, she stared at the ornate silver button that clasped his robe about his neck and held his signature scarlet cravat in place.

"I will lead with my right foot. Step back with your left." The professor moved forward. As Percy faltered he said, "No, the other—"

"I'm so sorry!"

"Stop apologizing, Miss Parker, and *move.*"

Percy stepped back, obedient if rigid. The professor added, "Repeat this, following my lead, stepping back when I step forward, interchanging." As he did so, Percy followed with hesitation but precision, and moved without stumbling. She felt a giddy rush.

"I see!" She dared a look up at him, and grinned.

"It's rather simple once you know the steps," he stated, and began again. "Can you feel the pulse?"

Their steps remained small and controlled. "Yes," she

breathed, shocked at her voice, which was a good deal more sensual than she intended. Their eyes locked, Percy stumbled and broke away. "I am sorry, Professor, but—"

He stepped forward and grabbed her by the hand, firmly turning her to face him again. Percy gasped. He clamped his other hand upon her waist, putting an abrupt halt to her cringing retreat. He stepped forward. She stepped back. They lifted and stepped and repeated without incident. They moved around the open spaces of the office, each turn imparting confidence. Finally, Percy could not hold back a delighted laugh as she realized she was waltzing. And Constance was watching, hovering above the professor's desk, smiling proudly.

"I'm dancing!" Percy whispered with glee.

The professor partially smiled, his eyes sparkling for one single moment. "Indeed you are," he replied, and Percy felt a tug upon her right hand. She allowed his pull—and twirled beneath his arm! As she spun to face him again, his hand returned to her waist. Percy nearly swooned.

The professor lowered his head in approval. "Not a bad start, Miss Parker. You see, if you pay attention to your partner, you can react without even being warned." He smirked, displaying a mischievousness Percy had never seen—or perhaps it was merely wishful thinking.

The music ended. The disk crackled beneath the needle. The professor released his hold on Percy and stepped back, bowed, holding her gaze. Percy curtseyed in return, wishing the music had gone on indefinitely.

"Now . . . no more moping about that damnable gala!" he commanded, moving to the phonograph and lifting the needle.

"Oh, Professor, how can I ever thank you for this—?" She ran forward and realized with sudden horror that she had unconsciously meant to embrace him.

"Good night, Miss Parker," he interrupted.

"Oh. Yes, of course. Good night, Professor. Thank you!"

She spoke hurriedly, awkwardly gathering her things to cover her dangerous intention. "I shall see you on Saturday?"

"Perhaps you will find me in a dark corner, hiding," he admitted, grimacing as he took to the chair behind his desk and busied himself with a cup of spiced tea.

"Well. Good night, then." She hurried to the door, wondering if the blush upon her cheeks would ever fade. However, her gaze fell upon the painting that earlier had done her such an ill turn, and she couldn't help but comment. "Do you know why that painting is so ironic to me, Professor?" She did not turn around to face him, instead stared at the woman being led down into the darkness.

"Do tell, Miss Parker."

Percy removed her glasses again and turned to face him. "Percy is just a *nick*name." Then she quit his chamber.

Outside, in the hall, she swooned. Constance bobbed at her side. "You looked so beautiful together," the ghost breathed.

"Oh, no, none of that, Constance, I've warned you against insinuations," Percy snapped. But then, suddenly: "Oh, my! I nearly forgot!" She fumbled among her books and drew one out. "This was in the library, and I believe it's yours. The writing in the margins . . . do you recall it?" She flipped to the appropriate page.

Constance stared, a translucent hand at her lips. "That's it," she choked, reading. A drop of water splashed the floor: an actual tear made manifest. "My greatest folly," the ghost admitted, "was to deny a lovely soul who asked nothing more than to remain by my side." She glanced desperately at Percy. "You and I seek such similar comfort, do we not? Shall I now find mine?"

"Perhaps your 'P.' wanders nearby, seeking you. Or perhaps . . . perhaps you are simply free to be at peace."

"Yes, yes! I feel peace, Percy, no longer any sickness in my hollow head. It's why I was pushing you toward your professor—because no matter what may stand between, love is the highest power on earth and our one true purpose. You realize that now, don't you, Percy?"

"Of course," Percy murmured, looking at the ground.

The spirit continued blithely. "Now that I know, and now that I've helped you, I can rest."

Percy waved the ghost onward, smiling. "Go! Go and find rest, my friend."

Constance nodded and grew blindingly bright. "At last. I shall see you on the other side," she said. And with a loving wave of her hand, at last the spectre dissipated. Only the hint of one word remained. *"Paul . . ."*

Percy wiped her watering eyes and darted back to her hall, ignoring the guard she passed along the way; she couldn't be troubled by murderers or fear when there was so much beauty in the world. Bursting through Marianna's door, she wailed, "He taught me how to waltz!" then clapped hands over her mouth.

Marianna looked up from her bed, a smile creeping over her face. "Who?"

"You'll never guess! After our lesson . . . he asked me to turn on the phonograph. When I turned, he was standing in the middle of the room. Oh, how grand he looked! And then . . ."

Her friend leaned forward, clearly titillated.

Percy clasped her hands and whispered, "I can't begin to describe how incredible it felt to be touched on the waist, held by the hand . . . Oh, this is silly and dangerous!"

"Waltzing?"

Percy looked around as if the walls had ears. "We should not speak of it."

"Because Miss Thompson might dismiss you out of jealousy? *Liebe ist wie Krieg . . .*"

Percy squealed. "Hush with your love and war, it was a *lesson*, Marianna. There was nothing untoward—truly! This was utterly innocent! I am his student!"

"Are not some people drawn to one another, no matter

their professions, age or circumstance? Does fate mean nothing? Are you not nineteen, no longer a girl but a woman? Back in my homeland—"

Percy shook her head, crushing down all hope. "We cannot pose such questions, Marianna, no matter where we are. I shan't risk my future at this academy. Whatever exists between him and the headmistress, so be it. And...there's been nothing remotely inappropriate. He's only trying to help."

Marianna shrugged, thoughtful. "Well, no matter. We must find you a dress."

"A dress?"

"For the ball, silly. You do not mean to tell me after that rousing lesson you plan to miss?"

"Oh. Well. Perhaps I'll go—but I'll still look a fright, and no one will want to dance with me."

"You will not look a fright, Percy," her friend promised. "Love's bloom becomes you."

Percy hissed. "Never say that, Marianna. How many times must I . . . ?"

She broke off as the German girl turned and ran to her closet, pulled down a mass of fabric from a shelf. "*Fräulein,* your evening gown!" A moment later, Marianna held up an incredible dress.

"Oh, how beautiful!"

"*Meine Mutter* sent me three gowns. Have one!" the girl cried. When Percy laughed, overcome, and nearly knocked her to the floor in an exuberant hug, she added, "Come, *meine Liebe,* there are errands to run, flowers to gather and dreams yet to be planned!"

The Groundskeeper stood looking through the portal, his gaze sweeping the river Thames up to the Tower of London. He was finally returned home, and he stood with calloused feet planted firmly on his natural soil, his arms folded. He had cleaned his face, which like a carnival mask was currently ill proportioned and eerily lit.

"Oh, my darling Lucy-loo!" he cried, not knowing where she was but only that she was there, in the very heart of the world, and would soon make the Whisper-world proud. "With you and The Guard on the loose, my dear, nothing will stop you. Not this time. Nothing between you and the last pin. Pry, pry, my lovey, it's up to you," he chortled, the pitch of his singsong voice rising. "We've loosened, we've loosened, and everything's ready. Now . . . shatter the seal!"

CHAPTER EIGHTEEN

The corridors of Athene Hall were filled with the soft murmurs of women, the rustle of expensive fabrics and the occasional giggle, and excitement had transformed Marianna into a force of nature. Only once she and Percy had donned their finery and done up all their buttons and clasps did she let either of them pause to breathe—and breathing was difficult with the tight press of their undergarments. With grand ceremony, both girls turned to look in the mirror.

Percy did not recognize herself. Pale lavender satin enveloped her in contemporary style. Paired with a snug corset, Percy's flowing skirt swept out into a bell, with a gathered layer drawn up on either side and cinched into a bustle at the back. A high-backed dress with buttons all down the spine, its neckline was elegantly sloped to allow generous amounts of flesh to be shown without scandal, the bustline accented by flowers embroidered in silver thread and seed pearls. The glitter of her necklace chain matched the sparkle of Percy's eyes, and her phoenix charm lay reassuringly tucked into her bodice. A perfect braid swept her hair into a circlet, and sprigs of heather crowned her a veritable fairy queen. Marianna had rubbed the oil of the flowers behind Percy's ears and around her wrists, and the smell filled Percy's nostrils with calm delight.

Marianna, elegant in burgundy taffeta with fitted sleeves and a slender V-line waist, spun about slowly. She produced a set of pale lavender lace gloves and presented them to her friend. "You are an incredible sight, Percy. You *are* Titania. This gala is yours."

"I . . . I do look all right, don't I?" Percy breathed. For the first time in her life, she was nearly pretty. Her perfumed hands flitted over each other, and she could not stop staring at her reflection. But there was one hesitation: she had never once left her room without a scarf. "Marianna, I can't, I'm frightened." Overwhelmed, she shook her head and reached for the muslin.

"Percy, I tell you, you look amazing. *Schöne!*"

"But you're accustomed to me." Percy paused. "Well, you and the professor. He's seen me, too. He demanded I be brave and not hide beneath shrouds while I'm in his office." She was surprised she'd never admitted as much to her friend.

Marianna seemed pleased. "Tonight, Percy, you'll be braver than ever before."

A second-floor chamber long locked away, silently ready, the ballroom of Promethe Hall was a dreamily glittering sight to behold. This gala was the academy's one grand indulgence, and Percy and Marianna stood hesitantly at the threshold. Marianna had to keep removing Percy's hands from her collar, foiling her instinct to cover up.

The ballroom was long, one side lined with high windows that made a dark, starry night visible above the rim of the courtyard. At the center, French doors opened onto little balconies. Past filmy white curtains rustling in the wake of a crisp fall breeze, the silhouettes of coupled men and women stood staring contemplatively at each other's faces or the evening sky. The opposite wall was golden and colonnaded, with wide doors at both ends. Alcoves exhibited gaggles of murmuring ladies reclining upon benches lined with crimson velvet. Busts of philosophers and literary figures stood silent sentry amid the frivolity. If living guards were posted, they had done well to dress finely and blend in.

After drinking in the sights, the two girls crept beyond the threshold. Percy glanced around. Marianna anticipated her, and nodded across the long hall. Like a guardian statue at the back stood an unmistakable figure, tall and swathed in black. Percy let out a choking sigh.

Marianna shook her head. "You are hopeless, my friend. Why is it you have set your sights only on the forbidden? Is it because you feel no one else will court you?"

The evening had made her friend bold, but Percy did not mind. In this atmosphere, it seemed as if almost anything could happen. "No. He just..." Percy found she had no words.

Marianna's friend Edward approached, cutting a dashing figure in a navy coat that fit him like a glove, a grey silk cravat tucked neatly into his vest. His tousled chestnut hair hanging adorably down over his eyebrows, he stared at Marianna with unabashed rapture. "Miss Farelei," he murmured, clearly relishing the opportunity to kiss her gloved hand. Their bodies shivered simultaneously.

After that long moment of rapture, he turned with a wide and welcoming smile. Taking in the sight of Percy, all of her, he nodded in approval. Her hand was kissed in turn, or rather the lace upon it. "Miss Parker, I am delighted you're here!" He squeezed her hand in his. "You are unlike anyone I have ever seen—and I mean that kindly. Come into the light, Miss Parker, for I'll not allow you to slink in the shadows. To do so would be to eclipse the moon."

Percy beamed. "Your kind words, Mr. Page, are a gift. Believe it or not, a professor of mine recently expressed similar sentiments. Perhaps I ought to listen." Her eyes flicked to the opposite corner of the room, where Professor Rychman was holding a conversation with a history teacher, looking thoroughly bored.

"Perhaps," Marianna supplied with a smirk.

The three students amused themselves with punch and confections, listening to the string quartet, watching and appreciating the gala's attendees. Everyone boasted breathtaking finery, the very latest fashions in sleeves, bustles and buttons. No one yet had made a scene regarding Percy's arrival, and she wished to remain inconspicuous by the door.

Edward held out an arm for Marianna. "Miss Parker," he began timidly, "would you mind if I escorted your friend about the room? I promised I'd introduce her to a fellow who recently returned from her homeland."

Percy nodded graciously, seeing how Marianna's eyes lit up. "By all means," she said, waving them off. Her friend replied with a look of gratitude, and Percy smiled again, happy until she was assailed by a tinge of jealousy, jealousy for the way Edward looked at the other girl's very normal and beautiful face. But she had no such admirer, and so, forcing herself to stop staring at her professor, she drifted to the corner and evaluated her peers.

A few of the women toted flowers. Many more wore corsages, produced by beaus, admirers or family members. Percy wished that she had a flower. She had no beau, nor admirers, nor family, yet she refused to let this daunt her, was determined not to lapse into a melancholy. She realized, too, that she did not seek the same throes of giddiness that Marianna and Edward enjoyed. She wanted something blissful, yes, but also something deeper and more inscrutable. Something eternal.

Valiantly she smiled, moving at last to sit alone in a chair by the wall. Some unwanted attention was indeed cast her way, murmurs and the occasional titter, but she ignored them as best she could and sought peace. Batted eyelashes, soft words exchanged by inviting lips, giggles, smiles and

butterfly kisses upon palms, scarlet flushes, fans held at precise angles and in unspoken signals: a whole world unfolded
around Percy in a language she didn't understand, a world in
which she had no place . . . This world's inhabitants twirled
past her without a care in the world.

After a bit, the living dancers failed to amuse. Percy
couldn't help but turn and watch the dead who hovered beyond the ballroom windows, hesitant to join the party. She
recognized one from her hall, and he lifted up a transparent
hand. Percy waved back with a smile—and then realized she
appeared quite mad. Quickly she changed the motion to adjusting a bud of heather in her hair, but she had a sense this
was unconvincing. The subtle pointing and whispers of her
peers increased, and Percy blushed, knowing she was on display.

Alexi was in the midst of an uninteresting conversation—
Mrs. Rathbine was droning on about Roman pottery—
when he first noticed the goddess across the ballroom: Miss
Parker had come, and admirably without her shields. A goddess indeed, for he had guessed her full name after her hint
about the painting in his office. She had the name of *his* goddess, though that long-ago oracle had never given it. Nonetheless, his work and his fate required faith, and he had
nothing left but to await the final sign. Prophecy had come,
surely, and in the surprising form of a student. He knew she
could not know that truth for herself, troublesome as her ig-
norance was. They would both have to await the final reve-
lation.

Miss Parker's elegant dress and elaborate coif were stunning. Her fine features had been painted with the softest rose
blush, and her pale eyes flashed like diamonds. She was by far
the most captivating thing ever seen at this silly event. He
noted her talking to various young ladies who drifted past,
strained into saying something polite. She was gracious and
returned their trivial, polite conversation, but when she oc-

casionally glanced away, he read her struggle and isolation. She alone, he was sure, understood why he dreaded this event every year. Such recognition was profound.

An enraptured young couple twirled past. As they did, they waved. Percy returned the gesture happily, then watched them twirl away, her warm smile fading. Something seized up deep inside Alexi. Perhaps she felt the weight of his stare, for she looked up. Eyes like snowcaps finally met his, and the rest of the world was muted.

"There you are—my favourite gargoyle!" came a taunting voice.

Alexi turned and saw Elijah Withersby leading a woman through one of the arched entrances and into the ballroom. Miss Linden. Having only seen her briefly, in the moonlight, Alexi was unprepared for what a well-lit room would do for her beauty. It was unparalleled. Her sensual ruby lips twisted in a smile, and her green eyes glittered with a pleased recognition. Her red satin dress was simple yet tremendously flattering.

"Here's the man of the hour at last." Elijah removed the woman's hand from his arm and offered it to Alexi. "Professor Rychman, here again is our dear Miss Lucille Linden."

Alexi kissed the woman's gloved hand with solemn courtesy. Rosy-cheeked, with black hair curled immaculately in place, she was indeed breathtaking. A foreign sensation wrestled deep within him. "A pleasure to see you, Miss Linden. I am sorry it has taken so long for our paths to again cross."

"The pleasure is entirely mine, Professor Rychman, and I forgive you your absence, sorrowful though it has been. Lord Withersby has been kind, as has Miss Belledoux. If you hadn't pointed me there, I'd have been without recourse! I am forever in your debt. Fate brought me to you, I am sure of it."

Alexi could see Elijah nodding eagerly.

"Of your little coterie, Professor, you're the only one I haven't gotten to know, though Lord Withersby has told me much about you."

"Has he now?" Alexi eyed his friend.

Miss Linden sighed. "It is difficult to be a stranger in such a large place, and to feel safe when the world is coming apart at the seams . . ."

She possessed a magnetic intensity Alexi had never encountered, and her regard surpassed custom. But then, just over the woman's perfect, bare shoulder, Alexi regarded the opal eyes of Miss Parker looking on in stricken sorrow. Her pale, heather-framed face quickly rallied into a hollow smile, and she tried to pretend she hadn't been staring. But eyes like hers could truly hide nothing; and when the music slowed, the couples parted and still no one came to speak with her, Percy rose from her chair and fled the room. Alexi's instinct was to follow.

"Professor Rychman?" called a musical voice, jarring him from his reverie. "Are you all right?"

Alexi faced Miss Linden. "My apologies. Something caught my eye."

"Ah, we interrupt his chaperoning, Miss Linden," Elijah taunted. "The good professor takes every task with the utmost gravity. He takes great care with his *students.*"

Alexi looked sharply at his friend, but Miss Linden smiled and he felt her smooth gloved hand graze his. "I admire gravity in a man." Her eyes were precious emeralds, and they sparkled at him. Yet they could not keep his mind from wandering.

"If you wouldn't mind, Miss Linden . . . I am terribly sorry. It was a true pleasure to see you, but I must beg your leave. I believe someone requires my assistance. A student," he added, staring at Withersby.

"I shall miss you," Miss Linden replied. "But I leave you to your duty."

Elijah was quick to take the hand she waved in languid dismissal. Giving Alexi a look of extreme scorn, he led her away.

Percy felt her very blood ache as she clutched the folds of her fine skirts and fled. She nearly ran, sweeping up the stairs to the third floor, far from the ballroom. "This must end," she commanded herself in a mournful whisper. "Your heart is dangerously out of hand! You're here to be a student, not a romantic. And if no one asks you to dance and you're jealous of a beautiful woman whose hair looks coiffed with serpents, so be it—but it cannot destroy you!"

The stairs opened onto a foyer, red granite columns rising like stone tree trunks in a forest clearing. The walls were plain and stately. White drapes at each window appeared silver in the moonlight. This place of solitude let Percy breathe again. She felt far more at home here than she had under the chandeliers. Music wafted from below in a spectral waltz.

The click of her dainty shoes echoed softly upon the marble. She made her way to the center of the open space, passing in and out of moonlight, and stopped inside a mosaic circle—Athens's seal, a golden eagle. "'As the Promethean fire which banished darkness, so Knowledge bears the Power and the Light,'" Percy murmured, reading the motto.

Whirling slowly in a dance, she released the tension in her arms, let her head loll and loosed a sigh. The waltz music lingered below. Percy felt the strings played as if they were kisses across her face, light touches of the feathers of birds. She was monarch of this moonlit hall: the air, light and shadows obeyed her command . . . Of course her mind placed her dear professor in her grasp, one hand holding hers and the other firmly upon her waist. She had, after all, a potent memory to invoke. And rather than fighting the image, or letting it embarrass her, she gave in fully and welcomed Professor Rychman into her dream.

Suddenly, Percy felt something cold graze her hand. Her eyes opened in a flash and she saw a worn, smiling old man in tattered Elizabethan garb—an old friend she never thought she'd see again. "Gregory!"

"Hello, dear girl," said the faint, raspy voice.

"How in heaven—? How did you come here?"

"I've only a moment before my weary wisp be finally laid to rest. But ye shan't take me, said I to the heavens, before my girl's first dance!" The wizened face widened into a smile.

Percy laughed. "Indeed, my dearest Gregory, how dare you not be my first?"

Cold air found Percy's left side. It touched also Percy's outstretched right palm, and with a nod she led the spirit in the new waltz beginning to be played below—a dance an Elizabethan would not know, but as there were no corporeal feet for her to trip on, it proceeded without flaw.

"Hast thou found happiness, my child?"

"Sometimes," Percy replied, as she and the ghost glided across the marble floor.

"Dost a brave young lad own your heart? Thou wert lost in reverie when I found thee, and—"

"Hush! None of that. Your hopeless romantic of a girl has merely grown older, not wiser, I'm afraid. My desired match is . . . unlikely."

"Foolish girl! Thou art mad, to fix thy heart on what cannot be, when thou hast so much to give!"

"Don't chide, dear Gregory. My fate is my own to choose . . ." Yet Percy faltered and slowed, looking into her friend's transparent eyes.

"But who shall care for my little swan?"

"God shall provide," Percy replied—the words Reverend Mother always used to assure her. She hoped they were true.

The waltz drifted to its dainty end. After a moment, a new and stronger tune began. Gregory reached out a translucent hand, and Percy felt a cold trickle of air down her cheek.

"Percy, my time hath run its compass." The ghost's voice was far off; he was beginning to fade. "My little one is now a lady. Dost thou relinquish me?"

"With all my heart. Good night, sweet prince, I wish you peace!" Percy blew her friend's diminishing figure a kiss. Gregory began to hum along with the music, until he was nothing but a lingering sound and a cool patch of air. "'Flights of angels sing thee to thy rest,'" she added, her voice breaking, hoping their familiar, final benediction could carry him home.

Suddenly, she realized that she'd never before been so terribly alone. Tears sprang forth, and Percy let them come.

"Now, now, Miss Parker, what's this?" a voice scolded from behind.

Percy whirled at the familiar, stern sound. A figure broke from shadow, clad in an elegantly tailored frock coat trimmed with ornate embroidery, and a white silk cravat. His black hair was combed neatly, framing that noble, stoic face at which Percy had spent countless hours staring. Percy's heart throbbed in her throat.

"Oh, Professor! Good evening!" She nearly coughed out her words, feeling all grace drain away, cut to the quick by his unexpected appearance. She tried to bat away her tears but his firm hand caught her pale, lace-covered fingers. He took her hand, their entwined fingers bridging the cold chasm between their bodies.

"May I have this dance, Miss Parker?"

"Oh . . . of course, sir." A blush bloomed ferociously in her cheeks but she was helpless to stop it.

As his hand grasped hers, she examined his full lips, which had just enough curve to make his expression inviting. There was just enough light in those dark eyes to make Percy wholly forget about breathing, and without words or even a nod he drew her hand to his side. He slid his opposite hand around layers of smooth lavender satin and placed the fullness of his palm assuredly upon her waist.

Percy's hand flew to his shoulder, alighting like a lark on a branch. She saw his nostrils flare, as if he took in the intoxicating scent of the heather she wore, and if her mind did not play tricks he stared at her as if she was his peer. But her mind did play tricks, and these were dangerous thoughts.

They began to waltz—slowly at first, their circles precise and narrow, their gazes locked. Percy, who had already memorized the professor's features, now savored each pore, crease and eyelash. The study of his sculpted lips forced her to close her eyes or else, truly, her knees would have buckled. In turn she knew she was being parceled; but from *him,* she welcomed the scrutiny.

Their bodies were one with the music, and Percy found she didn't have to think about the correct steps any longer. In and out of the moonlight they floated, silent save for the deft clicks of their heels, the whispers of the music rising from below and the occasional sigh escaping Percy's lips. Their orbit grew, expanded. Her sighs grew into giggles and laughs.

Professor Rychman spun her, and Percy swept fully against him, lingering there for just a moment. Her face brushed his chest and she took a deep breath. He smelled faintly of clove tea and leather-bound books. She did not want to remove her cheek from the thick black lapel of his jacket; she could have nestled in that warm darkness indefinitely. Perhaps, at least, until class. A giddy scream welled up inside her. This was surely a dream!

Had they not been interrupted, they might have danced till dawn, time slowing as they stared breathlessly into each other's eyes and dreamed volumes they could not voice. But their magical moment out of time was fleeting. A raucous squawk sounded. The professor's brow furrowed and his eyes clouded. He broke away, and a hand went to his temple as if he was pierced by a sharp pain. It was like a spell had broken.

They both turned to the noise at the window, staring at

the large black bird upon the branch outside. "Professor . . . ?" Percy said.

He turned, focusing on her, then sighed as if heavily burdened. "Pardon me, sweet girl. I must go."

Percy blinked, enraptured by his endearment and at the same moment distraught at his retreat. "My apologies, Professor. I did not mean to keep you—"

"It was I who asked you to dance, Miss Parker, but I'm afraid it may have been in error," he explained, raking his hand through his hair and taking another moment to stare at her.

"Oh." Percy stepped awkwardly out of his way and looked at the floor, her blush reignited. Was he sorrowful that they had broken the school rules of conduct, though this night was unique?

Perhaps he sensed her fear, for he reassured her with weary gentleness, "You've done nothing wrong, Miss Parker, only provided a welcome distraction. But work calls."

The raven squawked impatiently. Percy glanced over. There was something strange about the bird; something glistened upon its black breast, a tiny patch of blue. Was it not the same raven that had perched outside the headmistress's office?

Percy shuddered. What strange omens were these? What exactly did her professor hide?

A crisp evening wind blew through the open window near Lucretia Marie O'Shannon Connor, the woman commonly known as Jane. Her fellows in The Guard were never sure if her name was actually her own or rather a romanticized invention, but they fondly blamed it on her Irish heritage. They enjoyed her eccentricities where her actual family did not. Such as, her fondness for solitude: she was not a social creature, and certain secrets increased her proclivity for isolation. One of those particular secrets, if he had been present, might have warned her of the coming danger, but Jane's ghostly paramour was gone and so she was more vulnerable than she believed.

A white cat padded around the fireplace, as if looking for something misplaced. The wind whipped more strongly through the open window, blowing the damask curtains and rattling the pages of Jane's open book. She saw the cat stop pacing and stare past her toward the door, ears erect and tail pointed.

"What is it, Marlowe?" The cat looked up with flashing, intelligent golden eyes, and wrapped a long tail around her ankle, and Jane realized, "Ah, something's here, is it?" She closed her book and stood. "Well, Marlowe, we'll just have to encourage it to leave, won't we? We'll just . . ." She turned to face the open doorway and there was a pause. "Holy Mother of—"

"I've work to do," Alexi repeated hastily, backing to the stairs. "And you have a ball to attend. You must return." As Miss Parker moved forward, unconsciously maintaining their proximity, he held up a hand. "*Good night,* Miss Parker."

"G-good night, Professor Rychman." A hand rose to her lips but the girl caught herself, never actually blowing him the kiss. Exchanging such a token of affection would have been wholly inappropriate on any night, but Alexi allowed a flickering smile to nonetheless toy at the corner of his mouth. Then he bowed slightly and turned to hurry down the stairs.

"P-Professor?" she called. He turned back. "Thank you. Thank you so much."

"What else was I to do?" he replied, letting her interpret as she would. Then he turned and was off again, leaving her where she stood.

There was no choice but to abandon her. Alexi's temple throbbed, his chest tightened and his stomach churned, and he knew some evil had come to one of his companions. He was being punished for his foolish indulgence. Taunting Prophecy came with consequences. He was moving too fast, not waiting for the appropriate sign.

Rushing out the door into the cool evening air, past giddy partygoers and whispering couples, Alexi's anxiety was only heightened by thoughts of Miss Parker, who had stood unabashedly enraptured by the touch of his hand. Percy's laughter, the radiance of her sweet, innocent soul—every aspect of her had been aphrodisiac, gently alleviating years of weight upon his soul. Her eyes had betrayed both of them: they shouted her feelings and stirred up his own, unfamiliar and unsettling as they were.

Rebecca was awaiting him on the steps of the academy, tapping her foot in supreme irritation. "Where have you been?" she snapped as a carriage sped around the corner and shrieked to a halt.

Alexi shrugged as he climbed inside, following her. "Waltzing." The carriage set off.

"Waltzing? Are you ill?" Rebecca asked.

"Fevered, perhaps," he agreed. "Do we know what we're in for?"

"Marlowe came to my window."

"Really? You ought to have asked him to dinner. I have a question about Faustus—"

"Shut up." Rebecca scowled. "Marlowe, Jane's familiar. She's in trouble."

"She'll stave it off, whatever it is. I have complete faith in—"

"Remember the dog?"

Alexi's mind returned to the last encounter the group had suffered with the forces of Darkness, and he blanched. "I assume the others are on their way and will meet us there. Oh! Elijah was attending Miss Linden," Alexi recalled, seized with sudden guilt. "I assume he'll offer her some grand excuse and find us?"

"You mean, you weren't waltzing with her? Who, then?"

Alexi rolled his eyes. "What does it matter?"

Rebecca clenched her fists but said nothing.

Alexi stared at her. "I know you all think she's our seventh, but nothing's yet proven. If—"

Josephine's cry outside the carriage and the pounding of horse hooves beside them alerted him that their time was short. They were almost at Aldgate, and Alexi prayed they weren't too late.

"'Work calls...'" Percy repeated the professor's words, standing alone once more in the moonlit foyer. She wanted to laugh and cry all at once, but mostly she wished to scream. Had there indeed been a spark between them? Could she trust her memory and senses? She shook her head, feeling faint. Surely it had been imagination.

Darting down the stairs, she was out the front door before her mind caught up. "What sort of work at Saturday midnight?" she asked herself. "And what am I doing?" A guard called out to her to ask why she was running, but she was inside Apollo Hall before she even knew the answer, darting up the stairs and knocking on Professor Rychman's door with no idea of what she was going to say if he answered. Her heart thundered. She had no right to inquire of him, yet here she was following, compelled to question. She knocked again. There was no answer.

The door was unlocked. Boldly she opened it. The room was dark and uninhabited.

"What work has he to do?" she asked the empty chamber. "Please tell me your mysteries, Professor Rychman. Perhaps they shall illuminate mine . . ."

"My God. Not you again . . ."

Jane was not a weak woman. She trekked down the Minories to the Tower of London on a regular basis to face the local spectres. While none of her illustrious group could ever completely confine or expel the tower's many spirits, with a

gentle Celtic admonition she policed its boundaries, keeping
the antics of centuries of ghosts inside the ancient, worn
stone walls, bidding poor Margaret Pole and her brutal, ax-
wielding executioner remain within their usual bounds of
the Tower Green lest they disrupt the whole of Tower Hill
with the gruesome repetition of her death was a daily routine. But this black cloud floating before her was more terrifying than any of the tower's offerings, were there a hundred
Margaret Poles and a thousand chasing executioners and
were the flowing silver blood of ghosts to turn red. This
blackness was terror itself. It hovered at the threshold, taking
up her entire doorway. When last Jane had seen it, she'd had
the aid of her companions. Even then, it had almost taken
Elijah's life.

The cloud congealed into the form of a single-headed canine. That head then multiplied, and the beast stalked forward and began to circle her chair. From its feet, which
hovered a good six inches from the ground, blood appeared
to drip. Blood culled from Whitechapel. Blood drawn from
single, unaccompanied women . . .

The monster opened a hellacious maw and growled: the
whispers of a thousand damnations. It sniffed her then struck.
Jane screamed as blood poured from a deep rent across her
forearm, and a shriek flew from her lips as she pressed back
hard against her chair. The incantation worked, if only for a
moment; the abomination jumped back as if scalded.

"What do you want?" Jane demanded, as the infuriated
beast slashed her curtains. "Damned Ripper. What are ye
looking for?"

The monster turned and its invisible force lashed out. A
shallow wound began in each of Jane's cheeks, drawing
downward, stinging and creating tearlike trails of blood.
Like the Ripper's other victims, Jane would die ignomini-
ously, cloven and torn. She prepared herself, knowing that
wars always had casualties. She had just expected to remain
safe, a healer—

Her front door suddenly burst open and the back of her library exploded in flame. The beast turned, startled. Alexi Rychman, voice like thunder, chanting in an ancient tongue rich and beautiful, entered the room. A whirlwind surrounded him, and his dark eyes were blazing; with a wave of his hand, he extinguished the fire.

"Impeccable timing, my friends," Jane murmured—and promptly fainted.

"*Non, non, ne nous quittez pas.* None of us have your hands to heal, *cherie.*" Josephine rushed in. Ripping fabric from her dress and winding it around her friend's arm, she massaged Jane's temple.

"Hello again, you filthy creature of hell!" Alexi growled. He unflinchingly stared the beast down.

Rebecca appeared. A keening note rose from her throat, a call for The Guard to unite in their attack. It was a noise sweet and ancient, as if the wind were singing. The room filled with whispers, the beating of a thousand wings. A current of air circled above, and forked blue lightning.

Alexi's arms rose, his hands deftly flicking forward as if conducting violins to lift their bows to a symphony's seminal note. Ringlets of blue flame danced across his fingertips. Threads of lightning arced forward, sought to bind their foe and neutralize it. The abomination writhed, groaning like a sinking ship and spitting like a rainstorm.

Josephine, tending to Jane, was suddenly knocked to the ground. She rose up, hand to her forehead, and stared deeply into the center of the vapourous beast. Whatever she saw, it was a vast nothingness too terrible to comprehend, and she was transfixed by the spear of madness itself. But Elijah called out her name, and Josephine felt something warm wash over her, as if her veins were caressed from the inside out. She stepped back and into her lover's arms. "*Merci, mon cher.* That was needed."

As Josephine refocused on her half-conscious charge, Jane's head lolled to the side. "Ah, ah, none of that!" Josie snapped. Her friend's eyelids drooped. "Lucretia Marie O'Shannon Connor!" Jane's eyes shot open. "Good. Now, look." Josephine pulled a golden locket from around her neck, opened it and held out the shimmering image of an angel. The rest would take care of itself.

"Rebecca, dear, could you enlighten us a bit?" Alexi asked with mild strain. He did not want his companions to worry, but this creature was like nothing he'd ever contained. Anger, built up through countering the sheer evil of this monster, was getting the better of him.

Rebecca searched the library of her mind. As last she cried out, "'How you have fallen from Heaven, bright morning star, felled to the Earth, sprawling helpless across the nations! You thought in your own mind, I will scale the heavens . . . Yet shall you be brought down to Sheol, to the depths of the Abyss!'" When in doubt, the King James Bible often sufficed.

Alexi applauded as the creature snapped its many jaws and howled. "Well said, Rebecca! The puppy does not care for the word of God. Now, my friends, I think it goes without saying that all shows must eventually let down their curtains. Cantus of Extinction!" Clearing his throat as if preparing a lecture, he peered into the contracting form of their enemy and confided, "You should feel privileged, we've never had to sing this one."

Music rose in the room, an overture from the night sky, every star an instrument. However, just as the cantus swelled, their foe writhed from the grasp of Alexi's blue flame and burst out the window. "NO!" Alexi shrieked. Jagged shards of glass rained down on The Guard, and once again the creature was gone but not destroyed.

CHAPTER NINETEEN

Percy stood at the center of her room in a long nightgown of filmy white fabric. It swished around her as she rocked from side to side, humming softly. Absently fingering the contours of the phoenix pendant between her breasts, she hardly noticed how warm it felt. One sensation obliterated all else: the firm press of Professor Rychman's hand upon her waist. That memory was euphoria.

The obsession was silly, of course. Percy hated it. She had a powerful mind capable of numerous, divergent trains of thought, and this was mental slavery. She had prayed the rosary repeatedly to try and derail her fixation, but she remained in solitary study, in abject adoration. This passion outmatched her. Her very blood was restless.

A spirit drifted by her window but did not stop to say hello. Percy felt the draft, cooling the moisture upon her skin, but all she could think was, "Oh, my dear professor, you must have given me quite a fever . . ."

She lay back on her bed. The more she tried to fight her daydreams, the more scorching they became. She imagined him bent over her, easing her onto her pillow as carnality consumed them. Her back arched upward, and as she pressed herself into his covetous, illicit, imaginary embrace, the phoenix pendant slid up her body and rested upon her sternum.

"We demand Prophecy now!"

In their chapel, the voices of The Guard rose like the blowing sands of a thousand years. A hazy door burst through the air, swinging open at the altar. The Guard descended,

formed a circle, hands clasped and heads held high, responding in otherworldly liturgy as instinctive as their breath. Rebecca and Josephine continued to sing.

"In darkness, a door. In bound souls, a circle of fire. Immortal force in mortal hearts. Six to calm the restless dead.
Six to shield the restless living."

A ring of blue flame leaped from nothing into being,
harmlessly licking their ankles.

"Great spirit of The Grand Work, we are here because
we're weak!" Alexi cried. "Since childhood we've looked
for you, beautiful creature, to return and guide us. Be silent
no longer! Give us the friend you promised. *Seven* to calm
the restless dead. *Seven* to shield the restless living."

He lifted his head to the image topping the altar. "Great
One, let your feathers unfurl. Your wisdom!" A disembod-
ied burst of music sounded. "Your power!" The music grew
louder. "Your light!" A shaft of ruby orange fire leaped from
the center of the floor to illuminate a burning heart in the
white stained-glass bird above.

"We demand Prophecy! We cannot wait! Where is she?"

Someone was screaming, burning, his body encased in bloodred flames. A divine force was splintering before her eyes.
Lying back upon her bed, Percy cried out in empathy, arch-
ing upward, the terrible vision like hot oil upon her eyes.

There was a piercing, burning pain just below her throat.
She looked down in horror, bending forward to see that her
pendant was glowing red. Her ivory skin was sizzling. Percy
quickly unclasped the necklace and hurled it to the floor,
where its glow extinguished, but upon her skin, just above
and between her breasts, was now a perfect imprint of a
phoenix. Blood welled at its edges.

Her breath hissed through her teeth as she rushed to the
lavatory, and she stared into the large mirror at her white
form in her white gown, now marked with this blood-lined

stamp of symbolic rebirth. She dipped a cloth into a basin of cool water and pressed it to her chest, moaning.

"Such strange things! Mother, why did you leave me this bird, my only inheritance? Why won't you guide me now? Why aren't you a spirit that will speak to me when I see so many others? Why am I left in the dark? Please, tell me something."

Her stinging skin was her only response.

"Please, tell us something," Alexi begged.

Warm, vibrating power coursed through The Guard, making hearths of their veins, but the only sound was the hum of their combined power, a lingering note of music. No goddess appeared to help them.

His shoulders fell slightly but Alexi steeled himself; he would not show the others his defeat. While they had not received an answer, the ring of blue fire still surrounding them, a hazy beam of light dancing from each host's heart to the hearts of the others, linking them all in a misty, dimensional star, giving them a sense of hope, however silent.

Alexi's mind wandered as he held Rebecca's and Michael's hands. For a moment he thought he heard a feminine gasp, something familiar. But then he shook his head and turned. "Silence. Still."

"Yet we are renewed," Jane murmured, rejuvenated enough to place her hands on her wounded cheeks and heal them once more. "We are recharged, and that has ever been the purpose of this sacred space."

The circle of blue flame died, and the beams between the hearts of The Guard dissipated. The shaft of light illuminating the stained-glass dove slowly faded.

" 'Once more unto the breach, dear friends, once more'?" Michael asked.

Alexi nodded, fearing to say more. He had always grieved when his goddess declined to appear at their meetings, but tonight he had begged and still she was silent. He had never before begged. He had always dreamed that she would pay him heed. But perhaps—his heart quickened—it was because she was no longer the same and could not come to him in such a vision. Perhaps it was because she now wore skin of snow and had forgotten her lineage. If this was so, it was dangerous, the form she had chosen—or what might have been chosen for her—and his hand was still checked, awaiting a sign only she could give. If she even knew how.

The Guard broke into conversation as they ascended to the nave of the chapel. Michael remembered a pun he'd heard in the pub earlier that day, and he was quite desperate to tell it to Elijah who would surely denounce it as the stupidest thing he had ever heard. Jane, still a bit weak, discussed with Josephine through a minor coughing fit the romanticism of becoming a consumptive invalid and wondered if the scars on her cheeks gave her character.

Alexi's mind wandered to a moonlit foyer that had doubled as a ballroom. He could feel Rebecca looking at him, so he placed a hand absently upon the small of her back, guiding her up the stairs. This sent a tangible shiver up her spine and brought him back to himself, and he retrieved his hand.

Still, all Alexi could think of was waltzing.

CHAPTER TWENTY

As Percy crept into the professor's office for her usual tutorial, so close on the heels of Saturday's revelry, he was standing by the stained-glass window. Shafts of coloured light fell in patches upon his distinguished face. His expression was blank but Percy felt his pull upon her blood, drawing her near. He had said nothing about the gala night during their class today.

And she couldn't have expected him to; a dimly lit dance without a chaperone was the talk of paramours, not professors.

"Good evening, Miss Parker," he murmured without looking at her. A thrill raced up her spine. The winglike sleeves of his robe quivered as he, arms across his chest, tapped a finger upon his forearm.

"Good evening, Professor," Percy replied, unwrapping her scarf, removing her glasses and placing them on the table. Unconsciously she swept a few locks of pearlescent hair forward to cover the burn now visible above the bustline of her dress.

"And how are you this evening?"

"Well, thank you." There was a long pause. "And you?"

"There is a strange feeling in the air, Miss Parker. Forces are at work."

Percy gasped. "You've noticed it, too?"

The professor turned, raising an eyebrow. Her outburst had clearly startled them both, and she spun to stare into the small fire in the hearth at the side of the room. "You are a curious one, Miss Parker."

"Am I?" she asked, only afterward realizing the coy manner in which she replied. She bit her lip and looked at him, hoping he would not be disgusted.

He was not. The sparkle in his eye did not go unnoticed, nor did his flickering smile as he moved to take his seat. Percy's nerves forced a tiny giggle from her lips as he prompted, "You have work for me?"

"Indeed," Percy said, sliding a paper across the desk. Her fingertips brushed his and her temperature rose. She wondered at the volatile nature of her blood—or at the preternatural effect of his presence upon her.

He spoke, breaking the tense silence. "What think you of the new geometrics in the last chapter?"

Percy bit her lip. "Well, to be perfectly honest . . . I would rather it were a waltz," she replied. When he eyed her, she hastily added, "Sir."

The professor gave her a sideways glance and his small smile ignited fires all across her body. "Indeed. Our sessions would be less painful if I were your professor of dance." Then he stared down at her paper and said, "Actually, Miss Parker . . . you may be improving. A few of these are correct. Or perhaps my standards are lowering."

Percy grimaced, wishing he could see her excel at *something*. She debated asking his opinion of a burning pendant, but thought better of it at the last moment.

The professor rose and walked to a crystal bowl near the phonograph. His expression was inscrutable. After a small pause he said, "I've a test of a different sort today, Miss Parker. May I offer you a piece of fruit?" He picked up something Percy could not see and kept it cupped behind his back as he returned.

Percy fought back confusion. "I . . . suppose so. Thank you, sir."

"For you." The professor held out a half-peeled, waxen-skinned, orange-red fruit with seeds like rubies. A pomegranate. The smell overcame her. Immediately Percy leaped from her chair and began to choke, reeling backward.

The professor, clearly unprepared for such a reaction, cast the fruit aside and rushed forward. "Miss Parker, my apologies! I had no idea you would react so violently. Please—"

"That horrid smell! Those horrid seeds!" Percy cried, struggling against his grip, gagging. "It's like that vision!"

He held her safe in his arms. "Forgive me! I had to test my theory . . . *Persephone*."

She stared at him, startled, so he continued: "Am I wrong? You bade me guess your name. Is it not strange that a mere namesake should have had such a vision in this office—and such a reaction to that fruit? Persephone, Greek goddess, bound to the underworld after digesting pomegranate seeds offered her by Hades . . . Why, Miss Persephone Parker, there must be more to your story than you know yourself."

She had quieted somewhat, especially after hearing the

sound of her full name spoken in his delectably sonorous voice. When she could once more breathe, she became aware of the protective nature of his embrace—and that again made her gasp. A violent cough racked her, and she lurched forward, her hair falling aside.

"My God, what is happening to me?" she wheezed.

But the professor's eyes were drawn to her chest where it was pressed against his arm, to the swell of her bosom smooth and white against the black fabric of his sleeve. "What is this mark upon you?"

Suddenly and keenly aware of his fixation upon a rather personal part of her anatomy, her eyes flickered upward. Every inch of her flushed. "Oh! That—Well, it is a burn. From my pendant." Embarrassed, she again covered the mark with her hair. "I . . . I cannot explain it, Professor."

"Try."

Percy gave a laugh of weary hysteria. "Well, Professor, the strangest things have happened all my life. I've grown accustomed to them."

His eyes bored into her. "Yes, and?"

"I've worn this against my skin all my life," she remarked, pulling the chain from inside her dress and showing him her pendant, which glittered in the candlelight. "It has grown warm before, periodically. I thought nothing of it, and it is the only thing my mother left me, so I did not want to remove it. But as I lay dreaming . . . it burned me." She looked up at him helplessly as his brow furrowed, and wrung her hands. "And now you think I'm raving at last. Oh, Professor, why do you ask such questions when my answers will only appear mad?"

"*When* did it scald you?" he asked.

"After the gala . . . I suppose it was after midnight. I did not hear bells, for there was singing in my mind. Don't you see? Madness!"

"Singing?" The professor's eyes were wide.

Percy sighed. "In one voice, there were two. One spoke

an ancient language I've never heard, and one our native tongue."

"What were the words?"

"Why do you ask? Surely you do not care what—"

"I care very much!"

Baffled and rattled by his urgency, Percy began to recite what she remembered. Her eyes closed in a moment of exquisite pain. "'In darkness, a door. In bound souls . . . a circle of fire. Immortal force in mortal hearts. Six to calm the restless dead. Six to shield the restless living.' Angelic voices sang. It was how I always dreamed a mother's lullaby would sound: the most beautiful music . . .'"

Opening her eyes, she glanced at the professor, who was now leaning against his chair, gripping it with white knuckles. A light was in his eyes she had never seen. Surely she was dreaming, for this particular look . . .

He rose and quickly closed the distance between them. As if in a trance, he took her by the arms and lifted her to her feet. "Our seventh—surely it is you! You'll do so much for us, Persephone, especially for me. With things the way they are . . . I can't wait any longer. I asked for you to be revealed, and you come to answer my prayers!"

Percy was overcome by his words, by the sight of him gazing down at her, by his nearness, by the smells that were so inherently his—by the lurid intensity rising between them. "Your *seventh*, Professor? What will I do for you?"

The fire in his hearth flickered, and it was as if he suddenly realized where he was. *Who* he was. Flustered, he took a moment to recover. Stepping back, breathing shallowly, he stared at her with confusion and wonder. "Forgive me, Miss Parker. Perhaps now it is *you* who thinks *me* mad."

"Professor, please, you must explain—" But she was not allowed to finish; a vision came in a wave of heat: She was seized and cradled in the professor's arms. His eyes were a raging inferno, and his face moved closer. A strong yet gentle hand drove into her hair, tenderly grasped her neck. Professor Rychman was bending as if to kiss her, a lock of his lustrous dark hair brushing her forehead . . .

The vision faded as abruptly as it began. Percy's eyes unclouded once more to see him staring at her. A furious flush broke out across her skin, and her heart leaped in sickening waves.

Surely noting the change, he said, "And what had you in its clutches this time, Miss Parker?"

You, she thought, trying to mask her panic. She was desperate to flee, afraid he could read her mind. Oh, how she yearned for that vision to become truth! Light-headed and full of guilt, she ran to her chair, placing her hands upon her cheeks in an attempt to cool them.

"Miss Parker? What on earth is the matter?"

She fanned herself desperately. A firm hand clamped upon her shoulder and she whirled, backing away, gazing at him and then looking ashamedly in the other direction.

He closed the distance again, and touched her arm. "Percy, what did you see?"

She shook her head, backing off around the desk. "It was nothing. I'm terrible!"

"Was it an unpleasant vision?"

"Oh, no, it most certainly was not," Percy breathed, a voluptuous murmur. Then she clapped her hand to her mouth and cursed herself, biting her fingers.

He kept stride as she retreated. "Why do you flee me, Percy? What has you so rattled? Was I in this vision?"

Percy's blushing silence was her admission. Her fists clenched as she stole furtive glances at his face, and he continued to pursue with measured steps, his voice a veritable purr. Suddenly he was upon her, his hands at her shoulders, and he bent, unable to hold back a whisper, low and rich, that caressed her ear. "Tell me Persephone, *goddess* . . ." The tip of his nose brushed her earlobe, his breath lingering there, and Percy swooned against him.

Before his hands could catch her, she stumbled away and

faced him with a mixture of fear and desire. Dimly she realized that his pursuit had backed her up to his desk. He was
luminous, his gaze intoxicating. His noble features and suddenly otherworldly presence made Percy think she was wit-
nessing the coming of an angel.

He again closed the distance between them and cupped
her cheek in his palm. "Persephone Parker, you *must* tell me
what you see. I need to know everything."

Percy buckled again at the sound of his voice speaking her
name and the feel of his hand on her face.

And then she was seized, was suddenly cradled in the professor's arms. His eyes were raging fire as his face moved
closer. A strong yet gentle hand drove into her hair, another
grasped her neck. He was bending as if to kiss her, a lock of
his lustrous dark hair brushed her forehead—

Persephone cried out, dually in shock of his lips so near to
hers and the first exact culmination of a vision.

He gazed down at her, unable to let go. "My dear Miss
Parker . . ."

"Professor! The very moment you took hold of me was
my vision coming true! This has never happened! And . . ."

Their eyes locked, and his grasp about her tightened. "Oh
my," he murmured. And then he pressed his lips to hers.

The fusion was instant. His arms locked around her waist,
and in a rustling of fabric and soft breath he lifted her off her
feet and made her captive against a bookshelf. He was thirsty
yet gentle. His lips hungrily devoured hers, and she returned
the kiss with eagerness. The reality of what she had so ach-
ingly dreamed was pure heaven.

His lips finally broke from hers and he moaned, raked a
hand down her body. Percy gasped and threw her arms about
his neck, clinging to him as tears leaked from her eyes. Her
smooth, moist cheek wetted his closely shaven jaw.

He lowered her feet to the floor again, but refrained from
removing his viselike grip. "I am sorry, Persephone, I could
not help myself," he gasped. "Forgive me."

Percy laughed, delirious. "What's to forgive? I'm so tired of caution."

But her words caused him to shrink back. Releasing her, nearly sending her to the floor, he murmured hoarsely, cryptically, "Caution? Without a door, a portal . . . What am I doing?"

Percy, in a dreamlike state, yet noted a flush had mounted his prominent cheekbones. The absence of his hold was like a gust of cold wind.

The professor rushed to the window, as if seeking refuge. "You must think me a monster to behave in such an inexcusable way. I, your superior! I, who must be strong and just! I beg you not to think I have taken advantage of my station in order to . . ." He shook his head, distressed. "Such actions are uncalled for, and are certainly not my fashion. You must forgive me, Miss Parker. I don't know what came over me."

"Please, do not apologize!" Percy gasped. It was as if she'd been doused in cold water, and she rushed forward to rekindle the fire that had so fleetingly been theirs. "Oh, Professor—"

He raised a hand, halting both her and her speech. " 'Professor'? I am ashamed to be addressed so after what has just transpired!"

She looked gravely into his eyes, and a truth filled her that seemed irrefutable. "I cannot help being your student. But I'm older, and unlike every other student here. Many girls are married by my age, to men of your station. And there's surely something pushing us toward each other, no matter where we stand."

Rychman clenched his fists. "I cannot deny that, Persephone."

Seeing he would say no more, she shook her head, recalling how they had broken apart. "A door, a portal? You speak in riddles. Help me understand."

He stepped back, raking a hand through his hair. "I can't."

"Well, I can't help what I feel," Percy replied.

"What you feel, Miss Parker?" he murmured.

"Would you like me to tell you exactly?"

The professor cleared his throat. "I fear that would be extremely difficult for me at the moment. But . . . you must call me Alexi from now on, Persephone. I believe you have earned my familiarity."

"Very well then . . . *Alexi*," she murmured.

They stood in silence a moment.

A sinking feeling suddenly seized Percy, a fear of the worst. Her own attachment was strong, but perhaps the professor's reaction had been something baser. Men often punished women for their own loss of control. Her fingers fluttered at her sides and she whispered, "Please, Professor—Alexi—I know the rules of contact. Please don't have me expelled."

He looked horrified, retreated behind the familiar boundary of his marble desk. "I would not dream of it, Miss Parker. I'd never punish you for my mistake."

" 'Mistake,' " Percy repeated.

The look he turned on her was paralyzed and pained, but his voice was hard. "I dare not allow myself any other such indulgence . . ." His tone softened. "Thrilling as it was, I dare not cross such a line again. Not until I can be certain."

"Certain of what, Professor?" Percy asked. When he opened his mouth and closed it without reply, she pressed, "Until you are certain of *what?* You owe me some insight, Professor. You spoke of a number, a prophecy even. What do you mean? A prophecy for whom? And, where did you go after the ball? You know how mad I am for answers regarding my—"

"You will have to remain mad for the time being, Miss Parker!" he barked, staring deep into her eyes as if willing her to understand. "I . . . I beg your patience."

Percy touched her lips. "And what of this?"

"I suppose you'll have to keep quiet, my dear—out of respect for both of our places here," he snapped.

All Percy's happiness vanished.

Alexi's shoulders fell, and he sighed. "Blessed creature with such a gentle heart..." He skirted his desk and dared approach her, took her arms in his hands. "Miss Parker, Persephone, my dear goddess of a girl—however I am to address you. Look at me, please." She did as requested, but a tear fell from her eye, and Alexi drew his fingertips across her cheek. She leaned into his palm, but he drew back again, as if he could not trust himself to touch her. "Please listen. There are forces at work upon my life that are beyond my control. I know you, of all people, can empathize. Have you strength enough to bear with me until I see the signs I need?"

Percy blinked. "I don't understand, but I'm in your hands." She gave him a radiant smile, praying he understood the faith she was putting in him. As she moved to touch his arm, however, he turned away, and her breath hitched in her lungs.

"There is much to make us cautious, Miss Parker. I have a duty toward you; that much is clear. But do not ask too much of me or think too much of me—not yet. Those beautiful eyes of yours say so much, and I simply cannot... This is all rather sudden, untoward, and more than a little upsetting."

"For us both," Percy agreed, noticing how laboured his breath had become, how white his knuckles on his chair. She took a step closer. "However, I—"

"Get out," he demanded. "Get out of this office before you drive me mad," he begged. "Have mercy upon me, Persephone. I do not trust myself."

"I trust you," she said.

He smiled, and there, in the weariness of his smile, she saw years of loneliness and the toll they had taken. He said, "You trust the man who just set upon you? You are as foolish as I." Gently he turned her away and gave her a slight push. "Go, beautiful creature. Until next time."

"Alexi," she insisted, reaching for his hand.

"Percy," he echoed. But he drew his hand away.

"Alexi—"

He placed a finger upon her lips, hushing her. A thrill took her, and the bones of her corset were a sudden prison. He commanded, "Elsewhere you must call me 'Professor.' And—as I am still your professor, here and everywhere on these grounds— do as I say: get out of my office. And keep your silence or all is lost. More than you can possibly know."

"But—"

"I shall silence you by any method necessary," he finished, staring wistfully at her lips.

"Is that a threat?"

He smiled sadly at her breathy, hopeful reply. "Out. Mercy, I say. I'll call for you soon." Stepping out the door, she turned, but he waved her on and she could see the battle in his eyes. "Sweet dreams, sweet Persephone. Sweet dreams."

A tall dark figure burst into the headmistress's office, muttering to himself, and Rebecca jumped, her pen scrawling across her paper. "Alexi—dear God, knock, will you? Your presence is startling enough as is."

Her friend crossed to the window, brooding.

"What is it, Alexi?"

"Prophecy," he breathed.

Rebecca rose anxiously from her chair. "Did you see the sign? Was there a door?"

"Not exactly," Alexi admitted. "I . . . I need to clear my mind. But there's an answer here, timid as she is, *unexpected* as she is. But, must I not wait? This admission is just between us for the moment, Rebecca. Until I have more proof, until I have—"

"You've been speaking with Miss Linden?"

Alexi turned. "No."

Rebecca raised an eyebrow. "No? After everything I've alerted you to, in more than one infuriating conversation? Who do you think it is, if not her? The rest of us are sure she's the one! Placed in our path as she was . . . Didn't you sense it? Why else would you send her into the tavern? What in the world are you on about?"

Alexi scowled, dropping into the seat opposite.

Rebecca sighed. "Alexi, come now. Elijah spoke of how Miss Linden looked at you at the gala—as if she'd come home. I knew from the first that there was something powerful and fateful about her, but you've been nothing but rude. When you disappeared she was crestfallen. She said you seemed distracted. Where *did* you wander the night of the ball? If not Miss Linden, who in the world—?"

Alexi warmed at the thought of Miss Parker's face by moonlight, and foreign sensations wrestled in his stomach. "I was waltzing."

Rebecca snorted. "Ah, yes, that's right. With whom?"

"A girl far too unique to feel comfortable in that gaudy, flighty crowd. A girl who forsook the frivolous sparkle of chandeliers for the simple moonlight of the upper foyer."

Though Alexi attempted to remove the poetry from his voice, Rebecca was not fooled. "How popular you've become, Alexi. Who could have imagined?" She took a long breath and spoke through clenched teeth. "And so you yet place your bets upon Miss Parker."

"You should have told me about her the moment she stepped through our doors, rather than leaving me alone to think we'd enrolled a ghost," Alexi reproached. "We should have used all our gifts to glean her information. Did your instincts not cry out when you met her?"

Rebecca shrugged, unable to look at him. "A bit."

"A bit?" Alexi cried. "And you didn't tell me? Rebecca, can I not trust you?"

"For the love of God, did we not set boundaries?" she defended herself. "Need I remind you *once again* that she is a student? I don't like this, Alexi; it is surely a trap as your goddess warned. And, how am I to keep this school running if you fail to obey the rules of propriety? I ought to fire you and expel her!"

"Rebecca—"

"You're threatening everything we've worked so hard to create!"

"I'm doing nothing but trying to determine Prophecy. It isn't me who now has a problem talking about things—it's you! There are forces that press our boundaries, however carefully and sensibly we might have placed them. Do you know Miss Parker's full name, Rebecca?"

"I do not recall. Shall I find out?" the headmistress asked, exasperated. "So you may send a bouquet?"

"Persephone," Alexi replied. "*Persephone* Parker."

"Persephone," Rebecca repeated blankly.

"Yes. Don't you find that interesting?"

"What, are we now looking for the bride of the underworld?"

"Yes, since she was the one who appeared to us all those years ago."

Rebecca looked dubious. "You believe this because of all the references to the spirit world? You believe that is the reason we are here at *Athens* Academy, because a Greek goddess has entwined us in her mythology?"

His friend was trying to make it sound absurd, but Alexi would have none of it. "Yes, of course—because it makes perfect sense! She bears our clue in her very name. That, and the phoenix pendant she wears about her neck."

Rebecca leaned back. "A phoenix?"

"A pendant that burned her at the very moment I cried out for a sign the other night," Alexi explained.

Rebecca bit her lip. "It burned her? Couldn't that be a sign of the opposite, actually warning us against her? And these coincidences, Alexi, however uncanny, are nothing. Not if there isn't a door—the one definite we were given in a host of damnable ambiguities. Aren't you the one always counseling patience? I tell you, Alexi, we need more than a myth, a pale face and a pendant. And . . . the others are sure it's Miss Linden."

"It isn't up to the others."

"Alexi, we're all in this—"

"She's mine to find!"

"And ours to agree on!" Rebecca cried in response, her face reddening and her pitch rising. "Does Miss Parker know about any of this? About our work, and about the danger? Does she know that you're pinning your hopes on an untried girl who's a . . . On an untried *girl,* Alexi!"

Alexi shook his head, glowering. "I'm more cautious than that. You of all people should know my code." He rose and hovered over her. "But, Rebecca . . . she knew our incantation. She sang it to me. It came to her in her mind. She's the one—our seventh. You'll see that I'm right!"

He wasn't acting himself, and they both realized the fact. Rebecca just shook her head and said, "Alexi, the hour grows late. We've no time for games."

He sighed and, in a splay of dark fabric, collapsed into his chair. "Am I to have no support or encouragement from you? You, who are my oldest and dearest confidante?"

His friend shook her head, an ache in her voice that almost matched the uncharacteristic pleading in his. "Alexi, I do not mean to be difficult. I am simply frightened of mistaking Prophecy. Please, do not entangle your heart," she added. "It only will make matters worse. You need to give Miss Linden objective consideration. Remember your obligation!"

"My obligation?" Alexi hissed. "What else have I ever thought of? Has there been a door?"

"No, not yet. But—"

"Then I'm not concerned. I believe what I believe." A sudden frown furrowed his brow. "Rebecca, why are you so set on this woman when I'm so certain it is Miss Parker?"

His friend's eyes flashed. "Because, Alexi, as I've said more times than I wish to recall, Prophecy has nothing to do with you *caring* for our seventh, and—"

He gave her a cold look and interrupted: "Yet I've always known it would."

Rebecca glanced down at her desk, blinked and swallowed a few times before looking back up at him. "Alexi, why are you looking for love elsewhere? It has been staring you in the face since that day, forever ago, on Westminster Bridge."

There was a horrible, embarrassing silence. Alexi stared deeply into the eyes of his dearest friend, his confidante . . . but not his lover. Never that.

"Aye," he sighed. "There's the rub. I'm sorry, Rebecca."

"Don't tell me you didn't know already," she said with a sorrowful laugh.

"I care for you, Rebecca. I always have. Perhaps if we had lived other lives, I could have made you my wife."

Her face contorted. "Oh, thank you," she said. "Thank you very much for that declaration of pity. Dear God—"

"Certainly not *pity*, Rebecca."

"What, you cannot tell me . . . Do you love Miss Parker, then?" she hissed, almost inaudibly, staring at her desk.

Alexi made a face. "Rebecca," he finally sighed. "I am doing my best. This is not easy for any of us. I need your help."

"You had best make sure she stays quiet about whatever you have . . . done to her."

"I've not ruined her, if that's what you're—"

His friend held up a hand, wincing. "I don't want to hear it. Prophecy aside, we'll lose everything here if the staff is proven scandalous hypocrites. I'd not hesitate to send either of you packing. I will expel her if this becomes a problem."

"Stop threatening me," Alexi barked. "I've insisted on secrecy. The dear girl will do anything I ask. Anything."

Rebecca eyed him. "Don't you dare be smug about that, Alexi. Not about that."

He looked at her for a long moment before his expression softened. "I know you're in a difficult position, Rebecca. In many ways. Trying times befall every mortal given our destiny. We are no different than any before us."

"We know nothing of those that came before us," she spat.

"I wish they'd have left notes and a guidebook. But I suppose you are right, trying times is our lot."

Alexi smiled and gave her a tentative smile. "I would have hoped, after two decades, you might have learned I'm *always* right."

Rebecca just groaned.

"Well, I'm off!" He rose quickly, exhibiting a youthful energy she'd not seen from him for years. He anticipated her calling him back, however, and so he turned at the door and leveled a stare at her. "Caution. I know, I know," he promised gently. Then he disappeared into the hall.

Rebecca sat quietly, staring at the closed door. Finally, ignoring the pain searing her heart, she filed the documents she'd been handling and again cursed her life.

CHAPTER TWENTY-ONE

The crack began as a hairline fissure. The fissure then split. The window pane burst, and a shard of glass fell and struck Josephine's hand where she was stacking dessert plates. *"Merde!"* she spat.

Walking to the front of La Belle, Josephine stared down the alley to see a glowing woman in rags who was tearing at transparent hair and throwing her head back in a silent rage; she floated several inches off the ground, and it was her wails that had destroyed the window. Josephine returned and found Elijah, and pointedly drew him away from his conversation with Miss Lucille Linden. "Lord Withersby—a word with you?"

"Yes, my dove?" he murmured, leaning across the counter.

"We've got a shrieker heading due south. My, there's been a lot of them lately."

Elijah glanced to the window. "I suppose you'll make me replace that glass?"

"Tell Jane and Michael. What shall we do with Miss Linden?"

"I'll wipe her."

"Do you think she'll take to it?"

"Almost everyone does. It was said Prophecy won't have *exactly* our powers, so it should take. She didn't come running when the dog was on the loose, remember? Or when I abandoned her at the gala, either! We'll return with no time passed. Although, to tell the truth . . . would it be so harmful for her to see what we do? We have to address Prophecy with her, and soon. Let's just show her—"

"Non." Josephine shook her head. "Only with Alexi's blessing, Elijah. You know that."

"But he's never here anymore. I think something's wrong with him. We may have to take matters into our own hands. Let's just bring her along."

"Elijah, do you want to explain to Alexi why you broke our compact without his approval? And Rebecca isn't even here to ask."

The impetuous gentleman pouted and eventually shook his head.

Jane, who had forsaken her usual solitude to spend a pleasant evening at the tavern with her friends, sensed both the spirit and the blood on Josephine's hand. Rising from the table she said, "If ye'll be so kind as to excuse us, Miss Linden?" She eyed the woman with caution, no matter her self-professed desperate circumstances and the other Guards' approval. From the moment they met, Jane found Miss Linden a bit too nice and certainly too beautiful. But there was an unmistakable something about her, something to be learned, so she could not be dismissed outright.

"Of course," the woman replied sweetly.

Carrying her teacup to the counter, Jane grasped Josephine's hand, knowing which was bloodied without having seen it. Dragging a finger over the cut, she concentrated until the Frenchwoman's skin closed over.

Elijah approached Miss Linden. "We'll return in a moment, and you won't even know we were gone," he said quietly, staring deep into her eyes and waving a hand before her face. The beautiful woman stared blankly ahead, and the assembled company evaluated her.

"Is she out?" Josephine asked.

"Looks snuffed to me," Michael chortled, rising from the table and bounding out the door.

They tore down the alley toward the tortured spectre in rags. In her wake, glass windows had cracked or burst. Running past, the group wheeled around to block the spirit's departure. As they lifted clasped hands, sparks of thin blue lightning coursed between their bodies. The ghost stopped and stared at them, agape.

Random passersby approached, but Elijah sent them wandering off with a flutter of a hand and a sardonic smile. They wouldn't remember a thing.

The four opened their mouths and a sweet, simple lullaby rose into the air. The spirit clawed at her hollow face, and her form flickered. One by one The Guard moved their hands toward the spirit, and Michael let loose a jovial laugh. The spirit blinked. She opened a sagging jaw as if to recommence her netherworld wailing, but the four placed their fingers to their lips and a soft "Shhhh" echoed down the alley. The old woman's jaw closed and she hung her head. Her form slowly sank into the cobblestone street.

Lucille Linden watched all of this from the front door of the café with a wide smile. As the four made to return, she was quick to resume her seat at the table and play along for one last moment.

Laughing, the group walked to the bar, and Josephine began to pour glasses of wine. Elijah approached and snapped his fingers in front of Lucille's face. She looked up at him with a knowing smirk.

"Why is it," she murmured, her eyes alight, "that spirits are always hanging about you and your friends, and you feel the need to go and play with them? I simply must speak with that professor of yours."

Elijah Withersby stared at her, glanced at the others and squirmed.

"Why are you so quiet?" Marianna scolded Percy. The two were sitting at the courtyard fountain.

"Because I've nothing to say. Do you still think I wandered off with someone the night of the ball? Just because you and Edward were chatting until dawn and had to resort to all manner of trickery to sneak into your respective halls doesn't mean I was so inclined."

The German girl giggled uncontrollably. Percy hadn't seen much of her friend now that Edward was around, but she did not take offense; there was plenty to preoccupy her. While she dared not even a hint, she was dying to rhapsodize about the joy of being so near Alexi, to be kissed by Alexi . . . but she couldn't say a word and could only wonder if she'd ever be kissed again. She spent a great deal of time wondering that.

"Something is different about you. You seem less timid. Older, somehow."

Percy only smiled, her tinted glasses obscuring what naked eyes might have betrayed.

Miss Jennings startled them. "There you are, Miss Parker! I've been looking for you. This was tacked to your door," the bumbling woman blurted, eyeing the two girls suspiciously. Then she wandered off as if confused.

Percy and Marianna glanced at each other and laughed. "Poor old dear! Well. What can that be?" Marianna asked.

Recognizing the precise script, Percy took care to shield it from her friend.

To the pale nymph whom it concerns:
Our meetings must now commence more regularly. Tonight,
wear something fine.
Yours,
—A

Percy lost her breath, staring.

"Well?"

"Oh...Nothing at all. Reverend Mother wishing me well on an upcoming exam."

"Truly? I saw a spot of colour rise to your cheek, right there." Marianna poked her friend in the jaw.

"No."

"Let me see the note."

"Marianna, please," Percy begged.

There was an edge to her voice that Marianna dared not question further, so the German girl said, "You are hiding from me. Perhaps you must. But I do hope, soon, you will trust me enough that no matter how strange, or forbidden—"

"Of course I trust you, dear heart," Percy interrupted. "Just allow me my silence. There are certain things I am not at liberty to discuss. Not at present. Please forgive me."

"You do seem older," Marianna stated quietly. "Only, answer me this. When we first met, you told me your wish—to find someone or something that could explain your destiny. Have you found this?"

"I may have," Percy admitted.

"Good, then." Marianna nodded. "That is good."

"Yes." But as Percy looked up, past Promethe Hall, her blood chilled. The sky held a sparkling prismatic quality and also a new addition. Silhouetted horsemen rode the clouds. They were galloping in place between earth and sky, and she almost felt the distant beat of the horses' hooves as if they were the pounding of her heart. She had no idea what the shadows were, or what they could mean. Stranger still, she was surer than ever she heard dogs barking, deep growls and roars. She did not realize she voiced a whimper.

"What is it, Percy?"

Casting aside her weighty dread, she glanced to her friend and then again at the sky. The vapourous horsemen were gone. "Must have been a vision—something I thought I saw past those walls."

Still, there was yelping in the distance. Something was closing in.

Hours later, Percy paced her room. As the clock chimed quarter of six, she looked at herself in the mirror to find delirious panic upon her face. She'd done the best she could: swept up her hair with filigree barrettes, applied a bit of colour to her lips and cheeks, donned a midnight blue dress—a bit of finery sent by Reverend Mother. She clasped her pendant higher up on her neck so that it lay just over and covered her fateful burn. With bell cuffs of lace, a scooped neck and a doubled skirt, Percy hoped she was "fine" enough for whatever adventure lay ahead.

A sudden thought made her quake. Did he plan to take her out somewhere? Was he prepared for how people would stare? She fought back a fit of worried tears and tucked a thin scarf and glasses into her reticule.

Throwing a dark hooded cloak about her shoulders, she sneaked out the back door of her hall and kept to the courtyard shadows, avoiding any exterior doors where guards would be posted. She scurried to the professor's office and knocked.

Rather than bidding her enter, Alexi opened the door and drew her in. His hand on hers caused frissons through her body. "Good evening, Percy."

"Good evening, Profess—ah, Alexi," Percy murmured, her eyes huge.

His sharp features were inscrutable but his eyes sparkled.

With what Percy hoped was reluctance, he released her hand and moved to take her cloak. His firm hand lingered on her shoulder. She held her breath.

A fire and the candelabras were blazing. He moved to place her cloak on the coat tree where his professorial robe was draped. He wore a blousy grey silk shirt beneath a thick black velvet vest cut perfectly to fit his broad torso. Music crackled from the phonograph. Bach.

Handing her a glass of white wine, he did not seem to mind how she stared at him. "Thank you for coming, Percy. Of course, there's no tutorial tonight."

"What then, Alexi?"

"I thought I'd whisk you off to the opera. You look ravishing."

"The opera?" Percy exclaimed. "What a grand surprise! To what do I owe this honour?" Her eyes clouded in a mercurial and unexpected panic. "Oh, Alexi, tell me this is not some game to you, some fleeting fancy that dares scandal and cruelty. I'm too fragile for such sport."

"I dare much, Percy, but not cruelty," he replied. "I wish to do nothing but what is meant to be."

"So cryptic, Alexi!" she murmured.

"Forgive me, my dear, but I can speak no other way," he replied.

Percy felt feverish. As he kissed her gently on the cheek, his lips lingered too long to be polite; then he broke away, anxious. Percy nearly stumbled forward, having melted all too easily against him.

"I'm sorry, Miss Parker," he whispered.

"For what?" she asked, fisting her hands at her sides to keep from reaching out for him.

"For being unable to keep myself from touching you." He spoke through clenched teeth and moved to lean against his great marble desk, gripping it as if to maintain stability.

"Oh, Alexi, please! I never dreamed a man would have such a problem with *me*." She giggled in spite of herself.

"You can't know how much . . ." She trailed off, because he looked pained. "Don't apologize for what you've done to— *for* me." She blushed. "I didn't know life could be so thrilling until you first walked into my classroom."

His expression was fraught with secrets, and they drove Percy wild. He shook his head and remarked, "I hardly believe that my walking in a room could have much effect."

"Oh, but it did," she assured him, laughing nervously. "You terrified me."

"And do I still terrify you?"

"Always," she whispered. But a smile twitched at her lips.

Alexi smiled broadly. Such a smile was rare and beautiful. Delighted, Percy returned it, feeling so radiantly happy that her face could never contain the beams. "Why, Professor, to see such an expression on your face! I thought you too cool a character."

"Now is not the appropriate time to test my temperature, Miss Parker," he murmured, and gave her a glass. "To the number seven," he toasted, when they each held a libation.

"Whatever it may mean," Percy countered, leveling a gaze at him as she carefully sipped, unused to tasting wine in any place save for Holy Communion. "Were it not for the strange things that have happened all my life, I might think you suggest something wicked."

"You think me wicked?" Alexi asked, a small smirk curving his mouth.

"Captivating, cunning and, I fear, wholly above my grasp . . ." Percy stopped short, biting her lip. Perhaps she was going too far and there should be no discussion of grasps. She took a breath, leaned forward and continued, "You're not the only one sensing fate, Alexi. I'm seeing new and terrifying things. Beyond your window, silhouetted horsemen ride the sky. I hear the dull pounding of their horses' hooves and the terrible barking of dogs! Something is about to happen, Alexi. Something that I do not understand is *meant* to happen. I feel it in my bones, and I must tell you that as delighted as I am to be here in your presence, I'm also frighten—"

There was a loud knock at the door. Percy jumped. She and Alexi looked at each other and Percy went to the desk without a word, plucking up her scarf and throwing it around her head, taking a book into her hands and placing the wine out of sight.

"Yes?" Alexi called.

Headmistress Thompson entered the room. Her eyes seized on Percy, who was attempting to appear studious.

"Ah," the headmistress began, giving Alexi a wary glare. "Have I stumbled upon a tutorial . . . at this hour?"

"Yes."

"But it is a weekend." The headmistress eyed the lovely dress Percy wore, which was hardly attire for schoolwork. Percy's heart pounded. They were surely found out, and she would be expelled!

"Miss Parker requires my assistance—as you know," Alexi stated. "How might I assist *you*?"

There was a troubling strain in his voice.

"You have a visitor who wishes a word with you, Professor—Miss Lucille Linden," the headmistress stated. Her voice was similarly strained.

Partially hidden behind the headmistress, Percy turned to glimpse the beautiful woman she had first seen at the ball. Something exploded within her. A rebellious part of Percy wished to proclaim that she and Alexi weren't in the midst of a tutorial at all, but rather discussing the correct manner in which to commence a scandalous affair—and could they please be left to it? But staring at Alexi with a fierce mixture of panic and confusion, Percy simply shook her head.

Alexi, seeming similarly at a loss, hesitated. "Miss Thompson, would you allow us one further moment? I am advising Miss Parker on a personal matter in regard to a return to the convent. As she has no family to answer her questions, I consider it my duty to finish my appraisal. Would Miss Linden be so kind as to wait upon the bench outside? Miss Parker will send her in as she departs."

"Well, then," the headmistress bristled. "Good evening to you both."

The door shut behind the two uninvited women. Percy turned again to Alexi, and words tumbled forth before she could stop them. "Thank you for giving me a moment. I know that that woman outside is far more beautiful than I could ever hope to be, Alexi, and so I beg you not to trifle with my heart. If there should be something between you—"

"Percy, truly!"

She could not help herself. "So much is secret about you, Alexi. I'm wary of your silence. However . . . whatever may happen here between you and her, should you advance similarly upon her as you did me, remember, there are witnesses." She gestured to a floating figure near the phonograph. The spectral boy smiled and waved. "And remember, I can speak with them."

"Why, Miss Parker!"

"I only now realize that there are times when timidity must be abandoned, Alexi, and that there are things worth a fight. I'm weary of spending my life afraid of what I do not know." Percy sighed, weary beyond her years, and rose to her feet. "I wish we could've gone to the opera tonight, but then again, I never thought I could. Good evening, and I'll await your next instruction." She gave the window a glance and added, "Make it soon, Professor, as I've no idea how quickly those horsemen outside may advance."

She curtseyed lightly and glided to the door, where she turned. "Lastly, yes—in my opinion, you are worth a fight." Then she exited, leaving him staring after her, slack-jawed.

As she proceeded down the hall, Percy thought about the scarf around her head. Steeling her courage, she whipped it off and strode down to the dimly lit rotunda at the center of the second floor. There she found Miss Linden on a small marble bench, sweeping skirts a sea of emerald around an ir-ritatingly beautiful physique. Her eyes as bright green as her dress, Miss Linden's attention snapped to Percy, and when their eyes met Miss Linden gasped. A threatened fascination began to work its way over her beautiful, creamy-skinned features, and the look gave Percy a jolt of satisfaction.

She held her head high. If this was indeed a rivalry, she would stake a strong claim. "Good evening, Miss Linden, I am Percy Parker. Professor Rychman will see you now. The professor is very kind to me and spends a great deal of time concerned with my welfare, as would any truly gifted . . . tutor."

"Of course. I'm certain he's very talented," the beauty replied.

"Yes. I owe him much," Percy stated, flashing a smile and politely inclining her head. "Have a pleasant evening, Miss Linden."

The woman's eyes suddenly clouded. "Forgive me, Miss Parker, but . . . are you human? The professor seems to keep strange company."

The words cut to the quick, but Percy mastered herself. "I assure you: while I look like a ghost, I'm no spirit or demon. I'm nothing but a girl struggling to make her way in an intolerant world. I bleed, I love, and someday, I'll die. And you?"

Miss Linden smiled. "Much the same."

"Indeed. Good night." And with that, Percy swept off. But she could not help but turn her thoughts again to Alexi. *Strange company?* What would this woman know about it, or about him? To feel so close to someone and yet have no idea about his soul or his thoughts . . . Percy clenched her jaw and fled to her room.

Alexi shook the lingering effects of Percy's presence from his mind and opened the door to find the exquisite Miss Linden. "A pleasure to see you again, mademoiselle," he stated with a polite bow, gesturing her inside. "Do have a seat."

His visitor took her time evaluating his office and finally sat, turning to offer him a winning smile. "It is wonderful to see *you* again, Professor."

He nodded. "You're looking lovely as ever."

"Thank you, Professor." Her eyes sparked as she smiled. "Appearances are so important, are they not?"

"Perhaps," Alexi replied, uncertain if she referenced his being closeted with a student. "I trust you are well since last I saw you at the ball? I regret that work prevented me from bidding you a proper good evening, I hope you'll not find me hopelessly rude."

Miss Linden's smile remained flawless, but she spoke with crisp efficiency. "Professor, I have no doubt we could continue charming pleasantries for quite some time, but might I propose that we set such delights aside and press right on to the point?"

Alexi raised an eyebrow. "I did not know you and I had business."

"As a matter of fact," the woman promised, "we do."

"Well, then, Miss Linden, please be so kind as to enlighten me."

The beauty leaned forward, her green eyes both inviting and mesmerizing. "It would appear, Professor, that you need me."

CHAPTER TWENTY-TWO

The door of the café burst open and an impressive whirlwind of black fabric and wild dark hair made a direct line toward an unsuspecting Elijah Withersby. Lifting him from his seat by a thin arm, Alexi dragged the startled Elijah to a corner of the café and bent over him, transfixing him with an arctic gaze. The few patrons remaining at such a late hour who did not belong to The Guard looked on in titillated interest, while Alexi's friends looked on in alarm.

"Hullo, Alexi, fancy seeing you here—"

"What did you tell her?" Alexi hissed, inches from Elijah's nose.

"What?"

"What did you tell Miss Linden?"

"Oh, her." Elijah smiled nervously. "Well, she failed to take to the wipe, Alexi; we thought she was clean—"

"She wasn't. She watched your entire little dance with that shrieker."

"Well, yes, we gathered that."

"Just a few moments ago she told me all about it, in immaculate detail. I thought she might present me a dainty watercolour rendition of the scene. Now she wants to help. It came to my attention that you let on we were looking for an addition. Did you?"

Elijah squirmed.

"Did you?"

"Alexi, let go of me, and let's not make a scene, shall we? Sit down and I'll tell you what was said. Quietly."

Alexi reluctantly released his grip, and Elijah rubbed his arm. The two joined the table where Michael and Rebecca sat watching. Alexi glowered at them all.

"Alexi, listen," Elijah began. "Miss Linden has been so intrigued—particularly by you, if you've been paying any bloody attention. She's been taking refuge here at the café from God knows what, always inquires about you and feels connected to us . . . and, Alexi, we all feel it, too." He looked at the others, who nodded. "When I found out that she could see everything we did, I drew her aside and inquired more of her. She confessed that disturbing things have always happened to her, and she wanted to know if we could shed light on her condition. I said my friends and I enjoyed a good haunting, and would be happy to hear her experiences—"

"And that you were looking for someone! Someone like her! You had no right to impart our secrets!" Alexi snarled.

Rebecca's eyes widened. "Did you tell her that, Elijah? Without consulting us first?"

"I was terribly vague! I didn't share any secrets!" Elijah hissed. "I believe in nothing more than the subtle nature of our work, but she *saw*—"

"Did you ever mention me as anything other than a friend?"

"Well, other than my usual sarcasms . . . no," he replied.

"Whatever you may have hinted at, Miss Linden has without a doubt pinned me as your leader," Alexi stated. "I told her she was a lunatic for giving me such credit, though I couldn't fault her taste." An amused grin hitched at his lips.

"Alexi, open your damn eyes. She's who we're looking for!" Elijah snapped, emboldened by the sudden glimpse of levity. "The strength of my conviction is the reason I spoke of things I'd never, under any other circumstance, dare to reveal."

Michael and Rebecca stared anxiously at Alexi, who took a measured breath. He was careful to make his next declaration a calm one. "I would not be so sure."

"You just wait. I would bet the Withersby estate that we'll see a portal door any day now."

Alexi set his jaw. "But it is not the time to be loose-lipped."

It would not do to discredit Elijah's beliefs, for Alexi understood his friend's reasoning. Yet he himself had a different notion, needed Prophecy to be otherwise, though he had only corollary proof. He glanced at Rebecca, who simply stared at him in silence.

"Why are you so hesitant, Alexi?" Josephine asked, moving to join the group at the table.

"There is . . . something else," he replied.

Michael adjusted his vicar's collar and pressed, "If you have strong presentiments, you must share them. We have a right to be privy to your thoughts on this matter."

"Of course, and you will hear them," Alexi agreed.

"Eventually. But for now you must not speak of anything to anyone outside of this group. Until you see a door as Prophecy decreed, I want you to keep Miss Linden at bay and in the dark. There may be plots afoot. We cannot know whom to trust."

The Guard nodded, though it was clear they were all on edge.

Alexi offered to accompany Rebecca back to the academy. A carriage awaited them at the corner, so he helped her into the cab and took the seat across from her. The ride, save for the clatter of wheels over cobblestones, was silent for quite some time.

He felt Rebecca's eyes bore into him, and he waited for her to speak.

"So, after that meeting you remain fixed. You stand by her as your choice?"

"Hmm?" Alexi kept his eyes on the passing alleyways of the dark city.

"Miss Parker. She remains your choice. I mean, you had her in your office after hours and on a weekend! For God's sake, did I not tell you to be cautious? I'll ask you again. Not that it has anything to do with Prophecy, but will make things more complicated: do you *love* her, Alexi?"

He heard the words and could only turn to stare at his friend for a long moment. Finally he admitted, "I'm not sure I would know it if I did."

Rebecca's eyes narrowed with weary skepticism. "You would know, Alexi."

"No, I don't know that I would," he insisted, his broad shoulders tight with worry. "I forbade myself the very thought for so long, thinking only of that ethereal goddess we saw once in our youths . . . I forbade myself all sentiment until the time was right."

"And now the time is right." Rebecca sighed. "Is *she?*"

Alexi closed his eyes and leaned back into the leather of his seat. "In so many ways."

Rebecca's mouth contorted into an ugly grimace, but she kept silent.

The driver stopped in front of Promethe Hall. Alexi descended from the carriage and helped Rebecca out. Uncertain moments passed. Finally, she moved to embrace him and he returned it hesitantly. Ominous clouds began to tumble in on the whole of London, covering the moon with their dark mass. The salt taste of unsettled forces was potent in the air.

As she drew back, there was a moment where Rebecca lingered and watched his face, but she could see his mind labouring with conflict. She pulled away completely and murmured, "Bring her to us. Nothing else can be done until you bring her to us. We must see what you see, otherwise there shall be no happy end to Prophecy at all."

He nodded slowly. "Good night, my dear."

As Alexi turned and walked away, Rebecca felt something sharp drive deeper into her bosom. His footsteps echoed back from the broken stones of the narrow, pillared alley to the side of the great Athens portico, on toward Apollo Hall. She listened to those footfalls and waited for them to stop, to perhaps turn around, for him to come back and admit he was a fool for denying her all these years. Of course they did not.

She cursed herself for not taking advantage of his moment of hesitancy. She might have simply pressed her lips to his, to know what it would feel like, to know what she might have enjoyed were they not fated to such damnably odd lives. But a woman did not simply kiss a man, however long she'd known him and however much she cared for him; it would not do. These damnable standards of propriety kept her a gentlewoman but made her feel as hollow as the ghosts she saw.

While she was cursing things, she spared a moment for her morals. The damned Work kept her always on guard, never appreciated. If she wasn't sure that people would die without her contribution, she would have walked away from her fate long ago. Pressing her hand to the creases of her aging flesh, she wished a fleeting wish she would never dare utter: that her skin were younger and deathly white.

Heaving open the great front doors of the academy, she nodded curtly to the guard inside. Then, heedless of the hour, she went to her desk, listened in isolation to the coming storm.

The spirit who often floated near the chandelier in the main hall drifted through her door and bobbed up and down. Rebecca looked up and barked, "What do you want?"

The spirit frowned, and it appeared as though he was about to cry.

"Oh, for God's sake," Rebecca muttered. Exaggeratedly, she winked. Ghosts were creatures of routine, she had learned. It was always her custom to look up and wink at the young spirit, but she'd stormed past tonight and ignored him. Appeased, he remained staring at her with helpless sadness, as if he wanted to help but knew he couldn't. He mouthed something that looked like it could have been the word "Mother" before he vanished back through the door, but she couldn't be sure.

At one point in her life, she would have found the scene emotionally powerful, beautiful and endearing; it would have renewed her faith in her work and herself, in that she mattered to those around her. But tonight she found no comfort even in the storm that broke overhead, and saw other clouds that would darken all her remaining days. She could think only of Alexi, realize he did not and could not return her feelings, that he was captivated instead by snow-white tresses and eyes shaded by glass, captivated perhaps to the point of catastrophe.

She wondered how to stop him. After a long moment of contemplation, she wrote a letter to the reverend mother of Miss Parker's convent. She could, with these few simple sentences, send the girl packing. But . . . Alexi would not forgive her.

Her pen stilled on the page as another thought occurred: Was this about Prophecy at all, or did she, without warrant, hate that ghost of a girl for purely personal reasons? Was she, Rebecca Thompson, one of those fated, as Prophecy warned, to be a betrayer?

Her sadness hardened inside as she put her face in her hands to cry. When all was said and done, there would be no heart of hers left to love or to betray.

Percy had been pacing her room for hours, brooding and refusing to take down her hair or remove her lovely dress despite the time. A sharp rap sounded at the door, startling her. Flying to attend, she found nothing outside save a note tacked beneath the fading room number:

> Come to the office. Presently.
> —A

Making an eager bolt for Apollo Hall via out-of-the-way passages she had previously determined, she found dread gnawing at her nerves. The distant barking seemed nearer, and Percy could have sworn dark shapes were scurrying in the shadows. All manner of strangeness frolicked with un-usual menace this night.

Before she ducked into the hall, the night sky made her pause. There was something new and alarming about the closeness of that sparkling canopy of stars. It was as if, for the first time ever, she was aware of the heavens as a finite layer, and this was because a small line was being drawn above, a thin line like lightning, fractured and splitting further. The sky was *cracking*.

Percy ran up the few flights of stairs to Alexi's office, darted in without knocking and closed the door, her heart in her throat. He was there waiting, standing pensively at his mantel, drinking the glass of wine he'd poured himself ear-lier. Hers remained untouched.

Her churning heart was elated to see him, yet she was fearful of any new knowledge that this meeting might provide. Deciding to keep the madness of her latest sight to herself, she focused on trying to control her breath and on enjoying the wonders of the man before her—if indeed she had any opportunity.

"Are you all right, Persephone?" he asked.

She set her jaw. "Never mind me. You?"

"Thank you for returning."

"Of course."

The two fell into a long silence, staring at each other.

Finally, overwhelmed by emotion, Percy could no longer maintain his stare and broke from it. Eternity lay within his eyes, and all she wanted was to collapse in his hold and feel safe and loved. "What did she want with you, Alexi?" she blurted, unable to keep jealousy from her tone. "Beautiful as she was."

"She wanted to join my club," was his reply.

"You have a club?" Percy turned, raising an eyebrow. "Let me guess—a club of six, looking for someone new. To make seven."

"Yes," he replied.

"And what, may I ask, is the purpose of this club?"

"Public service, Percy, nothing more," Alexi remarked. "Now, I still owe you an opera, dear girl, but for now I need you to tell me—do you still see foreboding shapes on the horizon?" He directed her gaze out the window.

Percy looked. Nodding, she gulped, for the sky resembled an eggshell waiting to split. "Yes, the silhouettes are still there. I hear whispers, too, and strange noises. And I see . . . other frightening things. But I cannot make out what the whispers are telling me, nor why I'm seeing what I see. Every now and then I hear the ticking of a clock, though there be none near me. And barking. That barking! I feel fevered. Please don't think me mad, Alexi—"

"I never did," he interrupted.

"The air is full of dread. I'm tired of seeing doors and shadowy figures and flames when there's so much beauty in the world," she murmured, staring longingly at Alexi's face for a moment before turning away.

"The visions are coming to me nightly now," she admitted, rising from her chair and crossing behind the desk. She inched toward Alexi's throne of a chair, desperate to be closer to him. Expecting to be rebuffed, she was instead surprised when he reached out and took one of her cool white hands and pressed it to his lips; she gave a tiny gasp.

Percy could not take her eyes away from the shape and sensation of his mouth against her hand. A shiver worked up her spine, but his eyes stayed riveted to hers, his lips lingering on her flesh—the most sensual sight she could imagine. Her other hand was instantly required to steady herself upon the marble.

Alexi released her hand but not her eyes, and Percy felt her head spin with a glimpse of a vision: The city raced by. She held on to a strong form as their horse pounded onward, away from something terrible—

Percy blinked, returning from the blur of the vision to see that her hands were now clenched into trembling fists and she'd sunken into her chair once again. Dread of the vision lingered like acrid smoke in her nostrils.

Alexi was watching her. "And where did you just go, Percy?"

"I was on horseback, speeding away from London as if pursued. Something is . . ." She shivered violently. The distant barking had reached a crescendo and then fallen silent; it had not been silent in days. The temperature in the room dropped an immediate, drastic number of degrees. The hairs on the back of her neck rose and froze. There was a distant echoing sound, like glass shattering, though no glass rained down upon her. "Pursued," she repeated, suddenly terrified.

A shadowy form rose slowly from behind Percy's chair, a

pulsating black silhouette with the head of a huge, crimson-eyed, bloody-fanged dog. The form flickered and became a collection of canine bodies fused together, one head shifting into three, into ten, into forty. One dog or a hundred, they were all from hell. And this familiar foe rose over Percy, chilling Alexi to the bone.

"Alexi, is it just my imagination, or did the room just turn very cold?" she asked, and if her flesh could have gone a shade paler, it would have.

Alexi's mind spun at great speeds. "Percy, listen carefully. Close your eyes. Don't question me, just do as I say."

"Why? What—"

"Do as I say!"

Percy closed her eyes and trembled.

Alexi stood with silent ferocity, staring down the vapourous animal opposite him. Blue fire appeared along his hands, and he locked the creature in a battle of wills. It sniffed Percy, and she whimpered.

"Alexi, what in God's name is behind me?"

"Quiet! Rise slowly and keep your eyes closed. Swing widely to your right and run to the door. Run down to the stables, and get a boy to ready my horse and bring him to the portico where I shall attend you. Percy, you *must* do as I say." They would trust in her vision, if she had the courage to obey him.

Unsteadily, she rose to her feet, her eyes still closed as he'd instructed. But when the monster's strange, bestial growl erupted beside her, she cried out. "Alexi!"

"Do as I say!"

Percy ran to the door and disappeared, but not before she shouted, "I'll wait for you. Come quickly!"

The beast growled, swiping angrily at the air where Percy had been. Its gruesome maw shifted from flickering cloud into a more tangible mass, a single, horrific hound's head, and that snarled, preparing to strike.

Alexi called upon all the inner forces that had made him

more than mortal for years. Each subsequent beat of his heart fortified a separate particular anger. Facing this beast alone, he felt an ancient rage not entirely his own, and this tore out of him, fiery and defensive; it was an old wound, an old score yet to be settled.

From his lips thundered a powerful command. For a moment the canine nightmare seemed frozen, deflated. Gritting his teeth, Alexi felt lightning course through his veins. A wind swept the room, scattering papers and whipping his black hair across his forehead. Halos of fire surrounded Alexi's outstretched hands, crackling to be released.

The abomination leaned back on pulsing haunches and tilted a vague head, knowing that it had been commanded. Fire burst from Alexi's fingertips, and it yelped and retreated. Then, in a burst of frantic barking, the form shifted into a hundred doglike forms that disappeared like roaches from light, snorting as they vanished through the walls. Only barking lingered in the air.

Alexi bolted out the door as howls rang across the sky like inclement weather. The beast was not destroyed but merely regrouping, as it had done many times before.

Once the door to Alexi's office echoed closed behind her, the journey to the stables tucked behind Athene Hall was a blur. Without pause, Percy flung open the doors to find a boy asleep on a chair. Nearly hysterical, she shook him. "Please, sir," she begged. "A horse. I need Professor Rychman's horse. It's an emergency!"

The boy woke to quite a fright, thinking Percy a spirit. He fell out of his chair and scrambled backward.

"Please, sir, there is danger. I need help. Oh! No! I am not a ghost, I promise you, see?" Percy reached for his hand and squeezed it. The boy cried out. "Please, forgive my appearance, but I am flesh and blood! Professor Rychman is in danger and must get away! You must help me ready his horse!"

Seeing the tears in her eyes, the young man groggily acquiesced. He began to ready a beautiful black stallion whose huge dark eyes were fiercely alert and intelligent. Of course such an impressive, elegant, onyx creature would be Alexi's horse, Percy thought. The beast seemed to be well aware of the danger, too.

Percy anxiously waited at the portico, where the stable boy had been all too happy to leave her standing, reins of Alexi's large dark steed in her ghost white hands. Assuming telling the guard at the door that there was a demon on the second floor would get her sent off to the histrionic ward, she invented a medical emergency to dissuade the man from sending her to her room. The entire night watch seemed too spooked by her to care one way or the other, and they left Percy well enough alone.

A billowing storm of black fabric rounded the corner at top speed, and her heart leaped. "Alexi! Thank God you're not harmed!" Percy cried.

Without a word, he grabbed her roughly by the arm just as the barking began again above them. He mounted his horse and swept her up in front of him.

"Dearest Alexi, what was—Oh, dear God!" Percy had looked over his shoulder, pressing her cheek to his, and just above the gargoyles that guarded the front entrance of the academy, she saw a huge, fanged dog with eyes like burning coals. Its head flickered into three heads, then ten, then more; it opened countless salivating jaws in a roar. The beast perched above their only escape route.

Percy screamed and tucked her head into Alexi's bosom. He loosed a powerful shout, and spurred his horse forward. A paw swiped down toward their heads, but at the same moment a shield of blue flame burst forth. Alexi's horse reared and leaped past, tore off down a narrow alley.

Percy could not get her bearings. A dark mist enfolded her brain, a dread filled her body and damnations were murmured in her ears. She screamed as her sleeve was torn by something she could not see, the something that had likely pursued them.

Alexi roared a word, a command to desist in a tongue Percy had never heard yet still understood. There was a crackling of blue lightning, and then a cloud lifted from around them. That nebulous mass of whirling bestial forms rose into the night sky, but all Percy could make out were hundreds of teeth. And then there was only London. The nightmare vanished and the barking quieted.

"Are you all right, dear girl?" Alexi asked above the din of his horse's hooves upon the cobblestones.

Percy's shaking arms desperately clutched his chest. "I . . . believe so. What in God's name was that?"

Alexi sighed. "That, in *hell's* name, was something I never saw until recently. Running rampant through London, it is, and I can't help but think it's looking for something."

Percy shrank, catching his meaning. "Not . . . me?"

"What you just saw was the terror of Whitechapel. I don't know for sure why it came here, but . . ."

"Oh, God have mercy!" Percy cried. "You're certain that is the Ripper?"

"I only wish I wasn't."

Percy thought about her splintered heavens and wondered if, before this night, something had been in place to protect her. She looked upward, afraid what she might see, but low, thick clouds were her only celestial view. "Am I in great danger, then?"

"Fear not, dear heart," Alexi declared.

"I was terrified to leave you!"

"Indeed," he replied. "I was hardly overjoyed to be left. But there are times when expert direction must be followed, no matter the fear."

Percy dared look up into his resolute face. "Oh, Alexi. Whatever that was, whatever is happening . . . I need you."

He smiled and met her gaze. "Good."

Their faces were so close, the heat of their cheeks and the

parting of their mouths so inviting . . . Alexi forced himself to look away, but Percy could see the battle in his eyes.

Percy, held captive by the moment, by the kiss that should have been, put a hand to her forehead to quell the dizzying effects of desire. "What did you do, just then?" she asked, avoiding the magnetism of his eyes. "Did that fire erupt from the beast . . . or from you?"

"Many things will surprise you in the days to come," was Alexi's cryptic reply.

"I have no doubt of that. But where—"

"I told you, I have never seen that creature until lately. As for the fire . . . that was mine."

"Goodness!" Percy breathed, clutching him tightly. "You are magical, then."

"Mortal—at least mostly. With a few tricks. But, think no more of it. Think only of holding on. I beg you."

"I would do anything for you, Alexi. Do you realize that?" she murmured.

He cleared his throat. "Careful with your words, Miss Parker. You belie your pride—and your modesty."

"Oh, Alexi, I—"

"Say no more, Percy, please. Not now."

She pressed fully against him. "We cannot unclasp our hearts in the least?"

He shuddered beneath her, clearly tempted. "It would hardly be proper."

"Then tell me something of what you do, Alexi, or what we are running from. Else I shall go mad!" she cried, leaning against his shoulder. That she had been ignorant for so long seemed a travesty in itself.

Alexi sighed. "To tell you a mere 'something' may be even more maddening. All I can say is this: The living need protection from supernatural forces they cannot comprehend. There is a group charged with maintaining the relative peace of day-to-day mortality, protecting it from the dead by a mix of their own mortal talents and a few . . . special forces."

Percy pursed her lips. "That could not be more vague, Alexi."

"Oh," he laughed, "it most certainly could."

"Are you one of these individuals?"

"Sometimes *vague* is all one has to go on, Percy."

"Go on? Toward what?"

"The undiscovered country, my dear. But now I've said too much."

"Ah," Percy muttered. "Well, I'm not any less maddened, my melancholy professor of Denmark. Quite illuminating indeed."

"Ride with me, then, into the mouth of madness."

"Do I have any choice?"

"Of course. But shall I leave you at the roadside until that creature returns? That, of course, is your alternative. My dear Miss Parker, you're riding upon Prospero, the finest horse in all of England, and you're in the arms of a most accomplished professor. What more could a young lady hope for? It's almost like an opera, itself."

Percy couldn't help but chuckle and relax against his powerful frame. Alexi gave her a flickering smirk, clasping her hand in his.

"Where are we going?" she asked after a short distance.

"Out of the city limits. We must put distance between you and that thing. I would take you to my home but . . . my estate has not always been safe from spectral disturbance," he remarked. She thought she heard pain in his voice. "Also, trouble often follows The Guard, so I cannot take you to our collective command. Not yet."

" 'The Guard'? That's your little club?"

Alexi smiled briefly. "I can only hope I'm not leaving them to another fight on their own . . ."

Storefronts and darkened flats of North London sped past Percy's watering eyes. The spirits of the city parted hastily, some bowing, some darting into the bricks of townhomes but keeping one protruding eye trained on the mortals' hasty flight. These ghosts seemed as nervous as she, who was terrified that every gust of wind might be the breath of that ghastly canine presence who was "clearly looking for something."

Outside the city, north of his estate and the surrounding expanse of spirit-ridden heath, Alexi took in the open air and sensed its quality. "Safe. For now," he said.

Percy felt Prospero slow, and she broke from silence again, hungry for knowledge.

"Tell me *something* of yourself. I know so little of you outside your classroom."

"If I tell you, will you remain rapt in my presence? Dare I break the enigma, the mystery of my person?"

Percy laughed, nervous. "Has my fascination been so obvious?"

Alexi's eyes clouded as he glanced over his shoulder. "Father moved the family from Berlin to our London estate when I was very young, and came to London in pursuit of a great medical career. They left me there, with the property to myself and my sister, at sixteen, and returned to Berlin."

"They left you? So young? Whatever for?" Percy breathed.

"Because they were terrified of me," Alexi replied, his eyes and tone harsh.

Percy could not help but shudder and there lapsed an uncomfortable silence.

Alexi spoke again, cool and casual. "I was apprenticed to a secretly renowned and brilliant alchemist, a friend of my father's who, noticing my penchant for mixing powders and devouring old texts, took me under his tutelage. Alchemy was increasingly considered arcane, but thankfully Athens still held interest in its basic principles—provided I coupled those with mathematics."

"How did you come to teach there?"

"My dear friend Rebecca."

"Headmistress Thompson?"

"Yes, of course."

"I always thought the two of you were—"

"Friends, Percy, and have been for ages. We've worked closely together under incredibly trying circumstances. She, like I, was groomed for an academic setting since childhood. I can't say I recall exactly how she came to run the school. I suppose I was so caught up in my research at the time . . ." He trailed off, as if trying to access a memory he could not locate. "At any rate, the academy was founded in the Quaker model, so Rebecca could, as a woman, serve as administrator." He eyed her. "We continued thus until, one day, a ghostly young woman who was barely competent in my class unsettled my life."

Percy made a face. "You lie, sir. I? Unsettle the inimitable Professor Rychman?"

"Always," he replied, echoing her earlier sentiment as such.

Percy hid her flushed face in his chest, unable to hold back a giggle or stop her lips from pressing against his cloak in a phantom kiss. "But Professor, that is a rather large leap. Nothing happened between the start of your teaching career and my entrance into it?"

"Oh, quite a lot."

"Well?"

"The academic life is gratifying, noble work, but it does not constitute what you would call a 'thrill.' The excitement in a professor's life often comes from what he does away from his profession—but for me to answer that, my dear, would be rather personal," he intoned deliciously. He looked her over then added, "All in due time, my dear. I've told you what I do, Percy. I'm a bit of a police officer, nothing more."

"Did you have . . . lady friends in this time?" Percy blurted, having no idea how else to continue, and wanting desperately to know.

"Why, Miss Parker, how bold of you! I have had thousands of lovers." When Percy gasped, he added nonchalantly,

"We all have, at one time or another, from one life to the next. For each spirit, a thousand lives."

Percy narrowed her eyes. "You believe in reincarnation, then?"

"Of course. Don't you?"

She took a long moment of consideration, enough to stop bristling from her sudden jealous reaction to the thought of the many possible lovers Alexi had enjoyed, and then answered. "I've always been conflicted. Everything I was taught at the abbey denounced such a theory, yet surely it could happen; otherwise—"

"How could you see the things you've seen, or fall upon your knees in my office, spouting a foreign language while trapped in a painting? Or be so offended by the smell of a pomegranate?"

"But if this is so, my former life must have been wretched, for I see dreadful things." Percy fought back a sob.

"Tell me more of what you see."

"All in due time, Professor," she retorted.

Alexi pursed his lips. "Answer me this. You once mentioned there were certain aspects of your particular faith that fascinated you. May I ask what?"

"I don't suppose it will be of any use to you, but I have always been enthralled with the idea of the Immaculate Conception."

"Indeed?"

"Yes. The idea of something holy and godlike taking residence inside a mortal, to me, is a most beautiful thought. For something greater than humanity to inhabit a simple body, forsaking divinity for simple mortal flesh . . ." She sighed. "It seems so incredible."

Alexi was struck. "So, do you remember being queen of the underworld?"

"What?"

"Do you remember being a goddess?"

"I . . . No. Why would I?"

"You're Persephone."

"Hardly!" She laughed. "A name does not a goddess make. Though I clearly identify with that story—"

"Then why is Cerberus hunting you?"

Percy gasped. "You think that's what that thing was?"

"Perhaps. Do any of your visions give you a sense of your history?"

Percy searched her mind. Soaring angels, horsemen, cracking skies and fire . . . a patchwork, nonsensical history. She shook her head. "No. Surely, all my visions were to lead me to you. I think I'm just a strange, mortal girl with a strange fate who happens to have a coincidental name."

"Hmm." Alexi looked lost in thought.

A few small homes became visible in the moonlight. "Ah, we have arrived."

Alexi tethered Prospero to the garden gate of a quaint cottage. The appealing edifice of stately grey stone was surrounded by flowers of all kinds. Lace curtains rustled behind open windows. Prospero nudged his master, stamping as if expecting remuneration for his fine work. Alexi smiled and fondly stroked the horse's muzzle. Percy drew behind him to follow suit, quelling the urge to slide her other arm around Alexi's waist.

Imagination got the better of her, and she experienced a thrilling rush while gazing at the cottage. She dreamed she was to be mistress of the place, and that the man who had taken her by the hand was her newlywed husband, ready to whisk his young wife inside and . . .

Alexi stopped to examine her. "What now, wandering one?" he asked.

She turned to face him, and the thought struck her that all she wanted in the world was to proclaim three simple words of her heart—words he might accept and return. But staring into his stoic face, she could not go against his wishes. She instead turned to the flowers, shaking her head.

A maid rushed out the front door and stopped in her

tracks. "Professor! What brings you and—oh, goodness! Milady!" The mousy young woman seemed baffled.

"Isabel, would you rouse my sister and apologize for my late and unannounced arrival?"

"Certainly! But I need not rouse the mistress, she keeps such terrible hours. Come in! Come in!" the maid exclaimed, running back to hold open the door. Percy smiled sweetly at her, but Isabel just stared back in shock.

A woman in a wheelchair, dressed in folds of black taffeta and slightly older than Alexi, rounded the corner of the entrance hall. "Brother, darling!" she cried in a deep female voice. At that moment, the maid remembered her place and took their cloaks.

Grinning, Alexi darted to lift the woman from her wheelchair and into his arms, and he squeezed her tightly before gently lowering her back down. "Hello, Alexandra—and before you chide me, yes, I know, it has been too long. Please forgive this strange visit; we simply had to escape the city.

"Alexandra, Miss Persephone Parker, whom I mentioned in my last letter. Percy, this is my sister, Miss Alexandra Rychman."

Percy, thrilled to have been mentioned in a letter, smiled nervously at Alexandra. The woman's wide, watery eyes and chiseled features were similar but more feminine than her brother's, and her dark hair with streaks of grey was swept atop her head in a severe coif. Her pale lips nonetheless curved into a welcoming smile.

When Alexandra held out her hand, Percy took it, bowing her head. "It is a pleasure to meet you, Miss Rychman."

"And you, dear. My, my, Alexi certainly has a way with acquaintances. Never a dull moment or an ordinary soul. Though I must say, it is unlike him to take such care of a *pupil*."

"This one is rather special," Alexi stated. Percy turned a mottled pink.

"So it would seem. Come, my dears. I'll have Isabel put on some spiced tea."

Alexandra led them into her parlor, where she gestured for her brother and Percy to sit upon a divan accented with embroidered pillows while wheeling her chair to face them. The room was decorated with paintings that Percy recognized to be of Josephine's style that was neither classical nor modern but simply *lovely;* there was no other word for it. Moonlight spilled through the lace curtains of the French doors and mixed with the light of several stained-glass lamps.

"Alexandra, where is that large wooden trunk I brought here years ago?" Alexi asked.

"Upstairs in the guest room, where you left it. And yes, it remains locked!" his sister teased, before turning to Percy. "He can be so maddeningly secretive."

"Indeed," Percy agreed.

Alexi seemed to delight in the pointed glance she gave him; he appeared lost for a moment. Then, jumping up, he said, "Excuse me a moment, please."

The ladies watched him go in a swirl of dark fabric as he darted out of the room and up the stairs. Alexandra sighed. "I learned at an early age that it's best not to ask too many questions about my brother and his work. But whatever it is," she said, "it—he—is good. Despite his secrecy and strange friends, he's never faltered from a noble path in life. Never."

Percy nodded. A long silence followed in which she felt excruciatingly examined, but she sat and sipped the tea Isabel brought all the same. "When did you come to this lovely place, Miss Rychman?" she asked politely, admiring a bronze statue, a graceful couple dancing a stationary waltz across the mantel.

"Alexi bought this place nearly fifteen years ago, when it was clear that my state would make it difficult for me to be married off," the woman said.

"Ah." Percy nodded. "You have made it a lovely home."

"Thank you. I do my best. Fate dealt me a harsh blow," Alexandra stated.

"I take that to mean you were not always as you are?"

"I was eighteen. Alexi was fourteen, I believe. We don't talk about it. That day—it was the strangest thing, as if some sort of demon swept through our house, a horrible tempest of a being. I was knocked from the top of the stairs in my parents' old estate, where Alexi now lives alone. My family claimed it must have been the wind that crashed through suddenly and startled me, opening doors and cracking windows and causing my fall. My grandmother was there, and the shock of it stopped her heart! Alexi found us just after. He didn't think it was the wind, either, but no one said a word. But something was . . . different. And one day our parents simply left." Alexandra traded her grimace for a sudden smile. "A *demon*. You must think us mad!"

"Not in the slightest," Percy replied.

The woman stared at her for a long moment. "You believe in such things, don't you? I can see it on your face."

"I do with all my heart."

"You, Miss Parker . . . you have led a hard life, I can imagine."

Percy held the woman's stare. "I have led a *strange* life, Miss Rychman, and at times it has seemed hard. You understand. But I have been provided for. I'm grateful for Athens. I often wondered if I would ever be able to leave the walls of the abbey where I grew up. The sisters there were afraid that someone might whisk me off to some terrible sideshow"—Percy grimaced—"and there are moments when I still fear such an abduction. But your brother has taught me much, rallied me from self-pity, helped me to find confidence and makes every effort to keep me safe. So, I am blessed—at the very least by his presence in my life."

"Indeed, my brother has taken an unusual interest in you and your welfare. He told me a young lady was in his care, and that he was sure that I would see you both soon. I have been waiting so long to see him, I wish I had more prepared."

"No, please, it is we who apologize," Percy leaped to say. "Especially as the nature of the urgency which deposes me to you is still uncertain." Her heart had warmed at the idea of being thought of as in Alexi's "care."

His sister smiled. "Alexi and his many secrets. Ah well, it is good to have company. And it is excellent to see my brother with company. He's kept himself so bitter and lonely all his life, I feared he'd keep on with his odd friends and never take a wife. And so I welcome you as his lady, and as a sister to me."

Percy's jaw dropped. "His wi—His *lady?* Oh! I . . . Why, no—"

"You needn't explain yourself, dear girl. Isabel has put on a hot bath for you upstairs if you care for one. I am sure you have had a harrowing night."

"Oh! That would be grand!" Percy's grateful smile held many kinds of thanks.

CHAPTER TWENTY-THREE

Michael sat with a mug of cider, staring at the fire in his modest hearth. He kept a rustic little nook with sparse decor, priding himself on simple pleasures; he'd always saved the gilt and pomp for the church. In this room that boasted only a few threadbare chairs and a mantel topped with trinkets from various ancestors, Michael was content with his fire and cider. His abode lay near the academy, a few blocks from its unmarked passages, just up Montague Place. He was closer to Rebecca and Alexi than anyone else—though they tended to forget he was so near, pairing up and darting off toward work, leaving him often to fend for himself. He had gotten used to that, but every now and then he would confess to himself and to God that he was a bit lonely.

He had attempted to sleep tonight but couldn't. Even his impervious humour was rattled by the events of the past few days. He had smiled regardless, giving his friends the benefit of his warmth and light, but now in the privacy of his home he allowed his face to fall. A parochial vicar at a nearby Anglican parish, he tried to reconcile his melancholy as penance to an Almighty power. He was relieved to believe in something larger than him or his companions' odd fate . . . but he could not, however, admit that faith was an infallible salve. Especially not when he thought of Rebecca Thompson.

The very woman in question suddenly burst breathless through his front door in a rustle of thick linen skirts, her eyes wide and searching. "Michael, have you seen Alexi?" she blurted.

Always Alexi, Michael thought. Usually this sentiment was pondered with a sad smile and only a tinge of jealousy, but on this strange night everything pierced more acutely.

"No, my dear, I haven't," he replied. "Why, is something wrong?"

"You feel the air, don't you?"

"Of course," Michael replied. "But it has been this way for some weeks—or building to this. Alexi should be found round one of his usual haunts."

"I fear he's left without notice. I cannot sense the slightest trace of him."

Michael frowned. "And you received no note?"

"Nothing. I am at a loss! Come with me, Michael, we must all meet in town. I feel it in my blood."

He rose and worriedly accompanied her out into the night.

The bright moon glared down from above as four carriages sped through separate streets to halt in Trafalgar Square. The horses seemed to converge at the same instant, as if some great hand was guiding them to this confluence. Hopping down from their respective cabs, each of The Guard stood milling about, speaking in hushed whispers.

"Where is Alexi?" Elijah asked.

"It would appear he has left town," Rebecca replied.

"What?"

"He is not currently in London."

"Well, where in the holy name of the saints is he?" Jane demanded, adding a few well-chosen Gaelic curses.

"I can't say, but evidently he felt his business pressing enough to keep it from us." Rebecca shook her head and snorted. She was still burning with resentment, though she tried to shake it off.

"What do we do?" Josephine asked. "Something is about to descend at any moment. *Certainement,* Alexi has reason for his actions, but really, his timing is horrible!" She was taking note of how the clouds were making beautiful yet foreboding patterns, a nightmare scene she might be compelled to paint.

"It's Prophecy, isn't it?" Elijah asked.

"I'm sure he believes it has something to do with that," Rebecca replied.

"Well, what?" Michael demanded.

"I know very little, but he thinks he has found her." Rebecca sighed. "He will bring her to us soon, so he says, but he's being . . . difficult. He doesn't believe it's Miss Linden."

"Difficult isn't the half of it!" Jane insisted, suddenly shivering. "To abandon us at this moment?"

They could all feel the approach of something terrible. Wind whipped through Trafalgar Square and the temperature dropped drastically. The ladies pulled their cloaks tighter around them; the men buttoned their greatcoats. They all looked to the sky, worried.

"Let us not speak ill of him before we know the circumstances," Rebecca suggested, but her irritated tone betrayed her generous words, because she was tired of always making excuses for him. She had to remember that she owed him nothing. She was simply his *friend*.

"Shall we wait for a while, together?" Jane asked, feeling an instinct to maintain close proximity to her comrades. Oddly, eerily, Trafalgar Square was utterly empty. Where were London's finest? Her helpless?

"Why not," Elijah grumbled. "It doesn't appear we'll be getting much sleep this evening."

As if to prove Elijah's assessment, a gruesome form suddenly slithered, ran, galloped and skittered all at once above their heads. Terror breathed down upon them, a terror that had become sadly familiar.

"The hellhound hath returned!" Michael proclaimed. The barking, frothing creature glared down at them with one pair of eyes and a hundred. It hovered; growling, snorting, snarling.

"Bind!" Rebecca cried. All five friends took hands.

A glorious hum began to emanate from their circle, a light hanging on each of The Guard like halos.

The abomination was not impressed, and reached down vapourous paws in assault. The five stood fast against the constricting pain that tore at their lungs, and Michael breathed loudly, purposeful, reminding them that they indeed had control of their own organs. The pain eased.

"Benediction!" Rebecca commanded her compatriots. A verse lifted from their lips and into the air as a murmuring wave.

The ungodly creature spat and lashed. Though strained, The Guard held their ground, wondering if they could withstand the beast long enough for it to at least lose interest. Tears rolled silently down several cheeks. Even Michael's determined smile was belaboured.

Josephine coughed suddenly, faltering; the circle was broken. The creature turned a ghastly set of heads in her direction and pounced, and each of the five were knocked to the ground by chimerical claws. Wounded, their clothing torn and their skin scraped and bruised worse than ever before in all their years of The Grand Work, the friends cried out in alarm and cursed Alexi for his abandonment. If he were here, they had a fair fight; without him, they were doomed.

And then, suddenly, there was a door.

Alexi stared at the well-worn black leather-bound book in his hands, and opened to a nineteen-year-old entry, written two years to the day after his young life changed forever:

> Today is my anniversary. It is the anniversary of the day I became something new in that chapel, the day I—we—began patrolling the dead. Today I awoke from restless sleep with a keen sensation. Something additionally cataclysmic has occurred. I'm filled with longing, as if touched by a long-lost love upon waking. I yearn for that sensation again; the voice of that goddess is calling my name . . .
>
> I heard a newborn's cry in my sleep. When I woke, a feather lay at the foot of my bed. The specimen is unlike any I have ever seen. Translucent, iridescent and twice the length of my palm, the feather is luminous as I hold it. Life seems to hum within—and a strange blue light. It seems a talisman.
>
> I am unsettled by a torrent of emotions I cannot place nor discern, but something is indeed coming to find me. I long for it . . . for her, that voice. My destiny was born today . . .

He shut the book with a triumphant exclamation. October 16, as he'd thought! That was the date recorded for this entry. He thought back to the date in his office that Percy had mentioned as her birthday, and it was the same. How had they never thought to celebrate their turning? How was it that they failed to celebrate becoming more than simply mortal? Perhaps because The Guard was as much a curse as a blessing. Yet if Prophecy's alleged door was never to be seen, he'd need every last scrap of proof to bring to The Guard over to his side, to help them realize what he knew in his gut was the truth: Persephone Parker was their seventh.

"Percy!" he cried, bounding into the hall and toward the nearest door. He flung it open without thinking.

Percy squealed, hastily covering her body with her long white limbs. Alexi, seeing the bright blur of that slender, alabaster body, closed the door to the washroom with a similar exclamation. His heart became spasmodic, and a flood of heat sent him reeling. "Oh! Percy! Terribly sorry! I found something you should see, and . . . sorry!"

"What is it?" Percy called, still breathless from shock.

"Never mind. Take your time, Perc—Miss Parker. I'll tell you . . . later."

Inside, Percy stifled a giggle. She could hear Alexi fumbling at the door like a clumsy boy, and while she was scandalized that he'd seen a flash of her naked body, she was flattered near tears that it should affect him so. She'd never before seen him blush, and the look on his face seemed one of rapture . . . at least, it had been before his horror at the impropriety of the situation.

Percy couldn't hold back a beaming smile as she began to lather her body with scented soap and contemplate how perfectly magical it was to be even considered by a man like Alexi. Their strange behaviour aside, just to be anywhere in his private sphere was a blessing, especially as it dared scandal and expulsion for them both. She decided that even if he never revealed a single other thing about his mysterious ways, or about her possible part in it, she didn't care so long as she could be near him. To perhaps steal illicit kisses . . .

As she caressed herself with a small washcloth, she closed her eyes, leaned back into the water and couldn't help imagining his hand dragging the lathered linen across her, lingering lovingly on her bare white skin. Ashamed yet invigorated, her body tingled. The sensations overwhelmed and intimidated her. But, surely no one could see the entirety of her queer skin and yet be attracted to her . . . Percy was suddenly certain that Alexi had withdrawn in shock and horror. His arousal had been her imagination. He was repulsed, and so a frown replaced her girlish, giddy smile.

Percy dried and powdered herself. She appreciated the sensation of the thick satin nightdress she'd been given as it slid around her chilled body. The long braid of her hair damp against her neck, she slipped into the hall . . . and heard crackling music from a phonograph downstairs. A waltz?

Cautiously, Percy peeked between the rails of the staircase to behold Alexandra sitting in her wheelchair at the center of the living room, and Alexi bowing slightly across the way. His sister chuckled and batted her hand in the air as Alexi approached.

Carefully he bent over his sister, lifted her out of her chair and held her around the waist; her legs dangled limply beneath. She laughed a tired yet happy laugh, and laid her head upon his shoulder while placing her hand in his. Alexi effortlessly carried her around the floor in slow circles, as if he were dancing with a child.

"I remember when I taught you this dance. You were twelve," Alexandra said softly. "What an irony now, eh? I'm so lonely, Alexi. I don't know how much longer I can carry on."

He pressed his cheek to his sister's hair and replied softly, "I know, dear. I understand. I always have."

"Not now, dear, you don't. Not now that you have her," Alexandra countered. There were tears in her eyes, but she was smiling. "She is gentle and strange, Alexi . . . but charming. How those unbelievable eyes glitter for you!"

"I do not *have* her, Alexandra. You must not make such assumptions. And I shall forever understand loneliness," Alexi replied.

"Let's not speak of it. Simply dance with me."

As they silently moved around the floor, Alexi, as he often

did, indulged in regret that his sister had been struck down so many years prior, that her paralysis and his grandmother's passing were both somehow his fault. It was as if all evil in the spirit world had swung a warning paw that day, reminding him that no one close to him could ever truly be safe. No one but Prophecy.

Had he just cursed the sweet and gentle Percy Parker by bringing her into all this? Would she grow as frightened of him as his parents, who sensed something they'd never confronted? No. She was fated to be involved. Fearless. She was Prophecy. She *had* to be.

The disk bumped and scratched, the waltz complete. Alexi and his sister continued moving in the hissing absence of music for countless moments, unaware and unconcerned, but then, as gently as he had lifted her, Alexi returned her carefully to rest. There was a rustle of taffeta and a squeak of the wooden wheelchair.

Sensing another's eyes, Alexi looked over to behold Percy watching him, her face aglow and her cheeks glistening with tears. The moment she was spied, however, she ducked out of sight. Alexi smirked. "Good night, Alexandra." Then he climbed the stairs, tingling with anticipation for what waited above.

Catching sight of Percy standing wide-eyed in the hall, dressed in a flattering satin nightdress that Isabel must have procured for her, he moved forward, gently wiping away her tears. "My dear, what's this?" he asked, ignoring how utterly unheard of it was for him to see her in such a state of dishabille. Percy didn't seem to think of it, either.

"You are so beautiful, Alexi!" she sobbed.

With a warm little laugh, he opened his arms and Percy fell into them. His embrace closed around her and wrapped tight. Numerous moments passed as they slid closer and closer, their arms entwining and their palms pressing tight until there was no space left and they were helplessly and indecorously locked. Alexi became keenly aware of the fact that she was only wearing a nightdress, and he was quite sure no layers of clothing would have been able to conceal his body's reaction.

It would be so easy, to whisk her into one of the rooms, part her robe and gaze upon that snow-white flesh again, to worship it as the light of the moon itself, to unleash years of pent-up passion upon that marble body, to take, to claim, to seize and devour Prophecy as his own. It was his right; he had been denied it all his life and—

Perhaps she sensed his burning thoughts, for she pulled back, daring to look up and see the fire raging in his eyes. "Alexi," she began. "I lo—"

He suddenly reeled backward as if struck. Percy did not get the chance to complete her declaration. His hands flew to his head, as if he was in great pain.

"Alexi!" she murmured, frightened.

"Something's wrong," he muttered, sinking down to the floor, rubbing his temples. Percy recalled the night of the ball and how he had been called away by the same reaction. He looked up at her sadly. "My dear Percy. I hope soon you and I may . . . indulge," he said carefully, his jaw clenching, his eyes still flickering with desire. "But I fear for my friends. I must return to London. You must stay here in safety."

"But—"

Alexi reached out and clasped her hands in his. "I don't dare return you to the eye of the storm, Percy; it may not be safe for you. I'll come for you in the morning. There's nothing else to discuss. I must go."

Confused and exhausted, Percy could only dumbly nod, helping him as he rose shakily to his feet. His face pinched with pain and anxiety, he bounded down the stairs and called for his sister. Percy glided halfway down to listen to their conversation.

"I must be off to London again, Alexandra. I'm sorry . . ."

"Already? Why, you've barely had time for a breath!"

"I wish for nothing more than to stay, but there is something, perhaps something dangerous—"

"Yes, yes, you and your mad work. I ought to be used to it."

"You must do me a favor. You must hide Percy here tonight. I fear it isn't safe for her where I'm going, and I can't risk returning her to the school. I'll come for her again in the morning. Is there space for her?"

"There's always a room prepared, Alexi. Don't worry . . ."

Alexi gathered his cloak, hat and a small black book Percy didn't recognize, and darted back to find her on the stairs. Bounding up a few steps at a time, he swept her into his arms and buried his mouth against her neck, searing it with kisses. "I know I shouldn't, but I cannot help myself," he murmured against her throat as she gasped in pleasure. "Await me here and stay safe. I won't be long."

As he pulled back, Percy was struck by a terrifying thought. "Alexi . . . I'm not bringing this danger on you, am I?"

He smiled wearily. "Oh no, dear girl. It was brought on centuries ago. An old vendetta, between two antique creatures, that's still playing out in our dreary little lives. Mortals made pawns by immortals—isn't it terrible? But soon, my dear, we'll settle the score. You and I."

Percy tried to smile through her confusion, but it came out more a worried grimace.

Alexi seized her neck and moved in as if to kiss her goodbye, then groaned as his head pounded with a fresh, searing pain. Back in London, things were grim.

"Go, Alexi," Percy said softly, kissing him on the cheek and ushering him to the landing below. "And know that I—"

"I know, Percy," he said. Then he hastily turned and darted out the door before either of them could exchange a vow, was on his horse and tearing off down the countryside. There was work to be done before he could rejoice in her coming. He would not let Prophecy be tainted by premature declarations.

* * *

The sign they had been waiting nineteen years to see was now floating over the western lane of Trafalgar Square. The sign. The most important sign. Prophecy. It was a dark rectangle with a dim interior, much like the portal that opened when their meetings commenced in the chapel. But this one they had not made themselves, and none of The Guard was quite sure what was happening.

The canine abomination turned, ignoring his supine prey and staring instead at the portal. There was a sound—an unfamiliar, halting sound bellowed from a female throat. The monster's ears perked up, and it bowed its head in subordination. The Guard next beheld the beautiful Miss Linden, her arms outstretched, power radiating from her in a stunning manner, her beautiful face suddenly terrible in its ferocity. The beast broke into a thousand hound clouds and vanished in a yelping flurry through the door. The portal crumbled into nothingness an instant later.

Miss Linden shuddered and stumbled forward with a cry of pain, as if shaking loose the effects of poison. After a moment she raised her head again, her face once more noble and beautiful. She stared at the others and offered them an exhausted yet winning smile.

"I fancy a drink. How about all of you?"

Reeling from the evening's events, Percy wasted no time in falling into the bed Isabel had shown her. But, just as she was drifting off, a spirit floated through the wall and drifted close.

The entrance of spirits into her rooms was such a usual part of Percy's life that it never startled her. And she didn't always acknowledge them, because she couldn't handle conversing with them all. But this elegant old woman, dressed in fine clothing dated a few decades prior—dark heavy fabrics with high collars and puffed sleeves—seemed intent on speaking with Percy, for she was staring down at her fiercely. She looked familiar.

"*Zdravstvuyte,*" the old woman said, greeting her in Russian.

"*Zdravstvuyte,*" Percy replied. "*Ochen priyatno.*"

"Lovely to meet you, too, dear girl, but listen close, I've only a moment," the woman continued, still in Russian. "The firebird has come for you and you alone, child. I've been watching. Tell my grandson that he mustn't be fooled by the tricks of snakes. Tell him he needs to use fire to banish the darkness. His fire. It is the only way."

Percy recalled Alexi mentioning his grandmother was Russian. She didn't understand what the old woman meant, but she nodded in compliance, anyway. Alexi's grandmother nodded curtly back and vanished.

With a sigh, Percy tried drifting off to sleep, but she was restless with the barking that distantly rang in her ears. At last she attempted a prayer: "Dear Lord, please help me solve a few riddles before receiving new ones. And bring my beloved safely back to me." She pressed her phoenix pendant—her *firebird*—to her breast. She now believed the symbol meant Alexi. If so, then he was here with her, even in his absence. In fact, he always had been. She had to find a way to make sure he always would be, no matter the dangers ahead.

CHAPTER TWENTY-FOUR

Teacups rattled on saucers at La Belle et La Bête, which was closed to everyone but an exhausted, nervous group of six, their jaws set and expressions stern. Rebecca and Josephine sat adjusting their clothing. Jane first healed everyone's wounds, cuts and bruises, then went on to mend her torn sleeve, and she was now moving with an air of obsession to mend her female companions' bustles and skirts. Elijah and Michael left their shirtsleeves in tatters.

"You must think me mad for having burst upon you like that," Miss Linden laughed, finally daring to break the silence.

"After the events of this evening, which of us would dare?" Elijah replied. When he snickered, the woman tilted her head in demure appeal.

"How did you find us, and then, how did you do what you did?" Rebecca asked.

Miss Linden paused, taking care with her words. "An unmistakable taste in my mouth occurs when something is . . . I could taste something amiss. And it's not yet right."

"Ye made that . . . thing retreat. We must know how," Jane demanded.

Miss Linden shrugged. "All my life I've been plagued with strange company. Ghastly, nightmarish creatures, such as that one, are familiar. I've encountered all manner of the inexplicable."

Jane gaped. "A beast such as that? Here in England?"

"Your group must be a magnet for troubled souls," Miss Linden proposed. "But this was no mere troubled soul. No, when I speak of encountering other such nightmares, I speak of my time abroad, where there are many such creatures—forces of nature, really, things you've only heard of in myth." She paused as the group nodded in amazement. "Forgive me, but where *is* that unmistakable professor of yours? Shouldn't he be here?"

"We've been pondering that all evening," Rebecca replied. "We were in need of him."

Miss Linden looked troubled. "Indeed, how surprising! Elijah told me you were inseparable. I confess that I hoped to see him—his presence would have put me at ease."

"Is that so?"

Miss Linden blushed. "I mean to say . . ."

"Yes, yes, he has a calming effect upon most people." Elijah snorted.

Placing the glass of wine she held tightly in her hand upon the table, Rebecca leveled her gaze once again upon their savior. "Professor Rychman is currently . . . preoccupied with other business."

Miss Linden's green eyes flashed. "The pale girl," she blurted. "He's with that ghost of a girl, isn't he?"

Jane and Michael looked confused, but Elijah and Josephine exchanged speculative glances. Rebecca gritted her teeth. The two Restoration wraiths in the corner ducked their heads together to gossip.

"Perhaps," Rebecca finally replied. "He thinks her of great importance."

"I met her," Miss Linden murmured.

"Yes, I imagine. Your impression?"

"I would not be so bold as to conjecture about someone whom I know so little—"

"I ask only for your *impression,* Miss Linden."

"Well," the woman began hesitantly, "I'm not sure she is as unassuming as she pretends. She seemed to wish to challenge me. I tell you, something is—"

"Rotten in the state of Denmark," Michael muttered.

"Yes," was Miss Linden's reply.

Glances and nods were exchanged among The Guard. The Restoration wraiths in the corner seemed to hold their breath.

"Perhaps we can make it right, my dear Miss Linden," Elijah declared, rising from the table.

"Please, call me Lucille."

"I suppose the saving of lives does indeed invite familiarity," he replied. "Do you trust us, Lucille?"

"Implicitly. Though I cannot claim any intimacy by right, I . . . I feel I belong here. With you," she suggested eagerly. "We must stick together, our kind."

"Our kind? Have you met others like us?" Josephine asked.

"Never," Miss Linden responded in earnest. "I've been

looking all my life for people like you. I feel as though my soul has seen centuries, and all for this purpose."

The Guard looked around at one another. There was a door, and here was the reason for it. Something had to be said at last.

Rebecca cleared her throat. "Do you believe in prophecies, Lucille?"

"Why do you ask? Have you had one?"

"Yes, one heralded the coming of a friend to join our ranks, to aid in coming battles of this world we seek to keep at peace."

"This friend, then... You feel it is I?" Lucille asked, breathless. As The Guard rustled in their chairs, she laughed suddenly, joyfully. "It's all I've ever wanted. To *matter*. To finally be a part of something important. Surrounded by so many strange forces all my life, overshadowed by them at every turn—to now have you as my own, and that ineffable Rychman, is my dream come true!"

"Have you spoken such impassioned sentiments to him?" Rebecca asked.

Lucille shook her head. "While I sense he is fascinated by me, he's been unwilling to reveal anything. A careful, guarded man, he keeps his secrets well. A capable leader."

"Save for abandoning us tonight," Elijah muttered.

"An inscrutable man with many reasons for his actions, I've no doubt," was Lucille's reply.

Jane piped up, her infamous disinterest melting. "Ye take his side, Miss Linden. It's nice to see he has a supporter."

"Or an admirer," Josephine corrected. Lucille coloured and stared at the table.

"And, the door," Jane continued softly. "Have ye ever opened a portal to the spirit world before?"

Lucille blinked.

"It's what our prophecy hinges upon," Rebecca clarified.

"Oh. Well, doors between this world and the next have

always sort of... followed me," Lucille replied. "I wish I knew why. Perhaps this is my answer."

Rebecca rose and grabbed her by the elbow. "May I have a private word with you, Miss Linden?"

"Secrets, Rebecca?" Michael chided.

"Hush." Rebecca batted a hand in the air and drew Lucille into the alcove by the door. "Please forgive the strange manner in which we speak here."

"I assure you, I've dealt in odder exchanges."

"Indeed? Then, if I may be so bold, allow me ask you something private," Rebecca said.

"Anything."

"Do you feel that Alexi Rychman may have a very... personal place in your destiny?"

The woman stared into her eyes, and Rebecca could not describe the calming power those emerald irises possessed; Miss Linden's presence was an odd yet exciting balm. "I am certain, Miss Thompson, that my destiny involves him. I believe he is my destiny—even if he, at this point, does not share my conviction. He is a careful man, as you know, and very wise—"

"We'll see about that."

"For a mortal," Lucille finished.

Rebecca's lips thinned, and for a moment she was taken aback. "Why, Miss Linden, are you not mortal?"

Lucille's eyes flashed. "Sadly, I am. Yet I feel like so much more."

Rebecca nodded and the two shared a smile of understanding. "Indeed, I know that feeling well."

Lucy's eyes narrowed, as if she was considering the merits of asking a specific question. After a moment, she summoned the courage. "Since we are displaying the fullest candour, Miss Thompson... the professor's eyes, they burn for something, but not for me. Why do you ask me about my feelings on this topic?"

Rebecca sighed. "Alexi believes that our prophecy has an...intimate element. He's wrong. It was never directly said to be so. But, he's so damn stubborn. In his mind, the woman who fulfills Prophecy will be..."

Lucille drew in a long breath. *"His?"*

Rebecca nodded, grimacing.

"Oh, my," Lucille murmured. "How exciting." Then her powerful gaze clouded. "But he thinks the answer lies in that ghost girl!"

Rebecca nodded, knowing full well the snow-white creature who had claimed Alexi's attentions. "I am afraid so."

"How can I convince him?" Lucille asked.

"Convince him of what?"

"To love me instead!"

Rebecca blinked. "Well...that's just it; you don't have to. Alexi is misled on that point, making all of this more complicated—"

"But I'd *like* him to. All I've ever wanted is to be loved."

Rebecca pursed her lips. "Indeed."

"And I must tell you," Lucille continued. "I've seen that girl. I fear for you if you keep her near."

Rebecca scoffed. "Come now. She's a timid girl, hardly a threat—"

Lucille shook her head. "I have seen what you do to spirits. She's much of one, herself, I fear. Too much to be trusted." Leaning in, she whispered, "Recently, when you took me to the professor, that girl was clearly threatened by my presence. Could she not have been sent from the realm of your enemies? That guise of timidity, her awkward isolation—these things cause her to *appear* harmless. But if she is not a mortal, if something else has taken hold in that body and causes that odd pallor...she could do a deal of harm. But forgive me, I prattle on! How presumptuous—"

"Your apprehensions are valid, Lucille. I will share them with the others," Rebecca promised, and with that they returned to the group.

"You do realize, my friends," she addressed them bitterly, "that this will not be easy news for Alexi. He is sure he's found Prophecy in that student of his. He—"

As if on cue, Alexi Rychman burst through the door in an explosion of black fabric, clutching a book, his eyes bright. "Good morning, dear friends!" he began, filling the room with his presence. "I felt you were in trouble so I came running, but the storm seems to have subsided. Good work, then! And I have . . . such news!" After taking a good look at his companions. "You all look dreadful. What in the hell has happened to your clothes?"

"We haven't slept," Elijah countered bitterly. "And we're in tatters because we were nearly *ripped*."

"Sit, Alexi," Michael commanded.

"I'd rather stand, thank you," Alexi replied.

Rebecca whirled upon him. With unease, Alexi noted that the beautiful Miss Linden stood behind her.

"What in the name of our Grand Work did you think you were doing," his friend hissed, "abandoning us on an evening when the Balance was at its most precarious? We were crippled by your unexplained absence. How could you do such a thing?" Recovering herself, she glanced at Miss Linden and the rest of The Guard. Alexi did the same.

Lucille was picking up the black book he had set down, and she began to look it over. Michael recognized the need for privacy and kindly waved, gesturing Miss Linden upstairs, giving an apologetic smile. Nodding, Miss Linden politely and unobtrusively put down the book and glided away.

Once she was out of sight, Alexi felt he had sufficient leave to retort, "You question me as if I were suspect? I acted for the very sake of Prophecy! Did you think I'd go on sudden holiday for the fun of it?"

"And since when does an illicit escape with your lover— oh, forgive me, your *student*—constitute aid to Prophecy?" Elijah demanded, his pale face flushed.

Alexi's jaw dropped. "Slanderous fools, what right have you to say this? That hellhound came to my office, came for Miss Parker. I could not fight it alone, so I moved her to safety."

"It came for us," Jane said. "Since when has the fate of a student come before us?"

"Because Miss Parker is Prophecy!" Alexi cried. "Not that I should have to explain myself. I intended to share my findings at the proper time."

"It is well past the proper time, Alexi, seeing as we almost perished tonight," Elijah spoke up. "The prophecy wasn't just given to you; it's not your toy or alchemical formula to keep and meddle with. It's ours. We are all in this together. You've given us nothing, and yet we have something incredible in our midst."

Alexi's gaze pierced him. "I know you think Prophecy points to Miss Linden. I realize that she is indeed incredible, with a presence unlike any other, with a beauty unmatched, and with the power to see spirits and know the unknowable. But *Persephone* Parker, named for my goddess, also sees spirits. She can speak with them in any language. Did Rebecca not declare our need for just such a translator when we worked in Fleet Street? She has transporting visions, too. She was even granted a vision of our liturgy, the sacred text known only to us, which came to her in a dream!"

"Is that all?" Jane asked.

"No, it isn't, but what an impressive vitae on its own! She has worn a phoenix pendant around her neck since she was a child. She was scalded by that very pendant the night we demanded Prophecy be shown!"

"Alexi, none of that matters now. Prophecy has shown herself—to us," Josephine countered. "We would have died tonight, Alexi. Do you understand that? We would have died if Miss Linden had not lent us aid. Tonight, we lived, without you. We owe Miss Linden our lives, and Prophecy was fulfilled. She opened a door."

Alexi stilled. "What?"

"A portal," Rebecca explained quietly. "As was foretold."

There was a long and tense silence. Alexi shook his head, his body visibly taut. "No. This must be a trap. It isn't her."

Rebecca threw her hands in the air. "Oh, yes, it must be a trap! Of course, how foolish the rest of us are for believing we might have a part in this! You, who sacrificed everything to your fate, unlike we five . . . It could only be you to whom Prophecy would be revealed."

Alexi kept shaking his head. "No, my friends, I . . . simply know. I know it isn't her."

Elijah's nostrils flared. "And that's your answer, *Professor?* You deny the one hard fact of Prophecy just because you 'know' things to be otherwise? Is the one scientist here listening to himself?"

"You do not trust my instincts or my proof."

Rebecca held up a hand and attempted to explain. "Alexi, I've never seen you like this. You're trying to pin Prophecy on this young girl when it's supposed to be a peer. You're tearing around in a whirlwind over her, fashioning facts so that it can be her—not that it is. You're changed by her, as if by some spell. Where is our stoic, unfaltering cornerstone, willing to see only hard facts? There was a door to the spirit world, Alexi, through which the hellhound vanished. How much more plainly do we need the prophecy fulfilled?"

Alexi shook his head. "A trap. I . . . I don't trust her."

"Tell me, Alexi." Elijah leaned in. "Has your dear little Miss Parker *opened a door* for you?"

He ignored any double entendre his rakish compatriot might intend. "She sees them in visions, she draws them. And that painting, Josephine—it was like a door that she went through, as if she were from that very age and time."

Jane made a face. "Her visions and mythical past won't help us when we're being attacked, as we were tonight. I don't suppose Miss Parker had a vision of saving our lives, did she? Alexi, what're we supposed to make of this? Ye may think this girl of yours is Prophecy all ye like—we've yet to get a glimpse of her."

"I've seen her," chorused Elijah, Josephine and Rebecca.

Jane and Michael exchanged surprised glances. "And?" Michael pressed.

The three shrugged.

Josephine said, noncommittally, "I met her briefly. She's deathly pale and clearly enamoured of Alexi. There's something about her, certainly—but nothing like what we've experienced in the presence of Miss Linden."

Elijah nodded in agreement.

"But Elijah," Alexi protested. "You came to my house having just met her, having seen a burning image when you touched her—an image that matched how the goddess spoke of the phoenix! And Josie, that *painting*. She was your inspiration! And that painting sent her into a vision—"

"Alexi, none of those details connect to what we do or what we fight," Elijah interrupted. "I touch and see many terrible sights. Josephine is inspired by many things, not just our work. Tonight, our work included Miss Linden, and the one particular of our prophecy revealed itself just as we were running out of time! Can that really mean nothing?"

Alexi shook his head, unwilling to be convinced. "But Persephone Parker is the one. A phoenix charm burning her flesh just as we demand a sign? How could that be, if she's not linked to us? How could she know our invocation?" He brandished the diary he'd reclaimed from his sister. "And . . . I have an entry on the day she was born. I awoke knowing there was a great alteration in the Balance—and it was two years to the day from when our lives changed to this fate! We never saw my goddess again because she was born as Miss Parker!"

"Alexi, calm yourself, you're raving," Josephine said.

"And her pallor!" Alexi continued. "She appears as if she could be a spirit—and she can communicate with them!

Does this not make her useful to us? She is not possessed as we are; she is truly reborn." He whirled to face his friend. "Josie, we've never dared ask . . . but please tell me when those white streaks first appeared in your hair."

Josephine faltered. "Since the moment of my possession," she replied quietly.

"As I thought. And I believe that something has been with Percy all her life—within her, from the womb—to make her whole body white. It is the shock of an outside power—a divine possession itself!"

Everyone stared at him sadly, as if he were to be pitied. This riled him further. "I will bring her to you," he vowed. "You will know. By spending time with her, you will know. But damn it all, there's no reason why you should fight—you should simply trust me!"

"Alexi, facing death without you revoked your privilege of unconditional trust," Elijah snapped. "Oh, and did we mention there was a goddamned *door?*"

Alexi's fists rose, and sparkles of blue fire trickled out.

Rebecca flew forward. "Haven't you considered that there may be more than one kind of trap, Alexi? You must consider them all. How many times have I prepared you for this moment? We were warned of betrayals and false prophets, of *'the mistakes of mortal hearts.'* Prophecy warned of this very fight! Just because you"—she choked—"care for Miss Parker does not make her our seventh. However innocent and guileless she may appear, she may in fact be sent from the ungodly realm, possessed by something harmful who looks to betray us. Appearing as no ordinary mortal, as you mention, with the ability to communicate with spirits—these very facts you present might be used to damn as easily as elevate."

Alexi shook his head. "Nonsense!"

"Alexi, she may not even be human."

"She's human, I assure you."

"Why, what sort of experiments did you conduct upon her to reach that confident conclusion?" Elijah asked, giving an unnecessary, lecherous smirk.

Alexi's expression was fearsome. He pounded his fist violently upon a nearby table. The gas lamps on the walls roared suddenly out of control, threatened to burn the place down.

"Alexi, please!" Josephine squealed. "Do you mean to kill us all?"

He raised one finger and the lamps dimmed; then he pointed it at Elijah, who turned pale.

"Never impugn her honour, Withersby," he warned, his voice deceptively calmed. "And who are you to criticize me—you, who nearly caused a riot ten years ago by running off on a whim?"

"I was wrong, Alexi. I was very wrong," Elijah murmured, truly contrite. "And I've spent years repaying that debt. Don't you make my same mistake."

Alexi held Elijah in a vicious stare for another unbearable moment, the lamp flames again burning high, the walls beginning to smolder. Finally, he tossed a hand aside in a casual gesture and the danger vanished—though the group coughed from the resulting smoke, waving their hands before their eyes. Elijah loosened his collar, sweat beading on his forehead.

"Alexi," Rebecca said. She moved slowly toward him. "Alexi, look what this is doing to you. Don't become a stranger to us, as you seem to have done since you met Miss Parker. You must consider the danger. And, Alexi, however innocent the girl may seem . . . something may be working within her she does not even understand. Working to undo you. To undo all of us. Prophecy told us to listen to our instincts and stay together!"

Alexi's hands clenched and unclenched. "It is my life! Am I to disobey my heart, my instincts—?"

"Mortal hearts make mistakes, Alexi." Rebecca was shaking her head. "For the thousandth time, love has nothing to do with Prophecy; it's only confused and endangered us. You'd risk the whole of our work for this wisp of a girl, this timid curiosity—"

"Don't you dare speak of her so," he hissed.

Josephine and Elijah looked at each other in surprise, then at Alexi. "Love? Love isn't a factor here, is it?"

"Alexi, listen to yourself," Rebecca continued, ignoring all else. "We were warned of this. She is a trick, a pawn meant to test you. Clear your mind, stop and think of duty! You've never been so swayed by passion. What on earth is this mad light in your eyes? You have always been our anchor of reason."

Alexi smoldered. "How dare you. Reason and duty? I've sacrificed everything. I denied myself every possible scrap of companionship, pleasure and comfort in my life, and now that Prophecy has come, my duty is to protect her. And you five, turned against me by Miss Linden—"

"We're not turning against you, Alexi," Rebecca insisted, tears in her eyes. "You're biased. Evidently, you must see the door yourself to be convinced. You can't find it in your heart to trust us. I'm sorry it's come to this."

Alexi approached, stood nose to nose with her. She remained strong beneath his withering stare and added, "This isn't easy for any of us, Alexi. Hearts may be broken. I know all about that."

"You want Prophecy to be Miss Linden because it's obvious that I don't care about her, beautiful as she may be. Your jealousy is such that you'd rather push me toward someone I care nothing for, hoping that once the *number* is out of the way I might at last choose you—"

Rebecca slapped him across the face, rage in her eyes. "How dare you say such a thing, Alexi Rychman? You've fabricated Prophecy to be your lover when that was never so! How dare you blame me for trying to save you from yourself?"

Alexi's hand rose to his cheek. Tears spilled down Rebecca's flushed, defiant face. Everyone else stared on in horror, waiting for the walls to ignite.

"Has it come to this?" he growled. "You, of all people, Headmistress? Years of friendship and trust turned to petty violence?"

"Alexi," Jane interrupted, moving to place an arm around her friend. "Don't blame Rebecca. We were all in agreement before you waltzed in."

His knuckles, in tight fists, were white. The word "waltz" was a great and painful irony. "All my years of leading you fools, and in the end they mean nothing. Fate has turned you against me. Well, I damn this fate!" Alexi fumed, turning to exit. "I shall make my own."

Michael jumped up suddenly and blocked him. In their years together, no one had ever seen the vicar angry. Until now. "You dare to alter Prophecy to suit your whim? You ignore the signs we are all given? Let the Balance fall to pieces, and all the goblins of hell can have a holiday on your lawn with this talk of yours!"

"No." Alexi shook his head, trying to press past, but Michael would not budge.

"Alexi, don't think this isn't hard for us as well," the vicar stated.

"No, I see. Kiss me on both cheeks, my friends, and send me to the cross."

Elijah scoffed. "Oh, don't be dramatic—"

"Don't be cruel, Elijah," Alexi countered.

Rebecca stood weeping across the room. "Don't be utterly stupid and blind. Listen to us, for once. You're not omnipotent."

Alexi stared at each of his friends, searching for any ally, any hint of understanding, but there was none. Lucille Linden crept down the stairs and stood silently in the corner. Weariness broke through Alexi's anger. If there truly was a door, could he deny it? Could he walk away from the group he led? He would fail everyone and everything if he did.

"I hate this," he stated sadly, and felt something begin to die inside him.

He turned to gaze upon the beautiful woman in the corner of the room who was looking at him with sympathy and care, and a bitter taste rose to his lips. Could they possibly be right? Somehow, could it be possible that the innocent Miss Parker had blinded him? Could his dear, sweet Percy indeed be the trap of which he was warned so many years previous? He had indeed made a mistake before—one that had cost his sister her legs and his family their love. Could he afford to stand alone again?

"May I speak?" Lucille asked. Her voice was like warm music, soothing the chill throughout the friends.

"Yes," Elijah replied. Alexi set his jaw.

"Please, my friends, I don't presume to know anything about how your esteemed faction operates. I can't say exactly how the doors operate. I've only seen them in times of stress, and I cannot guarantee them. But . . . let me spend a bit of time with you and let us see," she suggested gently.

The Guard turned to Alexi, staring expectantly. They were still his to command, if he would do so.

His shoulders fell. "I curse the day I received the burden that is this life," he stated, taking in his comrades. "Looking now, I don't recognize any of you. It's as if you've turned to stone."

He turned blankly to Miss Linden. "Very well, we'll have a meeting. Perhaps our chapel might return all of you to your senses," he muttered; but he was defeated, his voice hollow. Drawing his cloak about him, he turned slowly and moved to the door.

"I'll make arrangements for Miss Parker to be returned to her convent. The safest thing would be to keep her out of the way," Rebecca suggested quietly.

Alexi whirled with dead eyes, pointed a warning finger at her. "Don't say one word to Percy. I will handle it," he said, and stormed out the door.

The Guard stood silent, staring helplessly.

Lucille glowed with soft warmth. She said softly, her eyes watering, "I feel for the first time in ages that I—and all of us—may at last be safe."

CHAPTER TWENTY-FIVE

Isabel roused her with a sharp rap on the door before scurrying down the hall, and Percy rose and dressed alone, assuming, as she always did, that she was too frightening to receive help. When she finally made her way downstairs, Alexandra was awaiting her with scones and tea. Percy did not have the heart to admit she didn't have an appetite.

"I'm sure you're anxious to get back to your campus and to Alexi," the woman said, "so I won't hold you with pleasantries, but you simply must eat something; you'll waste away."

"Thank you, Miss Rychman, for your generosity and kindness," Percy replied, biting into a scone.

"Now, Alexi hasn't come for you this morning, dear girl, but don't worry. He sent a driver for you and the man's waiting outside." Percy was certain she appeared as crestfallen as she felt, for Alexandra was quick to add, "He must simply be busy, don't you worry. I'm sure you and I both worry too much when so much of his mystery we would never understand."

"But, are you sure he's all right?"

"He must be; he sent the driver. I'm sure he'll be at the school when you get there. Lord knows he spends hardly any time at our old estate."

The two females ate in silence for some time before Alexandra reached out to take Percy's soft white hands in hers. "Take care of him, dear girl. You've such a gentle heart—I see it in every part of you. He needs that," Alexandra confided. "He so desperately needs that."

Percy smiled nervously. "But Miss Rychman—"

"Break past his cold walls, Miss Parker! You must. You're the only one who can; he's never let anyone else near. He's so frozen without, but there's a fire within."

Percy nodded, thinking of his grandmother's words during the night, words about the firebird. She considered mentioning it and then thought better; she didn't want to add more madness to the mixture.

Her hands fluttering nervously in Alexandra's, she rose. "Thank you, Miss Rychman, for everything."

"Anyone that Alexi has taken the time to care about, which is hardly anyone, is always welcome here."

Percy stared out the carriage windows all the way back to London, wringing her hands and wondering why her professor hadn't come for her in person. Her mind raced through countless scenarios, and she willed the conveyance to speed her back. Of course, in the full light of day, the thought of his brazen kisses, the thought that he'd glimpsed her naked body, the thought that, had they not been interrupted, *anything* might have happened—all brought blushes that covered her head to toe.

Surely it was in regard to school policy that they couldn't take the risk of being seen creeping back onto the grounds together—this was the only thing she could think might be his reasoning, and she understood. Still, she found it odd he had not sent a note or any other communication indicating her course of action when she returned. She'd simply have to seek him out under the guise of academic pursuit.

City bells tolled nine. Percy thought guiltily about missing religious services when her arms had been so recently locked around a man not her husband. For that reason, she attempted to assuage her sin through fervent prayer. And yet, the strange events bringing her and Alexi together had to be the work of God's hand. Or, so she hoped.

When the driver pulled up to Athens's portico, Percy flew from the cab and scurried across the courtyard. She dared to glance up at the sky, thinking perhaps she'd dreamed the cracks along that surface, but clouds remained thick, keeping the heavenly canopy hidden.

She darted immediately to Alexi's office and almost forgot to seek permission to enter. Recovering herself, she took a deep breath and knocked.

"Who is it?" barked a voice from within. Percy shrank back from the tone.

"Perc—It's Miss Parker, Professor Rychman," she called.

No answer. Percy's fear pushed her onward. His door was unlocked, and she dared to open it, peeking her head inside. Alexi stood there, staring blankly out the stained-glass window, its colours cast across his expressionless face. Percy crept into the room, closing the door behind her.

"Alexi, what is the matter?" she asked as he shifted to not face her. He didn't reply, so she added sweetly, "I was worried about you when you did not come, but I'm sure that was for the best, considering our situation. Are you all right? Are your friends all right?" She approached slowly and reached out a hand to touch his shoulder.

He gave her one brief, stony glance that caused her heart to freeze, then turned away and evaded her touch. "You came in unannounced and uninvited, Miss Parker," he began coldly, "and so I ask you now to leave."

Her heart stumbled. "My apologies, Alexi. I was presumptuous. Do forgive me; I didn't mean to intrude. May I visit you later this evening, then? We've much to discuss," she added gently, hoping he'd turn with a weary smile, take her hand and unburden himself.

"No. You may not," he declared.

Percy trembled. "Alexi, a–are you cross with me? In the time since we were last together, what on earth—?"

"I have realized your web of witchcraft, and I must distance myself from you."

Percy blinked several times, suddenly nauseated. "What do you mean?" When she stepped forward and brushed her fingers against his sleeve, he flung his arm aside as if scalded. "Alexi, what on earth . . . How sudden is this pique? Why, just hours ago you held me in your arms—"

"I broke from your spell."

"Spell? What do you mean?" Percy asked after a short silence, her breath failing. "I grant you, I do not look ordinary—nor has anything in my life ever been so—but I'm no witch! I speak no incantations. I wield no charms. Your protection and concern were a gift you gave me of your free and dominant will—the greatest gift I've ever been given. And, if I'm not mistaken, you care—"

"I cannot explain to you any more than I could before. I simply cannot see you."

"Alexi, please, I don't understand."

"No more. I can see you no more. That's all you need understand," he declared.

"But, all we have—"

"I should never have so blindly indulged in your company, Miss Parker."

Percy wandered numbly toward his desk. "Alexi, do you understand how frightened I am? Not even a day has passed since you shielded me from that horrid beast," she reminded him. "What about my safety? Even if you do not wish to . . . follow through on the promise of your embrace, you pledged to keep me safe! Why this change of heart?" She was trembling quite badly.

"I . . . I cannot care for you; it is ruining me."

Tears falling, Percy staggered backward as if slapped. "Ruining you? Alexi. *Professor?* Tell me what could have been ruined but my own honour, useless as it is with my freakish face?"

Alexi remained silent. Percy prayed for something, anything to counteract the horror of this unwarranted change of sentiment more terrifying than the fangs of that incorporeal dog. Her hand flew to her mouth. "Have I been made such a fool that you'll not even look at me? Of course. You are ashamed of me. I'm not Beauty, not Snow White, but the Beast after all."

His formidable figure did not move; he made no sound. Finally he cut the silence with a dismissive declaration. "Miss Parker, you're a very intelligent girl. Don't indulge this senseless romanticism. You've also no need for further education. And since there are established rules of conduct in this place that have been thoroughly and egregiously broken, I've arranged for a carriage to return you to the convent tomorrow. It is for the best."

Percy choked, falling against his desk. "What?" she was barely able to whisper as her fingers fumbled at her throat to clutch the phoenix pendant. "You send me away; you punish me with no explanation, after all you did to me? What am I to do? What about your little 'club'—all these strange portents, talk of spirits, the number seven and a prophecy? You owe me something, not this cold, sudden banishment to whence I came!" She approached him. "Look at me, Alexi. Will you not see my pain? Don't you know how terrified I am of the dogs, the horses, the blinking visions of fire? If you abandon me . . . might it not mean my death?"

Despite her proximity, his expression remained impenetrable. Perhaps he cringed; she could not be sure. "Don't be foolish. You'll live," he stated.

"Live with what—fond touches turned suddenly to lies while unnatural events and creatures drive me to madness?"

"I told you no lies. I promised you nothing," he growled.

"You promised me information! Something! Safety! Knowledge! Foolish me, I thought you might need me as

much as I need you! For some greater purpose, it seemed!
But moreover . . . why did you tease? Why play with my
heart if you were only going to break it? I begged you not to
toy with me, and now you've ruined my life. My chances
and opportunities here—"

"It is not your place to fight me, Miss Parker. Stand down,"
he scoffed, still unwilling to look in her direction. "Silly
girl, you shouldn't have been foolish enough to give me your
heart. I am not responsible for the 'breaking' of any such
thing. You overstep your bounds—"

"I'm not the one who did so, Professor!" Percy insisted,
finding a surprising, righteous fury within her. "You broke
the rules when you pressed your lips to mine. You kissed
me." She had to gasp so as not to sob, tasting that delightful
yet devastating memory one final time. "There's a purpose
for me. Don't leave me so ignorant. Is this merely because I
am your student, and so now I, the one who has no power
here, shall be punished? Does the headmistress demand
that?"

Alexi clenched his fists. "She does, actually. You must be
removed from my life, Miss Parker, no matter what we have
shared. I can say no more."

Percy nearly swooned. "You can say no more . . ." A crazed
laugh tickled the back of her throat. "That's all you've ever
said. How convenient! And now you leave your pupil to the
wolves. The very sky is breaking open, Alexi. I'd like to hear
what the headmistress has to say about that—about Prophecy, about your little club, about how you touched me . . ."

The words crawled from her lips like spiders. Suddenly,
she remembered the night prior. "Oh, I should tell you that
your grandmother came to visit me at your sister's house.
She warned me of snakes and told me to tell you to light the
darkness with your fire, firebird. But perhaps that's useless
information to you now, as I am useless to you now."

It was then that he whirled upon her. His dark eyes were
colder than she could have imagined, and his face showed no

glimmer of pity. Percy buckled beneath the blow of that stare. She sank to her knees on the office floor, tears spilling helplessly from her eyes.

"You are not what I thought you were," he said simply. "I truly wish it were otherwise, but you are not Prophecy. You are a trap. And so you must go. I cannot have you here."

Percy was too stunned to move. Above her was a captivating yet suddenly foreign demon dressed in black robes and quivering with unfounded contempt. She knelt, crumpled like a helpless, broken doll. The pain in her breast was sharp as a rapier point, and she thought she might lose consciousness. She wished she would. Behind Alexi, visible in the window, the shadows of the horsemen in the sky seemed somehow larger. Her fear intensified.

Alexi pointed to the door. It was not a request.

Despite his ill will and her fall from favor, Percy could not help but stare up at him, intoxicated. Defiant, she refused to withhold her passion; if he didn't wish to hear the words, all the better. "Sending me away won't change how much I love you, Alexi." She spoke the weighty words like proclamations from heaven. She loved him dearly; there was no shame in that. What had begun as fascination had grown into a true love born from his unfaltering acceptance of her and everything about her, perhaps even delight in her. She could not credit it had vanished entirely.

Alexi's eyes closed. His conflict was betrayed by a shaking hand raked through his wild black locks. Percy rallied for a moment at this crack in his facade. Perhaps he would break down, confess his undying passion . . . But such a victory was not to be.

"Get out!" he cried, and lunged forward, meaning to drive her away.

She could bear no more. Percy crawled to the threshold, clambered out like a wounded animal. The door boomed shut behind her, its echo accompanied by the unearthly gasp of grief that tore from her throat.

On the other side of the door, Alexi Rychman dropped to his knees and put his head in his hands. He bit back an angry, pitiful wail.

Percy watched the sunset track across her wall.

Marianna knocked upon her door. There was a long silence. Marianna knocked again.

"Percy, it is I, are you there?"

"Yes, Marianna," Percy replied weakly.

"May I come in?"

"I . . . am not feeling well, Marianna. I think it best not to see me this evening. I fear I'd make you ill in turn." Percy found it difficult to think or speak in complete sentences.

"You are not well? May I get you anything?"

"No, Marianna. There is no medicine to cure this ailment."

"Oh."

"I will see you soon, my friend," Percy added, attempting to sound valiant.

"All right. Tomorrow then. Good night!" Marianna called, and Percy heard her slow, hesitant footsteps wander away.

Percy sat perfectly still, knowing the truth. There would be no tomorrow. She would never see Marianna again. She would be whisked back to the convent in shame, where she would live out an unfortunate life in silence. Or, she would cut that mercifully short with a sharp blade and hope God would understand. Or that canine abomination would find her and she desperately hoped its fangs were quick.

When she blinked, she saw fire beneath her eyelids. The sound of barking increased. Percy stared at the wall and waited for something to destroy her.

In the drawing room of Lord Elijah Withersby's grand estate, the chatter of The Guard and Miss Linden fell silent as Josephine ushered a swirl of black fabric and brooding shadow into the room.

"By all means, don't let me interrupt," Alexi said, his expression cold as he gestured for them to return to their conversations. He drifted to sit in a Queen Anne chair and stared into space, detached and silent. Rebecca stood across the room, an arm upon the mantel supporting her; but no matter how distraught his old friend appeared, Alexi did not acknowledge her. This was not the same group of comrades that wrought wonders.

His compatriots watched him with caution. Finally Jane rose and approached Miss Linden, who nodded and left the room.

Michael cleared his throat. "My dear Alexi," he began, somewhat sheepishly, "what on earth are we to do?"

Resting his elbows upon the arms of his chair, Alexi joined his fingertips at his chin. "Now you seek my guidance."

"We're lost without it, Alexi. You know that."

Alexi took a long moment before he chose to reply. "I told Miss Persephone Parker that our acquaintance could no longer continue. She'll be sent off and away from my sight," he declared, every word tasting like poison. As his companions took a relieved breath, he added, "However, I do not condone my own actions."

"Alexi, we are grateful for your compliance. But you must believe in Miss Linden, also, otherwise—"

"Otherwise Prophecy is a fallacy?" He snorted.

"Please, Alexi," Michael begged. "This is new for all of us. We are concerned both for our mission and your welfare. We're at a loss."

"Your sentiments baffle me. If you cared, you'd have respected my heart. I forsook Miss Parker and I don't know what will become of her. I assume she knew I . . . cared, and I do not flatter myself that she . . . Well, what does it matter? I wish you'd leave me to my fate rather than demand this charade of niceties."

"There's no charade, Alexi," Josephine breathed. "We've never seen you like this."

"I'll do my damned duty. I trust you'll do the same."

"We're accustomed to your cool melancholy, Alexi, but this bitter cold of yours is suffocating. We cannot do our duty with this strain."

"Ah, you are strained! Perhaps if you saw the utter devastation of a sweet young lady searching desperately for answers—an innocent who did nothing wrong, whom I've abandoned to the ravages of a strange and certainly harsh fate—you might understand true strain and the true extent of my bitterness!" Alexi spat, jumping to his feet. "If you will believe it, I am actually restraining myself in aid of retaining some semblance of professional manner."

Rebecca had all the while said nothing. She and Alexi now stared at each other, but she did not back down from his merciless gaze. "After so many years together, I can't bear this!" she whispered, her fist clenched upon the mantel.

"It pains me as well. More than you know. And if you'd like to speak further about such pain and suffering, Miss Thompson, you may seek me out in private, where I'm sure even more painful rumination awaits."

Rebecca's throat visibly constricted.

Alexi turned curtly to the assembled company, sardonic bitterness dripping from his words. "So. After denying my instincts you now ask for my edicts. Well, let's take Miss Linden's advice and have a meeting. Perhaps she'll open up the spirit world and it will be perfectly clear we're . . . meant to be. I expect she awaits us in the next room?"

Josephine nodded.

Alexi briskly departed, and his absence allowed his friends to breathe again. Jane attended Rebecca, who had sunk into a chair against the wall. Josephine, unable to bear the silence, went to the phonograph and set it viciously to playing. A sentimental piano piece burst forth, doing little to assuage the unsettled company that had been taking refuge in tea and wine.

In the adjacent chamber, Miss Linden had lit a perfumed candle and made herself comfortable at a small Turkish suite. Bent over a notebook, she looked up as Alexi burst in. He coolly evaluated both her and the rich dressings of the room.

"Good evening, Professor," she said. "Will you sit with me a moment?"

He swept his robe aside and sat at the small table, eyeing the small book in which she had been writing. "Your memoirs, Miss Linden?"

She laughed softly. "Exactly!" Her emerald eyes reflected the diffuse light, and her red lips were soft and plump. Her creamy skin, set against the dark green of her garb and eyes, and her impeccable black curls, was flawless. Miss Linden was, Alexi had to acknowledge, with her beauty and regal carriage, everything that he and his compatriots had originally expected of a goddess.

"You will come with us to our hall tonight," he commanded.

"I shall do whatever you bid me do," she agreed, green eyes sparkling.

"My dear professor," she continued, reaching out to brush his locked and folded hands upon the tabletop. "All of this is very sudden, very overwhelming. I'm sure you feel the same. However, I trust you and know that you'll guide me." She blushed and looked away. "I was drawn to you from the first . . . Though I know you cannot say the same."

Alexi shifted in his chair and blankly absorbed her sad smile. Her eyelids fluttered, and he thought he glimpsed the glitter of tears. "Miss Linden—"

"No, Professor," she interrupted. "There is no need for you to make excuses. I feel for you, and abhor the duty which forces you to forsake your heart. You and I are thrust into a most strange situation."

"Indeed," he replied.

"Miss Thompson told me of the provisions of this prophecy, and what you believe it to mean." She sighed as Alexi gave a slow nod. "The prophecy, as you see it, would call for us . . ."

"To be lovers," he agreed.

Lucille visibly shivered, causing her back to arch, pressing her voluptuous body against the table and toward him. "Yes. Lovers. But your heart lies with a paler face, doesn't it?" she whispered. "Such a strange girl—so timid and yet so passionate. What a poor, unfortunate creature!"

Alexi swallowed hard. "Please, do not speak of her."

"Very well, then. What can I do to make you . . ."

"To make me fall in love with you?"

Lucille gave a shrill, nervous laugh. "This is so terribly odd! Must we throw aside all propriety? How this turns my world inside out. I, beautiful as I know that I am, find myself struggling for a man's notice, despite the fact that it has been preordained," she mourned. Alexi found he had no wish to comfort her. "Though I wield no sword, I'd gladly fight my rival."

Alexi stared at her with hardening heart and a clenched fist.

She softened. "If only for your sake, Professor, I feel I may do anything—and it terrifies me."

"Indeed?" Alexi sighed. "You no doubt possess powers, the full spectrum of which we've yet to discover."

"You're trying to convince yourself," she recognized.

"This is very difficult for me, Miss Linden."

"Call me Lucy, won't you?"

"Lucy, then. It is very difficult for many reasons."

"Tell me."

Alexi snorted. "Though my social graces have before been impugned, I'd rather not try the patience of a beautiful woman with the scattered thoughts of a dour and tedious man."

"Please, Professor, you're nothing of the sort. Let's put simple courtesies aside. If you and I must suddenly care for each other without the benefit of courtship—though I've betrayed my sense, modesty and pride in admitting that I care for you already—it might help if you ... 'unfold to me why you are heavy,'" she pleaded with a small smile. "I hear you like Shakespeare."

There was a long silence as Alexi processed her words. He found it ironic that Lucy should quote Portia's plea to Brutus—Brutus, who was noble and yet a murderer, a betrayer. Alexi himself was no less. And where Brutus came to a dire and undignified end upon his own sword, Alexi wondered grimly if he'd someday do the same on some spectral threshold.

Chasms within him opened wider, but he forced himself to speak. "I prepared all my life for my coming fate, was obligated to lock my heart for countless years. Recently I saw the opportunity for my loneliness to end."

"Miss Parker?" Lucille prompted.

"Yes. I believed so ..." Alexi's voice faltered. "But that could not be proven on all counts. I, unused to such feelings, am at a loss. I've known duty, diligence, omens, spirits and loneliness. But nothing like this." Having unclasped far more than was his custom, he felt ill and resentful.

"Dear Professor," Lucy said gently. "If you allow me, I can abate that loneliness of yours." Moving around the small table, in a gesture that somehow did not seem out of place given the circumstances, she knelt and looked up at him in earnest.

The sight of Percy's pale, stricken face stared up at Alexi, the memory of her similar earnestness as she sank to her knees on his office floor. Her sweet voice accosted him, a voice he'd grown eager to hear, now begging for kindness and the answers rightly due her. He relived the wretched sound of her sobs as she fled his office, inexplicably cast aside, passionate ties sundered. He could think of nothing else.

He leaped to his feet, breaking out in a cold sweat, and was uncomfortably pinned by Lucille's gaze. As thunder roared outside the window, he turned and said, "I'm sorry Miss Linden, but I cannot continue this conversation at present."

He burst out of the room and returned to his compatriots, who looked expectant as he faced them.

"My fellows, we cannot have a meeting tonight; I've grown distract, and it will only create weakness in our sacred space. We shall reconvene soon, but I beg you, not tonight." And with that, he ran out the door.

He had no desire to return to his empty estate—he would likely set it on fire and let it burn to the ground this time—and he did not believe he could face his sister and the questions she would doubtlessly pose. Instead, he escaped into academic paperwork, his only solace for years, and listened to the tempest break viciously outside his office window.

When the clock down the hall chimed a late hour, he was certain it tolled the doom of all happiness he'd ever hoped to have.

CHAPTER TWENTY-SIX

Things had been growing increasingly grim. A thunderstorm raged outside Percy's window, the night sky unleashing its atmospheric fury upon the whole of London and the city's sprawling outskirts. Percy lay in pain upon her floor, limbs twisted in the lacy folds of her nightdress. Something sharp had begun to heave within her. It was a strange, inhuman sort of pain, not entirely emotional and yet not wholly physical, as if something deep inside was waking in rebellion. Something inside was eating her alive.

There were whispers in her mind, sounds that pelted her brain like the raindrops against her window. The lightning illuminated her writhing white body. She felt a close presence but could see nothing. Certain that her wits had fled, she feared she had turned demon, and longed for a priest to exorcise her.

Daring to look out the window, she saw that the horsemen trod closer on the horizon, and that horrid barking continued to echo from the clouds themselves. Curling into a ball, she drew back from the vantage and sobbed.

Her sorrow did not aid her churning stomach. Instead, her sobs seemed to bring something up. She gagged on the immediate sensation of something palpable and sour in her mouth, and, not having eaten that day, she found the pulpy kernels that were suddenly burgeoning from her throat an additional terror. There was the same sickening smell of fruit as had nauseated her in her vision, and she coughed up seeds onto the floor. She knew just what mythic sort of seeds they were, mysteriously and disgustingly expelled, and it did nothing for her sanity. When the goddess Persephone, kidnapped by Hades, king of the underworld, ate the fruit of the pomegranate, she'd been bound there and to him.

To a silent God, Percy prayed that the shadowy horsemen on the horizon were not galloping in to drag her away. She did not remember being the bride of a god, namesake or no, nor did she ever wish to be. She heaved again, desperate to void the pulp she herself had never ingested.

The clock down the hall chimed a late hour. A bolt of lightning flashed so near her window that she cowered, thunder reverberating in her bones. She needed, now more than ever before, to be wrapped securely in Alexi's arms. She was sure she was meant to be nowhere else. An invisible force was urging her on, demanding at all costs that she run to him despite his betrayal, despite the fact that he was sending her away in the morning.

Something sharp twisted again within Percy's body. More pulp burst into her mouth. An uncontrollable shivering took over. Her pendant burned, but she paid it no mind. The thunder roared, and there came a rending shriek—something pressed in toward her, intending to snuff the candle of her soul. Something sought to destroy her. And perhaps, she realized dimly, it sought to destroy Alexi, too.

She had to warn him. They were not meant to be separated. Beyond their hearts, something larger was at stake. A balance was sliding from light to dark.

As if to force Percy out into the storm, with a sharp crack and explosion her window shattered and the gale poured in. With a cry, she stumbled backward. Blood seeped into her white gown from many tiny wounds made by glass . . . matching the dribbled ruby stains of half-digested pomegranate.

Percy stared at the blood, her shattered window, her patches of lacerated skin, and loosed a scream. She flung open her door and flew into the corridor, ashamed and terrified to seek Alexi out. But to whom else could she turn? The headmistress? Marianne, who knew nothing of the darkness that surrounded Percy? Through her increasing horror and dimming sensibility, only one thought remained. She was not meant to have been shunned by the man she loved. Of that, Percy was sure.

Alexi, inconsolable and exhausted, put down a dreary book of Russian politics and went to his stained-glass window. The tempest roaring outside fit his mood. Staring at the courtyard below, his gaze clouded. He tried to ignore the pounding of his heart. He imagined life without the mysterious snow-white girl who held his mighty heart captive, he who had once forsworn love.

Love. The word made him ill. It was foreign, unfair, and

he'd done fine without it. What good was any such feeling if he could not have the one he wanted? What of those who could choose whom they loved? Jealousy scorched his heart, jealousy of normal men, faced with no other requirements than their personal desires. He dug his nails against the windowsill.

Restless, he moved to the opposite corner of the office, turned the knob of his phonograph so that an evocative aria filled the room, and began pacing. An intense lightning strike drew him back to the window. There, he contemplated throwing himself into the torrent.

A few ladies, frightened by the storm, had gathered in the hall. They shrieked with fear at the sight of an uncovered Percy, whose door was flung open with a cry, revealing her mad-eyed and tousle-haired, patches of crimson bespeckling her spectral whiteness. Percy heard muffled squeals of "Murder!" "Madness!" and "The Ripper has come for the ghost girl!"

The mortified ladies of her hall screamed and ran, hurrying into their rooms to gossip or faint. Percy didn't care. She flitted past a gasping Miss Jennings to rush headlong into the thunderstorm.

She was the only one daring the outdoors; even the school guards had taken shelter. The rain pelted mercilessly down on her tearstained face, and in moments her snowy locks became sodden strings that grasped her cheeks and shoulders. Her ruffled gown plastered against and chilled her slender form. The spots of crimson on the lace of her gown spread in watery, haunting traces. Nonetheless, she welcomed the stinging downpour, sobbing into it as she ran across the courtyard. Cold rain and hot saltwater mixed in her mouth.

Somehow, tonight she could see the sky. *Her* sky. Above her appeared a gaping hole where a shell of comfort had been broken open, revealing a starker atmosphere beyond. It was as if she'd once been shielded but was now completely open to all possible assault . . .

Apollo Hall loomed ahead. Percy's wounds from the glass throbbed. Lightning blazed. Thunder screamed. Percy stood, staring up at a stained-glass window and opened her mouth in a weak wail. She shook violently. There was a form in the window.

Her heart stopped. The figure above was unmistakable, her only chance for safety and salvation. He was the answer; he could make the horsemen vanish and the dogs silent, and he could close up the broken heavens.

"Why reject me?" Percy wept at the window. "You need me, Alexi, for London is rotting. An apocalypse is coming if we part, so don't send me away."

The cold rain was freezing her to the bone. Faint, she dropped to her knees and quailed. She was not meant to withstand this strain, the eviscerating misery of what was inside her, screaming to be acknowledged. And she could fight no longer. Whatever power had shattered her window and pressed in upon her would now get the better of her. Percy cried hysterically. She loved Alexi so. And now, more than ever, she needed his understanding. For she understood nothing.

All faded to black.

Alexi froze.

A shade—a frail, beauteous nightmare—stood beneath his window. White hair whipped in all directions, her head thrown back, mouth wide-open, white dress soaked and blotted with red... his dear Percy was there, torn by the storm's fury. The lament of the soprano keening from the bell of the phonograph could just as well have come from the mouth of this spectre below, who suddenly collapsed in a lifeless heap onto the sopping flagstones.

"Oh, dear God. Percy!"

Alexi bolted down the stairs, out the door and into the rain, toward the motionless bundle of limbs and wet fabric, ignoring everything else. He scooped Percy into his arms. She was light as a feather, unconscious yet shuddering. The downpour clubbed him. Alexi gazed down at the lifeless marble face, that visage which, even in this half-drowned state, he could not help but find beautiful.

"Persephone, you godforsaken romantic, what drove you to this?" He moaned, sickened by the sight of the blood on her gown as he whisked her off toward the infirmary. "Please, not me. Please let this not be my fault," he cried, knowing full well it was.

A sight indeed swept into the infirmary. Tall, black and billowing as he moved, wet hair hanging over burning eyes, he was a veritable angel of death holding an apparition more fairy than human in his arms as he burst through the doors.

"Professor!" a nurse exclaimed, rushing to him and the limp form he cradled. Alexi charged to the infirmary beds without care or clearance, and laid Percy upon the nearest one. An entourage of nurses clustered around.

"Professor Rychman, what on earth—"

"Take care of her," he commanded, raking a hand through sopping hair. "She collapsed outside my window. I happened to notice."

"But why—" a nurse began.

"I don't know!" Alexi cried. "Tomorrow she was supposed to return to a convent. Make sure she goes nowhere until she is well."

"Yes, sir," they all agreed.

The medical staff dispersed to gather supplies, and he was given a moment alone to hover over her wet, bloodstained body. He knelt beside her, imagining her an angel that had plummeted from the heavens and into the sea, there perhaps to be drowned.

"Poor Ariel, my sweet cipher. Don't let the tempest claim you. I only wish I could," he murmured, kissing her moist forehead.

His lips lingered upon her a moment too long, for he was desperate to place his aching lips upon her lifeless ones, rouse her like the prince did Sleeping Beauty in one of those tales of which she was desperately fond. But finally he drew back, fighting a wealth of emotion he could not indulge, and fled. He must kill his heart once and for all, for it was a useless mortal contrivance that he abhorred.

Soaking, he stormed back to his office, stoked the fire in his hearth and sat at his desk. Emotions he was violently choking down were refusing to die. Stricken, he collapsed his face into his hands and remained frozen there in grief until sleep overtook him.

Perhaps it was mutual instinct and loneliness that drew Rebecca, at so early an hour, to seek out Alexi. The vicious storm had only just broken. Dawn's first light was licking the horizon.

She had wandered about her apartments at the top of Promethe Hall all night, wringing her hands, thinking she heard screaming. She'd troubled to travel all the way to Alexi's estate, only to find him absent. Upon her return, she dimly supposed he must have taken to his office. Wracked by nerves, she flitted across the courtyard in the same manner as the restless spectres of the academy who, one by one, turned to stare at her with odd mistrust. Even their sombre forms were agitated.

His office door was unlocked. Upon his desk was a head of tousled black hair. The fire was smoking in the fireplace.

Rebecca's blood ran cold as she approached the desk. "Alexi . . . ?"

His breathing was laboured, his brow furrowed in a painful dream. Rebecca reached out a questing hand and brushed a lock of hair from his moist forehead. With a start he bolted upright, his dark eyes blurred and unfocused.

"Alexi, it's me," Rebecca fumbled. "I didn't mean to startle you."

He growled and rubbed his face in his hands, raking back tousled hair with quivering fingers. After a moment of purging the horrid vision of a pale girl in a coffin from his mind, his eyes focused. "What do you want?"

Rebecca took the chair opposite him. "This anguish in your heart, I cannot bear it. I must apologize. The night I struck you . . . something within me died."

"You killed something inside of me as well," he countered. "I never thought you and I would end in such childish acts."

"Forgive me, please, Alexi, I beg you." She reached a shaking hand across the table. He withdrew his own, pinning her with furious eyes. "Alexi, I never wished for this."

"Nor did I. But don't you dare speak words of contrition to me now, traitor."

Rebecca's mouth went slack. She had nothing to counter that terrible blow.

Something snapped in Alexi's eyes and his shoulders convulsed. His head fell suddenly into his hands. "She may be dying!" he cried.

"What?"

"My Percy—my dear, sweet girl . . . She wandered into the tempest. There was blood on her gown; she was feverish, shaking. She collapsed outside my window, crying up to me. I was watching the storm . . ."

"My God."

"Rebecca, I feel her slipping away. Terrible forces are at work upon her, and I feel her passionate, innocent soul draining from me. I'm so confused! I promised to keep her safe and I don't know that I can!" He wailed, tears springing to his eyes. "Damn my heart! Cut it out! Cut it from me, Rebecca, please . . . !"

It was an unprecedented act, but Alexi Rychman began to sob.

"Oh, Alexi!" Rebecca's hand went to her mouth and she rushed to him, clasping him in an embrace.

"I promised I'd explain everything. I told her I'd protect her, but instead I may have killed her! What if she dies, Rebecca, without ever knowing? This damned prophecy aside, I love the girl!"

He acquiesced and fell helpless into her arms, weeping like a little boy. Rebecca cried with him. She reeled with a mixture of sympathy, the sting of his confession of love, and the bittersweet feel of her arms around him.

"Dear God, Alexi. What are we asking of you?"

Percy lay like the dead, Snow White without a glass coffin, below a large window. Only pale, bluish shadows distinguished her body from the pristine white sheets.

"Oh, Percy!" Marianna rushed to her corpselike form. She knelt and took her friend's colourless hand and found it uncommonly warm, the arms covered with small bandages. "What horrid distraction drove you to this?"

A sheen of perspiration covered Percy's semitranslucent skin. Her eyes fluttered beneath white lids, lost in a dream-filled unconsciousness.

A wide-eyed nurse was making her rounds, and she paused at the foot of Percy's bed to glance at Marianna. The German girl asked, "Miss, may I ask how long she has been here?"

"Since late last night. Are you her dear friend? She's been murmuring for a Marianna."

Her friend's eyes filled with tears. "Yes, that is me. I've been inquiring of her everywhere. The girls in my corridor said they heard she went mad and rushed out into the storm. Who brought her here?"

"I did not see, miss, but I was told Professor Rychman found her. Oh, my, miss, how she's been murmuring!" The nurse spoke with noticeable discomfort. "Desperate pleas, but all in foreign tongues. I can't catch a word." Then, bowing slightly, she hurried off.

Marianna picked up a small towel at the bedside to blot the moisture pooling on Percy's forehead. "Percy, my sweet, you know what myth we learned about yesterday in class? I now know your namesake. We learned of poor Persephone, kidnapped and dragged below the earth. Please don't let the underworld take you, Percy, I could not bear it!"

Her friend's eyes suddenly shot open, and Marianna gasped as her arm was clenched tightly by white hands. With a sick and ashamed chuckle, Percy let her head fall limply to the side in order to gaze up at her friend. "Hello, darling. Sorry—thought you were a demon come for me."

"Who has done this to you?" Marianna asked.

Percy shook her head gravely, and after a long pause decided to reply with a bit of verse. "'Nobody, I myself'!" she murmured.

Marianna shook her head. "No, no, my Desdemona, I'll not take Shakespeare for an answer. What Othello brought you to this?"

"From the moment he sent me away, everything is falling apart!"

"Who, who sent you—?"

"I am mad, dear Marianna! Can one suffer their very own apocalypse, meant only for them? My world is coming to an end, and I see it all . . . As prophe—" Percy choked.

"You are not coming to an end, Percy," her friend argued. "What is it that you see?"

"Dogs—horses and dogs, approaching closer, snapping their hundreds of jaws, closer, closer, my fever burns, here a feather, there a portal, a burning bird, snakes . . . hounds . . . one or hundreds . . ."

"What drove you into the storm, Percy? And why are there bandages on your skin?"

"Wounds of a shattered heart."

Marianna shuddered at the sound of her friend's rattling lungs. "Shattered by whom?"

Percy set her lips.

Marianna shook her head. "You leave me to guess?"

"It does not matter," Percy murmured.

"Oh, no, of course not! You are bloodied, driven to madness, out in a maelstrom to catch your death, but of course it does not matter," Marianna replied. She leaned close. "If that professor of yours—"

Reacting as if stabbed, Percy clapped a hand over her mouth. "Please!"

"I see." Marianna gritted her teeth. "You would shelter and defend *das Schwein* to your very death."

Percy collapsed again on the bed. As her eyes rolled up beneath her eyelids, she began to mumble. "I am on fire." Marianna took a towel, dipped it in the washbasin and placed it upon her forehead. Percy's head lolled to the side and she murmured, "Sick with the scent of scorched feathers—"

"Feathers?"

"Something terrible from another time," Percy breathed, unable to focus. "Something's after me, and none of it's what we think . . ."

"What isn't? Percy, stay—look at me."

"Hell is not down. It's sideways," Percy murmured, and her eyelids closed.

"Percy?" There was no answer. Marianna felt for her friend's pulse, terrified, and found it racing. "Dear God, Persephone Parker, what is happening to you?"

CHAPTER TWENTY-SEVEN

"Miss Linden," Alexi said carefully, bowing.

Lucille swept into his office, shimmering in an immaculately tailored silver dress. "Professor Rychman." She curtseyed in return.

"Shall we take a turn about the courtyard?" Alexi offered. "The weather has broken. Perhaps only for a moment, but I suppose we must seize our chances."

The woman's ruby lips formed a delicious smile. "What a lovely idea. Quite peculiar weather we've experienced of late, don't you think?"

"A portent," Alexi replied.

"Ah, of course."

Descending the front steps of Apollo Hall, they both took a deep breath of air pregnant with moisture and the fragrance of decaying leaves. A flock of birds swept around the corner, taking refuge in an evergreen to weather the next onslaught of the storm.

Percy's eyes shot open. She heard horrid noises of indescribable creatures. Her mind had just been staring at the charred face of a once-beautiful man.

Things were crawling on her. Flinging the covers aside, she jumped out of bed with a cry . . . but her own body was the only strange thing that had been writhing in the bedclothes, and her bandages fell away to reveal little red hash marks.

"Miss Parker, darling miss, you've just had another dream. Back to bed with you," a nurse commanded, rushing over and putting a hand on her forehead. "My God, your fever burns yet."

Percy trotted awkwardly to the terrace doors. "I need a breath of air." The nurse opened her mouth to reprimand such sudden exertion, but her words fell short as Percy stared at her; the sparkling madness burning in her eyes stemmed all protest.

A heavy breeze cooled Percy's enflamed body, whipping through her thin hospital gown, and she closed her eyes to relish the air, trying to avoid staring at how the sky remained broken into two separate layers. Her momentary peace was disturbed by a familiar, strong sound of footsteps in the courtyard below. None other than her very own black-clad heartbreaker walked two floors below. She shook violently.

In Percy's heightened state, she could sense an energy about Alexi that was as dire as her own, a desperate aura between strained hearts. On his arm was that beautiful woman,

Miss Lucille Linden. The pair neared the fountain, almost directly beneath the balcony where Percy stood frozen. Several spirits passing across the courtyard were scoffing, but it was behind Miss Linden's and Alexi's backs.

Watching them, Percy felt a sickening cry begin inside her throat like bile. An image before her was coming clearer, and she was overwhelmed by a wave of new horror. When she'd first glimpsed the woman at the gala ball, Percy had imagined Miss Linden's coiled black locks as serpents. This time, she didn't just imagine them. Writhing and slithering over the woman's head, asps leered up at Percy with menace; their red eyes were made of fire, forked tongues hissed flames.

Alexi halted as if he sensed something, but he did not look up.

Percy wailed aloud. Clapping a hand over her mouth she sank to the floor, curled into a huddled mess against the wall. Biting her palm, she fought as her body convulsed with dry heaves. Hot tears coursed down her cheeks.

"Miss Parker?" The nurse rushed over, having heard her cry. She bent over Percy and lifted her feeble form in strong arms to return her to bed. "Poor dear," the nurse sighed, her red cheeks flushing further as she helped settle Percy under a sheet. "Your dear friend said she would return to sit with you soon. Until then, you must calm your nerves."

Percy's eyes rolled as her breath hitched, and she felt the darkness of unconsciousness claiming her once again. "All the creatures of the Old World, and nothing to protect me! The spirits are crying 'Beware,' but for what? He can't hear their warning! Oh, the snakes ... what his grandmother warned—"

Percy fainted.

Alexi heard a wretched cry above him, and he turned to find the source of the sound, looking first to the terrace of Pro-

methe Hall and the infirmary floor. A white figure flickered
out of view. His heart burned in his chest, and he looked at
Miss Linden curiously as a shudder ascended his spine.

"What is it?" she asked gently. Not a hair, bead or dainty
bit of lace was out of place on her immaculate figure.

"I . . . thought I saw something," he choked out, his eyes
flicking again to the terrace. Unsure if the form had been a
ghost or indeed Percy, he prayed that it was her and that this
meant her frail body was recovering.

With a growing unease, he noted how the spirits of Athens, men and women of various ages and periods, stared at
Miss Linden. Aware that she could see them as well, he tried
to make his evaluation as surreptitious as possible as he attempted to discern their attitude. Their moods were of no
help, for their transparent faces were inscrutable. Yet each
ghostly mouth moved. Alexi wished more than ever he
could hear their words, or that he had Percy by his side as
translator, for he desired to know if these spirits were offering a benediction or a warning.

"So," Miss Linden began gently. "Tonight we have a
meeting?"

"Yes," Alexi replied.

"What shall I expect?"

"Well. I'm not sure really."

"You have a common meeting place, then?"

Alexi nodded. "Yes, a secret place we found upon our
possession, the location and entrance of which came to us
like an old, dormant memory resurfacing after many years."

"Upon 'possession'! Why do you call it such a thing? How
on earth—"

"We were around the age of thirteen, some fourteen,"
Alexi said, attempting to explain what he had always considered inexplicable, "when something slid through our bodies—a soul into each of our veins, claiming us for our Grand
Work. We were led to a sacred place where we received our

prophecy from a goddess, the divine creature who told us what we are. We have a vague mythology."

"Oh! Do you now?" Lucille looked enthralled.

"I beg your patience, Miss Linden. I cannot tell you the whole of our history, or what scraps of it we may have gathered over the years, in one brief turn about the courtyard. Did you ever experience such a thing?"

"What? A possession? No. Not exactly."

"Well, then. What about you?"

"I was born strangely," Lucille began, and at the sound of her words let out a sparkling laugh. "As if I was born specifically for someone. I knew I had a magnetism, something that kept people . . . and spirits . . . *staring* at me. I knew I was meant to see all manner of incredible things in my life, and have all manner of incredible things see me." She paused and tilted her head. "Professor, what shall we do once we arrive at your meeting place?"

"Well." Alexi took a breath. "We will form a circle, sing incantations, I'll ask the Great Force for a benediction and see what, if anything, happens. There's no rule book for this thing, Miss Linden. I wish it were a science but it is not. Of course, we'll also be looking for that door of yours."

"Ah, yes, the sign."

A drizzle of rain began to fall. Lucille squealed and dragged Alexi by the hand, running beneath the portico of Apollo Hall.

"Miss Linden, I must attend to business. May I lend you a parasol, escort you to your carriage and leave you until later this evening?"

"By all means, dear Professor. And again—do call me Lucy, won't you?"

Alexi hurried to his office and plucked a parasol from a rack. Lucy followed silently. He felt her watching his every move as he led her back down the stairs, out onto the path to the waiting carriage, and opened its door.

"Thank you for the company, Professor," she stated warmly, her perfect cheeks rosy and her gaze just as inviting. She cocked her head to the side, closed the distance between them and stood staring, her wide green eyes searching his. Then, lightly, she placed her mouth to his cheek and kissed him. He stood rigid and allowed it. Lucy lingered, breathing him in. When she drew back, blushing, and ducked inside the carriage, Alexi folded her parasol and placed it on the seat next to her.

"It will become easier," she said as he closed the door, his face blank. She poked her head out the window and said in a sultry tone, "Soon you'll want to kiss me back! Until this evening, then."

Alexi nodded.

"Thank you, dear Professor," she murmured. Waving daintily as the carriage rolled off, Lucille kept her eyes upon him to the last.

Alexi felt the rain again permeate his robes. He walked slowly, dragging wet footsteps up the stairs of Promethe Hall until he stepped into a cavernous white room that smelled sharply of medicinal fluids. A blonde girl at her side, Percy lay as if entombed yet still looked angelic.

Marianna turned, sensing movement. She stared blankly at Percy's professor, taking in his tall form draped in damp black fabric, the crimson cravat around his disheveled collar open like a wound. He stood like a statue, chiseled features harsh, hypnotic eyes drinking in the sight of the supine body before him.

"What did you do?" she demanded.

The professor grimaced and said nothing. The sight of something above Percy seemed to rattle him. Marianna looked up to find nothing. The professor turned and exited, trailing black fabric and raindrops, leaving a keen emptiness where his piercing presence had just seethed. Marianna watched as the door swung shut and clicked. She sighed, turned once again to her friend and started.

Percy's eyes had suddenly shot open, and she was staring in abject horror at the ceiling. Marianna felt the air around her grow unnaturally cold. Percy shuddered.

"Percy, what is it?"

"They're all watching."

"Who?"

"All the haunts. They are all above me, staring down. Waiting for me to die."

Marianna paused. "There is nothing above you, Percy. I just now looked."

"Well, there they are, waiting for me to join them. I wonder how long they've been watching." She coughed, turning to Marianna with eyes full of tears. "I am in such pain, my friend. I don't know what is inside me. Or outside me."

All of the spirits of Athens Academy had indeed gathered above Percy's bed and stared down at her. Numerous sets of ghostly eyes were watching, wondering. They pointed. They offered no explanation, only stared blankly.

One of the spirits moved closer. Marianna shivered as he did. Percy recognized the spirit as the young boy who hovered around the chandelier near Athens's front door. His soft brogue murmured just over her head. "Miss, I still don't know what you are, but are you goin' to do somethin' about the mess you're in, or are you goin' to join us?"

Percy pursed her lips, her nostrils flaring. She didn't know if she was relieved the boy had broken the spirits' dread silence, or if she'd have preferred the quiet. Marianna squirming nearby reclaimed her attention.

"I do not know if I should tell you this," the German girl began, "considering I know not the role he may have played in this . . . but he came by. Your professor."

"Oh!" Percy's body flooded with both joy and fear. "A-and?"

"He was all brooding power and sour expressions. I asked him what he had done. Forgive me, Percy, but I had to—"

Percy's hands fluttered at her side. "What was his response?"

"He said nothing. He stared at you—intently, sadly, I think—looked above you and left as abruptly as he came." The German girl halted as Percy doubled over and burst into tears. "Oh, dear. Percy . . ."

Wordlessly Percy wept, the last of her tears and strength draining away. She cried herself into unconsciousness while Marianna sat sentry next to her, clutching her hand, begging her softly to hold on.

Alexi paced about his estate. As the clock struck a quarter to eleven, his temperature rose. Nearness to the exquisite Miss Linden had not cleared Percy's taste from his thoughts, and he feared those reflections would influence the course of the coming ceremony. He tried to shove thoughts of her snowy face from his mind, but she haunted him; he saw Percy's eyes through his bedroom window, heard her voice in the corners of his mind, felt her vibrant heart in every shadow of his house as the pressure from her lips rested upon his in a phantom kiss. A sinking realization came to him: Persephone Parker would haunt him forever.

With great effort, he imagined bringing Miss Linden to his estate, imagined her lovely and poised, sitting with him in his drawing room. He tried to picture her lounging in the arched alcoves of his parlor, dancing on the veranda, caressing his flesh behind the thick curtains of his four-post bed . . .

These things he had, with an oft-thrilling guilt, imagined with Miss Parker. Thoughts of Percy had been known to fever him in the privacy of his midnight hours, where he dreamed of educating her not on mathematics but the finer points of seduction. Such thoughts of Lucille brought no such fire, no matter how exquisite her face and form. Percy's face, however singular her pallor, was infinitely more breathtaking to him. She had shaken his steeled, embattled foundations and shone a curious light inside just when he had begun to lose faith; nothing else had ever brought such warmth to his existence. Hers was the face painted like a locket portrait on the inside of his eyes.

Would it be for naught, the power and experience he had accrued throughout the years? So long he had toiled, leading The Guard, maintaining the Balance. But now was the moment of truth. If he chose incorrectly, if he was still pining for a marble angel with whom he had waltzed by moonlight when he was supposed to love a raven-haired temptress, would that require him to fail? Would he be betraying his goddess, his friends and his destiny? Jealousy for the commoner who could love freely again took hold.

Or, was Rebecca right after all? Was love indeed not part of Prophecy? Was he free to love Percy no matter her relation to the Grand Work, or would fate always keep them apart?

The clock struck eleven. He fell to the floor and began to pray. He had never been one for heavenly supplication, but he supposed if there was a time for it, the time was now. He prayed for presence of mind, to know what to say and do in the coming hours. He begged for Percy's continuing life and strength, for her to be kept safe at all costs. And he prayed that, even though he was sure that Prophecy was meant to be his lover, that he might be able to love Percy anyway . . .

He stared into the long mirror by the door. His dark eyes were empty; he was devoid of the usual energy with which he burst into a room and commanded it, making flames roar to life by the mere wave of a finger. But, rousing himself from his morbid reverie, he donned cloak and top hat to leave his large, empty house all the more empty. After readying the faithful Prospero, he set off for the intimate chapel that housed their divine mystery.

The air was sick. A virulent force was tearing through the streets toward a specific destination, ready for a reckoning. It growled and roiled and cut a path like a whirl of ancient blades. Its casualty would be an unspeakable shame. Neither

Alexi nor his cohorts had any inkling that there would be another mutilated corpse in the morning, nor that this would be the worst. There would be nothing, when all was said and done, to ever suggest that this woman, torn utterly to pieces, had once been a human being. The Ripper had struck again, swiping ferocious, merciless, unthinkable paws down Dorset Street, en route to the evening's festivities.

CHAPTER TWENTY-EIGHT

The faint roll of Percy's white eyes beneath her white lids was the only sign of life. Her odd fever had not broken. It seemed, rather, to worsen. As did her vision:

Light was the most welcome sight, after Darkness. Running into the field, she laughed. The sound brought Spring, and her love would be waiting: beautiful, winged, safe. Not cold and lonely like her husband in name but not in her heart. She had heard Love's rich voice, deep within her breast, his feathers murmuring upon her ear in her most shadowy hours. She knew he would come.

The call of a great bird sounded, and a warm wind surrounded her. Strong arms swept her into a cradle hold. Laughter greened the trees. The Muses rushed into the field, delighted by the reunion of their dearest friends.

"Darling!" murmured a rich voice. She beheld the speaker, winged and magnificent, chiseled, stoic and true; Balance, Truth and Light, he was. Her heart swelled.

"Love . . ." she breathed, as his dark eyes stared deeply into her own prismatic irises. "You waited for me!"

"Did you doubt 'forever,' we who created the word? We shall create so much, you and I, shall we not?" He smiled, irresistible, and placed a powerful hand upon her stomach.

Her insides grew warm with fertile desire, and she knew she would bear his body, take him in and then bear a god of Balance like the father. This would make the world right again.

The noble face of her love grew grave. "Has he harmed you?"

She shook her head. "Other than stealing me? No. Speak not of him. There is only you within me." She took in the scent of her lover: fresh air, foreign spices. He pursed perfect lips in a delighted smirk. She felt the weight of Darkness fall away like heavy linens, revealing her free and naked body for her beloved's appreciation, so different from her husband's cloying prison where she was meant to keep the dead at bay.

Her love kissed her deeply, his dark hair entwining with hers in the spring breeze. Tracing the lines of her body with his fingertips, he pressed against her, aching, desperate . . . In centuries to come, she would curse the day she had been so careless. She would forever curse the day she failed to look behind to the cave opening where burning eyes watched and hardened.

He, winged and supposedly eternal, the Keeper of Peace, the Balance, her *true* husband in love, drew back and stared at her, a woman who should never have become another god's bride. She should have foreseen the danger. So foolish. But she could only stare at her lover, transfixed. She did not hear a growl from distant shadows.

It was then that her true love's body burst into flame. There came an unforgettable, ungodly shriek of agony. She herself screamed a scream that rent the heavens.

Her lover's form exploded, his feathers scorched and smoldered in terrifying bursts. Her own terror made the rain come, and it doused him. But it was too late. Hysterical, she cradled the charred, reeking, unrecognizable body of her true love in her arms. The Muses watched, frozen in horror.

The wind lifted a huge feather into its gentle hands; the consoling wind, murmuring sweet sympathies, blew the feather upon the breeze. It began to float away of its own volition, stirring to life. Five Muses ran after it, while four others ran away in terror.

She watched her true love's corpse crumble to dust. She backed slowly away as madness began to overtake her. Wailing, she beat her fists into the ground until her hands bled. "This is far from the end!" she shrieked into the crimson mud. "The world will not release you! I cannot release you! It will not end this way. We shall return—!"

With a retching cry, Percy came to consciousness, found herself pounding her fists violently against her bed. Realizing she was not in a distant, ancient land but rather a London sickbed, she moaned, fell back and threw the sheets over her head. This did no good. To her great dismay, she still heard the distant growling of hounds. But there was a new sound. Percy removed the sheets and opened her eyes.

A humming, translucent feather made of blue fire floated before her eyes. This feather of cerulean flame was strangely comforting, and it eased Percy's boiling blood. The feather floated closer and then retreated, away from her bed, beckoning.

She stared at the feather and asked a silent question: *Am I to follow?*

The feather burned brighter; its blue fire sparkled.

Yes, Percy realized. *I must follow. And this is the end of me.*

Six candles burst into spontaneous flame as Alexi threw wide the chapel door and strode down the aisle. The Guard, clumped near the altar inside, looked to him, full of anxious hope. His eyes were dead, his face unreadable. From his lips burst a decree, and his powerful arm shot forward, emitting a burst of lightning that spun toward the altar. A black door rent the air wide, and The Guard approached it inexorably.

The chapel door behind them opened again, and they

turned to see a new vision. Lucille Linden stepped into the chapel, and everyone lost their breath as she threw her cloak aside to reveal her immense black satin gown. Everything about her was the picture of beauty.

Lucille approached Alexi with an outstretched hand. He stepped close to her, and she responded by sliding her arm into his.

"Lead on, Alexi," she said. He nodded slowly, as if trapped in a dream.

The feather bobbed and pulsed, impatient.

Are you leading me to my death? Percy wondered. The feather suddenly changed shape, its wispy blue barbs transforming into a burning Sacred Heart. The symbol evoked such yearning that Percy couldn't refuse to follow, no matter if it led to the undiscovered country after all.

She attempted to stand, but an attack of nausea sent her sprawling back upon the bed, sweat pouring off her brow. She reached toward the heart, asking for its help. The image again became a feather. A beautiful music played somewhere close. Percy felt suddenly lifted by a great, tingling hand. Her thin hospital gown clinging to her body, she stumbled forward but hesitated at the foot of her bed. The feather receded toward the door of the infirmary, pulsing, waiting for her to join it.

The nurses darted busily about their work, none of them seeming to notice her. It was as if she were already a ghost. Perhaps she was.

"Am I dead, then?" she wondered. The feather pulsed and sparkled, not an answer, only a beacon.

Outside, past the infirmary windows, fierce dark thunderheads galloped across the moon. This feather of flame seemed an infinitely better acquaintance than those horsemen of the horizon, who would eventually find their way through the hole in her sky and descend upon her, dead or alive. Thus Percy placed one unsteady foot in front of the other, scared that the nurses would at last see her and shuffle her back to bed with admonishments.

Fumbling with the knob of the infirmary door, she was almost free when the dearest of the nurses turned to her, rosy face flushing bright. Percy was sure she was trapped. And yet, the nurse somehow didn't quite see her; the woman's eyes lost focus and her mouth went slack, as if she had been dazed by a brilliant, hypnotic light. Percy looked down at her hands to find them glowing.

With Miss Linden in tow, The Guard descended into their sacred space, that secret place not quite beneath Promethe Hall but more parallel to it, inaccessible by any other means. The fact that Miss Linden, ostensibly an outsider, was able to set foot upon the stone stairs that had materialized from their inexplicable, private altar entrance, they felt, was not to be dismissed.

Once inside their circular room, Lucy Linden gazed about with eager wonder. Alexi stood nearby. His stern face was ashen, hers flushed; he a statue, she a flower.

Moving liquidly into their ritual circle, Alexi led Lucy to the center. Her smile was dazzling as the crystalline bird above her head.

He returned to the perimeter. A breeze and an ancient harmony filled the air, the first chord struck in a symphony tuned by angels. Their circle of blue fire leaped to life, licking their ankles with harmless affection. Lucy stared with evident excitement.

Alexi closed his eyes.

"Great guiding force, hold fast within us now, each to the other," he said carefully. "As myth would have it: from the Flame of Phoenix, Feather did fall and Muse did follow. If we are birthed from that flame, then our fire needs a new candle. I submit the humility of my mortal judgment to your higher wisdom. We know no other way than to humbly present our choice. Is this she?" He opened his eyes.

A breeze coursed around the circle, becoming a whirlpool, urging them to draw close. Lucy held out a hand. Alexi moved forward, breaking from the circle of fellowship that closed again behind him, and the pair stared at each other, faces mere inches apart. The Guard glanced around, uncertain.

"Alexi Rychman," Lucille said softly. "You are mine."

Alexi slid his arm around her black satin-clad waist, drew her against him and kissed her ruby lips.

Percy spat blood, crimson fluid welling up suddenly in her mouth. Stifling a cry, she leaped over the threshold of the infirmary, her bare feet pattering against the smooth wooden floor beyond. The halls were quiet. It was late. Only she and the ghosts were awake, she realized, as she moved down the corridor; and they turned to her, their eyes wide. They bowed.

The halls should have been dim, for it was night, but Percy suddenly realized she could see as if it were day. Bright day. Passing the glass windows of darkened office doors, she saw her reflection and could not recognize it for the nimbus around her body, burning from inside and glimmering on her skin. She stopped near one glass pane and stared, her hand before her eyes.

The feather floated close, and it brushed her cheek with a warm kiss before slipping again down the Promethe Hall corridor, coaxing, urging Percy to keep moving, no matter if she was shocked by how much she appeared the angel. No matter if she still tasted blood.

"*Mine,* Alexi . . ." Lucy repeated as she drew back from the kiss, caressing his cheeks with both hands.

Alexi found that kissing her had done nothing to thrill

him, and her touch made him cold. Her eyes shifted colours, emerald to ruby to black. Part of him shivered in dismayed recognition. His goddess had cycled through hues just the same.

Lucille's hands left his face. "Now then, let's begin." She moved her arms in a grand gesture, as if drawing an invisible arrow back against a bow. In response, a circular tile on the wall shuddered and shifted, twisting out of place in the same way a huge screw would pull from a stud, spiraling out. The cylinder lengthened, parallel to the floor as it invaded the room, glistening with indeterminate crystal and metal grooves, silt and debris falling from its edges as it extended farther. With a final belching sound, the extraction fell at an angle, leaving a gaping hole beyond. A dim, hazy shaft of light emanated from behind the seal: an opening.

Another portal, as Prophecy had decreed! Their sacred space had proven responsive to Miss Linden's commands, and murmurs of excitement flew among The Guard. Rebecca and Alexi stared at each other, and at the transformed wall. Lucille's beautiful face grew lovelier still.

"I've always wanted to come find you, to play with you. This time, when everything is at stake I've caught up with you and I'll never let go. He will be so proud!"

Rebecca's eyes narrowed. "What do you mean?"

Lucy's smile tightened. "I mean, you're fools. Once upon a time, if you recall, there was a vicious score to settle. Once upon a time there was jealousy, betrayal and justice dealt by fire to put a whore in her place. But let us forgive and forget, shall we? We could join, could reign in both realms as they become one! The sepulcher is pried open at last!" she cried, and flung out her arms.

"What the devil do you mean?" Alexi demanded. His very soul felt frozen.

"The division between worlds, held fast by the seals . . . Wait."

The Guard looked blankly at the stone pin, and then at her.

"Don't you know what you're keepers of?" Lucille asked, incredulous. She laughed. "You truly are useless mortal fools, if you don't even know your own purpose."

"We police spirits," Rebecca scoffed. "Of course we know—"

"Yes, yes, but when you run about and perform your little tricks, don't you realize you're holding the seals fast? The more spiritual havoc you allow up there on your mortal streets, the more this seal loosens." She gestured to the pin upon the floor.

"It seems that our teacher left that part out of our tutorial," Alexi muttered.

"For centuries the latch between life and death has been held safely closed by your little chapels. But now that you've let me in, we can fling wide the door right here and now! 'London Bridge is falling down, falling down . . .'" Lucille grinned.

The hearts of The Guard froze. Their fearful gazes snapped to the crevice in the wall, where deep from within a familiar growl sounded. Then, suddenly, their enemy leaped from the abyss, and that tumultuous mass of combined spirit mongrels loped around the circle of blue flame with its one or one hundred heads snarling and snapping. Fresh blood and bits of flesh dripped from its ungodly fangs.

A laugh that sounded full of sand erupted from Lucille.

"What are you?" Alexi demanded.

"My fable has changed so much over the years! Careful! Don't stare too close—you'll turn to stone!" Lucy sniggered. Something shifted and rattled on her head.

Serpents shot from her skull, the black locks slithering outward, hissing, wrapping around the necks of The Guard. Forked, flaming tongues licked the ears, nostrils and lips of the six friends as they struggled. Michael attempted to rally them with a moment of hope, or even half a chuckle to warm their hearts, but he could not speak or breathe. Alexi's neck, so close to Lucille's, was wrapped double by a serpent, driving him to his knees.

"Such passion!" Lucy cried, eyes becoming feline. "Let me taste it—suck it from you!" Reptilian jaws opened their mouths and spat. "Master, receive my gift—the scales of the Balance will tip in our favor as the division of worlds is destroyed! At last you see how much I am worth!" She glanced at the broken seal. "The door! The prophesied door!" she mocked with glee.

"Oh, dear God, what have we done . . . ?" Rebecca sobbed.

"Phoenix help us. And Percy, forgive me—" Alexi gasped, staring into the gaping hole where a dank dungeon of souls awaited command.

Lucy turned to the ghastly host. "Come, come! Come back to your beloved lost world and make noise at last! Be as loud as you like!" she called into the darkness, before whirling back to The Guard, licking her lips. "And imagine just such a release happening all over the world—it occurs as we speak!"

Vile spirits began to pour from the wall, as if a gurgling sewer pipe of eternity had been unclogged and refuse now flowed free. Alexi pictured the horror of other orifices vomiting such phantasmagoria around the world, with no one there to stop the spillage, and he felt a wave of defeat, worse even than the snakes that suffocated him.

"Oh, Alexi," Lucy said, staring down at him, her eyes once again emerald. More snakes slithered round her head, caressed her cheeks and slid down her body. "Forget that weakling girl. You and I were meant to traverse the ages together. Come. Taste of me. I've been so lonely and neglected. Just like you. Do you remember what you used to be? So magnificent! Wisdom and Light, the very Balance itself! But ever since you were foolish enough to fall in love, when you lost your lady and burned to ashes, you understand nothing but loneliness and pathetic human pain. What a humiliating fall."

She crouched so that her face was level with his. "I will cure it all, Balance be damned," she murmured in one of his ears. The sounds of his choking friends filled the other.

Percy's throat constricted. She stumbled down the stairs to the ground floor, tearing around the corner to see the open chapel door ahead at the end of the hallway. A new sensation swelled within her, a heat beyond her high temperature, a seething power that obliterated her weakness and infused her with unknown strength. The throes of her heart began to clear into a sea of singing, wind and peace. And her hands—Percy suddenly knew she could command any force before her, through her light, through her revived power.

"What am I?" she murmured, "And what am I sent to do here?"

Ancient words of a tongue she had never spoken yet always knew were suddenly on her lips, a stream of blessings and curses all at once. She stumbled as if pushed into the white, empty chapel of Athens, but there everything seemed as it always did: the plain altar was draped in white cloth, the stained-glass angels stood silent sentry. But a sound grew in the silence, originating at the altar—a tearing sound—and her blood chilled.

A dark, gaping maw of a door began as a small square and grew before her, obliterating the sight of the altar for its dense blackness and wisps of dancing blue flame—so much like the vision she'd drawn in Alexi's classroom! Terrible sounds could be heard emanating from inside. Percy turned to the feather. It bobbed, impatient, swelled and suddenly burst apart, leaving only smoke. There was a cry from beyond the portal threshold.

"Alexi!" Percy realized.

The sound of his strained, faltering voice caused her to run forward, heedless of what might await her below, and she threw herself into the void.

★ ★ ★

The Guard tried to murmur curses, benedictions and prayers, but they couldn't connect to wield their collective power. They, despite experiment and the best of intentions, had failed. Through their mortal weakness, that chink in the armor of their every incarnation, a wound birthed anarchy. Malevolent spirits poured through the seal, wailing and cackling, anxious to terrorize the populace of the world's fulcrum city, to tip the balance from sanity to chaos and shatter divisions between journeys of the human spirit. All the while, an ancient foe, that chimerical hellhound, shifted his canine forms and waited, stoking his ravenous appetite.

"Why resist?" Lucille cried. "We don't have to fight anymore. All debts will clear and we'll begin anew. This was, at first, supposed to be about her, since Master lost his damnable bride again. Sending his faithful dog, I encouraged the beast to search out whores, expecting to find his errant girl in good company. Pity there were so many to choose from."

"Demon, what on earth—?" Alexi broke free of the serpent around his neck and leaped to his feet, diving forward to clamp his hands around Lucille's delicate throat.

Unhurried, she placed a finger on his forehead and he was again on his knees, as if his blood were suddenly turned to lead. "All politics, love and antique fables. But none of that old news matters. Now that we're together and there's something more than an ancient, pitiful love affair at stake, now that you'll join me—"

"Never!" Alexi cried.

"Truly?" Lucy pouted softly, her snakes undulating. "You're such a lovely man. I'd hate to lose a mind like yours."

"I knew you were never one of us, demon witch," Alexi spat.

Lucy sighed. Insects poured suddenly from every crack in the walls of the sacred space. Screams were issued from the faltering company who could draw breath, for arachnids, roaches and beetles crawled indiscriminately over marble floor, petticoats, arms and legs.

"Tell whomever you serve that we do The Grand Work, not that of the devil!" Alexi cried.

"Don't you remember *anything?*" Lucy bellowed in a harpylike shriek. "There is no 'devil.' There is no 'hell.' There is only Unrest. There is no down, only sideways; the transparent beside the opaque, and a thin wall to separate them. I'm so damn sick of fallacies!"

Josephine and Jane had slipped into unconsciousness, were held up solely by their serpentine tethers; the rest were fading. Alexi supposed oblivion was best, for spiders crawled over them in a most wretched manner. "Whatever suffices for hell—wherever there be suffering and horror—go there, where you belong!" He lashed out with his last bit of strength.

"And I was trying to be so kind," Lucy murmured as insects scurried up her skirts.

The entire room around them burst into true and harmful flame, not the blue fire of their Work, but an inferno that would ignite and burn their bodies. Michael and Rebecca tried to clasp hands, to wake the others into prayer and power, but all effort was futile. Spirits bent on harassing the living kept entering their world, floating through the fire, jaws wide with insatiable hunger. The world would be overrun; there would never again be peace.

Lucy's snakes were poised to strike, mouths wide and ready, fangs dripping. The encircling blaze was closing in. "What a pity your lover never did find you this life around!" she giggled. "Maybe it was that unfortunate Miss Parker, after all. I wish she were here; I'd have liked to show her this final scene, this end to your nauseating epic drama once and for all. I did think once I brought you to your knees she'd come running. Ah well. She's a coward, I suppose."

She took a moment to stare around at the foundering

companions, shook her head and shrugged. "Well, mortal arbiters between life and death, foolish romantics—sorry, remnants of a charred, dead god and his friends—your ends have come! It's time for you to cross the river!"

"NO."

The female voice boomed behind them, and an amazing, blinding white form burst into view at the threshold of the altar door. After her bare white feet stepped into the space, the portal snapped shut with a thunderclap.

Eyes blazing like stars, hair wild and raging, snowy arms outstretched and glistening with light as her thin white gown whipped in the wind of her own power, Persephone Parker descended through fire and entered the circle where Lucy stood staring, struck dumb and quizzical. The spiders scattered and the dog squealed, tucking incorporeal tails between its legs. The inferno vanished.

Lifting a hand, every muscle in her compact form taut with energy, Percy spoke, and her words cast a marvelous echo. "Demon, you'll not destroy my world!"

The serpents retracted, and The Guard fell to the floor, free. Lucille scowled.

Alexi stared up in desperate wonder as his beloved stood before him, the answer to his prayers, radiant from within. His friends began to rouse and stared on in awe.

Percy looked around at the spirits madly careening about the space. She frowned then admonished, "Go home." Her upraised hand closed into a fist. The pin between worlds roared, stone on stone, as it ground against the floor. Commanded, it lifted, shuddering and shedding debris as it began to twist back into place.

Everything reacted. The spirits shrieked, but their disquieting noises were audible only to Percy, who winced yet remained stalwart. As if pulled backward by strings, the horde was drawn one by one back into the black hole. Clawing and screaming, angry spectres were sucked again into the netherworld, blinking out, unable to shake London loose as they wished. And once the errant spirits were reclaimed, the tunnel closed with a resounding *Shhhh;* the fulcrum upon which the entire Balance hung slid back into place with a final stony and metallic crunch. The earth shuddered and settled, once again sealed.

A strange sound erupted from Percy's throat, an ancient, beautiful command that surprised her as she sang it. Obeying, a new door opened. A vertical, rectangular portal swung into place directly behind Lucy, opening to a dark and indeterminate realm, where dim figures waited in the vast shadows beyond, patiently in formation.

"Oh," Elijah murmured sheepishly. "That door!"

Up from the base of the opening came a finger bone, then another. Skeletal hands began clawing at the edges of this threshold, scrabbling and clicking upon one another as they sought purchase.

Lucy turned and pursed her lips. "How dare you? Who do you think you are?"

"Who do you say that I am?" Percy asked in a murmur that made everything tremble.

Michael stirred. "You are the one whose coming was foretold," he murmured. Percy turned to him, her face shining with love.

Lucy crossed her arms. "So it is you after all. A fine mess you've gotten us all into. What the hell do you expect to do now?" she demanded, her crown of snakes slithering and hissing.

Percy laughed, her inner light brightening like a fresh ray of sun. "To settle the score!" she cried, her confident words pouring forth; a mysterious vintage.

Suddenly, her head was thrown back. Percy's body arched. Her mouth fell open and a painful, feminine gasp flew from her pale lips as a shaft of blinding blue-white light impaled her body in a humming cylinder. The column of incandescence, floor to ceiling, pierced Percy's body at the sternum and held her just above the floor, arched in agony and radiance; an illuminated butterfly transfixed by a pin.

After a moment, Percy recovered herself. Throwing a vanquishing arm out toward her adversary, she cried a brief command in that ancient tongue she was speaking for the first time, her voice containing an echo older than itself.

Lucy pouted. "I was hoping it wouldn't come to—"

A wave of light and power exploded from Percy's form in a deafening gust of blue flame and angelic chords, and it sent Lucy sprawling back toward the portal, which pulled her like a magnet. The insects and arachnids Lucy summoned were sucked in as well, carried like tiny leaves in a gale. The hellhound followed, its many heads howling in defeat and punishment.

At the threshold of the portal, loosing a wretched squeal, the thing known as Lucy began to harden. Her skin greyed and froze like stone. Fissures appeared. Her face cracked and split. An arm broke away. Her body disintegrated, falling in a heap of hissing dust that was drawn ash by ash into the deep nothing. The skeletal fingers around the sides of the portal clutched at her particles, emitting a millennial rattling until each speck was consumed by their scrabbling hands. Everything disappeared inside, and only the open portal remained.

Percy floated toward the door, where she alone could dimly make out figures reaching for her. Light hummed around and within her body. Her arms hovered at her sides, and her thin gown clung to her flesh like gauze. Eyes fixed on this entryway to a foreign world, in a body not entirely her own, she drifted nearer the portal's edge, unsure where she was meant to go.

"Alexi," she whimpered, "take me away from this unbelievable scene. I want to be with you . . ." She forced her head down to gaze at him, pleading.

"Percy," he choked out, scrambling to his feet, tears

streaming down his face. He whirled to face his companions. "Now, do you see?"

Stunned, he and the rest of The Guard watched Percy, wrapped in light, drift closer to this new and unknown door. They could hear water lapping within.

Alexi's senses returned. "Persephone, you mustn't enter! None of our kind have ever been able to cross such a threshold and return with their wits! Please, come away—"

"Alexi, help me," she cried in return, reaching out a shaking hand.

He rushed forward, knowing through and through that his future was her, no matter what the future might be.

The moment he touched her fingers he cried out, pulled immediately up and into the light. Their eyes now level, Alexi and Percy floated in close proximity. They put their arms around each other with a sigh from their souls. Their arms could not clutch each other close enough.

The moment they sealed their embrace, the portal shut, leaving their sacred space at last closed. A tether of light began winding like ivy from inside Percy's pounding heart and into Alexi's.

"Darling..." He pressed his head against her bosom, directly into the shaft of brightest light. Percy's arms slid around his neck, and she pressed her trembling lips to his head.

The others scrambled to their feet. Taking hands hastily, still choking and shaking, The Guard began to murmur a gentle incantation of praise and thanksgiving. The wind that was already present in the room turned sweet, a musical caress.

There came a whimper from Percy's throat, fever overtaking her once more. What burst from within, she didn't know or understand how to control. Her body still felt on fire, and her fever poured forth in light. She wanted to close her eyes and sleep for years.

A cataclysm had occurred after all, justifying the madness

that had led her to this moment, the horsemen on the horizon and the cracked sky. Now, the sound of dogs barking was gone. The foul air, too. The flashing visions were gone, and all the demons. But her consciousness was slipping. Percy's mortal weakness was giving way beneath the strain. More than mere humanity coursed through her veins, but in the end, her veins were human and had limits.

The room itself trembled with Percy as her breath hitched and rattled. She squirmed in the binding light, still held transfixed, hovering off the floor. Alexi's body, once suspended with her, began to sink again to the ground.

"Alexi, accept me," Percy begged, her plea a strange counterpoint to her aura of power. Their eyes were locked, dark and light.

"Accept you as *what,* my love—what are you?" he asked.

"A mortal girl who needs you . . . and, I pray, whom I need, too," she choked out.

"Percy—"

"I've no strength, Alexi. I used it all in coming here. Whatever is inside me is tearing me apart," Percy gasped, her blood feeling thin and insufficient. "I don't know what's happening . . ." Her words were labored, a wheeze in her lungs. "All I know is that I was drawn here, wherever this is, for a purpose you surely know far better than I. Thus, I give what remains of me to you, Alexi, whom I love with my whole heart. Whatever you need of my soul, it is entirely yours and always has been—Ah!"

Pain claimed her body in a brief seizure. The shaft of light collapsed suddenly, as did Percy, crumpling into Alexi's arms, a limp heap of white limbs and fabric.

"Oh, God," Alexi cried as he sank with her to the floor.

And suddenly there was commotion. Jane attempted to focus her rattled heart enough to manifest a healing aura. Michael had closed his eyes, and with recovering cheer was attempting to quiet the frenetic nerves of his fellows. Josephine placed her locket that contained a tiny portrait of their magical, angelic icon around Percy's moist neck.

Elijah crept forward. "We were looking for her door. How terribly confusing! Well, I suppose we've found her now, haven't we? I daresay I liked her door a good deal more than that first one . . ." He would, perhaps, have continued to ramble had Jane not rapped him soundly on the skull.

"Thank heavens she found us," Rebecca murmured, and moved to the center of the room, where Alexi's black-clad form nestled Percy's fragile white mass. "Oh, Alexi!" She placed a hand upon his shoulder.

"Hush!" Alexi shirked away from her hand, cradling his beloved. His forehead against hers, he murmured, gently rocking her. "Don't leave me. After all this, you mustn't leave me."

"Alexi," Rebecca called. He looked up, and she glimpsed the mad light in his eyes.

"She's barely alive, Rebecca!" Spittle flew from his lips, strands of wild black hair stuck to his damp brow. "If she dies there will be no one to save us; we'll have failed Prophecy twice! That gorgon will have won in the end, the sepulcher will be thrown open entirely and our world will be overtaken!"

Rebecca retreated fearfully into the shadows.

Shaking Percy, Alexi began to cry out something in the beautiful tongue bequeathed only to The Guard, and the rest began to chant furiously with him, invoking ancient prayers of healing and rebirth. Their unparalleled sound grew into a heavenly crescendo, and then there was rapturous silence as they awaited the effect.

Percy lay lifeless and unaffected in Alexi's arms.

He grasped her face, calling her name. Nothing.

"Forgive me, Persephone, I do love you! My love never faltered, though I failed you . . ." He madly clutched her to him.

The warm wind of their prayers turned a bitter cold, and the ground began to tremble. Dread filled the room like water into a sinking ship. Rebecca whimpered his name, but Alexi paid no heed. Thunder roared and the stained-glass window above cracked. The group began to scream as the stone that had revealed itself as a guardian pin in their chapel began to wrest again from its moorings.

As their faith and sanity began to slip away, their fragile hope again dashed, Alexi could only whisper to his lifeless beloved, cradling her, murmuring praise and desperate regrets into her ear. His tears drenched those cheeks he repeatedly kissed. "This is the end after all," he said. "You tried to save us, but my failure doomed us all."

Tiny shards of glass began to fall from above. There was a violent thunder of horses' hooves. After centuries, it would be his leadership, his incarnation that failed the world.

"Percy, please save us," he whispered. "It's your fate. My love, please be strong for me against this terrible darkness…"

Suddenly he remembered his grandmother, what she'd said to him and to Percy. If there was ever a darkness that needed his fire…

In a burst of furious desperation, Alexi closed his eyes, using the last of his energies to turn the whole chapel into a small sun of cerulean flame. It poured out of his hands as he caressed Percy. It danced in sapphire waves over her alabaster body, entwining her limbs and licking at her cool skin as if kissing her toward consciousness.

Suddenly, enormous wings, cloudy visions of feather and flame, shot from Alexi's back and unfurled with a surge of blinding illumination. The rest of The Guard stumbled back. His black robes whipped about him. The wings were made of blue light, barely tangible shapes of mist and sundered divinity; these same wings had burst forth as an omen in the academy above, and they were now his proclamation of power, demanding that his lover come home to his arms.

Helpless tears of wonder poured down the cheeks of The Guard as their leader's glorious phantom wings wrapped his beloved in a cocoon of resurrection.

"From the Flame of the Phoenix, a Feather fell and Muses followed," Rebecca murmured, huddled beyond the circle, her face ashen and her throat bruised purple.

"My God, the old tale indeed," Michael sobbed, and he rushed to her side, lifting her to her feet and grasping her hands.

Limbs the colour of moonlight shuddered. A strong will and gentle heart stirred back toward the mortal life Percy wanted more than anything, and invincible love prodded her to consciousness as she became aware of the musical wind and dancing aurora lights around and within her. She'd fought too hard to allow this frail body to abandon fate. She'd not permit the wheel of the world's fate to turn to darkness, but would rouse to the lover who woke her with fire.

As a new peal of thunder shook The Guard's bones and apocalyptic horsemen threatened to bear down upon them, from Percy's dry lips came a sound, a soft feminine rasp: *"Shhh . . ."* The rumbling cavalcade dulled to a whisper. The ceiling held, and their sanctuary remained intact. The stones of the chapel settled back into place, the pin sealing the sepulcher once more.

Alexi's fire and his wings faded until wisps of incenselike smoke were all that remained. Percy stirred in his hold. Her eyes shot open to pierce him with a crystalline stare.

"My love," he choked.

She evaluated him for a long moment. "You have some explaining to do."

Dark eyes pouring with tears, Alexi laughed; an echoing sound of pure joy.

Percy placed a finger to his lips, a chuckle turning into a sickly cough. Her head swiveled as she listened to the silence. There was no more barking, pounding or murmuring in her mind. Only relief. Taking in her surroundings as best she could, she glanced at the six pairs of eyes that hovered over her, comforting in a distantly familial way.

"What was all that . . . ?" Elijah asked, dumbly breaking the silence. Rebecca elbowed him.

"I was hoping you could tell me," Percy murmured, her eyes focusing. "Oh, it's you, with the touch. And—oh! Headmistress! Why are you here?" She stared up at Alexi in confusion, her body wracked by shivers. He held her closer, but she clawed at him. "Please don't send me away tomorrow . . ."

Cupping her face in his hands, Alexi kissed her passionately. She gave in to the press of his lips, her body trying to shake the lingering effects of her epic battle, but she soon pulled back and gasped. A blush patched her cheeks. Glancing bashfully at the company around her, she turned her head, murmuring Alexi's name with shame, ducking and hiding inside the safe darkness of his cloak and giving an overwhelmed, youthful sigh. "Alexi. Goodness, does that mean—?"

Bringing her blushing face up again, he was sure to make this covenant eye to eye. "I failed you, Percy, but never again. Everything will be made clear to you."

"You made that promise previously," she reminded him.

"Yes. I was lost, my duty here unclear, though my heart was not. I beg you, forgive me."

"You will see me again, then?" she murmured, aching. "You'll not send me back to the convent?"

"See you? I'll not allow you out of my sight from this moment on! Say you'll forgive me."

"Forgive you?" Percy coughed again. "Well, I am rather angry."

"You should be angry—with all of us." Rebecca stepped forward. "Your rejection had everything to do with us and nothing to do with Alexi; he is not the one to blame," she admitted shakily, glancing humbly at her friend and colleague.

"Bless me for I have sinned!" Elijah cried, prostrating himself at Percy's feet.

"Get up, silly man," she laughed weakly. "You don't need a blessing; we all need a good night's rest. However . . . what in the name of Holy God just happened?"

"You're a goddess," Elijah whimpered.

"No, I'm a mortal woman with a horrid headache and a confused identity."

"No mere mortal girl could open a gate to the other side!" Elijah assured her.

Percy shrugged and winced. "Well, it would seem that serpentine friend of yours could, too, and I'd like to think I'm nothing like her . . ."

"No, no, you're clearly the greater power here. What incredible proof! Your business with those doors was very well done, if I may say. You've certainly proved us the consummate fools!" he exclaimed, his foppish sleeves flapping as he gesticulated absurdly. Rebecca made a move to elbow him again, but then realized it was no use and only shook her head and sighed.

"Well, it would've been nice to know my power, whatever it is, long ago. It might have saved us all a lot of trouble. No. I can't be a goddess. If I was, I wouldn't be in this much pain." Percy smirked halfheartedly. Alexi could only stare, drinking in her every word.

"Were you one, then, once? Full of *sorcellerie et puissance?*" Josephine asked. "Do you remember ever coming to us, years ago? Giving us a prophecy?"

"Oh, why . . . it's you, too—the painter. *Bonjour.* Well, mademoiselle, I don't know whether I've had such dreams or memories, but I've never before been capable of magic or divine acts." She turned to Alexi, giving in to the warmth of his embrace. "And I don't remember ever seeing *you,* my dear." She bit her lip. "I assure you, I'd never forget if I'd seen you before."

He drew his covetous embrace tighter, and pressed a finger to the soft skin over her racing heart. "Herein lies the magic," he declared softly, and Percy's face lit with a rapturous smile, unwittingly proving his point. "Inside this incredible, radiant heart is all the divinity we need. 'Tis the whole of my salvation."

Rebecca bent carefully over them. "Rest is what is best for you now, Miss Parker. Let answers come later. You're in good hands with your professor."

Staring up at Rebecca, that word struck Percy with sudden horror. "You won't...expel me for this, will you, Headmistress?"

The group laughed, albeit some a bit guiltily.

"No, dear heart—since you rescued the world, we may have to make you faculty."

Rebecca gave Alexi an anemic smile; Percy, even in her weakened state, could see many complex things cross between their gazes. Alexi nodded slowly, as if all might eventually pass.

"Give us a moment, please," he instructed his friends. "Regroup at the Withersby estate, where Percy and I will soon join you. Don't worry, there will be time enough for repentance." Flashing each and every one a caustic smirk, he waved them away.

Without protest, they quietly filed out. As they turned toward the stairway, the door to Athens and their normal world materialized with the sound of a small rip. Only Jane lingered, shifting for a moment on her feet and wringing her hands.

"I am so sorry, Alexi," she murmured. "There was a time when I did not trust that vile woman. I ought to have fought for Miss Percy. I failed you."

Alexi shook his head. "Every one of us failed. But all has been made right."

Jane wiped her eyes, crossed herself, and was the last to leave the sanctuary. The portal closed behind her, leaving Percy and Alexi alone.

Attempting to sit upright, Percy found she couldn't and collapsed once more into Alexi's clutch. Never had she been so exhausted, yet her heart pounded in this embrace and her body thrilled. "I've no idea what has happened to me. Where are we?" she murmured.

"A special place reserved for us alone, within the academy walls and yet far from them, neither here nor there. But if not for you, this delicate place would have been destroyed—along with much more."

Percy shuddered. "Oh, Alexi, I've had such visions and terrors! If I'm meant to be here with you now, why did you send me away? You were so cruel."

"I fear it was all a horrid test, bringing us to this catastrophic point. I had to act cruel, to make you hate me, otherwise I'd have never been able to let you go. I was in agony—"

"Good." Percy's eyes flashed. "You deserved to suffer, you were awful . . ."

Alexi's expression grew pained. "The rest of The Guard feared I was too taken with you to allow Prophecy to be fulfilled. More than just our own desires were at stake—"

"You thought it might be that Gorgon," Percy accused.

"*They* thought it was, but I believed in you . . . and your power proved everything tonight!" Alexi gasped, pressing her to him. "Signs of Prophecy were seen in that . . . woman. The others were enamoured of her, but I never . . . I knew I was meant to love the Prophesied, and we were so terrified of fate we'd have ruined everything were it not for you."

"So . . . *did* you love her?" Percy breathed fearfully, wondering what might have transpired while she was in the infirmary, the exact period of time of which she had no accurate awareness.

Alexi shook his head. "Never for a moment. Loving a

goddess that appeared to me as a young man was nothing like what began to happen to me when you would come to my office, fascinating me. I began to live for our private moments, unprepared for my reaction, unprepared for what you do to me," he professed, his words a groan of need as his hands roved her shoulders. "As your professor, it was unbearable. Unattainable as my student, and yet . . . the difference in our status did add a titillating dynamic to this entire ordeal," he purred, drawing a finger over her cheek.

"Maddening, in fact," Percy murmured, moving her face to kiss his fingertip, her lips lingering there as he reacted with a yearning exhalation.

Her expression suddenly grew grave. "Alexi, promise me you'll not leave me alone tonight. I can't bear it. These terrible events have nearly killed me. Promise me you'll not turn from me like you did at your sister's, toy with me like before?"

Dark eyes burned with desire and adoration. "Percy, the sanctity of our love is tied to the balance of our world and"— he drew a shaking breath—"my very life depends on it." Loosening the cravat around his abused throat, he pulled at a thin metal chain. A small silver ring was revealed.

"Strange that we've both worn symbols of our fate against our skin," Percy murmured, staring as he slipped the ring from the chain and held it before her. Delicately crafted, a single silver feather was wrapped into a slender circle. It took her a moment to realize what his presenting a ring to her meant, but when she did, she nearly shrieked in delight.

"I waited for ages to give this to my destined love, growing older and bitter, losing all hope. Then you waltzed in, Persephone Parker. You lifted me from the ashes. I love you. Your nearness is the cure to my cold, lonely life." Alexi pressed the ring into her palm, his hands trembling helplessly. "Heal me by becoming my wife."

The joyous cry from Percy's lips could have made flowers bloom. Perhaps it did, somewhere in window boxes above.

"Oh, my dear professor!" She laughed. "I've been helplessly yours from the very first." Her pale eyes burned with the blue flame that bound them all, that fire triumphant over darkness at last. "My God, your *wife!*" she squealed as he slipped the ring upon her finger. "I could only dream someone would have me so, and for it to be Alexi Rychman—"

"It must be me," Alexi interrupted. "My goddess may live on in you, but even if she doesn't . . . I need you, Percy."

He fondled her arms and nuzzled her neck as tears of joy and relief from the night's unearthly terrors spilled down her cheeks, all horror draining away with each salty drop. "You will stay at my side tonight," he commanded, arms locking around her waist. When Percy drew back, blushing, eyes widening with excited uncertainty, he anticipated her nervousness. "I'll respect your modesty until we are wed, sweet girl, but you and I have much to discuss."

She nodded, shifting in his hold, and he gave a hiss. "Michael may have to wed us immediately!" he groaned, no longer able deny the contours of her body, so evident beneath the thin fabric of her gown.

Their eyes locked, desperate. The betrothed were permitted such passion . . .

All inhibition aside, Alexi slid an arm around her neck and his lips fell to devour her throat, her shoulders. Her senses sharpening with desire, she felt his fingertips upon her rib cage. His hand trembled upon the cloth and crept upward. Percy gasped as she felt his palm graze her breast then cup it. Her skin thrilled, flushed and tingled in places she blushed to acknowledge.

Responding to her sounds of pleasure, Percy's beloved caressed her with increasing hunger, his hands roaming and questing. Their bodies joined in a symphonic movement of touch and response, and the light in the sacred chamber grew brighter. The mosaic bird above them glowed as if the heat of their pressing bodies had ignited a divine hearth.

Percy wept softly, joyously. Her hands seized and fluttered

over him alternately. "You delight in this body, then, Alexi? It arouses, not repulses?" she whispered with thinly veiled fear, while every trace of his fingertips caused entirely new delights.

"Is this not proof?" he panted. "Pale as you are, your features and body are singularly, beautifully perfect—my flawless sculpture come to life, warming to my touch. I warrant, dear girl, that respecting your modesty shall be a—I'd best take my hands from you else I be unable to help myself! Oh, forgive me! You shiver with cold. Have my cloak," he begged.

"I don't shiver from the cold, Alexi!" Percy laughed. "How I rejoice that my strange skin could receive such a loving treatment! I imagined you, imagined this . . . but the truth of it!"

He looked down at her and grinned. "I am a man who searches for truth. Truth and a reason." And with a smile, he descended upon her again, ravaging her lips, his hands began to once more wander.

There was a tearing sound. At first Percy assumed it was some part of her clothing, but then the corner of her eye saw that the altar door again gaped. "Ah. The door," she stated.

Alexi turned and groaned. "Perhaps the heavens know, as I do, that I'm about to lose all hope of control and make these stones our marriage bed," he muttered, reluctantly drawing back. "Come, love, our friends await." He unclasped his cloak. "Though we should let them. Lord knows I've waited for you forever! Yet . . . you do deserve an actual bed."

He wrapped his cloak around her with great care, and she giggled, quaking with nervous anticipation of the prospect. A sudden dreadful thought clouded her gaze. "Alexi?"

"Yes?"

"Am I still being sought after, sniffed out by that Cerberus we fled, holding a grudge from a mythic past? Are we to be hunted, you and I, by . . . do we dare say Hades himself? Pursued by other strange minions like that Gorgon revealed herself to be? Or have I been able, in any way, by powers I do not understand, to set us free from those horrors?"

"I cannot say, Percy, for we were given our myth alone. I know only of the phoenix and the Muses. I've no memory of them; I know only what was told to us by that goddess long ago."

"I had a vision you—what was surely you—died in flames, in my arms," Percy wailed, recalling the horror.

"Whatever we were, or we are, we've returned to each other. We certainly have foes yet to face; there was too much talk of settling scores for it to be over. But for now, darling . . . ?"

"For now I, Persephone Parker, am content with you, Professor Alexi Rychman, here in the Queen's England, enamoured with anything you do and anywhere we go!"

Alexi swept her into his arms and she squealed in delight, clinging to him as he carried her up through the portal door and past the altar beyond. The sacred chamber closed dutifully behind them. He bore her down the church aisle and out of the silent, empty chapel, then through Promethe Hall's front doors and into a now-peaceful evening.

At the threshold of the academy, Alexi placed her on her feet and they gasped in unison at the sight before them. Dozens of peaceful spirits had gathered in greeting, the sorts of spirits that The Guard allowed to roam without censure, souls that just couldn't quite let go or were tethered by the living who couldn't let go. Patiently floating on either side of the portico, an incorporeal receiving line had formed for the newly betrothed duo. These spirits' expressions were filled with warm anticipation, and Percy smiled at each in turn.

Turning to Alexi, she kissed him reverently, a shaft of moonlight falling on both of their faces like a spotlight. The spirits applauded—and many remarked that it was about damn time.

"No matter future foes, Alexi, look what a life we will lead," Percy cried. "Look at our entourage!" Clutching his hand, she could hear murmuring tongues in all manner of accents and languages, and all were offering their regards and congratulations. "Oh," she breathed, blushing, flattered.

Percy stared at each spirit with a respect that acknowledged the inner soul, perhaps in a way that was never realized in their mortal lives. Each ghostly countenance took on an expression of peace before the glowing form dimmed into the darkness. Many spectres waved or blew kisses before they departed to their rest, granted in return for their felicitations a much-needed sleep by a wondrous, compassionate force. The air felt at peace, never so balanced.

Venturing to look at the sky, Percy was relieved to see it no longer torn. The heavens, and her heart, were now whole. The scales were level.

"What do all these spirits tell you, my translator and my love?" Alexi asked softly.

Percy turned to him. Pale and powerful, she was a beaming, heavenly sight on the academy steps, bathed in and reflecting moonlight.

"They tell us, love, that eternity awaits."

☐ YES!

Sign me up for the Love Spell Book Club and send my
FREE BOOKS! If I choose to stay in the club, I will pay
only $8.50* each month, a savings of $6.48!

NAME: _____

ADDRESS: _____

TELEPHONE: _____

EMAIL: _____

☐ I want to pay by credit card.

☐ **VISA**   ☐ **MasterCard**   ☐ **DISCOVER**

ACCOUNT #: _____

EXPIRATION DATE: _____

SIGNATURE: _____

Mail this page along with $2.00 shipping and handling to:
**Love Spell Book Club
PO Box 6640
Wayne, PA 19087**
Or fax (must include credit card information) to:
610-995-9274
You can also sign up online at **www.dorchesterpub.com**.
*Plus $2.00 for shipping. Offer open to residents of the U.S. and Canada only.
Canadian residents please call 1-800-481-9191 for pricing information.
If under 18, a parent or guardian must sign. Terms, prices and conditions subject to
change. Subscription subject to acceptance. Dorchester Publishing reserves the right
to reject any order or cancel any subscription.

GET FREE BOOKS!

You can have the best romance delivered to your door for less than what you'd pay in a bookstore or online. Sign up for one of our book clubs today, and we'll send you *FREE* BOOKS* just for trying it out... **with no obligation to buy, ever!**

Bring a little magic into your life with the romances of Love Spell—fun contemporaries, paranormals, time-travels, futuristics, and more. Your shipments will include authors such as **MARJORIE LIU, JADE LEE, NINA BANGS, GEMMA HALLIDAY**, and many more.

As a book club member you also receive the following special benefits:
- **30% off all orders!**
- **Exclusive access to special discounts!**
- **Convenient home delivery and 10 days to return any books you don't want to keep.**

Visit **www.dorchesterpub.com**
or call **1-800-481-9191**

There is no minimum number of books to buy, and you may cancel membership at any time. *Please include $2.00 for shipping and handling.